Contemporary Romance

Wedding Vows

A Collection of Wedding Love Stories

Contemporary Romance:
Wedding Vows –
A Collection of Wedding Love Stories
by E. Ayers
Published by Indie Artist Press
Eagle Mountain, Utah
www.indieartistpress.com
First Edition
With This Ring by E. Ayers
I Thee Wed by E. Ayers
To Have & To Hold by E. Ayers
copyright © 2015
All rights reserved.
ISBN-10: 1-62522-043-X
ISBN-13: 978-1-62522-043-1
May 2015

Dedication

To George, who believed in me.

Book One

With This Ring

One

DeeDee Drayden had nothing but ideas in her head. Glorious, grand ideas for her own bridal business. She looked around the starkly furnished studio apartment that she had rented for the last few years in the Big Apple and decided there was nothing left except for a few memories.

High fashion was a dirty business and far from the glamorous one she had envisioned as a child. Talent and ability only got her so far. She was thirty-one years old. If she was going to strike out on her own, now was the time to do it.

She pulled the apartment door closed, stepped onto the elevator, pushed the ground floor button, and held her bittersweet tears in check. Dreams of her own design house in New York had come to an end, but had been replaced with a new vision. She put on a brave smile as she stepped out of the elevator.

"I'm going to miss you, Mack" She stuffed a hundred dollar bill in the doorman's pocket as she gave the older man a hug.

"I'm gonna miss you, too, Miz DeeDee. Don't you worry about nothin'. Don't forget to write me. I wanna know how yous doin'." He held the door and hailed a cab for her.

"I promise." She jumped into the back seat of the yellow cab. "JFK Airport."

Eight hours later, she stepped from another cab and looked

around the small town. The plain green door contained a basket filled with fresh-faced pansies that almost hid the alphanumeric address, 323A. She rang the doorbell and waited. The floral shop window next door was filled with ordinary arrangements. *Six months, I'm giving myself six months to do this. Failure is not an option!*

She rang the bell again and waited. Walking three doors to the left put her in front of an insurance office with gold lettering proclaiming Ferguson Insurance, Meeting Your Every Need & Taking the Worry Out of Living. She pulled open the heavy glass door and stepped inside. Several pitiful potted plants stood by the window. An older woman greeted her.

"Hello, I'm Deanne Drayden and I'm looking for Mrs. Anderson."

"She's with a client. Was she expecting you?"

"Yes."

"Hmm. I don't have you on her schedule. That's very odd."

"I was supposed to meet her at lunchtime. My flight arrived later than expected."

"Oh, you must be her new boarder. Have a seat." She waved to a row of wooden chairs surrounding a coffee table filled with old magazines and insurance brochures. "I just made a pot of fresh coffee. Would you like a cup while you wait? I expect she's going to be awhile."

"Thank you for the kind offer. But would it be all right if I left my bag? I'd much rather walk around town and become acquainted with my surroundings. I've been sitting all day."

"Oh, go right ahead. She's going to be at least a half hour or more."

DeeDee parked her rolling case with the fancy designer label next to the tree-like plant that immediately dropped three leaves.

"Thanks."

She exited the building and looked both ways. The street looked like a movie set for a quaint little town. She began walking towards the 400 block before retracing her steps. The little coffee shop on the other side of the florist seemed to be calling her name. Pulling open the wooden and glass door of the tiny cafe, a bell jingled over her head, and the scent of brewed coffee filled her nose. Several tables of various styles packed the little space. Two women sat chatting at one table and two police officers sat at another, the rest were empty.

One woman from the table hurried behind the counter. "What can I get for you?"

"Sixteen ounces, dark roast, six sugars, extra cream, to go." She fished in her purse for actual cash. "Do you take plastic?"

The woman nodded, took the card, rang up the sale, and poured the coffee into a paper cup. "The fixings are over there. Help yourself."

DeeDee took the cup and turned to the old-fashioned sideboard that contained stir sticks, and everything else anyone might want for their coffee.

A few minutes later, she was standing in front of a corner building made from blocks of granite. She put her nose to one of the glass doors and tried to see inside. It was nothing but a dark hole, but it would be her dark hole. Four big windows fronted Main Street and four more fronted Elm Street.

"It's been sold," a deep male voice said from behind her.

Her stomach and heart collided as her hot coffee sloshed from her cup and dribbled over her hand. She turned and faced the voice. It came from a man who must have been her senior by at least ten years. Piercing blue eyes were partially shielded by a black Stetson.

"Sorry, didn't mean to scare you. Cody Montgomery, at your service." He lifted his western hat with his left hand before setting the hat back on dark hair that showed signs of silver. "We're you looking for a piece of property?"

"Mr. Montgomery? I'm Deanne Drayden." She licked the spilled coffee from the back of her hand and winced at the tender pink spot. "We're to meet here tomorrow at nine a.m." She took in the custom-cut black wool suit that covered his well-portioned frame and had already noticed that he wore no wedding ring.

"If you want to see it now, I'd have to get the keys, and we won't have any light inside."

"Tomorrow will be fine." She glanced at her watch. "I'm supposed to be someplace in about three minutes."

"Then I won't keep you. See you in the morning."

She nodded and scurried away. He looked about as out of place as she felt in a small town. Delicious thoughts of Cody Montgomery ran though her mind, but too many years in the fashion industry taught her that the good-looking men were either gay or players, and the players didn't play with women like her.

***

DeeDee followed Mrs. Gloria Anderson through the green door and up a flight of stairs. She guessed that the woman was probably in her late forties. Her big golden brown eyes went perfectly with her walnut-stained skin. Her wig was no cheap synthetic - real human hair probably from China.

"Welcome home." The woman opened another door at the

top of the steps.

DeeDee looked around. Everything was pink, burgundy with pink, pink, and more pink. The sofa was pink, the chairs were pink, the walls were pale pink, the carpeting was lipstick pink, and the silk flowers on the glass coffee table were pink and burgundy. The only relief from the pink was the black of the large flat screen TV that hung on the one wall and a few black table legs that held up heavy slabs of glass. The color was too much, but she gave Gloria credit for freely using the color pink.

"Laundry room is beyond the kitchen and off of that is the back door. I have four parking spaces in the alleyway."

"I don't have a car. Haven't driven since I was eighteen, and I have no desire to start driving again."

"You'll have to get a car. This isn't the big city."

"I'm used to catching the bus."

The woman laughed. "What bus? There are no buses around here."

Uh oh! She followed the woman up another flight of steps.

"Make yourself at home. I put your boxes in here as they arrived." The woman turned an old cut-glass doorknob and pushed the door open. "I'll have dinner ready at six."

The room was white, stark white. After all the pink, it was an oasis. The bedroom was larger than her New York studio apartment. An archway led from the sitting area to the actual bedroom and beyond that, were two more doors. One belonged to a walk-in closet and the other to a modern bathroom. *This is heaven! How did I get so lucky?*

Quickly, she unpacked and arranged everything in the closet and bathroom. Living as a minimalist kept life simple. She checked her watch and decided she had time for a quick shower.

Dinner was plain. Pulled pork with a tangy gravy, sweet potato bread, and a fresh salad was ample fare. As she sat with Gloria, she learned much about her new home and the tiny community.

"You're a fashion designer, eh?"

DeeDee nodded. "I took my degree and ran off to Milan. Did an apprenticeship with a minor house there before going to Paris. Three houses there, and then a real design job in London. Naturally after I leave, is when she becomes famous. I've spent my last few years in New York with various houses."

"Sounds exciting, so why here?"

"Hardly exciting. To be honest, I was tired of the outrageous: animal print lamé held together with sheer fabric that doesn't cover what needs to be covered; that little black dress is getting skimpier and skimpier until there's almost nothing there." She picked up her cup of tea and sipped it.

Gloria shook her head. "I have one black dress. I bought it to wear to my husband's funeral and I've never worn it since."

"Oh my, I'm sorry. How long have you been widowed?"

"Ten years."

"Does the dress still fit?"

"Of course not."

"Then it's time to get rid of it."

Gloria's hands flew to her ample chest. "Oh, I can't do that. If I can lose thirty-five pounds and get back to one-twenty-five, I'll be able to wear it again."

DeeDee rolled her eyes. "The last time I weighed a hundred twenty-five pounds, I was twelve. I have the bones of a lumberjack. I'll never be petite. I don't look fashion forward and I can't wear what I was supposed to be designing. The last time I tried to diet, I almost landed in the hospital." She held up both hands. "That's when I decided I like food too much and no diet was worth it. That's also when I came to the conclusion, that all women want to feel pretty and have the right to be pretty no matter how much they weigh." She grinned. "And when do women want to feel their best? At their wedding."

"I wore my grandmother's wedding dress. My great-grandmother made it."

"Do you have wedding pictures?"

"Do I? Oh, honey, I have pictures. I still have the dress."

"I'd love to see the dress and the pictures."

At nine o'clock, DeeDee climbed into bed and every part of her relaxed into the soft cushioned mattress. *This beats a futon by miles!* But instead of her brain relaxing along with her body, it spun in a million directions.

She got up once and padded across the thickly carpeted floor to peer out the windows that overlooked Main Street. Old-fashioned lamps illuminated the empty street. Far in the distance she could see the dark building that would be hers, a former department store that had sat empty for years. The price was cheap for the square footage, very cheap. *Somehow I've got to make this work.*

***

As soon as morning light began to filter into DeeDee's bedroom, she scurried from bed. A quick shower and shampoo felt invigorating. She styled her light-brown hair so that it framed her face with its feathered ends that were supposed to be slenderizing. Her only good feature was her eyes. They were hazel and the shape had a slight upward tilt. She applied her long fake lashes, brushed on mascara, and lifted them with an eyelash curler. Once her lips were lined and filled in with a bright red, she dabbed a little powder on her nose, thankful for always having clear skin, and left the bathroom.

She looked at her clothes and pulled on a beige knit dress that fell to just below her kneecap. The short plum-colored bolero sweater made her look even longer when paired with the elongated dress. Dropping a multicolored set of beads over her head and slipping on a pair of wild-printed, way too high, Karina Karr heels, she was ready to face the day as a new entrepreneur.

Sleepy Main Street was no longer deserted. Traffic was non-stop. She made her way to the coffee shop. Inwardly she groaned, as the woman ahead of her ordered a spun mocha hazelnut sugar-free with soymilk, upside down.

"Plain coffee, sixteen ounces." She handed over her plastic card, then took the coffee. Checking her watch, she had just enough time to walk to the next block and meet Mr. Dreamy. She pushed those thoughts far away and concentrated on not spilling her hot coffee as she walked along the sidewalk.

Cody Montgomery was waiting for her. *Silver toe tips on his boots? What man wears silver tips?*

He dangled a set of keys in front of her as he bid her a good morning. "Ready?"

"Yes. Very." His wide smile was contagious and she smiled back.

She stepped inside. Large and cavernous, it was much more room than she'd probably ever need. The morning sunlight streamed through the large windows and showed off every flaw. At the very back, there were offices. Two more floors just like the first were above them. She swallowed the lump that had formed in her throat. *It'll be years before I'll need this much room. What have I gotten myself into?*

Two hours later, she sat in Mr. Montgomery's law office and signed the papers that made the building hers.

***

To prevent her frustration from getting out of hand while she waited on everything to happen, she set up her computer in her sitting room at Gloria's and went to work designing a website. She had bought her domain name six months before making her decision to leave New York. The final straw had come when she heard one of the senior designers refer to her as Miss Pig. She was in the wrong place and she knew it.

She wasn't fat; she was female with curves. Constant walking and running stairs had kept her in good shape and doing five flights of stairs and not getting winded was a source of pride. She had muscle or at least that's what she told herself, muscles and curves to go along with her extra thirty-seven pounds.

She paid a company that specialized in setting up websites as stores to create the backbone for her site. All she needed to do was fill in the fields and she was filling them in as quickly as she could. Twice she called the company to ask a question. With their help, her website was turning into a professional store that rivaled the best in the business.

Her phone rang and she grabbed it. "Hello, DeeDee Drayden speaking."

"This is Big John. You called about getting a renovation estimate on a piece of property on Main Street."

"Yes, 400 Main Street. Is there any chance you can meet me there this afternoon?"

There was the sound of breath being exhaled. "I've got to come into town to pick something up at twelve thirty. Could we meet in the next hour? I'd hate to make that trip twice."

She looked at her watch. "Not a problem. I can be there in a half hour."

"See you then."

Dressed casually in a multi colored cape over beige slacks and a pair of Karina Karr clogs, she met the contractor. Gloria Anderson had recommended him. She promised he was the only man to have working on the building and that he was completely honest.

No wonder they call him Big John. The man was huge. Standing next to him, he dwarfed her. At five foot ten inches, few men made her feel small, but she had to put her head all the way back to look into his face. But in spite of his height and bulk, he reminded her of a gentle giant.

He wanted to look at all three floors, even though she only wanted the first floor finished. Then he went to the roof.

She checked her watch. Minutes felt like hours, but she refused to follow him all over the building, especially to the roof. She showed him sketches of what she had envisioned and he made several notes on a tiny spiral pad he had pulled from his shirt pocket.

She watched as he strode to a corner and lifted an edge of carpet. He rapped his knuckles on columns and on walls, shot laser beams around the room, and stared at the ceiling.

"Well?" She crossed her arms over her chest and waited.

"Big job. How soon do you want it?"

"Yesterday would be nice."

He looked at her and laughed. The sound was deep and rich. It echoed in the empty space and matched his molasses coloring.

"I'll give you an estimate next week. You understand I handle all of it. I bring in the electricians, plumbers, et cetera. All you need to do is tell me what colors you want."

She nodded. "How long will it take?"

"Some of that will depend on the subcontractors. I'll have it in the estimate."

Anxiety climbed up her back and pounded in her head.

He pressed his lips together. "It's not going to be done in a week, but I promise if this place stays empty, it won't take us long."

A week later, she had her estimate.

Written in plain English, it spelled everything out including several factors that might slow the job. She punched his number into her phone. After an impossible and useless conversation over the background noise on the other end, she picked up three words: tonight, Gloria's, and dinner.

She headed for the coffee shop. In severe need of a break, she realized that working for herself consumed her. If she wasn't working on her website, she was busy locating and buying equipment and supplies that she would need. She also was networking like crazy.

Fashion was a tight-knit industry where everyone knew each other. She enjoyed her conversation with her old friend, Karina Karr, especially when Karina promised to create a special line just for the bridal store. From wild and crazy to classic footwear, Karina would do it.

Karina let everyone think she was some European aristocrat,

when in truth she was from a dirt poor, Cajun family from deep in the Louisiana bayou. They had met in Milan and had instantly bonded. Not to mention, DeeDee had loaned her two thousand dollars when Karina was desperate, and Karina never forgot it.

DeeDee trod up to the counter of the almost empty coffee shop, stared at the woman who was old enough to be her mother, then held out her arm. "I need a gallon by IV if at all possible."

"Oh, honey, I don't know what you are up to, but whatever it is, it needs to come to a halt. Grab a seat. I'll bring you a cup."

DeeDee sat at a table near the front window, the woman placed a cup and an egg salad sandwich on the table.

"Eat something. The coffee is decaffeinated. You look like you're drinking too much caffeine and not getting enough sleep."

DeeDee's fingertips touched the puffy area under her eyes. "Ugh! It shows that much?"

The woman nodded.

"You're right. I'm probably lucky if I'm getting five hours of sleep at night. I have more to do than I ever imagined."

"What are you trying to do?"

She looked at the woman with a friendly, motherly face, and poured her heart out. "I can't believe I just spilled my guts to a perfect stranger."

"Sounds to me like you need help. You are biting off way more than you can chew." She pulled a paper napkin from the holder and began to write on it. "You need Vanessa's mom, Winnie. Any chance you took French in school? Because the woman barely speaks English, but she's the best seamstress you'll ever meet. You'll find Vanessa at the beauty salon."

"My French is excellent."

"Good." She wrote the names and the street on the napkin.

"And Edith and Mary are both retired, but I know they are looking for work. No one can live on social security these days. Edith works at the pharmacy two days a week, but Mary's not up to standing on her feet to run a cash register. She really could use a job. I promise that both women can sew up a storm." She pulled a phone from her pocket and wrote down the phone numbers on the napkin. "Now who else do you need?"

"A good photographer, a wedding planner, some musicians, a DJ, and a few good men with muscle."

Two more cups of coffee and DeeDee had the names of probably half the town or at least it seemed that way. And she had confirmation that Big John was the best man for the job. She was about to bid the coffee shop's owner a good day, when Mr. Dreamy walked through the door. He tipped his hat and smiled, shook hands with one of the police officers sitting at a table, then chatted for a moment with two women who had been busy typing on their laptop computers. As quickly as he had come, he left with a small coffee in his hand.

She had blown a few hours, but she also had a long list of people to contact. And seeing Mr. Dreamy again was worth every minute she'd spent at the coffee shop.

Feeling refreshed and a little more confident, she stopped by the florist. Each step put her closer to reaching her goals. And after talking to Jim Lapinski, the owner and designer, she knew she could count on him to create beautiful arrangements and bouquets for any occasion.

Back in her room, she transferred all the information she'd gathered into her computer. The day had been the positive jolt that she needed.

As DeeDee and Gloria finished their evening meal, the

doorbell rang. It was Big John. That's when DeeDee discovered that Gloria and Big John shared the same grandfather. He sat at the table with them and polished off a slice of Gloria's raspberry with chocolate ganache pie, then sipped Russian Tea with them as though he was at a garden party. Watching his big brown hand hold a delicate teacup seemed totally amiss.

Big John explained everything and DeeDee listened carefully. Her stomach rolled over. "What do you mean the elevators must be replaced? How do you know they won't work when I turn the electricity on?"

He put his cup down. "I could see they won't make it past code. The newer ones are safer. You'll have two options, replace or refit those. Refitting might be cheaper. If you'd give me a key, I can meet the elevator company and have them look it over. Newer ones are going to be quieter and smoother, and they'll look better. You said you want everything to look modern. Which brings me to another thought." He drank more tea and asked for a refill. "Those showcase windows upstairs... Certainly you'll want to utilize them, correct?"

"I wasn't planning on doing it right away."

"Why not?"

"Ah..." She hadn't thought that far ahead. "I-I mean... Yes... I guess it would be a good idea to use them."

He nodded. "Okay. It's in my estimate, but two are leaking and the others will be."

Money figures spun in her head. It wasn't that she didn't have money - she just didn't want to spend every penny of it. And she had no desire for anyone to know how much money she did have.

Before Big John left, she had signed the contract and wrote a check for the deposit. It was a lot of money, but it was still less than she had expected.

She fell into a pattern. Her workday started at eight thirty and ended most evenings by six. Then after dinner, she'd draw for an hour or more in the evening.

She created several lines: from classic to casual; from white to dramatic black, and every shade in between. She wanted something for everyone and every figure. What looked good on a petite size-two woman wasn't going to look good on the woman who wore a four X.

Women didn't want to be considered extra large. She created her own numbering system and divisions. There would be a certain number of rack-like items available in plain cotton that could be used for fittings, but each dress would be made for the individual bride.

Faithfully at nine o'clock, she turned out her lights and sat by the window that looked over Main Street. The town was quiet. Peace settled over her, releasing the tension from her shoulders and neck. Mentally she made plans, not just for the salon but also for her life.

The fashion industry wasn't filled with eligible men. And her long hours didn't allow her to drop everything and go have lunch or even promise that she'd be available for Friday night dinner and a movie. Besides men didn't like independent women, and she had more alpha qualities then most men.

But in the quiet moments before retiring, that estrogen side of her wanted a man's arms wrapped around her, and someone who looked like Mr. Dreamy would be perfect. She pushed that thought away.

What she needed was a good supplier for pearls and other

beads. She had the name of one but they were expensive. *Another source, but where to find it?*

Two

Cody Montgomery shut down his computer and turned out the light in his office. His receptionist who also doubled as his secretary had left early to pick up her son from school. Now he was running late picking up his boys from the babysitter. He should have called Melissa and had her pick up Colin and Logan, but he didn't think it was right to impose on her.

He cut across the alleyway, down two blocks and over one more. Two marriages had yielded seven children. At least they had each other.

"Hi Donna," he called, as he pulled open the kitchen door of a brick house on a quiet street. "I know. It's the third time I've been late this week. Carlie had to pick her son up from school after lunch. Apparently he had a stomachache. I needed to finish something before I left."

The young mother walked out of the laundry room carrying a basket filled with whites and dumped them on the kitchen table. "There's something going around. I've made Tommy stay in his room. He's come home with a stomachache."

"Oh, no."

"I've kept the twins away from him, but they all rode the bus together."

"Daddy!" Two little towheads grabbed his legs and almost

knocked him off balance.

He grinned as he grabbed them into his arms and hoisted them to his hips. "Stop tackling me."

"I need twenty-five dollars for our class trip and you've got to sign this." Sean didn't even look up from the game he was playing on his phone as he handed over the permission slip to Cody.

Donna sorted white socks and undies according to their size. "Ian isn't here yet. He and Jimmy have basketball tryouts this afternoon and Barb Clayton was going to drop them here afterwards. Why don't you let him stay for dinner and I'll bring him to you after he's eaten. I've got to go to the grocery store this evening anyway."

"Thanks." He lowered the twins to the floor. "Guys, go get your stuff. We need to get home."

He and the twins walked the three blocks to their home, with Sean trailing behind, acting as though he didn't know his stepfather or the twins. Cody knew part of it was Sean's age, but that didn't stop the worry that niggled inside of Cody. That boy lived to play computer games.

Quiet and introverted, Sean created his own world and lived within it. Cody saw himself at that age, the loner who didn't get involved with other kids. But he wasn't certain how to draw the young man out.

Cody knew he was still a loner. The difference was, he learned to live in a world with people. He'd spent the last ten years working with Project Release, a nonprofit group that worked to protect and prove the innocence of convicted felons. He'd managed to prove the innocence of two men and one woman. Along the way, he'd stumbled upon countless violations of rights, which gave the inmates new trials and often reduced sentences. Most of the time, those serving time were guilty. His job was to search for the proverbial needle in the haystack.

Occasionally, he'd handle some private legal matter for a friend, but most of the time he pushed it off on the local law firm. He wasn't interested in making money. He had money. Thankfully, he was in the position to give back to society.

Darkness was settling as he approached the front door of his home. His children were his first priority. He unlocked the door and keyed his entry on the small security pad in the foyer. It was important to keep the children safe. His clients weren't exactly model citizens and they had plenty of family and friends that would do anything to free them.

"Melissa! Chelsea! We're home." He heard the car in the driveway and knew by the sound of the engine, it was Julia.

"Sean, do you have homework?"

"Yeah."

"Were you planning to do it anytime soon?"

The boy shrugged.

"Please do it and get it out of the way. I want to talk to you about something tonight. I found a summer program that I think you might like."

"Oh, spare me. I'm not going to sleep in a tent and sit around a campfire singing *Kumbaya*."

A chuckle rose in Cody's throat. "I'll remember not to send you to Camp Granada."

"Isn't Granada in Nicaragua?"

"Never mind. I'll talk to you later."

Cody made his way to the kitchen, washed his hands, and began to prepare dinner. He was no chef, but he managed, and the kids didn't complain too much. His next hurdle was getting them all to the table at the same time. Forbidding cell phones at the table was the only way to manage conversations with any of the children.

With Ian missing from dinner, it was a little less boisterous. That boy had enough energy for three kids and his mouth never stopped, but he wasn't considered to be hyperactive, just active, and his grades were good. Julia struggled with schoolwork but managed to get average grades. Of all the children, Chelsea looked the most like him with her dark hair and blue eyes.

He looked at his second oldest daughter, Melissa. With dark brown curly hair that hung almost to her waist and dark eyes, she was a beauty. It was almost two years to the date that Melissa got sick. Her right hand had cramped and curled her fingers. For almost six months she lived with pain. The doctors never did figure out what caused it, but they looked for everything and asked for DNA testing. That opened the biggest can of worms he'd ever personally experienced.

He had been young when he married Julia's mother. Julia wasn't a year old when he met Jenna. That marriage produced two girls before it ended. Then after several years, he married Patty. She had Ian and Sean from a previous marriage. That marriage produced a set a twins. He thought they were happy and mourned her death. The memory soured his stomach. He pushed his plate away and sat back.

"What's wrong, Dad?" Melissa asked.

He grimaced. "Not very hungry tonight."

He scraped his plate and added it to the dishwasher. "I want all of you on your homework as soon as you're done eating."

He cleaned up the kitchen, then called for Sean to meet with him.

The boy shuffled into Cody's home office and plopped into a chair. "What?"

"Come here and look at this."

"Email it to me."

"No. I want you to actually look at it so we can discuss it."

Sean tipped the monitor slightly and grabbed the mouse. "You're joking? You'd let me do this?"

"I thought you'd like it."

"How'd you find out about it?"

"My father sent it to me. He's on the board of the University."

"Whoa. You think he can get me in?"

"No. *You* have to qualify. I can fill out all the forms, but you've got to write the essay and show them why you deserve to go."

"Six weeks - and I get to stay in a dorm and everything?"

"Yes. Now finish your homework so you can start planning your essay. You don't have much time."

"Six weeks of intense programming so I can write games!"

"Certain you don't want to go camping?"

Sean held up his middle finger.

"Behave." He waited until Sean had left before allowing his laughter to surface.

As he was about to turn out the light and leave, his phone rang. Looking at the Caller ID, he hesitated. Had someone gotten wind of his idea to decorate his home for Christmas with a few million lights timed to music? Prepared to use his most professional voice, he picked up the receiver on his landline. "Hello."

"Hi, it's Elizabeth. Have I caught you at a bad time? I have this incredible idea."

He slumped his shoulders into the padded chair. "I've got to get the twins in bed in a few minutes and the older ones are finishing up their homework."

"Okay, I'll be quick." There was the sound of an inhale. "You are going to the Downtown Business Association Christmas Dinner, right?"

"Yes."

"Great. Please tell me you do not have a date for it."

"A date?"

"A woman."

"No. And if I really needed a date, I'd ask Julia to accompany me."

"She'd probably be pleased to think you'd ask her and bored to tears the entire time. I have a better idea."

"What?"

"Trust me. I've been on this earth a lot longer than you have. I've got the perfect date for you, and you won't be disappointed."

"Who?"

"I'm not telling. Besides it's just an association dinner and hardly intimate. If things click between you, that's great! If they don't, you'll tell her goodnight and that you'll see her at the meeting in January."

"Who are you talking about, Grace Bickers?"

"Grace is almost old enough to be your mother. I already said I'm not telling."

"Whatever. I've got to put the boys in bed."

"Tell Ian I said congratulations on making the team. I'm sure he's busting his buttons."

Why am I the last person to know about my son? "Thanks. I'll tell him."

"You can pick your date up at the coffee shop. Night"

The following morning he got a call from the middle school to come get Chelsea. He had no sooner settled her in at home with a bucket, clear sports drink, and plenty of tissues when he got called to the high school to get Ian. But when the elementary school called for Colin, he said he'd take Logan, too.

Logan managed to get all the way home, but as soon as he opened the car door, the child tossed up his breakfast and probably everything he'd eaten for the last week. Over the course of three days, Cody had picked up every one of the children, except for Melissa, who swore she wasn't even nauseated.

Whatever the children had, it was short lived. At least they all had it out of their systems before they flew home to Utah for Thanksgiving. His parents loved his large brood.

Forty-six family members gathered for dinner. It was wonderful, chaotic, and exactly what a family Thanksgiving was supposed to be. The next day Cody and his sister took all the children skiing.

Strangely enough, it was Ian who loved the ranch. The boy followed Cody's oldest brother like a glued shadow.

But it was while watching the gaggle of young female family

members that Cody's sister roped him into a disturbing conversation.

Barbara gripped his shoulder. "How much have you talked to the girls about sex?"

"I-I've given them the pamphlets and I've told them they can come to me with any questions they might have."

"You dumb jerk. Just talk to them. They are your children."

They're my life. "What am I supposed to say?"

"What did you tell the boys? Or did you skip that too?"

"No, I talked to them."

"Well, talk to the girls."

"What am I supposed to say? I'd like to discuss your vagina? I'd rather not think that my girls have such parts or even intend to use them until they are thirty."

"Do you realize that Julia has a boyfriend and is sexually active?"

"Whatever gave you that impression?"

"When was the last time you checked up on her? Looked in her room, her computer, read her text messages, or even looked in her purse?"

"I'm not doing that to my daughter! That's a violation of her privacy!"

"You'd better talk to those girls before you've found out that one has had an abortion or is pregnant."

"What am I supposed to say, it's time to discuss the birds and the bees?"

"No. Julia isn't actually doing anything at the moment. Grab your coat and hers and tell her you are taking her for a walk. Then just talk to her like a grown woman."

"Now?" His guts twisted into a knot.

"It's as good a time as any."

He turned away from his sister and found the coats. His skin prickled as he walked up to the oldest of his brood. "Put your coat on; we're going for a walk."

In silence, they walked down the fence-lined driveway as he tried to pull together what he was supposed to say to Julia. Plowed snow lay in dirty rows on each side of the asphalt. A steer mooed. His stomach knotted. "We need to talk."

"Is something wrong?"

"Maybe. Maybe I should have told you a few things when you were younger. Now you're grown and…" He held his hand out to her and she took it. Cold stung his eyes.

"And what?"

"When you needed a mother, you didn't have one."

"Obviously, my mother didn't care to stick around, and I didn't like Patty."

"I know." He walked a few more steps. "There were things I should have told you, but I didn't know how. I'm still not sure I know what to say."

They walked for two hours. He gave her his opinions and listened to hers. He heard things that, as a father, he didn't want to hear. And as dusk settled, they sat on the back patio and talked some more. Maybe it was the best conversation he'd ever had with Julia. In the end, he knew he'd raised a sensible young woman in spite of having no idea how to raise a child.

He didn't have any advice on picking spouses. He had

obviously failed miserably. *How do I ever trust any woman?*

Sunday evening they were back home, but before tucking the twins into their own beds, he called to all of them, "I want the dirty clothes now. I don't want anyone telling me they have nothing to wear in the morning!"

As he sorted through the array of dirty jeans, sweaters, and socks, he thought about the upcoming Downtown Business Association Dinner. He was nothing more than a lawyer with a small practice. He liked that. There was the time that Bill Colton, who was president of the association, asked if he was related to Charles Dakota Montgomery. People didn't need to know who he was, or that he was the grandson of America's greatest oil baron, and an heir to all that wealth. Brushing it off was easy.

The paperwork that allowed him to be a legal entity of Cody Montgomery kept a lot of problems away and allowed him to focus on his children and his job. Besides he didn't want the children to think they were privileged or special in any way just because of their last name. Even when they went home for visits, they only saw their grandparents and other family members as family. Not one of them ever questioned the wealth. They only saw a big ranch.

He tossed the jeans and dark tee shirts into the washer, added the detergent, and turned it on. He hated doing laundry, hated housework, but he didn't want the children growing up with a passel of servants. *This is better.*

It was after midnight when the last load of laundry was folded and he tumbled into his bed. As he lay in the dark of his room, he wondered who Elizabeth had intended for him to escort to the meeting. He wasn't into blind dates, but Elizabeth was one of those people in a small town that you wanted on your side. Telling her no was not an option.

Three

DeeDee woke to the sound of her alarm. Quickly she dressed and headed out the door. First stop was for coffee, then she'd meet Big John at her salon.

The coffee shop was busy, but no one was sitting at any of the tables. There was a line that moved along quickly. The scent of cinnamon buns filled the air. It wasn't her intention to have one, but by the time she ordered her coffee, her taste buds were screaming for the sweet treat. She ordered two buns, one for her, and one for Big John.

"Excuse me, please." She wiggled her way between two men chatting by the sideboard that contained the coffee fixings and overheard bits of their conversation.

"That's what I told the city council. Ever since they closed the mill, this place has been a ghost town."

"Too many people out of work. Real estate prices have fallen to nothing."

"Heard Montgomery unloaded that white elephant to some unsuspecting out-of-towner. I wouldn't give fifty thousand for that pile of rubble."

So the bastard ripped me off! She turned and faced the two men. "Are you taking about 400 Main Street?"

The older man with pure white hair chuckled. "Montgomery stood on his head to get that whole block and two more under the historic preservation before the town leveled it. Said it was to protect what we have. He just didn't want to lose his wallet when the city offered him thirty-five thousand. Damnedest man I ever met."

The younger of the two men with a severe case of bedhead started spouting, "Then he stands up and supports that new road. It's gonna take traffic away from here. How are we supposed to survive if all the traffic is on some other road? We'll be lucky if we can get a delivery truck in here if he has his way. No trucks allowed on Main Street? That's just damn stupid!"

She forced a smile and slid past the two men. Anger burned in her gut. If half of what they said was true then she was taken for a major ride on that property, and if Mr. Dreamy was intent on keeping trucks out of the downtown area, how was she supposed to operate? *This place will be a ghost town.*

With a bag of cinnamon rolls in one hand and a cup of coffee in the other, she was in need of a third hand as she approached her building. She shifted her coffee to her left hand and attempted to hold the bag and the cup while digging through her coat pocket for her keys.

"Need some help?"

Her heart and stomach collided, and her cup fell to the ground showering her pants and shoes in hot coffee. "Dammit!"

She faced the voice.

Cody Montgomery stood there with a surprised look on his face. "I'm so sorry, Miz Drayden. I was going to offer to hold something for you."

"I think you enjoy sneaking up on people. I don't find it the least bit funny, and you had better not do it to me ever again! Do you understand that?"

He stepped back and smirked. "A little too early in the morning for you? I'll replace your coffee."

It was then that she realized he had two small boys with him. She raised her gaze to his face. "I'm sorry for cursing in front of the children."

He raised an eyebrow. "I'm sure they will hear much worse as they grow up."

She watched as he picked up the paper cup and lid and put them into a nearby public trashcan.

Her blood boiled. *So much for Mr. Dreamy. Married with children. And a money grabbing--*

Big John pulled his van to the curb.

She watched him climb out and snatch a clipboard from the front seat.

"Howdy, ma'am. We're going to have chilly one. Look at those clouds. Seems like a snow blanket to me. What the heck happened to you?"

"Coffee. I think the cinnamon buns survived." She held up the bag for him.

"Thanks." He took the bag, unlocked the front door, and held it open for her. "I love Elizabeth's cinnamon buns. That was real kind of you, ma'am."

Her gaze swept the entire space and tried to take in everything. "It's beautiful."

"Phil will be here to install the mirrors this morning and the alarm company will finish their installation this afternoon. Follow me."

She toured the large dressing rooms with their private viewing and fitting areas, the bathrooms, and the service areas, which included a break room with a kitchen area. It was exactly what she wanted. It was opulent, spacious, and more than enough to make any woman feel like a true princess.

They walked though a door and entered the actual work area. The small dark offices had been removed. She had several large offices to one side and a huge open area for dressmaking. Racks and shelves had been made to hold bolts of material. There were banks of drawers for notions, buttons, and other small items.

"Are you sure you want all this open area? Seems like a waste of space."

She put her hand on Big John's powerful arm. "This is perfect. If someone wants a train on their dress that's fifty foot long, I can do it. I'll have the space."

Big John looked at her as if she were insane. Anything was possible, and she was prepared for it.

He took her upstairs and she looked around. It had been gutted, and now sat barren but clean. Everything was painted white and commercial grade vinyl covered the floor. What had once been flat picture windows now were showcases with lighting.

"Ready for the grand finale?" Big John crooked his finger for her to follow.

She crossed her fingers. It had been a last minute idea, something that was probably very much needed in a small town where brides had few options. They stepped into the service elevator and rode to the third floor.

Her skin prickled with excitement, as she walked through a large service area that also contained a kitchen. "You've done an amazing job."

Big John opened a set of doors and she stepped into the wedding chapel. Room dividers allowed for several weddings and receptions to take place at the same time. She poked her nose into dressing rooms and bathrooms. Near the very front, there was one small intimate area for that couple that only wanted to be quietly married.

She bit back tears as she walked to the area overlooking Main Street and pressed an elevator call button. Silently the doors yawned open. Even these elevators were a cut above and screamed luxury.

It had cost her a fortune, and she prayed that she could make her dreams come true. This was it; Main Street Bridal Chapel. It had a separate entrance. She had planned everything for a one-stop wedding. From flowers to cakes, dinners, tuxedos, and dresses – she could do it all. "You are amazing, Big John!"

"Nah. Just doing my job." His warm brown eyes twinkled. "I watched my daughter last year trying to plan a wedding. Wish you were here then. Sure could have used you. She ordered her dress from some big company and then it didn't fit. She dissolved into tears. My wife finally called Winnie Kochang. Don't know how that woman managed to make that dress fit my daughter, but she did it. Then the only place my daughter could find to hold the wedding was at one of the hunt clubs. My wife had me making silk purses out of sows' ears, as my momma used to say." He shrugged. "My fault I guess. I sent her off to that big university and she came home with even bigger ideas. She didn't want any little wedding."

Big John opened another door and she was back in the salon. Three men were installing mirrors. But leaning against the wall by the front doors was Mr. Dreamy-turned-nightmare.

"I brought you more coffee. Hope it's still hot. Elizabeth seems to know how you like it." He held out the cup to her.

She took the coffee. "Guess this is where I'm supposed to say thank you for making me spill my coffee."

He lifted his shoulder and let it drop. "I said I was sorry. I'll pay for the dry cleaning of your pants. The dry cleaner is located between Maple and Second. Just take whatever there and tell them to put it on my tab."

"How generous. In that case, I have a nice full-length suede coat in need of cleaning."

He rolled his palm upward. "Go right ahead. You wouldn't be the first female to take advantage of me, and I doubt you'll be the last."

That little pressure cooker inside of her wanted to explode. She clamped her lips together, but she could feel the steam rising to her ears.

He scanned the room. "The place looks great. I never imagined it could look this good. But what are you going to do with the rest of it?"

"Why should it matter to you? You've already ripped me off and charged me ten times what this little white elephant is worth, and now you are trying to stop the trucks from coming into the town?" She brandished her finger at him. "Why don't you just cut my throat now and get it over with!"

She suddenly became aware of the deathly silence within the building and saw Big John standing with his mouth slightly open. She looked at the coffee in her hand and gave it back to Mr. Dreamy-turned-nightmare. "No thanks. I'll buy my own coffee. You probably poured antifreeze in it instead sugar."

She watched his eyes narrow and the muscles around his jaw tense. Then she turned her back to him. Over the next two weeks she had delivery trucks bringing everything from boxes of buttons to clothing racks and sewing machines. She had plenty to do and it didn't include chatting with him.

Big John handed her the permits that had to be posted and the stickers that went on all the doors that the city and fire department required. It all took more time than she thought it would, and the last thing she did was write a check to Big John. Gloria was right, his prices were more than fair, and he had done a superb job.

She set the alarm and walked out of the building.

Friday night she had that dinner to attend for the Downtown Business Association. She smiled at the thought. Elizabeth had said to meet her at four thirty at the coffee shop.

DeeDee realized this would be her introduction to the community and she wanted to make a good impression. Elizabeth said it wasn't real formal, but most people did dress up for it. She needed to think about what she'd wear, but her mind was still on her business.

Boarding with Gloria was the smartest thing she could have done. She was only a half block away and even as the cold air whipped around her, she enjoyed the walk. The town was decorated in Christmas lights and green garlands made from real pine boughs.

Thoughts of creating window displays for that perfect Christmas wedding flit through her mind and then came back to the reality of today. She had eight large windows downstairs and eight upstairs to use. That was enough to showcase sixteen dresses and she didn't have a single one made. She was hiring three women based on the word of others. A chill raced through her system. *Have I completely lost my mind?*

As she approached the green door where she lived, she stopped for a moment. This wasn't New York. She had a feeling, an eerie feeling that gripped her neck and quickened her pulse. Something said she was being watched. She turned slightly to catch a glimpse of her store and discovered Cody Montgomery watching her. That cowboy hat was unmistakable. *Bastard!*

She opened the door to Gloria's and went up the stairs to her rooms. Something smelled good and her tummy rumbled. She hadn't eaten anything all day and she hadn't even had a cup of coffee. Remembering that cup she had handed back to Cody, she inhaled. *He deserved it.*

Someplace in this little town had to have a store where she could buy her own coffee pot and a few mugs. She mentally ticked off a mini list of things for the break room. Having spent a large chunk of her money, the thought of spending more grabbed at her empty stomach. She ran her fingertips over her forehead, then changed into a pair of comfy old jeans and a baggy sweater.

"What am I going to wear to that dinner?" she mumbled to herself as she looked around her big closet.

Lifting several things from the rod, she considered each one for only a moment, then put it back. But when her hand touched a green wool dress with a gored skirt she knew it would be perfect. Her gold lamé jacket would be just the thing to pair with it.

She normally wore the jacket with her black dress, but over the green, it would add a festive touch, yet still be conservative. She hung the two pieces together, then she went to her jewelry box and found a necklace and earrings. Bright green Karina Karr heels with a matching purse would set it all off.

She made her way to the kitchen. "May I help by setting the table?"

"It's going to be simple tonight. Fiesta Chicken." Gloria reached into a cabinet. "Here. Use these bowls for the meal and those smaller ones for the salad." Gloria then lifted the lid to the slow cooker. The rising steam filled the kitchen with a strong aroma of spices and chicken.

"I'm starved! The only thing I've had all day is a sip of coffee early this morning - that was before I sent the rest of it to the ground."

"Oh, no! You need a coffeepot at work."

"I was going to ask if someplace nearby would have one and maybe a microwave."

"Tyson's Appliance closed several years ago when the big super store was built. They couldn't compete with the prices. Lots of folks thought it was terrible, but in the end it was better for all of us to pay less for such things. Competition benefits everyone except the competitor who can't compete."

"True. I've got a lot of competition out there. I'm hoping I can give them a little more for their money. Better styles, better fit, and a place where they can get it all."

Gloria tossed the salad and ladled it into the small bowls. "From the sketches you showed me, you've got some beautiful dresses."

"Thanks."

They chatted about their day in general, and Gloria offered to take her to the big super store.

"If you don't mind. That would be perfect. There are several things I could use."

At nine thirty, she fell into bed exhausted and at six a.m. her alarm was ringing. She intended to be at her store sooner, but as tired as she was last night, she knew she'd need the extra sleep. It helped.

She carried the tiny microwave to the store, returned to the apartment and picked up the little cube refrigerator. As she made her last trip with the coffeepot, coffee, toilet paper, creamer, sugar, and a half dozen other small items she'd picked up at the grocery story, she realized how out of shape she had gotten in these last few weeks. She also didn't need to run into Cody Montgomery.

"Let me help you." He reached for her packages.

"Do I look like a helpless female?"

He grinned. "Do I look like the kind of guy who is going to rob you of your packages?"

She glared at him and kept walking.

"What is your problem? I said I was sorry about scaring you, and I even brought you more coffee. You handed it back to me and inferred that I'd probably poisoned it."

She cut him a sideways glance. "I bought your property. That's all I bought. Take your charm someplace else. There's no point in wasting it on me. Besides I don't mess with married men!"

"I was trying to be a gentleman. That has nothing to do with being married or not married. This is a small town, and you're new here. Is there something wrong with my being nice?"

She lowered her packages to the ground long enough to unlocked the doors to her store. "Good day, Mr. Montgomery."

She pushed her packages through the door with her foot. Although she wanted to slam the door in his face, she couldn't because they had an auto-close mechanism. The door quietly slid back into place. She pressed the button and locked the doors behind her.

At least this morning she'd have coffee and Butterscotch Krimpets.

She set up the coffee pot and breathed a sigh of relief as she listened to the sound of water heating. She'd have coffee - her coffee - in *her* store.

Satisfaction was short lived as her mind turned to other things, including greeting the three women who she had recruited to work for her. Elizabeth was right. All three were obviously skilled, but it was Winnie Kochang who was the most proficient. She could actually cut patterns. And they all seemed anxious to be working, especially Mary.

As her deliveries began to arrive, she unpacked and set each item up. It was her clothing racks that stumped her. Her little toolbox only contained a few tools, but she assumed it was enough. She sat on the floor as she stared at the pieces. There were no directions. No paper that said add this piece to this. Frustration chewed at her. Knowing that giving into that aggravation was useless, she persevered. After trying several times, she finally figured out which metal tube went where. Once she got the first one together, the other eight went quickly. She picked up the one rack to place it on the showroom floor and realized that none of the bolts were tight enough. Annoyance from deep within flew up her throat and came out in a loud surge. *Why? Why does every little thing have to turn into a major project?* Tears spilled down her cheeks. *Have I made the biggest mistake of my life?*

Friday morning, she went into the store and awaited more deliveries. Each step of the way put her closer to her goal, but she was also whittling away her money. She needed to protect what she had. It wasn't an endless supply.

When the last delivery truck left, she checked her watch. She barely had enough time to get ready for the Downtown Business Association's Holiday Dinner. At the apartment, she showered and fixed her hair. Taking a little extra time with it and her makeup made her feel special. She liked dressing up.

I spend way too much time alone. She stared into the mirror and admired the way she looked. She stepped back, turned, and looked over her shoulder. *Oh yeah. I look good. Nothing is going to ruin this night. This town is going to know who bought the white elephant and who is going to put them on the map. I'll fight to my death to keep the trucks rolling through the downtown area.*

Four

Showered, shaved, and dressed in a good black suit, Cody looked in the mirror as he cinched the fancy gold Christmas bolo tie clip that had once belonged to his grandfather. *Too childish?*

Memories of his grandfather filled him with sweet sorrow. He could barely remember his father's mother, but his grandfather had left a strong impression that wasn't going to leave anytime soon. Of all the family members, Cody was the one who resembled the old man the most. There weren't many family photos of the man, but in each one, the resemblance between them was remarkable.

Cody stared into the mirror. His hair was still black, but the threads of silver were there. It made him look older than he was. He turned away and ran a cloth over his boots. A chuckle rose in his throat. *Elizabeth. I'm Elizabeth's date. She just didn't want to have to sit with Mr. Tyson.*

A little part of him relaxed. "Julia!" he called, as he walked down the hall. *"JULIA!"*

"I'm in the kitchen."

"I'm getting ready to leave." The oldest of his pack met him in the foyer.

He grinned at his adopted stepdaughter. "I should be home

probably no later than ten. This dinner should end at nine. If for some reason I'll be later than ten, I'll text you. Are you going to be all right?"

She rolled her eyes. "Dad, I can handle them."

"What about dinner?"

"Hot dogs, rolls, baked beans, coleslaw, chips, stuffed celery, and for dessert, ice cream. I can handle it."

He put on his heavy coat. I'll be at the Grand Hotel on Main and Market. I left the number for the hotel's desk in the kitchen."

"I have your cell phone number. Why would I need the desk number? Get out of here!"

"I'm going. I just hate sticking you with everyone."

"Leave!" She pointed to the door. "And stop worrying."

He wrapped the Black Watch plaid scarf around his neck and tucked it in the front of his coat. Then hopped in his SUV. When he reached the coffee shop, he parked in the front.

Elizabeth still had the paper taped to the front door saying she would be closed early for the Downtown Business Association's Christmas Dinner. *That is so not politically correct. It's the Holiday Dinner.*

Laughing to himself, he opened the door and spotted Elizabeth chatting with several local businessmen from the community. He also saw DeeDee Drayden standing in the huddle, looking like a million bucks in a green and gold outfit. There was something about her that appealed to him. She was confident, and poised, but there was something else... He couldn't put a word to it.

His gaze caught hers but hers was icy. Why did he care so

much? He'd given up on women. There were a few in this town that practically threw themselves at his feet, and he didn't want anything to do with them. He'd been burned twice and that was more than enough.

"There you are." Elizabeth smiled brightly at him. "Come meet DeeDee Drayden, our newest downtown merchant."

He looked at DeeDee and smiled. "We've met."

The glare she returned was enough to send the room to sub-zero temperatures.

"Wonderful!" Elizabeth pulled him closer to DeeDee. "I suspected as much when I found out she bought the old department store. I'm sure the two of you will have a grand time getting to know each other. DeeDee, you ride with Cody and we'll all meet at the hotel."

"I'd rather--"

He grinned. "Miz Drayden, it's merely a business meeting. There will be many more. I assume you have a coat."

She practically snarled at him, and he found it charmingly funny.

Her eyes narrowed.

"May I help you?" He attempted to take the fancy wool cape but she yanked it away from him. He did manage to hold the coffee shop door for her and then open the door to his vehicle. "It's only a few blocks."

He slid behind the wheel. "Miz Drayden." He offered his right hand to her. "Truce for the evening?"

She sat motionless.

He put his hand on the steering wheel. "I promise, you do not want to disappoint Elizabeth."

"It was very considerate of Elizabeth to provide me with a ride to the hotel, being there is no bus system here. For that, I thank you."

"You're welcome." He pulled from his parking spot in front of Elizabeth's little coffee shop onto the road. "The Downtown Business Association is a bunch of stodgy old coots who are scared of change. If they don't wake up, the downtown will be a ghost town. We almost lost the pharmacy last year. The City Council stood on its head to prevent the home office from pulling it out of here when the…"

"I don't care about your local politics."

"You'd better. It's called grassroots. It starts here and ripples to the state and federal levels."

"My understanding is that you are trying to keep trucks off Main Street."

"Yes. Main Street needs to be preserved for its historic value. We don't need tractor-trailers thundering down our narrow street to reach their destination on the north side of town. When that warehouse is finished, Main Street will be destroyed if the city doesn't build the access road to the interstate, but the Downtown Business Association seems to think that access road is going to take business away, so they keep blocking the funding."

He pulled into the parking lot of the hotel as sleet began to fall. "Wonder how much of this we'll get? The kids love when school is canceled."

***

DeeDee looked at Cody and bit back her anger. She already had a half-dozen tractor trailers delivering supplies to her bridal salon and with luck, her business would grow to the point of needing them daily. She didn't want her business to be so huge that the dresses were being manufactured in the Far East. She wanted them custom made for each bride. If she could fill that second floor with seamstresses, she'd have more than enough business.

He opened her door and offered her his arm as he held a large umbrella over her. She wanted to growl and bare her teeth. Instead, she ignored him.

The black pavement shimmered under the large floodlights, and in places looked white. Icy pellets hit the umbrella, cars, and pavement, creating a noisy staccato. Part of her was glad she wasn't walking the eight blocks, but Cody Montgomery was probably the last person she wanted accompanying her.

She watched where she was stepping and realized he was wearing black snakeskin boots with gold tips this time. The desire to touch them and see how they were made overwhelmed her. She wanted to feel the leather and take notes on how they attached the metal tips. Why did they have to look so good? Why did he have to look so good in them?

When they reached the protective covering of the hotel's baldachin, he closed the umbrella. The doorman opened the door and they stepped inside.

Victorian elegance screamed from every direction. It felt as though she had stepped back in time. In the very center of the room was a Christmas tree that had to have stood more than twenty feet high and was decorated in feathered ornaments and cut glass bubbles. Tiny candle-like lights flickered and added a magical touch to the tree. She wanted the name of whoever had decorated the tree. That took talent, and it was that kind of talent she wanted in her shop.

"This way."

Cody's words brought her back to why she was standing in the hotel's large reception room. She followed him past the old curved mahogany desk that must have been fifty feet long. Brass bells sat every few feet along its polished surface and old-fashioned brass keys hung on the wall behind it.

This place is unreal! It's gorgeous.

Cody yanked on her.

She gasped.

He chuckled as she tried to compose herself. If he hadn't almost pulled her off her feet, she would have walked into a large column.

"Hello, Mr. Montgomery." A woman sitting at a long table smiled as she handed him a name badge along with a handful of papers and several tickets. "Hold onto your tickets for our drawings. You wouldn't want to miss out on all the fun."

He nodded. "And this is Miz Deanne Drayden, our newest business owner on Main Street. I'd like you to meet Miz Margaret Olsen; she's the secretary for our group."

"Oh, yes. Elizabeth told me you'd be bringing her." She looked at DeeDee and smiled, except it looked way too forced. "It's here someplace. Oh, she picked up the nametag. "I'm afraid we have your name wrong. I thought Elizabeth said DeeDee."

"That's fine. DeeDee is a nickname. Pleased to meet you." She offered her hand, but the woman placed the badge and the papers in it.

"Go right through those doors. Your seats have been assigned." She pointed to a set of doors to their left. "Elizabeth made sure you were both together."

Great! I'm stuck with him the entire night!

One long table sat near the wall and in front of it, there were several large round ones set for eight. The room was quickly filling with people. Cody kept his distance, but introduced her to everyone and made certain she knew who the important people were within the group.

After the usual dinner, a group of young scouts entertained them with carols. Then Carol Brady, who owned an income tax service franchise, took the mic and began to reiterate the year's financial standing and accomplishments. "I'd also like to announce that we succeeded in our goal to collect over four hundred thirty-seven toys for needy families in the area."

The room clapped and cheered, forcing the woman to stop until the revelry died.

"And as you know at the last meeting, we were under in our goal to raise money for fuel assistance to heat the homes of those less fortunate in our area. Since the mill closed, the needs of the community have risen significantly, and we expect this year to be even colder…"

DeeDee's mind wandered to her own salon. She was standing on her head trying to get it off the ground and it had taken a fortune to do it. Now she'd be asked to contribute to the community. *I cannot fail!*

"But I'd especially like to thank Cody Montgomery for his

anonymous donation of fifty thousand dollars to our community outreach fund."

What! DeeDee gazed sideways at Cody who had dropped his head into his hand as the entire table muffled chuckles. DeeDee whispered, "Did she just say anonymous?"

"Well, it's not anymore."

Dr. Karen Hoovaar patted him on the arm and in a low tone said, "Thanks. It was much needed."

By this time the entire room hummed in soft chuckles, giggles, and whispers.

Mr. Tyson spoke up, "Carol, anonymous means no one is supposed to know who donated the money. But I think everyone in this room appreciates what Mr. Montgomery did. That was very generous. I'll remind everyone here that it was anonymous, so please keep the information to yourselves. What happens in this hotel stays in this hotel."

A few minutes later, DeeDee was asked to stand, as she was welcomed to the association.

Then the DJ took over and tried to lighten the mood.

Cody put his hand on her back and whispered near her ear, "May I have this dance?"

She glared at him and he shrugged.

He held up both hands. "No coffee."

She couldn't hold back the smile that pulled at her cheeks. "Why not? I'll warn you I'm not much of a dancer. I've had very little practice in my life."

He held her chair. "I find that hard to believe. You have a natural grace."

She raised her eyebrows and stared into his very blue eyes. "Chubby little girls don't take ballet. They take tap."

He chuckled. "Let's see what you can do."

He stopped by the DJ's table and said something, then waited until Bill Medley crooned *I've had the time of my life* before escorting DeeDee onto the dance floor.

Butterflies rose in her stomach as he took her hand.

"Nice and easy, just follow me."

It took her a second to catch onto the footwork.

Cody talked her through most of the steps. His grin was contagious and the room sort of fell away. It was just the two of them. He spun her around and even dropped her back over his arm. His arms encased her and she was pressed to his body. Her heart beat with the music but something deep inside her burned from his touch.

He spun her off, and inside she froze until she realized he was shedding his suit jacket. There was something about a man wearing a tailored vest and it caused that little fire to glow brighter. Then he grabbed her and they started again. It was the same basic steps done over and over. Some were closer and slower and some were faster and at a distance.

The music was inside of her. She was thirteen and dancing in her bedroom. Closing her eyes, she raised her arms above her head. She found herself smacked against his hard body. His breath was on her face, his hands on her waist. He lifted her into the air, and then slowly returned her feet to the floor as if she were a little feather. Her heart still pounded as the music died.

Still against his chest, *Bless the Broken Road* played as she found her breath during the slow dance. Her one arm rested over his shoulder while her other hand was entwined with his. His free hand pressed against the small of her back. A few minutes later, she rested her head on his shoulder and swayed to Elvis Presley singing *I Can't Help Falling in Love with You.* The trance began to break and she realized she was on a dance floor with Cody Montgomery.

He escorted her back to their table, then out of the hotel, and into the freezing cold. "My place?"

Instant red flags rose in her. "No, take me home. I'm not some desperate female looking for a hot night. Besides, where's your wife? Away for the weekend?"

He chuckled. "Oh, you are quite safe with me. And you don't have to worry about the last female in my life, I dropped her in the compost pile years ago."

Her insides turned to ice.

***

Cody pulled his vehicle directly into the garage and then wondered if he had made a huge mistake. *Maybe I should have used the front door?* "Welcome to my insanity."

The laundry room was overflowing in dirty laundry and someone was washing something. Fortunately the kitchen looked to be fairly clean. He dragged DeeDee to the front of the house and called up the stairs, "I'm home and I'd like for you to meet someone."

Melissa scrambled down the stairs first, followed by Chelsea, then Ian and Julia appeared.

Melissa spoke first. "Sean is watching over Collin and Logan in the tub."

He nodded. "This is Miz Deanne Drayden. She bought Patty's building."

Melissa extended her hand. "Hi. Pleased to meet you. I'm Melissa."

Each child present followed suit.

DeeDee decided they were a ragtag group of children, none of which looked like their dad except maybe Chelsea because she had dark hair. Half appeared in pajamas while the others were casually dressed in jeans.

Julia asked, "What are you doing with the building?"

"I'm a fashion designer. I'm opening a bridal salon."

Her eyebrows shot up. "The whole building?"

"Not exactly. I'm a dress designer. Part of the downstairs will be the store, the rest is where the dresses will be made, and the third floor will be available for weddings and receptions."

"Fashion designer… That's so glamorous."

DeeDee smiled at the young woman who seemed totally enthralled. "Much like any job, there's always the drudge side of it."

Julia looked at her father then back at DeeDee. "Will you be hiring? Dad said I could have a part-time job as long as my grades don't dip. I'm a senior."

"I'll be hiring quite a few people." She reached in her purse and jotted her info on a sticky note. "Here." She tore the note off. "Everything is online. Look under careers."

"Thanks!"

"This way." Cody leaned his head in the direction of a hallway.

"I have a home office."

She followed him into a rather large room. Everything about the house had a lived-in but quiet, understated elegance about it. His office was no different. She didn't recognize the wood of the furniture, but it was light, and the accessories were all in sandy-gray whites. Pictures of the children hung on the walls creating huge collages.

"Do you drink?" he asked as he opened a cabinet.

"Not much."

He poured some brandy into a warmer and lit the candle under it. "Have a seat."

Several overstuffed, micro-fiber upholstered chairs created a pleasant sitting area. She chose one and sat. It enveloped her in its squishy softness. Her whole body relaxed including her shoulders.

"Your wife?"

"She woke up one night with abdominal pain, one ambulance ride to the hospital, and a half-dozen tests later and it was determined she had a tumor. My mom stayed with the children while I took her to Texas to one of the finest cancer treatment centers. Two and a half weeks after that ambulance ride, she was dead. Total shock."

"I'm sorry."

"Don't be. As my grandfather would say, it was a lifetime ago with lots of water under the bridge. She was cremated. She loved the garden." He shrugged. "Here." He flipped open a panel on the side of the chair where DeeDee was sitting. "A little heat, a little massage, lean back."

A footrest rose from the chair and lifted her feet. The chair began to warm and rumble under her. "Omigosh, I want one of these."

"Now you know why this is my hiding place." He handed her a brandy.

An audible sigh escaped her throat. She sipped her brandy and then set it beside her. *Why do I hate this man?*

***

Cody watched her close her eyes and when she failed to answer his question, he knew she was asleep. To allow her to sleep undisturbed, he dimmed the lights and left the room. He warned the girls that DeeDee was napping and made his way up the stairs to the twins.

Greeting them was like greeting overly large puppies. They bounded into his arms with excess energy. They smelled of soap, shampoo, toothpaste, and freshly laundered pajamas.

Two bedtime stories later, he had Collin and Logan tucked into their beds. Then he checked on Sean and Ian. They informed him that school would be two hours late. "Doesn't surprise me. Do your sisters know?"

Ian laughed. "They told us."

Sean held up his phone. "We get alerts."

"Is your homework done?"

They both nodded.

After returning downstairs and checking the weather outside his door, he knew he needed to make a decision. He either needed to walk DeeDee home or let her spend the night. There was a slick layer of ice on everything.

"DeeDee," he called softly from the doorway of his office. He watched her stir. She was different from other women he had dated, truly independent, and obviously driven to succeed. He liked that. She wasn't needy and looking for financial support. She also didn't seem to be in need of a man. That thought stopped him. Had he read her wrong? He didn't think so. *Maybe she's been burned?* "DeeDee."

She sat up quickly and touched the back of her hands to her eyes. "I'm so sorry. I can't believe I fell asleep. How do I turn this off?"

He came over and pressed a few buttons.

"I can't believe I fell asleep. I'm so embarrassed."

"Obviously you were tired. We all have those days." He glanced at his watch. "Almost a two-hour nap. I hated to wake you, but you need to make a decision. The weather is bad. There's a heavy layer of ice on everything. You're welcome to stay here or I can walk you home. We've got plenty of boots in this house. I'm sure you can a find pair so that you're not walking in heels."

"Oh, no! I can't stay here. I've got to go home. I have to be at the store at eight in the morning."

"I do have a guest room. And you don't have to be anywhere at eight. This town is closed until the ice melts."

"No, you don't understand." Her eyes narrowed. "I have a shipment due in and people coming."

He couldn't control the chuckle that burst from within him. "Maybe in New York, but not here. There are three snowplows for the whole county. If it doesn't warm up tomorrow you're going to find out just how frozen this place really is."

"No, don't tell me that. I've got to be up and running by January 1. Brides don't wait until three weeks before their wedding to order their gowns. The dress has to be made and there are fittings! You don't understand."

"No, not those aspects of it, but you need to be able to accept that plans can change. So you do other things tomorrow that maybe you weren't planning to do until later. I'm not going to be traveling tomorrow. Is there something I can do for you?"

"Yes. Take me home."

"No problem. Let's find you some boots."

He loaned DeeDee an extra ski parka he had, as it was much warmer than her cape. With a heavy pair of socks, her feet snuggled into Chelsea's boots. The walk should have taken only a few minutes instead it took over a half hour as they slipped and slid on the icy surface. But by the time they made it to Gloria's green door, they were laughing.

"Just a sec." He took her key from her. "I can't recall having so much fun walking anyone home. I've enjoyed your company and for someone who doesn't know how to dance, you looked very good on the floor."

She shrugged. "Last time I danced, I was in Milan with a pack of other interns and we were all drunk."

"Really?"

"Yeah, young and stupid." She snatched her keys from him. "I had fun, too."

"Goodnight."

"Yeah, goodnight." She turned away from him.

He watched her go through the green door before he turned

and walked home. As he approached his block, he noticed all the lights were out. But the neighborhood kids were outside with flashlights and ice skates.

He vowed he'd check on DeeDee in the morning. He'd also sworn he was done with women, but DeeDee was unique. And he was certain the attraction was mutual, in spite of her protest. *But why does she act as though I'm going to eat her for breakfast?*

Five

DeeDee woke to her alarm and immediately ran to her window. Everything looked like a fairytale bathed in ice. *Argh I don't need this!*

In less than an hour, she was at the salon. Deep inside, she knew Cody was right. The town had come to a standstill, but she couldn't. She scanned in her new sketches and then put them on her website. She scanned in swatches of material in different colors. Blue used to be the color for a virgin, then it became white. Today such nonsense no longer applied. A woman was entitled to wear any color she wanted and often it was the second wedding that was the formal one. Huge bolts of material hung on racks at one end of the back room. If it was available in more than one color, she brought it in. But it was the satins and plainer fabrics that were available in the most colors, giving her the widest range. Some of her designs were traditional, but even those she put her very own stamp on. What she wanted was for women to have the widest choices and in styles that flattered. From cute and flirty, to elegant, she had designs to fit every budget.

Karina had emailed pictures of the shoes she had designed just for Main Street Bridal. DeeDee laughed when she saw them. But it was Karina's personal note that made DeeDee think. Karina wanted to know if the dresses and accessories would be available to other bridal shops. DeeDee mentally knocked out several large chain stores that carried their own brand of cheap dresses. She picked up the phone and dialed her friend.

"Karina, that's a fabulous idea. Now how do I pull it off?"

As Karina talked, DeeDee searched the web. There were hundreds of small stores that carried wedding dresses and special occasion clothing.

"Karina, I can't do this alone. I'm over my head."

"Honey, I'll let you borrow Chrisy. He's mine, but if you cover his living expenses, I'll loan him to you for a month."

"Chrisy is a he?"

"Oh yeah. I promise he's the best marketing and PR person in this business. I'd still be peddling in some back alley if it weren't for him." Her old southern accent came through loud and clear. Karina never put on airs around DeeDee.

"You're on. I'll fly him down here A-S-A-P. Tell him to call me tomorrow morning."

"And if it weren't for you bailing me out when I was flat…well, I don't want to think about that. I swear, he knows everybody who is anybody, and if he doesn't he'll be their best friend in less than an hour."

"Hope you are right, because I've got so much money tied up in this dream."

As she ended her conversation with Karina, DeeDee had another bright idea. She could create a kit. She found a supplier for inexpensive tape measures. DeeDee began to make a booklet that showed exactly how to measure and had a spot for measurements to be written into boxes. For a few dollars, the kit could be ordered and the amount deducted from the actual cost of the gown. It contained a checklist, and tips for the perfect wedding, along with a dozen small items such as a pen, a magnet, a luggage tag, and a key chain. She wanted to keep her name in front of the perspective client. She was so engrossed with creating and ordering things for her kit, she almost didn't hear the doorbell.

She smiled as she opened the door. "Are you applying for a job?"

"Personal chef?" Cody laughed. "Thought you might like something warm." He stepped inside and handed her a plastic container. "I'm not the best cook, or the worst."

She lifted the corner of the lid and sniffed. "Smells good. Thanks."

"It's homemade. I cooked the chicken last night. I figured if the kids were off from school, it would be there for lunch, if not I'd have it for dinner. You're my guinea pig."

"Am I supposed to be honored?"

"No, forewarned."

It was the twinkle in his blue eyes that made her laugh. Looking at him like this made her realize that he wasn't GQ handsome. His boots and hat made him appear taller than he really was. His dark hair contrasted with his pale skin, and he wore well-tailored clothing. Take all that away and put him in a tee shirt with jeans and sneakers, and he'd be an average guy.

She motioned for him to follow her. In the break room, she divided the container between two disposable coffee cups and found two plastic spoons. "I think I should be honest with you.

Are you man enough to handle it?"

"Is this where you tell me that you prefer women to men?"

"What would give you that idea?" She took a sip of the soup and let it slide over her taste buds. It was divine.

"Well, what do you think?"

"I asked you a question first."

"Let's call it my lousy luck with women."

She raised her eyebrows. "You're the kind of guy who has women falling at your feet. And the soup is delish."

"Maybe it could use some more salt?"

"No. It's fine just the way it is." She took a few more spoonfuls. "So what's with you and women?"

He swallowed then chuckled. "Seven children. That sends a lot of them running away. Furthermore, I'm not looking for a desperate housewife. So what were you going to tell me when we walked in here?"

"I have a whole like/hate thing going on with you."

"Huh?"

"On one hand you seem like a really nice guy, but on the other, I hate being taken advantage of, especially when it comes to money, and that's what you did."

"What gave you that idea?"

"This building."

"What do you mean?"

"I heard you charged me a dollar when it wasn't worth a dime."

"Where did you hear that?"

"I overheard some men talking at the coffee shop."

He shook his head. "You were not overcharged. I practically gave it to you. I'll show you the assessment on it. Patty Shillings was my former wife. The sale of that property finally closed her estate. And for the record, the money goes to her boys. It's held in trust."

"And what about the delivery trucks?"

"I have no clue what you're talking about."

"Seems you want to keep the delivery trucks out of the downtown area."

He shook his head. "In the past twenty years, this town has suffered huge employment losses. There was a small mill that closed way back when, and behind that went Sally Jenkins, a company that made little girls' dresses. Then the big paper mill closed about two years ago. Trying to keep this town afloat has been darn hard. The city council and board of supervisors have been working together to bring in businesses. They acquired hundreds of acres on the north side of town to build an industrial area, but one of the problems is the road off the interstate becomes Main Street. Everyone is afraid that if an access road is built from the interstate to the industrial area, that business in the downtown district will come to a screeching halt."

He leaned back in his chair and sighed. "I've been trying like crazy to support the historical society to preserve our downtown, and bring in new business such as yours, while protecting what we have and enhancing it maybe with a larger arts community. We want to increase the tourists. Make the area more productive, but we can't do that with big tractor trailers rolling through town, and big businesses don't want to be hauling through our little town anyway."

He tented his fingers and brought them to his lips for a moment as if deep in thought. "I'm not trying to stop any trucks from making deliveries. It's the through-traffic that isn't needed or desired. Several times a year, Jim Lapinski, who's the florist, has a tractor-trailer that brings potted plants to his shop, and another one brings supplies. The pharmacy has deliveries several times a week. If we stopped those trucks, this downtown really would fold."

"You said that they closed a dress manufacturer. How long ago?"

He shrugged. "Ten years. I'm not certain. It's been awhile. It was before I came here and I've been here eight."

Inside DeeDee wanted to scream with joy. "I need to find those people who made those dresses."

"I think the whole town is waiting to see what you are going to do with this place. Rumors are flying. Why don't you invite the newspaper for a visit and give them the scoop. Certainly won't hurt, and they need something worth printing."

Two days later, she had the newspaper at the salon taking pictures and asking her a gazillion questions. She was opening her store New Years Day with a big open house and drawing for a free gown. Thanks to Cody's connections, she'd have life-sized pictures of her dresses to decorate her store. The same company was making beautiful signs for outside and would put gold lettering on her glass doors.

She had fire inspections and a dozen other things that she wasn't expecting, but she was also interviewing people who actually knew how to sew and many more who knew how to do machine and hand embroidery. Part of her felt like she had landed in heaven. And the other part was in complete panic mode worrying about every tiny detail.

Ten days before Christmas, Chrisy arrived. Wearing purple heels, hot pink trousers, and a short purple and red jacket, he'd be rather shocking to the general public, but DeeDee was used to such men in the business. He burst though her doors and checked every nook and cranny before saying much of anything to her. She just handed him the keys to the third floor, all the storerooms, the service entrance, and elevator.

An hour later, he reappeared. "Oh, baby, we need to talk!"

"Let's save it until dinner. I have two more interviews." She realized that was probably the wrong thing to say to him by the pout it caused. "Make yourself at home and have some coffee. I won't be too much longer."

He turned and headed for the break room.

With a gray ponytail that hung to his waist, she wondered if Chrisy was another mistake to be added to the list that seemed to grow daily. She tried to remember Karina's exact words about the man, but only remembered that Karina had total faith in him. *If he can put me at the top of the heap…*

She shook her hands at her sides hoping to relieve the tension that had built within her before she went to greet her next perspective employee. As she typed in her notes from the interviews, she spotted a new application from a young woman who wanted to work part time. Julia Montgomery had absolutely no experience, but was anxious to learn. She emailed her back, said yes, and would discuss her hours later. *Everyone needs to start someplace.*

Then she faced Chrisy. "I'm sorry to keep you waiting."

"This place is gorgeous! You've spent a fortune. Ready to spend more? I've been making notes."

"Well, I still have a little advertising budget left."

"Never use *little* around me. That word doesn't exist. Not in my business. I took Karina from nothing to what she is, and I'm going to do the same with you."

"Let's eat. I've paid for your suite at the hotel. It's yours until the end of January. There are no other accommodations, except on the outskirts of town and the hotel is the closest thing to here. It's still a long walk. Karina said you'd pay for your own food, but tonight's dinner is on me."

Discovering that Chrisy was a vegetarian didn't surprise DeeDee. The hotel's restaurant was quick to provide a lovely dinner for him that was more than just salad. They talked until the restaurant closed and then talked more in Chrisy's suite, which was as lovely as promised.

They went over her web pages, and he showed her his ideas for advertising. The amount of money was staggering, but the idea of co-op'ing with Karina was brilliant. Karina was trying to get into more small boutiques and doing it with DeeDee made it easier on both of them. And sharing ads in all the big magazines cut the cost in half, meaning more exposure for both of them.

"You've got to have a New York première! It's a must and you know that."

"I've thought about it, but I have no idea how I could do anything like that at this point."

"Baby, don't worry about it. I'll set you up and fill that room with all the right people."

He gave her a price and her dinner instantly rolled up the back of her throat.

She swallowed hard. "I don't... Really... Oh, my... Maybe I should talk to Karina before committing to such a thing."

"Baby, from what I see of your designs, you'll be doing this for the stars. You'll make more money on that show than you can imagine."

He was right and she knew it, but her money wasn't an endless supply. Panic seized her.

"It's well past my bedtime, and I'm sure after traveling you need to unwind and rest, too."

He walked her to his suite door. "I know it's more than you were expecting, but my job is to make you famous. Trust me, baby. I know what I'm doing, and I believe you know what you are doing. Otherwise, I would have called a cab and walked out of your salon this afternoon."

She nodded and walked the eight blocks home. Her head spun with ideas and finances until she had a headache. She dealt in hundreds and he did everything in millions. Looking at the clear bright sky, she asked, "What do I do, Mom? What? It's your money. Do I risk it?"

***

Cody had spent the day at the federal penitentiary. He had a thirty-eight-year-old man who had been sentenced to life and had already spent twenty years behind bars. The whole case was flimsy and based on almost no evidence other than being in the wrong place at the wrong time.

Cody kept telling himself that we have the best justice system on earth but mistakes happen. It was his job to rectify the mistakes, but every time he found one, it dragged a pall over him that he couldn't shake. He'd spent over two hours driving home and didn't want to face the children while still dragging his foul mood with him. He pulled to the side of the road and called DeeDee. "Are you free for dinner tonight? I could use a serious change of pace."

"Um, I guess. What time?"

"I'll meet you in about twenty minutes at the salon. After that, it's up to you."

"Okay. That'll be fine. I'm trying to finish a few things."

That's all he wanted to hear. "See you in a few."

He called home and Chelsea answered. He told her he was having dinner with DeeDee and he'd be home late.

As he pulled up to the front of the store, he noticed that the windows were covered with white paper and announced the grand opening on Jan 1. He checked the door before he rang the bell.

"Yes. How may we help you?" a man asked, wearing tight jeans, a denim shirt, and a set of heeled boots that came to his knees and looked as though they belonged on a hooker.

"I'm Cody Montgomery, and I'm here to see DeeDee."

"Just a moment." The man left and then returned. "Come in."

Cody stepped inside and the man practically circled him. "Oh, A Raymond Bedham suit, but where did you get those boots? You have very good taste in clothes. Whose tie is that?"

Cody shrugged as he pulled off his outer coat, wondering how this man knew whose suit he was wearing. To Cody, suits were just suits, but he did like Raymond Bedham's wool suits and Acquitrino's lightweight suits for summer. But still how did anyone tell one suit from another? He found DeeDee in the back talking with Winnie Kochang. There were bits of dresses everywhere and it was obvious DeeDee was starting to make bridal dresses.

DeeDee held up a finger to him as if she wanted him to back away so he headed for the break room. There was a half filled carafe of coffee. He sniffed it and the aroma of fresh coffee filled his nose. He poured a cup and sat at a table.

He wasn't alone for long as the man who greeted him at the door came into the room.

"You didn't tell me where you get your boots. I love them."

"Brooks Saddle and Leather Shop on the outskirts of Santa Fe. Yes, they are custom."

"Do they have a website?"

He chuckled. "Not that I know of. But I can give you're their address and phone number. You have to go there to get boots."

"I must go."

Oh I'd love to be there when you ask for a pair of boots. "Call ahead. It's a small shop."

A moment later, DeeDee walked into the break room. "I see you've met Chrisy"

"Not formally."

"He's my marketing person. He works for Karina."

Cody raised his eyebrows as he looked at DeeDee. "Am I supposed to know Karina?"

"All my heels come from there. Karina and I interned together in Milan a million years ago. Surely your girls know about Karina Karr shoes."

He rolled his palms over.

"Anyway, she's providing me with my shoes. It's very exclusive."

"Oh, it is. She would have laughed at anyone else who had asked for such a deal." Chrisy waved both hands in the air. "But you are her most favorite person in the world. You must have some great blackmail on her."

"Hardly. Two glasses of wine and I'm lights out."

Cody chuckled. "I'd say one sip of cognac."

"It was more than one sip and I was exhausted."

"I might actually have fun trying to get you drunk." Cody polished off his coffee.

She turned and put her hands on her hips. "No such luck."

Chrisy laughed. "Oh I want to see baby drunk."

"Anything more than a single glass and my clothes fall off."

Cody laughed. "Then I definitely want to see you drunk!"

She narrowed her eyes.

Chrisy laughed until he was wiping tears from his cheeks.

"It's not funny." DeeDee's stern look did nothing to relieve the situation.

Cody stood and went to her. He slipped his arm around her waist and whispered in her ear, "Is there another way to get you undressed?"

"No!"

"Then I'll have to work on getting you drunk, because I'd love to see you naked."

She reared back and looked at him askance. "I'm not exactly Playboy material."

"Oh, I had one of those and I've got the issue to prove it. Let's go have dinner. I'm starved."

***

On the far side of town near the interstate there were several chain restaurants by the shopping center, but in the downtown district, there were very few choices. The old hotel seemed to have the best food.

Their drive to the hotel was silent but as Cody opened her door, DeeDee fired off at him. "How can you say you want to see me naked?"

He chuckled. "Why wouldn't I? You're beautiful."

"I am not. Do you know they called me Miss Pig behind my back in New York?"

He pulled her close to him as he closed the car door. "Why? Because you didn't look like an androgynous female model? Maybe they forgot what a real woman looked like."

She could feel his breath on her face and her heart beat twice as fast in her chest. Her whole body quivered.

He let her go. "Hungry?"

Her tongue forget how to form the words. "Y-yes. Very."

"Good."

He held her hand as they walked into the hotel. Her stomach growled and grumbled. Her breath hitched and she prayed he didn't hear the protesting within her. As they walked to their table, her stomach rumbled, and it did it again as he held her seat.

"You must be starving. When was the last time you ate?"

"Does a package of chocolate cupcakes with cream filling count?"

"No."

"Oh, then I'd have to say last night."

"Why didn't you eat something nutritious for lunch?"

"Because I didn't want to stop long enough to get it."

He shook his head. "Promise me you'll stop midday tomorrow for some real food."

She lifted a shoulder and let it drop. "Depends on what is going on."

"Do you realize it's almost Christmas?"

"Yes." The lobster Newburg sounded delicious. Just the thought of that creamy sherry-laced sauce made her stomach growl.

"I'd like to have you join my family for dinner on Christmas Eve. Afterwards, I take everyone to the park for the festivities there. Then Christmas Day is a little more relaxed but I'd like to have you at the house for that, too."

"Thanks, that's very kind of you to invite me. Gloria had said something about the festivities, too. It seems to be the big thing around here."

"It is."

His smile was so warm and welcoming. She wanted to wrap her arms around his neck and look up into it forever.

Their waitress filled their water glasses. "May I bring you

something from the bar?"

DeeDee shook her head, but Cody just grinned. "I think we'll save it for dessert. Are you ready to order?"

"The lobster Newburg special sounds delish."

"It comes with a salad. What dressing would you like?" The waitress scribbled on a pad.

"Thousand Island"

"And you, sir?" The waitress smiled extra brightly but her voice oozed with sensuality.

"I'll have the steak rare, new potatoes, and blue cheese dressing on my salad. I'd also like the seafood sampler appetizer."

As soon as the waitress left, DeeDee burst into giggles. "Omigosh. I'm surprised she didn't crawl into your lap to take your order."

He chuckled. "She was a little obvious. Probably wants a good tip."

"You're a very handsome man."

"She's also probably not much older than Julia."

DeeDee attempted to stifle her giggle but it still escaped. "I'd say she has very good taste in men."

"I'm not so sure her taste is altogether that great."

"How can you say that? You obviously have some money. You're impeccably dressed, you have a nice home, you have several nice vehicles in your driveway, and you are handsome to boot. I'd say she had excellent taste in men."

"Oh, do I have you snowed!"

"Let me guess, you are up to your ears in debt and on the verge of bankruptcy?"

"Not even close. I'm very solvent."

"But I thought your job didn't pay much."

"It doesn't. It pays a small stipend and I don't accept it. They pay me a dollar per year, because that is all I will accept."

"You must have one hellava trust fund."

He smirked. "I do. I just don't flaunt it. I let people assume my job is like any other. The money that is raised goes for things like DNA testing and court costs. Why pay me when innocent people need that money? I write everything off."

She put her hand to her chest. "Wow. I had no clue."

"Most people don't, and I prefer that it stays that way."

"You're very altruistic."

"I believe in giving back to society. I was raised to do that. I'm making my children, except for the twins, work at the soup kitchen on Wednesday afternoons, and at the food bank on Saturdays. They need to realize that life isn't kind to everyone."

The waitress set the seafood appetizer in front of them and flirted with Cody again. DeeDee picked up a ring of calamari and held it midair. "And what exactly are the children learning? Have you asked them?"

"Good point. Maybe I should ask each one directly." He lifted an oyster from the shell and ate it. "Ian has talked about a family that he knows. The father worked at the mill and has never found a steady job since. Apparently they lost everything."

"That's so sad, and it happens more often than we want to consider."

"Unemployment and under payment of wages. When my parents were growing up, a man could be a clerk in the store, buy a house, and feed a family of four without a problem. Today, it takes two incomes or more to survive."

"I noticed the people I've employed are thrilled to have jobs. And I'm not paying them that much, just a little over minimum wage. I'm hoping to increase that amount as soon as I get things rolling. Plus I've hired several home workers."

"The scuttlebutt is that you've hired Mary Singleton."

"How do you know that?"

"Coffee shop. I think half the town is thrilled that you've given her a job with benefits. Couldn't meet a nicer woman."

DeeDee shrugged. "It's piecework."

"Right after the mill closed, she had a stroke. Her ability to get around is hampered, but I'm certain she'll be a wonderful employee."

"I've got to make this work. I've got too much money tied to it."

"With your determination, I can't imagine that not happening."

Six

When they finished their meal, Cody ordered Irish coffee for both of them. DeeDee seemed relaxed but not sleepy. He paid the bill and took her to his house.

As they drove down the street, he tuned his radio to the frequency of his personal Christmas music. "Hope you like it. It's been quite a family project, and the kids have had a blast."

He watched her eyes as it dawned on her that it was his house with all the lights that danced with the music.

"How do you do it?"

"The lights are all hooked to a computer. Sean did the computer work. On weekdays, it's lights out at ten p.m., but on weekends, I keep it running until midnight."

He drove down the light-lined driveway and directly into the garage. "I'm terrible. I'm constantly bringing you in through the service areas instead of the front door."

The twins were already asleep, as was Chelsea. With DeeDee settled into his office, he poured her a glass of cognac. "Let's see what happens."

She shot him daggers as she accepted the warmed drink.

He laughed. They chatted and slowly what was left of the evening slipped away. He fixed her another drink. She wasn't drunk, and she showed no signs of being drowsy, just relaxed. "I should take you home before Gloria thinks I'm keeping you all night, and we ruin our reputations."

She raised her eyebrows. "You have a reputation to protect?"

"I most certainly do. I've been the role model for upstanding single parents with teenagers in the house."

"Seriously?"

"Yes. And apparently it hasn't done me much good. Which is why the hall closet upstairs now sports the biggest box of condoms I could find. I say nothing, but they are slowly vanishing one by one."

"Oh, dear. Do you know which child?"

He nodded. "Let's say one admits to a certain amount of activity, but I also suspect a son. I'm presuming that I'm supplying their friends, too. That or somebody is spending way too much time having sex."

DeeDee giggled. "I wish my mom had been as open minded."

"I'm not really, but I don't want one of my children diseased or pregnant. One evening after dinner, I had a long discussion about condoms and their proper use. Let's just say a salt shaker was used for a purpose it was never intended."

"Eww."

He grinned. "I used a disposable one, the kind you take on picnics. And yes, I tossed it."

"That must have been awkward."

"It was at first. I've had a difficult time talking to my girls. I had the five oldest ones at the table, but once I got started everyone was fine." He took a sip of his cognac. "As soon as they got over the embarrassment, we talked about everything. It took the taboo out of sex."

"I admire you for that."

"You can thank my sister who forced me to talk to Julia at

Thanksgiving. It opened the gate for me to really talk to the children."

"I totally understand. I know I'd have a problem talking to a son about some things."

"Ever want children?"

"Oh, I've always wanted children. At the rate I'm going, I'm going to be too old to have them. I figure I'm supposed to have a husband to go along with children. I don't want a sperm bank baby or to raise that child alone."

"Try seven."

"I'm not sure how you do it."

"Neither am I, but I do it. They are everything to me."

"None of them look like you."

An old pain hit him and twisted inside of him. He sipped his cognac and tried to figure out how to say it, except there were no words to camouflage his betrayal. "None of them are actually from my seed."

"But I thought--"

"Julia existed when I met her mother. We married six months later when she told me she was pregnant. That was Melissa. Then we had Chelsea. Chelsea was a baby when Jenna decided she didn't want to be married. She wanted out and she didn't want the children. I stayed single for several years and then met Patty. She was a natural blonde with pretty blue eyes. She had Sean and Ian from a previous marriage." He opened a desk drawer, pulled out a Playboy magazine, opened it, then handed it to DeeDee. "She was very beautiful."

"Oh, you aren't joking. She's gorgeous." She giggled. "And it's more than I wanted to see of your wife."

Seeing the pictures seemed to poke at a distant memory - one he'd shut out a long time ago. "The photos were taken shortly before she had the boys. They are twenty-one months apart. Sean is the oldest. He's about to turn sixteen."

Snippets of events flashed through his mind. "Patty and I met and dated for about two years before we married. We weren't married very long when she tells me she's pregnant. The twins weren't quite two when she died. I was a widower with seven children."

"Oh, dear. That must have been very difficult."

He took the magazine from DeeDee and put it back in the drawer. "The boys don't know about Patty's photos. I figure one day I'll tell them."

He slumped into the desk chair as painful memories swept over him in rapid succession. "Then Melissa got sick and the doctors weren't certain what she had. They had done so much blood work on her and everything kept coming back negative. Her doctor asked if he could do DNA testing to rule out a few things. Naturally, I said yes. They tested all three girls then they came after me. No match, not even a long shot."

He buried his head into his hands and held the heels of his palms to his eyes. "That's when I had the twins done. I suspected it, but I didn't want to believe it. The four children that I thought were mine weren't." The pain consumed him. "I was mourning Patty's death, yet she, too, had deceived me. Not one child is related to the other except by their mothers. They all have different fathers - the twins being the exception. I was swindled out of the most basic thing a man desires. Not once but twice. Two different women, who seemed to have no respect for me or their marriage vows."

"I can't imagine and yet I can. Fidelity seems to be a thing of the past. I saw it all the time in New York. Both the men and the women, they were always sneaking off with someone. Even the gays would go out on their partners. I learned to ignore it."

"I had a lot of pent up anger in me for months. Even the kids could see it. Then one day it hit me. They were all alone, and I was all they had. They needed me and I needed them. It was a turning point. I am their father. I'm the one who is raising them and cares about them. Somehow, I think it's made a difference. They all know I'm not blood related; yet they see me as someone who gives a damn. And that's a whole lot more than most kids have today." He shook his head. "I can't believe I just poured all that out on you. I'm sorry."

She smiled. "I'm glad you did. Your dirty laundry is quite safe with me."

"I have no idea why I just told you all of that. I've never told anyone including my family."

She stood and swayed for a moment before stabilizing herself by catching the arm of the chair where she had been sitting. "Woo! I think I've had way too much to drink."

"Really?" He reached her side in three long strides. "Is this the part where your clothes fall off? I'd be more than willing to help them."

"Probably not, but it is time for me to go home."

"I can't let you do that until I've been properly kissed." He slipped his arms around her waist and gently pulled her tight to his body.

She stared up at him with the most beautiful eyes. Her breath fluttered across his face. He leaned down and touched his lips to hers.

***

Yeah, this is the part where my clothes fall off. Her hands ran up his chest to his shoulders. She wanted him. Her body warmed, and her heart beat faster and harder. His lips left hers and traveled to her ear. They found that soft spot below her ear and followed it all the way down her neck. She moaned. Her skin was on fire and the heat deep inside of her begged for release. His lips were on her cleavage. Her back arched. Another moan escaped.

"Tell me that you're really not drunk, and I'm not taking advantage of you."

She ran her fingers through his hair. "Oh, I'm drunk, and please take advantage of me, because it feels delicious."

He continued to kiss her. His hands were on her shoulders sending delightful waves of heat down her back.

She ground her hips to his. He was packing plenty for a man. His hands went down her back and tucked her tight to him. It was a primal dance. His lips were on hers. This time she opened to him. Their tongues danced in time with their hips. She was soaked in desire.

Fireworks went off inside her and she lost her breath.

No man had ever done that to her with just a kiss, but that was no ordinary kiss, and Cody was no ordinary man. She gazed into his blue eyes. Her still body tingled as his chest pressed against hers with each breath.

He held her for another moment. "Women have an advantage that men don't." His voice was raspy as he spoke. "I need to excuse myself before I ruin my pants."

Her gaze followed him as he entered a small bathroom and vanished inside. *Why not?* She crossed the room and tried the door handle. It opened easily. "Mind if I watch?"

He groaned.

Seeing him and knowing what she had done to him increased her desire. She hadn't seen a man do such a thing since she was a teen and her boyfriend used to do it after their hot kissing sessions.

That thought almost made her laugh aloud. She was fifteen and he was sixteen, hardly a man, but full of hormones. Cody was a man and he was beautiful. She reached out and touched him.

He exploded.

Her breath hitched and she chewed on her bottom lip. A feeling of power surged through her. Knowing she could do something like that to him filled her with a new sensation. One she had never experienced.

Other women talked about the hold they had on their men, but she had lacked the men in her life. She leaned against the door jam as memories of the only man she'd ever had drifted through her. She understood Cody's feelings of betrayal for it had happened to her.

Her eyes met his. She saw only sadness in the piercing blue. Reaching out, she touched his jaw and ran her fingers through his hair. "Maybe next time?"

***

It wasn't quite eight in the morning when DeeDee opened the door to her salon. Chrisy was there and on the phone. He'd already downed half a pot of coffee. She fixed a cup and went into the sewing room. She pulled a bolt of white cotton and laid it on the cutting table, then she pulled another bolt of satin. She needed actual dresses for her catalog and for her mannequins that still sat in boxes of legs, arms, hands, and bodies. That sent her mind in a different direction.

She picked up the phone and called Cody. "Hi, I need to borrow your daughters. I'll pay them and I promise I won't use their faces."

"Certainly, when do you want them?"

"This afternoon after school?"

"School is out for the holiday, do you want them sooner?"

"Yes!"

An hour later, the girls appeared and she explained what she wanted. Winnie and Edith took measurements.

"Your father is going to die." DeeDee laughed as she stuck little pillows under Melissa's breasts and made them look twice as large.

Melissa giggled. "You mean there's hope for me?"

"Oh, honey, you have a few more years before you'll know for certain what size you'll actually be," Edith said as she continued to measure.

"I'm the slowpoke." Chelsea's mouth made a downward turn.

"No, you're not." DeeDee put her arm around the youngest but tallest female in the family. "You're on the verge of womanhood. It's a beautiful place to be. Embrace what you have." She turned to Winnie and in French told her she wanted the ballerina dress with the spaghetti top made for Chelsea. "What I have in mind for you is so sexy. It's not for the large breasted woman. They need a different bodice made of silk. This takes confidence to wear."

Chelsea groaned.

Julia jumped on her phone and soon had a variety of friends

there along with permission from their mothers to be part of this.

Thank goodness for digital cameras!

Several days later, she had a bevy of young girls at the salon along with a young female photographer.

"Just a plain screen, I can isolate their photo and put it on any background that I want. But I love the pink screen. It matches my website."

"Why do we have to have makeup on and our hair done if our faces aren't going to show?" Chelsea asked.

"Because part of your face might show and your hair might show."

Chrisy ran into the room. "They're here!"

DeeDee fanned her hand over her face when she saw the cartons with the Karina Karr labels.

The girls oo'ed and ah'ed over the shoes. Chelsea couldn't walk in the heels that laced to her knees.

Chrisy held onto her and helped her onto the platform for her pictures. "You'll get used to these, pumpkin. I have a feeling your future is paved in Karina Karr shoes."

DeeDee chose a single rose and handed it to Chelsea. "Sniff this."

Chelsea was a natural in front of the camera. One by one the girls had pictures taken and then changed to a different dress. Hair went up and hair came down. As the session continued, the girls loosened up. They laughed and giggled. They caught the hang of what they were doing, and at one point Chrisy stood slightly off camera and turned a fan on several of the girls as their pictures were being taken.

Winnie's granddaughter was there as well as several of her friends. DeeDee had a wide variety of body shapes and types.

Thrilled, she could barely contain her joy. But her real work was ahead of her. She had to get it all loaded into her website. And she had the grand opening on New Year's Day. There wasn't much time left.

When the session had ended, she found Cody in the break room. He had a cooler filled with sodas and enough pizzas for a small army.

"You know models don't eat pizza, which is why I'm not a model." DeeDee grabbed a slice of pineapple, banana pepper, and ham. "I love Hawaiian pizza."

"I'll remember that."

She paid the girls and let them take the shoes they had worn. The girls squealed with delight. Karina Karr shoes were beyond luxury for most of the young women.

When the pizza was gone, the models disappeared, except for Cody's three girls.

DeeDee grabbed her laptop and showed Cody the photos of his girls.

"No way, that's not Melissa. She's not that... you know...she doesn't..."

DeeDee motioned for him to follow her. "Pillows." She showed him the small wedges packaged for sale. "It makes anyone look fuller and even enhances the larger woman by lifting what she has."

Then she showed him Chelsea's pictures.

"That's...oh, no...she's too..."

"What? Beautiful?"

"That's my daughter. I'm not supposed to be noticing this about any of them."

"Embrace their beauty. They need you to see them as young

women, beautiful young women. A father's attitude is important. It's not sexual to recognize them for who they are and take pride in what they are becoming. Your acceptance gives them the confidence to face the world." She sighed and continued, "Chelsea feels like she's nothing because she's lagging behind her peers. I have a feeling she's going to be quite tall and probably never as busty as Julia."

"Jenna wasn't very big."

"Tell her that. She's worried because she hasn't gotten her period."

"She hasn't?"

"You're her father. You should know these things." She crossed her arms. "I think it's time for you to have a long walk with Chelsea."

"Oh."

She nodded. But it was the look of terror on his face that worried her. "Now get out of here. I've got a ton of things to do tonight and I don't need your distraction."

"Really? Well, I intend to give you something to distract you."

He pulled her into his arms and all reason went out the window. She turned into putty as his lips trailed her neck.

He whispered in her ear. "Tomorrow night. You may have the guest room, or if you desire, you may share my bed. I hope you choose my bed."

Her body screamed bed as his breath flowed into her ear, heated her blood to the boiling point, and left her trembling under his touch.

***

Cody walked away from DeeDee, but he was certain he'd stirred her flames. That was one woman who needed her flames stirred, and he intended to be the one to do it.

Maybe he'd chased the wrong women, looked in the wrong places for them, but he was certain he'd found one that was worth pursuing. She didn't need him, but she wanted him. Jenna needed him. Patty wanted him for all the wrong reasons. This time, he was smarter. Having been burned, he knew the difference.

He stopped by the salon about one o'clock on Christmas Eve to find DeeDee on the phone and buried in paperwork. Chrisy was not around. As soon as she got off the phone, he asked, "Where's your buddy?"

"He flew out last night to see his son, but he'll be back."

"His son?"

"Oh, he's straight, but strange. Let's just say he marches to a different drummer - his own." Her giggle was soft. "He loves clothes and color. He's a peacock."

"Could have fooled me. I don't want to talk about him. I want to talk about us."

"No us until after dinner. I promised Gloria I'd be home tonight with her. Besides I have to give her my Christmas gift. Want to see?"

She left the desk where she was sitting and opened a gift bag. "One little black dress."

He furrowed his brow. "Am I supposed to be impressed?"

"Yes!" she showed him the tag. "Custom made for her. And…" She held up two jackets. "Date night and day wear. Plus, shoes to go with it. It's actually a bridesmaid dress for a black and white wedding. It's extremely versatile." She put everything back into the colorful bag. "Since you seem to be so good with the female anatomy, I could use some help."

He followed her to where she had several boxes in the salon.

"Can you put these gals together for me? It's not difficult; it just takes time. I need to finish a few things before I can leave."

He lifted a flap and stared at the jumble of arms in plastic sleeves. "I'll do my best."

He didn't think it would take very long, but it did. *Maybe I need a ponytail to do this?* In a way, it was like fixing a doll that had come apart. Having never paid any attention to mannequins, he found them interesting. DeeDee's mannequins looked very realistic. *Sorry.* He took his hand off the breast of one as he tried to attach her head.

There was a whole box of wigs but he didn't touch those nor did he mess with the other stuff that seemed to be part of the mannequins' accessories. Just bodies. When he stopped, he put his hand on a tall rack and the whole thing wiggled. "DeeDee! I need a wrench."

It was after five when he walked DeeDee home, but she seemed relaxed and happy. "I will pick you up at quarter past seven and you are mine until tomorrow evening."

She raised her eyebrows. "I don't think so."

"Pack your nightgown. It's totally optional as to which bed you prefer, but I'd rather it be sans the gown and in my bed."

"In your dreams."

"A man has the right to dream. And I've dreamt of you plenty of times."

***

DeeDee smiled when Cody came to the door. Dressed in warm clothes, she headed to the festivities with his large brood. They listened to carols, the high school band, and then there was a live nativity and prayer service done by the Main Street Christian Church. Afterwards they all walked back to his house.

Once home, it was hot chocolate with marshmallows for everyone. Collin and Logan kept stifling yawns and protesting the idea of going to bed.

"Wait, they can't go to bed yet." DeeDee reached in her generous purse and withdrew a small package that contained several slices of carrots. "Reindeer food. Got to feed the reindeer."

She took the boys outside and split the bag between the two of them.

Collin looked at his hands. "This is bird food."

"No, it's grain. Sunflower seed to be exact. Reindeer love sunflower seed. It's their favorite, especially when mixed with carrots. Sprinkle it down the walkway."

They did as they were told and then ran inside. This time Cody got them into bed without any problems. Slowly the other children disappeared to their rooms.

Cody vanished to the garage. When he returned, he had a new bike in each hand. "The twins have learned to ride bikes without training wheels, but they've outgrown them. These are from Santa."

DeeDee was surprised that there weren't more presents.

"Why? They have everything a child could want or need. I try not to spoil them. Well, at least not to overly spoil them. Thank goodness for gift cards. I barely know what to buy the girls anymore." He pointed to several large boxes. "Makeup, all in one place. A million shades of eye shadow."

"I'm sure they'll be thrilled."

When he was done arranging everything, including the gifts DeeDee had brought with her, he came to her. "DeeDee, we're adults. I want you in my bed. I want to see your clothes fall off, and I don't want you drunk to make it happen."

She gulped down the lump in her throat.

He pulled her tight to him.

His breath was on her face and her lips slowly met with his. Every part of her body screamed yes, but her head said no. "I'll take the guest room."

He walked her down the long hallway past his office and opened a door. "If you change your mind, this is my room."

She looked at the well-appointed room with a large bed. It was done in the same shades as his office, except this room had touches of black everywhere, including black shutters at the windows. It smelled of sandalwood and patchouli, and a whole lot like Cody. Several large oil paintings of the Rocky Mountains hung on the walls. It was masculine yet beautiful.

He steered her away from his door. "I figured you wanted the guest room."

He opened another door and she was staring at a room done in neutrals but with touches of green. There were fresh flowers in a vase and a plate filled with dark chocolate. There was also a small box, beautifully wrapped sitting next to the flowers.

"You did this for me?"

He nodded. "I want to seduce you, but to be honest, I want you to be a willing participant. You're not the average woman. I could be reading everything wrong, but I doubt it. I think your heart is saying one thing and your head another. I don't want to blow it this time. Go open your present."

She crossed the room and when she reached the flowers she read the card. *To the most amazing woman I've ever met.* Her hands shook as she picked up the package. But it was the quivering inside of her that made it almost impossible to remove the fancy wrapping.

Underneath the paper was a box with a golden crown. She opened the box and inside was a solid gold watch. Diamonds surrounded its face. "Thank you. It's gorgeous. But I can't accept such an expensive gift."

"Yes, you can." He took the watch from the box and showed her where he had it engraved.

To DD From CDM

Then he slipped it on her wrist and fastened the catch. "You need a good watch. Every CEO of a multimillion dollar company needs a good watch."

"I'm not a multimillion dollar company, not yet."

"But you will be, because you have that faith in yourself."

"Still, I can't accept anything like this."

"Yes, you can. I only needed a simple thank you, and you've already given it to me."

She stared at the watch, then whispered, "It's positively beautiful."

Her insides quivered, and her skin was covered in goose bumps.

"Merry Christmas. I'll see you in the morning."

She watched as he strode out of the room. She took several deep breaths. Never had she met a man who bowled her the way he did. Yet he never pushed her. He was just there for her.

She looked around and realized her overnight case was in the room. He had read her like an open book, and she wasn't certain if she appreciated it or if it scared her. Maybe a little of both?

Seven

Christmas day flew by. It was fun and noisy with all the children. Having been an only child, she'd never had such a Christmas. Cody had fixed a delicious ham with all the extras, including plum pudding with a lemony sauce. When it was over, he walked her home and said goodnight.

Panic began to set in, as she had less than a week before her grand opening. She had sticky notes and check lists everywhere.

DeeDee dressed mannequins and decorated the salon. On December 30, the florist shop sent over several van loads of flowers including the silk ones for the windows. Everything was top of the line and she was thrilled. Elizabeth from the coffee shop had promised plenty of hot beverages and the bakery had sent over several wedding cakes. Julia and her friends would be modeling their dresses during the open house.

DeeDee found herself moving things around for the third time and decided there was nothing else for her to do. Her grand opening had created a buzz through town and even the hotel had called to confirm the opening date. People were viewing her website and her hits were steadily climbing.

As she was about to turn off the lights and leave the salon, Cody rang her doorbell. "No way; not tonight. I have too much to do."

"Then I'll do it with you. What do you need?"

She looked at him and fought back the moisture that was determined to pool in her eyes and overflow down her cheeks. "I've got to have all my social media ready to fly. I don't have time to be social."

He laughed at her.

"It's not funny."

"Bring your computer to my house and we'll deal with it together. That's what friends are for."

If I'm going to post all the photos…maybe… She narrowed her eyes. "Are you certain?"

"Absolutely."

"I'll need to go home early in the morning and get my clothes."

"We'll get them now. That's one less step in the morning."

"I have to get all the paper off the salon windows in the early morning. I'll be lucky if I get three hours of sleep."

"I'll get the windows in the morning."

No matter what roadblock she tossed up, he was ready to clear it. And clear it he did. They worked together the entire evening. Then in the morning, he had breakfast waiting for her. She was formally attired and he wore a tuxedo.

She bit back the feelings he created inside of her. She didn't have time for them, but he looked like a million dollars in his custom-tailored Edward Gallows tux that probably cost him more than the average person's car.

"I figured you'd need help, and at least, I'd look the part."

She fanned her hand in front of her face. "You are drool worthy. Maybe I'll just leave you next to a mannequin."

As they left the house, snowflakes fluttered through the air.

"Oh, please tell me this isn't going to turn into a blizzard and ruin everything."

"No, just flurries."

By eight o'clock all the windows were uncovered and DeeDee ran outside to double check everything from the street. Communicating with Cody by phone, she had him make slight adjustments to positioning.

At one o'clock, she opened her doors to a small crowd that had begun to gather. At two, she started her program with a fashion show. At five ten, almost every speck of the wedding cakes had been eaten, the tea and coffee urns were empty, and all but two little goodie bags had been taken. The winner of the free wedding dress was thrilled. The bakery had followed with a free cake to another winner, and the photographer also gave away a wedding package, as did the florist.

DeeDee locked her doors, then went to the break room. She leaned against the counter as tears rolled down her cheeks. Every speck of anxiety that she had experienced for the last few weeks flowed away with her tears.

"Why are you crying?" Cody asked.

She shook her head and left him. There were no words for what she'd been though and no way to explain it. She had succeeded. Looking around the salon, the place was a mess. Someone had spilled a cup of coffee on her new rug and there were enough crumbs to make her wonder if adults had eaten or a bunch of rowdy children. She grabbed the steam cleaner and began to suck up the mess as she swiped the tears from her cheeks.

Cody took the cleaner from her. "Go sit down. You're exhausted."

She bundled the bags of trash, washed the crystal plates, rinsed the urns, and cleaned up the tiny kitchen. She heard Cody turn off the machine he was using, and a few minutes later, she heard him park it in the utility closet.

"Is my beautiful date ready for dinner?"

She shook her head, found her laptop, and checked online. Not only had she gathered orders for quite a few dresses at the open house, she had even more orders online. The desire to scream and shout with joy was only met with more tears.

Cody looked over her shoulder as he rubbed them. "You've done very well. It's amazing. You've opened this business with a bang. I'd say you're going viral."

"Did you post those pictures you were taking?"

"Go check your website, under events. And it hit the feeds, or at least I think it did."

She checked the various places where she had an online presence and the pictures were there. "I see an abundant number of photos of your girls."

"Well, I was proud of them. But it scared the crap out of me to see them in wedding dresses, especially Julia."

"She's going to be a real asset around here. She's got a killer smile, and she's very poised for her age."

They walked out the back door and got into his vehicle. He drove her to the hotel and they had dinner. But it was as they were eating their dessert that Chrisy called.

"You need how much?" Her heart fled to her stomach as ice water flowed through her veins. "No can do. I don't have that kind of money. You're insane. You what?"

***

Cody dropped DeeDee off at Gloria's. She was upset but wouldn't talk about it. She never talked when she was upset. Instead, she bottled things. DeeDee was a tough cookie to crack, and he hadn't managed to break her thick exterior.

As soon as he entered his house, he pulled off his tuxedo and got the twins into bed. Ian had left a note with the days he had practice and Julia and Melissa had their own schedule that actually left Chelsea coming home alone two days a week. There was no way he was going to allow that. She might not like it, but he wasn't going to permit her being alone for hours. She'd have to come to his office.

He called her to his home office. "It's just two days a week."

"No! And I don't need a babysitter. I'm old enough to stay by myself." She burst into tears. "Do you think I'm going to play with matches and set the house on fire?"

"I don't think anything of the sort. You know me better than that."

More tears followed. "Why are you being so unreasonable?"

He took his youngest daughter into his arms. "Will you compromise with me until we can find a suitable alternative? Just come to the office for now until we can work something out. I promise I won't make you do it forever."

She pushed away from him and ran to her room. "You don't understand!"

He went to her bedroom door and lightly tapped. "Chelsea, you're right. I don't understand. And I don't understand why you're this upset."

"Go away!"

He shook his head. Mentally he ticked off where his children would be. Sean was in a science club that built robots; Ian had practice most days after school; the twins were at Donna's with her son; Melissa was part of the literary club and was on the school newspaper; Julia had her first real job working for DeeDee. Being in middle school, Chelsea only had an after-school program option available to her, and she wanted no part of it.

He went into his office and opened his desk drawer, pulled out a folder, and looked at it. DeeDee's parents had divorced when she was three. Her father had a string of DUI's, then seemed to settle down. He was working as a clerk in a convenience store when he was shot and killed. DeeDee would have been nine at the time. Her mom was a registered nurse at a major university hospital.

Apparently DeeDee was latch keyed most of her life. She had graduated from high school with honors and had gone to a design school before moving to Europe. But when DeeDee moved to Milan was when everything changed. Her mother won a lottery, thirty-four million dollars, then died less than a year later.

But he had no idea just how much of that money DeeDee might still have. *If her mom took a lump sum...* He calculated the approximate amount. But there was still no way of knowing what DeeDee actually had at her disposal, how much of it she may have spent, or how that money may have been tied up by her mom. *She seems to watch the pennies.*

Paying a private eye to dig for info had been worth it. At least he knew who DeeDee Drayden was. He didn't want to make another mistake.

His cell phone vibrated and he looked at it.

It was a simple text message from Chelsea. *I'm sorry.*

He texted her back. *U R 4given. I <3 u. Get some sleep. We'll talk l8r.* A smile crossed his face. When had he learned the shorthand of texting? And who thought of spelling later with a numeric eight in the middle of it or making a heart with two keystrokes? Would people forget how to spell after constantly using abbreviated wordage?

He had plenty on his plate, including a convicted man that should have never been arrested in the first place.

Morning broke too soon for him. Seven children made for noisy, busy mornings. Chelsea whined about her stomach aching, and she didn't want to eat anything.

"Fine. Stay home from school. I'll call Carlie and tell her I'm working from home today."

Chelsea vanished faster than a mouse into a hole. He checked on her once around ten o'clock, and found her sleeping soundly. At noon, he called her to the kitchen. She looked pale and he didn't like her color. With a little cajoling, she managed to eat half a bowl of soup and drink some Russian tea.

"I want to go back to sleep." She put what was left of her soup in the garbage disposal.

That's when he noticed the bright red mark on her pajama bottoms. "Chelsea, check the hall closet. Seems to me you've crossed over to womanhood."

She turned and raised her eyebrows.

He nodded. "I lost the last of my little girls today. She's grown up."

"Huh?"

"Your pants. There's blood on them."

Chelsea flew from the kitchen and up the stairs, while he fought back tears. Memories of walking the floor with her in his arms flooded him. Little white socks with lace on the edges and putting her hair into ponytails with bows... Tiny mental videos filtered through his head like a gigantic collage of time.

He'd give her a few minutes before he went to her. Julia and Melissa had crossed over without skipping a beat. Only once had Julia complained of being tired, and the doctor put her on some vitamins with iron. He finished his lunch and cleaned up the kitchen.

He knocked her door. "May I come in?"

"Yes."

He entered her room. All pink and frilly, it belonged to a little girl. "Do you want to go to the doctor? I know she put Julia on vitamins with iron because she became anemic"

"Do I have to go to the doctor? Can't I just take some vitamins, too?"

"I think they have to do a blood test. It's just a little thing. I think they stick your finger. They only need a few drops."

She shrugged.

"I'll call the doctor. If you're up to it, I'll take you out for dinner. Just the two if us, you'll be my date for the evening. Our way of celebrating."

"Just the two of us?"

He nodded. "Wear something special. Fix your hair. This is your first night out as a woman."

"For real?"

"Yes."

Later that afternoon, Chelsea appeared in the living room, wearing a few things from her sister's closet. It was nice to see her dressed in something other than the baggy stuff that she normally tended to wear. But her choice in clothes somewhat shocked him. The black leather skirt and silky, vibrantly patterned blouse had been paired with a sparkle belt and a velvet jacket. This time she could actually walk in the heels for she had practiced prior to doing the open house for DeeDee. Chelsea's hair was piled on top of her head and she wore enough eye makeup for six women, but he wasn't saying a thing. He helped her with her coat and offered her his arm. She took it and smiled at him. His little girl had grown up.

He took her to the hotel restaurant and almost laughed to himself as he hardly ever ate there until DeeDee had entered his life. Now it was a frequent thing. Chelsea's manners were impeccable. Years of fussing at the children were paying off, for each one seemed to know how to behave when necessary. They ate their meal and Chelsea talked about the bridal salon. It was obvious that she was jealous of her older sister's job.

"And that job is impacting you. Do you have any other ideas as to what we can do with you during those two afternoons when

Melissa isn't home?"

She put her fork down and lowered her hands to her lap "Would DeeDee hire me? I'm sure there's something I could do."

"You're too young. You can legally work domestic-type jobs at fourteen. But you'd have to be family to work for DeeDee. You wouldn't even be allowed to use a sewing machine because it's a machine. But being you are family…" He rolled the idea around in his head. Carlie had whined so many times that it was becoming harder and harder for her to manage with her son in school. *If I give her a slight raise. That might work.* "I have an idea. What if I employed you? As my receptionist? I could give Carlie those few hours off, unless I was going to be away that day or in court. But we always know that ahead of time."

Chelsea rolled her eyes.

"Consider it. I'll pay fifty cents over minimum wage. You'll have to do some typing, and you won't be able to *kibbutz* on the phone with your friends. It's a real job. And no jeans on those days, I want you dressed for work."

"Seriously? You mean I'd really be working for you and not just watering the plants or something?"

"Yes. Are you up to it?"

***

DeeDee smiled brightly when she saw Cody standing in the salon.

He smiled back. "How's our town's newest entrepreneur?"

"Crazy!" She circled her finger near her ear. "I'm out of the kits that go to every bride. Julia spent most of this afternoon ordering more for me. She's wonderful. I should have hired her when I first got this place. She's a wiz on the computer."

"She loves it here."

"I'm going to teach her every aspect of this business including the sewing. She doesn't seem to have the drawing skills, but she's got a great business head. And people like her."

He nodded. "I'm glad it's working out. I've never seen her get into anything with real enthusiasm. The rest of my brood all seem to have something they love to do, but not Julia. This is good for her."

"And it's great for me." She held up a finger, did an about-face, and went into the back. When she returned she asked, "How's your newest employee doing?"

He shrugged. "I'm teaching her to research. I don't exactly have a booming practice so she gets bored. But she's learning how to look up court records and seems to like it."

"That's good, right?"

"Very. That, with a few years of law school, and I could have a partner."

DeeDee laughed. He liked the way her laugh sounded. It was quiet but genuine. He helped her into her coat. In her wild heels, she was every bit as tall as he was in his boots and he didn't like that she probably topped him in what she wore today.

She locked the door as he asked, "Your place or mine?"

"As much as I'd love to spend time with you, I can't do it. I'm swamped. I got fifteen more orders today. The salon itself has been quiet, but the online is booming. I've got to decide if this is an initial rush because I'm new, or if I'm going to need to hire more people."

"Maybe we need to seriously talk about your business. You've got your laptop, come to my house."

"I'm not spending the night."

***

DeeDee took off for Cody's office while he fixed dinner and got the children settled down. She found another order for her Hawaiian collection. Those beach designs were flying in popularity, as were her Country Simples, which included several western designs.

Julia knocked on the door. "Want to join us for dinner or would you prefer yours in here?"

"I'll come to the kitchen in a moment" She realized Julia was walking away. "Julia!"

"Yes."

"Are you going to college, or will you be looking for a permanent job?"

"I hate school. Dad wants me to at least go to the local community college, but it's not what I want to do. Why?"

She smiled at the young teen with the flawless complexion. "I'll give you as many hours as you want and I'll work around your college class schedule. But your dad is right. You need a college education."

"Thanks. Working for you is so much better than what I hear from my friends who work at the fast food places or waitress at one of the pizza places. They are just working. I feel as though I'm really doing something meaningful."

"You are."

Julia smiled and walked away.

Cody was still standing by the microwave as DeeDee entered the kitchen. She watched as he pulled an odd looking container from the microwave and removed a vented lid.

"There are times when I think I need to hire a cook. Tonight is one of them." Cody put several dishes on the table.

Ian came though the front door, washed his hands, and grabbed a chair."

"You stink." Melissa covered her nose.

"Take a shower," Cody said. "Don't come to the table all sweaty."

"But I'm hungry."

"You're not ruining everyone's dinner. Hit the shower." Cody flipped on the exhaust fan. "Don't do that again." He looked at DeeDee. "Sorry. No one gets seconds until Ian has firsts."

DeeDee laughed. There was something about being with this noisy family that was fun. Having grown up an only child and living a quiet single life, this was amazing. And watching Cody cope with all of it… She smiled at him as he took his seat.

The fare was simple but tasted fine. Ian returned wearing pajama bottoms and smelling shower-fresh. Sean was the oldest boy, but Ian already stood several inches taller than his brother and every bit as tall as his father. He probably would grow even taller.

DeeDee sensed that Ian and Melissa didn't get along very well, but they managed to be polite to each other. In fact, as she watched the children interact, she realized there was a divide between the girls and the boys and Ian seemed to be the reason.

He was full of energy, boisterous, and reminded her of a partially grown puppy. Tall and skinny, with big hands and feet, he hadn't filled out yet, nor had he settled down into his young adult status. If any of these kids were going to get into serious trouble, it would be Ian.

Twice Cody told him to leave his siblings alone, and when Ian failed to rouse the ire of the older ones he started on the twins.

In an attempt to divert his nonsense, DeeDee asked, "Ian, what sports do you play?"

"Basketball and baseball."

"Are you good?"

"Of course I am. If I wasn't, I wouldn't be playing."

"I've noticed that there are some athletes that seem to rise above the others. It's not all physical ability. Intelligence has a lot to do with it, and probably some of the best players never make it to the big teams. They bail out and use their brainpower for other things - often sports related businesses." She took a sip of her water. "Someone has to completely understand how a man uses his feet when he plays basketball to design footwear. Or he's got to understand what it takes to repair a tendon or a knee and get that player back into the game." She realized she had the boy's total attention. "Several of our great Olympic athletes have become doctors, others design equipment for their sports. It's all very interesting."

"But they aren't making the money."

"Don't bet on that." She cut a bite of chicken. "Most athletes are washed up before they are thirty. They have a short window of time to make money. Some of the designers have built businesses worth far more than anything they would have ever earned."

"So?"

"Do you have practice tomorrow?"

"Yeah, everyday."

She nodded. "Pay attention to your feet on the court. Really pay attention. Feel your toes in your shoes, your ankles, calves, how do the shoes help or hinder. Where are you getting support or not getting it? What part of your foot works the most? Then email me your answer."

He didn't answer, but left his siblings alone for what remained of the meal.

When her phone buzzed, she excused herself from the table and answered it. "Hey, Chrisy, what's up?" "You did what?" "What? I don't have that kind of money." "Well, yeah, of course I do, but I can't do that!" She held back the tears that mixed with anger brewing inside her. "You call that little? I have a business that isn't three weeks old and you do this to me? You are out of your mind, a complete lunatic!" "No way! Undo it." "What do you mean you can't?"

She put her head on Cody's desk and cried. Everything she'd worked so hard to make happen, Chrisy was tossing down the drain. She didn't have that kind of money. She'd never have that kind of money. Her life was seeping away, oozing from her with every sob. It was over. She couldn't do it. Every designer wanted to be another Bill, Vera, or even Coco, but she didn't have unlimited funds. Her tears ended, but a heavy pall fell over her, sinking her deeper and deeper into unknown depths. Everything she wanted was spinning away and taking her soul with it.

Eight

Cody walked into his office and saw DeeDee with her head on the desk. Instantly he knew something was very wrong. "What happened?"

"Chrisy. I should have never allowed Karina to talk me into using him. I'm done. It's over. He just set up a complete fashion show in New York. There's no way I can do it."

"Why not? It sounds wonderful. Isn't that what all the big fashion houses do? Isn't it what you just did but on a larger scale?"

"Except I'm lacking the few million dollars to go along with it and he's committed me. He's signed the paperwork."

"Oh. Maybe we need to talk about your finances, which is what I had in mind earlier this evening."

She narrowed her eyes at him. "I don't discuss my finances with anyone."

"Maybe you should. I know your mom won thirty-four million dollars so let's discuss what you have and what you can and cannot do. You want Main Street Bridal to succeed. Let's talk about what it's going to actually take to make your dreams come true."

"How do you know--"

"It doesn't matter. The only thing you need to concern yourself with is getting your business off the ground. Talk to me so I know how to help you fulfill your dreams."

He winced a few times as she told him where the money was and what she wasn't getting from it.

Chrisy had set everything into motion for her to have a huge show in March. And no matter how he looked at it, Chrisy was right. She needed to do this. If she wanted to play with the big names in this business and be recognized as a powerhouse, she had to play in their sandbox and on their turf.

"Let's do it. I'll put up the money, but you *are* going to incorporate."

"Why?"

"Because I have a daughter who has climbed out of her little shell and has discovered something that she loves more than boys. And because I believe in you."

"Let me guess, you have a few million laying around as disposable income?"

"Not exactly, but yes."

She ran her fingertips over her forehead. "I'm not sure I can think that far ahead."

"You'd better. Furthermore, if that show is a success, you're going to have even more work than you can handle. That brings us back to what I meant to talk to you about."

He reached into the cabinet and retrieved the bottle of cognac. "There's a building that once housed the children's clothing manufacturer. I think you need to consider it. I talked to the owner the other day. He doesn't have the money to do anything with it and needs the money from the sale. I think you could probably get a good price on it. You're going to need more space than what you have at the salon."

"But I can't handle what is going on now. And what Chrisy has just done to me...my life is over. It's done."

He poured a small amount of the sweet liquid in the warmer and lit the candle. "DeeDee look at me. You are doing fine. But you're trying to do it alone. You can't do everything by yourself. You need help; more than just Julia. There are people who used to work for that clothing place and could use jobs. Let me help."

Her eyes narrowed and he knew he had raised her anger before she opened her mouth.

"Is this because I'm a female and therefore, I don't know what I'm doing?"

"No, and don't ever think that about me. There's no question that you know what you are doing. I'm saying you are trying to do it all yourself. There's not one successful businessperson out there who has not surrounded themselves with administration people to handle operations. Furthermore, every successful business person has partners who put up money to expand the dreams."

"You think I should go along with Chrisy?"

"You said he put Karina Karr out there, and that he'd do the same for you. You trusted Karina, so trust him. He apparently knows what he's doing, and I'm assuming you know how to run a fashion show on that scale, so let him have his way. You let your backers figure out how to cough up the money, and you need to be prepared for the sales it will generate. It takes money to make money. Put the people in place to handle the business you generate."

"You mean hire more sewing-floor people?"

"Yes, and hire the people who know how to handle the day-to-day operations. I'll have your papers drawn up for incorporation. I'll be your CFO."

"What? You're just going to take over?"

"Somebody better take over your finances before you collapse."

***

DeeDee jumped in the shower and wondered what she had committed to doing. Cody Montgomery drove her nuts, but he also was a calming force. He told her to concentrate on designing, and gave her several names of people to call, starting with the local newspaper for an ad.

Water sluiced over her face, washing her anxiety away along with the bubbles from her shampoo. She held her breath for as long as she could. Dallying wasn't on her agenda, and for every negative sensation she managed to wash from her skin another replaced it.

The more she considered the situation, the more she realized Cody was right. Every big designer concentrated on the designs and merely told the people around him or her to make everything else happen. But giving up that control, putting it into someone else's hands... She shivered as she stepped out of the shower.

Chrisy wanted her face on the cover of one of the biggest bridal magazines out there. She understood him. He got his kicks out of finding talent and launching it. He believed in her and

Main Street Bridal, just as he believed in Karina Karr shoes. He was impressed with what she had done and wanted her to succeed. She owed him a major apology.

By nine o'clock in the morning, she had the newspaper on the phone. By ten thirty she was on the phone with Cody wanting to see the building they had discussed. Her email from Chrisy had not been returned. She had no idea what city he was in or what he was doing.

A few hours later, Cody picked her up and took her to see the building. They drove to a seedy side of town and were met by two people, the owner and the owner's agent. The odor of stale oil, concrete, and mildew as they entered the building hit her and her stomach instantly revolted. She gazed around and shook her head. It looked like something from the 1950's.

"And over here, you'll find--"

She slipped her hand into Cody's as she turned to the owner. "Sir, I've seen enough. This isn't what I want. I'm sorry."

She almost yanked Cody off his feet as she pulled him out of the building and to his car.

"Okay, okay, I get it. You hate it."

"Didn't you say the town is creating a new industrial area? Where?"

He drove her a little further north of the town. "Here."

She looked at fields. "This? There's nothing here but weeds."

"That's right. No one wants to build here until we get that access road."

"Great. Just how much money can I spend, Mr. CFO?"

***

Cody held in laughter as he attempted to answer DeeDee's question. "What do you have in mind?"

"A building, modern, with all the proper lights, state-of-the-art computerized equipment such as cutting saws - the works. But also I want it to be a place that will make people want to come to work. I don't want to outsource to some country half way around the world. I want a..." She giggled. "A positive environment."

"Maybe you are crazy, but let me see what I can do."

He dropped DeeDee off and went back to his office. Chelsea was due in any second and he was glad he was there before her. He didn't like being late even though Carlie was still there.

"Did the lab results come in?"

Carlie shook her head. "That police chief called. Said he wasn't even on the force back then, but left the name of a retired officer who might be able to help you."

He took the written note from her. How could he make her understand that she should send her notes electronically? It didn't matter, for she was good at research, and actually a pleasant face with a good voice on the phone. She needed a job, and he needed her.

He looked over his mail, sorted a few things, then picked up the phone and called the mayor. Time was ticking away, and he knew he needed more time with the mayor. "Let's meet tonight at Trabeck's. I want you to meet DeeDee. Dinner is on me."

He picked up the boys, took Chelsea home, and headed over to DeeDee's salon. She was just leaving as he pulled up. "Oh, am

I glad I caught up with you. Dinner tonight with the mayor."

"What? You're joking, right?"

"No, now."

"I've got to at least freshen my makeup and I'm covered in threads."

"How fast can you change? It's going to take me twenty minutes to get there and I've got fifteen minutes to do it in."

"You'll have to do it in ten."

He dropped her off at Gloria's door and watched her enter the building. Anxiety crawled over him as the car's digital clock changed numbers. The minutes ticked away. DeeDee reappeared. He opened her door from inside the car and as soon as he heard the click of her seatbelt, he made a U-turn, and floored it.

"Geesh! Must you drive like a maniac?"

"I figured you were used to the New York cab drivers." He looked at the clock and sucked in a breath. "Larry Krabbits doesn't take kindly to people being late."

"Why are we meeting with the mayor?"

"That building that you want… He can make it happen. So smile and let me deal with him. I'll let you know when you need to chime in. Let me talk money. You talk vision."

***

DeeDee followed Cody into Trabeck's Bar and Grill. Situated in a shopping area, it looked slightly out of place, but suburbia had changed from when she was a girl. The whole storefront area had a slightly upscale look to it, yet looked almost empty except for the parking around Trabeck's. Once inside, it took a moment for her eyes to adjust to the lighting or rather lack of it. The large screen TV's were showing basketball games. Cody steered her to a booth and introduced her to Larry Krabbits.

The whole way over she pictured a man who either looked like a crab or a rabbit. She smiled. *Cranky rabbit.* His squashed nose, probably from a bad break, looked too small for his face, and his eyes were close-set and beady. She offered her hand. "Pleased to meet you, Mr. Krabbits. I've never lived anywhere that has been as warm and welcoming."

He took her hand and looked her over as if undressing her. "Very pleased to make your acquaintance. Heard you got quite an operation going."

He's got the teeth for a rabbit.

Cody edged her over so that he was sitting almost opposite Larry and she was crammed against the wall. She unbuttoned her coat and inched her way out of it.

She listened to Cody and smiled at the cranky rabbit with two front teeth that almost crossed at the bottom. To call the man homely was either a compliment or an understatement.

A pitcher of beer appeared with glasses and Cody poured for everyone.

She had briefly looked at the menu when the waitress appeared to take their order. "I'll have the…" Her eyes scanned the page one more time. "The Ruben"

"Chips, fries or onion rings?"

"Onion rings" *What have I done?* She sipped her beer. "May I have some lemon wedges?"

The woman looked at her slightly confused. "For your sandwich?"

She smiled at the young thing who showed plenty of cleavage. "For my beer."

"Whatever."

A few minutes later, a small bowl appeared with several wedges of lemon in it. DeeDee picked one up and squeezed the citrus wedge into her glass of beer. Cody did the talking and she realized he was trying to convince the mayor not only to give her a deal on a piece of property, but get the city to invest in the building, plus give her a huge tax break.

"Look what she's done in a few months. She's got over fifty employees…"

Yeah, if you count the piece workers at home.

"She's revamped a rundown piece of property that has sat idle for over a decade and turned it into a showplace…

About that rundown piece of property you sold me…

"Look at the traffic she's brought to the hotel. This is not a little business. She's got her New York debut bridal show coming up and a spread in every bridal magazine known."

Not hardly. What spread? Have you been talking to Chrisy? Is that why he hasn't answered my email?

"That multi-million dollar show is going to bring the town so much work that she's going to have to hire back every employee Sally Jenkins ever employed, plus some."

She was grateful when the food arrived for her last sip of beer was going straight to that spot between her eyes and her brain was its next target.

"That much, eh?" the mayor replied, with his mouth full of food.

"She needs more space."

"What about the Sally Jenkins building? I would think it would be perfect."

She couldn't keep her opinion to herself. "No way! Totally out of date. Today's equipment is different. The--"

Cody's foot intersected with hers and he continued, "It's all wrong for her. She's checked there." Cody grinned at her. "She's the perfect solution for the city. You put her out there and others will follow. No one wants to be the first."

"We do have the big grocery store chain warehouse…if we get the access road."

"And if you get the people of this town employed, they are going to go along with that road. She already has a picture of her bridal salon on her website. When she can show the beautiful modern facility where these dresses are made, she's going to have even more work. People like to know they are buying from a reputable company that takes care of its employees. And people like knowing the dresses are made here and not in some horrible sweatshop. Custom dresses for the woman who wants her day to be special, yet won't cost her an arm and a leg, or half her father's salary for the year."

The mayor sat back. "That big, eh?"

"Yes. That big."

She pulled her sandwich apart and tried to redistribute the ingredients that seemed to have been thrown on the bread from the far side of the kitchen. To make matters worse, she was certain she had a rye seed between her front teeth. She sipped her beer hoping to dislodge it. Then took a few more bites of the grilled sandwich before deciding it was a hopeless, greasy mess. She added the rest of the lemon slices to the beer along with a packet of sugar. It was the best tasting thing of the entire meal. It also was attacking her brain.

The waitress stopped by the table and Cody practically shooed her away.

"Coffee!" DeeDee hoped the young woman heard the request.

A cup of hot java appeared and something inside of DeeDee relaxed until she took the first sip. It tasted like it had been made hours ago and left to boil on the hot burner. But one more sip of beer and she'd be under the table. *Why can't I drink alcohol like normal people?*

The men chatted for another hour, then suddenly they were leaving.

She looked at Cody as he slipped behind the wheel. She really hadn't eaten and the beer was giving her a headache. "Is there anyplace to get real food?"

He grinned and took her to his house where he fixed her a potato in the microwave and gave her plenty of butter and sour cream.

"You really can't drink."

"If you had warned me, I would have told you that I hate beer and I *cannot* drink on an empty stomach." She placed her empty plate in his dishwasher. "I feel much better now." She turned back to him. "Now explain to me why you are so intent on helping me."

He stood beside her, trapping her into the corner of his kitchen. His breath flowed over her face. Blue eyes stared into hers. Every speck of her body felt as though he'd set it aflame. She didn't have time for this. She didn't need a man in her life. She needed to escape. He lifted her hands to his shoulders as though she were a rag doll, except she was. Her head was saying one thing, but her body was responding to him. His lips met with hers.

All sensible thinking left her as he held her tight to him. The whole world vanished. She needed her knees to hold her upright but they had failed. Cody was holding her, breathing for her, making her body feel things it had never felt before. Little mews escaped from someplace within her.

Every inch of her was pressed tightly to him and begging for more. Her head was saying no. Her body was screaming yes. His lips were on her ear. His words were hot. His lips dipped lower to that spot on her neck. She was melting under his touch. Her head could no longer think. He possessed her. His tongue circled the rim of her ear. More words flowed with his breath. He smelled like a man, all woodsy and sweet. Her body pleaded for his as one set of her fingers gathered his silky hair and her other set twisted his shirt. Her pelvis met his in a slow grind. Intense and primal, their dance began.

***

"Damn, Dad. In the kitchen?" Ian's voice broke them apart.

Cody looked over his shoulder at his son. "Just a kiss between two lovers." A fist connected to his ribcage. "What was that for?"

"How dare you insinuate--"

He turned back to his son and winked. "Feisty is good, and she's good."

119

Ian laughed.

DeeDee pushed against Cody. He turned back to her. "One of the joys of having children is having very little privacy."

"It's not funny. Let me go."

"Oh, no. You are mine. I know a good thing when I see it."

Ian grabbed a drink from the refrigerator and left the kitchen.

"And I want you to see this." Cody held her hand firmly in his and took her up the stairs to where the children resided. "Sean, I need you to put Collin and Logan in bed tonight."

He opened the hall closet and grabbed a handful of condoms. "Just in case."

"There won't be any--"

His fingers covered her lips and she shoved him.

"Save it for later." He dragged her downstairs, into his bedroom before releasing her. "Okay, now scream at me. Tell me what a cad I am for kissing the most delicious, intelligent, and sexy woman that I've ever met in my life."

She stood with her hands on her hips, her eyes narrowed, and he was certain that steam flowed from both ears.

He tossed the condoms on his bed. "You're call, but I'm willing to bet you're as wet as I am hard."

She pushed past him but he captured her. "Oh no, you don't. We are, at the very least, going to talk. You've not been kidnapped and I'm not going to rape you."

"I don't have time for a man in my life and I'm not so sure I like you barging in on my business operations." She plopped on the edge of his bed and crossed her arms over her chest.

He pulled a chair over near her and sat. "Which do you want

to handle first, the business or the personal? I prefer to get the business out of the way first."

"Whichever."

"Here's the deal. You've got tremendous potential. Investing in you is like investing in a gold mine. For every dollar I put in, I'll make more than double. You need help and I have the capitol to do it. And just where is Chrisy?"

"I have no clue. I emailed him this morning, and he's not returned it. It was my apology for calling him every name in the book when he dropped the bomb on me."

"Okay. Did you happen to tell him that you've got the money to do it?"

She nodded.

"He'll get back with you. Maybe he dropped his phone and broke it...or lost it." He leaned forward and took her hand. "Let Chrisy do his thing. You need ten more Chrisys to handle everything else, so that you can concentrate on what you do best - designing dresses.

"You need people you can trust to do their jobs... And you just oversee them. It's called leadership. Henry Ford used it. He knew nothing about building cars, but he knew to hire the best people and let them do what they do best."

She nodded.

"I promise, I know more about money then you can imagine. My grandfather was Dakota Montgomery. Does that name mean anything to you?"

"That's that oil family...oh...oh...o-o-oh."

"Yes. SunWest, the largest privately owned oil company in

North America and one of the largest producers in North America." He took her hands in his. "I'm Charles Dakota Montgomery. I promise I have the money to back you. I also live here as Cody because my kids get to have normal lives and create their own dreams. They see my family several times a year. They know I have money and they know the family does, but I don't drag it in front of them. It also keeps them from having cameras flashed in their faces and from being held to unrealistic standards. Plus, it keeps them safer."

She pulled from his grip and buried her face in her hands.

"By being Cody Montgomery - Mr. Nothing, with a passel of kids in a small town, I don't have gold diggers chasing me. My kids know how to make their beds, clean the bathroom, and be responsible with a small allowance. Do you think Julia would be working for minimum wage, if she had any real idea? She'd be wanting to jet off to some concert or film festival. She'd be blowing money rather than learning to use it to her advantage."

"I pay slightly more than minimum and much more to my seamstresses."

He shook his head. "That's not the point. Every day these children are worth more and more. They don't need to work. Julia could be driving a four hundred thousand dollar car instead of a five-year-old box on wheels, but she doesn't need more than what she has. When the day comes that she starts receiving money, she'll appreciate it and won't take it for granted."

"But she's not your--"

"She *is* mine. My family knows who has come by marriage. They are all legally adopted and legally entitled to their share."

"You are very generous."

He nodded. "I'm also making sure they all know how to handle money. They know I sold that property to you, way under value and they knew why."

"So tell me why."

"Simple. It wasn't producing. It was actually a liability and costing money. I wrote off the depreciation and I'd have to recapture that money on taxes if I sold it to you for more and showed a profit. Plus, I had a gut feeling that Deanne Drayden needed a break. I should have done the background check on you before I sold it so cheap, but now I'm glad it's worked the way it did. A lot of people in this town have benefited from your dream."

"My mom tied up that lottery money to keep me from blowing it all away. She made me promise I'd make it last a lifetime."

"We're all under restraints of some sort. So now you know that your dreams can come true. Let's do what Chrisy wants. He's a handler, an agent, it's what he does…and does best. You need an operations manager, someone who can run the dressmaking."

"There was a woman who worked for Sally Jenkins."

"If she's truly good, contact her." Once again, he took her hands into his. "I'm done talking business for the night. I want to talk about what happened in the kitchen because that was one hot kiss and you had no clue who you were kissing."

She looked at him. "Now I do."

"Does it make a difference?"

He watched her swallow.

"Why should it matter? Has anything here changed?"

"Because you're no longer Cody; you're this super guy and I

can't compete."

"Is this some sort of race? And you have to be the one calling it?"

She stood up and paced the room. She looked back at him several times but continued to pace. Then she walked to the far end of the room and crossed her arms as she leaned against the wall by his chest of drawers. "Maybe. I don't want to be somebody's plaything or the little woman."

The guffaw that broke loose almost choked him. "Ever hear of partnership?"

"I want to be on top. I want the accolades and the fame."

"And the mansion?"

She furrowed her brow. "Yeah. I want it all."

"I understand. I've also been there. But since that's your attitude, why are you building this business on Main Street and not Fifth Avenue?"

She paced some more, then stopped. "Because I could afford Main Street, and I couldn't afford a single square foot in a building on Fifth Avenue. Besides if I upped my overhead, I'd have to charge more for my dresses, and I want them affordable."

"We could build a house on the outskirts of town, but here you'd be within three blocks of where you work. Your heart is here on Main Street."

"What's this bit about we could build a house?"

He stood and opened his arms. "Come kiss me. I think your answer is in your kiss."

Nine

Chrisy breezed into the salon as if nothing had happened, told DeeDee he wanted a word with her, then vanished into the small room he'd taken over as an office.

DeeDee motioned to Julia. "This just came in a few minutes ago. See if you can contact Linda Ridgeway by phone. Be very cautious how you ask. This woman is either deformed or she's messed up her measurements. Do you think you can handle it?"

"The soup kitchen has taught me a few things."

"Good girl." She went to see Chrisy. She rapt lightly and opened the door. "Hi. Long time, no see."

Chrisy looked up. "Are you over your little snit?"

"Yes."

"Good, because we have work to do."

Three hours later, her stomach audibly rumbled. "Chrisy, we've got to eat, or I'm going to keel over."

He drove her a few blocks to a Chinese restaurant where they continued the conversation. She kept adding dates into her phone's calendar.

"June is the month for brides and everyone knows it. We're doing the end of March. Your face on the cover will come out one week before the show. You are going to be the face of the American bride. Two hundred dresses and something outrageous, extravagant, and insane; I want to see it."

She rolled her eyes. "I'm not doing a toilet paper dress."

"It's been done and so has the soda pop cans."

"I don't do that stuff."

"Well, find something. I want sensational. You wouldn't believe what I had to do to get this for you. Don't disappoint me."

"What did that cover and spread cost?"

"Don't ask. Pay the bill when it comes in." He expertly picked up a square of bean curd with his chopsticks and ate it. "Who did you get to back you?"

"Cody."

"He's a good guy. Sleeping with him?"

"No." Warmth began to flow up her chest and was headed for her cheeks. "I chickened out."

"Cody Montgomery hiding in a small town. It's almost laughable."

"How do you know who he is?"

"Baby, I make it my business to know everyone who is anyone. And why are you turning him down? You should be jumping his equipment every night."

"I don't know. Maybe I'm not ready for that kind of relationship."

"Baby, we've all been burned. Get over it."

When DeeDee returned to the salon, she found Julia working at the computer.

"Did you call the bride?"

"Yes. Those are her measurements."

DeeDee inhaled. "Thanks."

She mulled the situation over in her mind, then ran a text message to Chrisy. *I have an idea.*

Monday morning, DeeDee had her answer. Linda Ridgeway agreed and would be coming directly to the salon for a gown designed especially for her. Chrisy was ecstatic, and had made contact with a national news program that was extremely interested. They would be sending a film crew to watch the design and fitting process, then follow Linda all the way through her wedding day.

DeeDee knew she couldn't do it for every handicapped bride, but she'd consider it on a case-by-case basis. DeeDee also knew that something inside of her had changed. She was looking beyond just her little store.

Her eyes were on the spotlight and she was chasing her dream. But it was Chrisy who really was making it happen. She needed that competency in all areas of her business. She made a few more phone calls and found the woman she wanted to run her sewing operations.

But what had amazed her was Julia's ability to do things. She had a knack of taking over and making things happen. She also did well at organizing people. Her bright cheery smile kept the sales clerks busy and doing things when there were no customers in the store. And Julia was also excellent with helping brides and defusing tension between mothers and daughters.

DeeDee sat with her sketchpad and allowed her mind to wander. She had Linda Ridgeway coming and that fashion show.

Linda wanted to be a fairytale princess and the other required pure excitement. Sound caused her to look up.

"Hi." Cody stood there with two cups of coffee and a pastry bag. "Hungry?"

He looked fantastic and his smile seemed extra bright. She moved her sketchpad to one side, and cleared several papers from her desk. "What did I do to deserve your presence at..." She looked at her watch. "Three in the afternoon?"

"Town Council tonight at five, and I know you too well." He put a cup from the coffee shop in front of her, then reached into the bag and handed her a cream-filled doughnut. "Eat so you aren't starving during the meeting. I'll take you to dinner when it's over."

He took a bite from his doughnut and the cream filling squeezed out.

She giggled as he attempted to wipe his mouth and cheek.

"Isn't the filling why we eat them?" He licked his fingers.

Cautiously, she took a small bite but had to catch the oozing cream with her other hand. "No napkins?"

He looked in the crumpled bag. "Nope." He crossed the room and took a few tissues for himself then handed her the box. "Here."

"You seem to be in a cheery mood."

"Got a new trial for my client. They have nothing to hold him on."

"Is that the guy who has already served twenty years?"

He nodded. "Problem is, he'll never get his life back. He's luckier than most. He has family and they all seem stable." He finished his coffee. "You seem more relaxed than normal. Have a good day?"

"Did you see your daughter on the way in?"

"No."

"She's probably upstairs, redoing my windows. Spring is coming and she wanted to try her hand at some decorating. So I let her. She can't draw a straight line, but she's full of ideas and knows how to pull them off." Another bite of her doughnut sent more cream to her fingers.

"Julia and Melissa get these brilliant ideas to redo everything at home. I've walked in and wondered if I was in the right house. They'll see something in a magazine and they take off with it. It's when they start moving the glasses and silverware around in the kitchen that I get freaked."

"Oh no!" She pushed away from her desk and stared at the glob of cream filling.

"What? What's wrong?"

"I've dribbled cream…" She attempted to lift it off her blouse with the tissue. "When did I do that?"

Cody chuckled. "Need to go home and change?"

She nodded.

"Let's go."

"I can't just leave. Who will lock up?"

"Give the keys to Julia."

She found Julia and passed her the keys, then gave the young woman her security code for the alarm.

Cody took her home then followed her all the way to her room. She stopped and turned to him. "Wait here."

"Why? And miss seeing you without clothes?"

She shot him her meanest look, but he laughed at her.

"You've seen my closet. I want to see yours."

She swung her arm wide. "Go ahead and look."

He walked past her and into her closet. "This is it? How do you look so good all the time?"

"Accessories. Now out!"

He laughed. "When do I get to see your clothes fall off?"

"Maybe never. Furthermore, I'm nothing near wifey number two."

"Thank goodness or I would have left town." He grabbed her shoulders and planted a quick kiss on her lips. "You are so much better."

She ducked into her generous closet, closed the door, then quickly changed her shirt and her heels. "I want to go back and see the windows. I want to see what Julia's done. She's doing the windows in our new bridal colors."

He raised his eyebrows.

"Bridal dresses tend to be traditionally white or ivory. I have tints of colors such as green, pink, yellow, blue, purple, etc. But I've also designed dresses that are white with bodices that contain colored embroidery and beading. It's exciting to see women embracing these new colors. Yet it still gives them the white-gown effect."

"I really don't care about bridal gowns. When do I get to see you naked?"

"Never. Let's check the salon windows."

DeeDee felt as if she'd walked this street all her life. The folks within the offices and stores along the way knew who she was and would smile and wave as she passed. She could see the downstairs windows of the salon clearly. Each held a white dress with the colored designs and the second floor held dresses in various tints. "Oh, they all look so lovely. And I'm not saying this because she's your daughter – I'm thrilled that I hired her."

"She's ecstatic to be part of it. I haven't heard her mention a boy's name since she started working here. This is all she talks about." He opened the passenger door to his vehicle. "Ready for tonight?"

***

Cody listened to the debate over giving DeeDee property. His sister's architectural firm had spoken briefly to DeeDee. From that conversation, they had drawn a few pictures of a simple but modern building that was spacious and filled with natural light. She didn't need an access road if placed at the front entrance to the industrial park. She wouldn't need a road at all. The old road that ran in front of the area was sufficient.

Cody wanted to groan or at least strangle a few council folks, but he kept his feelings from showing and listened.

DeeDee fiddled with her watch the entire time, turning it around and around on her wrist. Only twice did anyone ask a question and each time she responded by referring to a page in the proposal. She went into the meeting expecting they would table the decision, which would set her back for time. But each time, Cody tried to assure her he was reasonably confident that they would grant her the property.

After more bellyaching by two of the councilmen, the one

councilwoman called for a silent vote. Cody reached over and took DeeDee's hand. She glanced at him, and he could tell that the tension had seriously affected her.

The secretary collected the ballots and counted them. DeeDee got her property. He leaned over and whispered in her ear, "Told you."

They sat through another half hour before the council meeting was adjourned.

DeeDee practically floated out of the building and to his car. She jabbered almost nonstop to the hotel about her vision for the building and her business. All through dinner, she talked about the bridal show and some of her designs.

"Color! Lots of it. Crimson and gold. Can't you see it?"

He didn't want to tell her no. To him, brides wore white. He didn't quite get it, but she was over the top with excitement.

Yet through it all, one thing was obvious; DeeDee was herself. She didn't put on airs, nor was she clingy. Never once did she demand his time, but seemed to genuinely enjoy his presence. She never asked for things, and always thanked him for everything. There were nights he'd ramble and she'd listen attentively. DeeDee was different from other women. Her closet matched her personality.

He knew he should take her home, but that's not what he wanted. "My house for coffee?"

"Why not?"

"Because I want more than coffee."

"Meaning?"

He could feel the smile tug at his cheeks. "Let's discuss that when you get to the house."

***

DeeDee gasped as she stepped into his kitchen. "Food fight?"

"I have no clue."

They picked their way through the spaghetti, into the hallway, then up the stairs. Bedroom doors were closed but the heavy strum of music was a dead giveaway that something was still very wrong. Cody opened the door to the twins room and found them playing with Lego toys. At quarter past nine they should have been in bed. They were still dressed.

Cody helped the boys clean up and then got them into pajamas. He turned to DeeDee. "Do you mind reading a bedtime story to them. It might take me awhile to get to the bottom of what happened. One book, not sixteen. It's well past their bedtime."

Both little boys brought her books and she picked one. Half way through her reading, Logan fell asleep and Collin was fighting to stay awake through the whole story. She finished the book even though she was certain Collin had fallen asleep on the next to the last page. She put the book back on the shelf and turned out the light. Behind one of the doors, music still blared. She stood for a moment contemplating the situation, then went downstairs.

If there were a place to begin... She shook her head. Then she recognized Julia's computer, except its screen was cracked. Whatever had happened was wicked and from the looks of things, it involved all the older children.

"Don't touch anything. It's probably a crime scene."

DeeDee turned to face the voice and found Julia standing there.

"Really, don't even think about cleaning up. I have a feeling that Sean, Ian, and Melissa will be up half the night cleaning."

"Who started it?"

Julia shrugged. "Sean and Melissa were in the kitchen. I already told Dad what I know. There was no point in spoiling your evening. It was over in a matter of seconds. He's really pissed with all of us."

"All? Including you?"

She nodded. "I'm the oldest and the most responsible. He said I should have called him immediately."

"Does your computer still work?"

Julia shook her head. "My homework is there."

DeeDee had no pearls of wisdom for the young woman, she merely turned and walked to Cody's office, but it too had been hit with what appeared to be cola on everything. If this was the result of anger, she was glad she wasn't here when it happened. This was beyond a simple food fight.

She checked Cody's room and it was untouched, then she checked the guest room. It wasn't destroyed but someone had been in it. She went back to Cody's room and sat in the chair. Time ticked by.

Her eyes no longer wanted to remain open. She had two options: she could walk home alone in the dark, or sprawl across Cody's bed until it was over and he could take her home. She kicked off her shoes, pulled off her jacket, and curled up on his bed.

Running water registered in her mind. Muffled sound and then slight movement next to her caused her to open her eyes.

"Go back to sleep." Cody covered her with a blanket, except he was next to her.

"What are you doing?"

"I'm going to spend whatever is left of this night sleeping."

She felt his hand on her back. The feeling of panic that began to rise was quickly offset by the sound of his slumber. She rolled over and in the darkness realized he was between the covers and she was still lying on top of them. The hand that had been on her back was now above his head. From this position she could see his clock glowing. She groaned and settled down, pulling the blanket around her.

Her eyes opened, and she realized Cody was pressed to her back with one arm around her. Cocooned and protected in his embrace, she drifted off again. Then the stillness of the night was interrupted by the sound of his alarm; faint at first but growing louder. He rolled over and silenced it.

She watched him as he got out of bed. Wearing only pajama bottoms, he looked amazing. He went to his bathroom, and she listened to the sounds of him preparing for his day.

"Your turn. I put extra towels out for you. And there's a brand new toothbrush waiting for you."

"Thanks."

She walked out of the bathroom in time to see him hitching his pants up over the tails of his shirt. "I could get used to watching a man do that every morning."

He turned to her and grinned. "We could try doing it again tomorrow morning. I promise I'm the safest man you could sleep with after last night."

"What happened?"

He sat in the chair to pull on his socks and shoes. "I never dreamed I could be that angry with my children. Never thought they'd ever push me to that extent. Would you believe I offered to remove my belt and use it on Ian and Melissa?"

"You didn't!"

He shook his head. "No. But I was on the verge of storming out of the house before I did do something stupid."

"I assume the house is cleaned up?"

He rocked his hand. "The worst of it."

"Now what?"

"I need to apologize to Julia. I was a little too hard on her, and it wasn't her fault. In a strange way, I realized that the four middle children would probably all benefit from some counseling. Maybe I, too, could use some help with my parenting skills. I've chalked up the problems between Ian and Melissa as being differences in personalities, but failed to realize they all have problems that go beyond their inability to get along. I don't want to wake up one day and discover they are doing drugs." He slipped on his watch and filled his pockets. "I'll take you home then wake up the twins. I'm really sorry about last night, but not about having you in my bed."

Dawn was breaking as she slipped the key into the lock on Gloria's green door and then ran up the steps to her room. Deep inside, she knew Cody was hurting. Not only had his children made a mess, but because he, as a parent, had somehow failed.

By ten thirty that morning, she realized just how tired she was and how worried she was about Cody. She picked up her phone and called him.

"How's your day going?"

"I got everyone in school and I'm doing my third wash load of towels. How's yours?"

"I'm tired and I had much more sleep than you did."

"Can I sneak you out of there for a little while?"

"Let me check." She touched the screen of the store's computer. "I can scoot out for a little while, but I want to be back here before Julia comes in to work."

"I'll pick you up in five."

***

Cody took DeeDee back to his house. "You've been on my mind all morning and I know that tonight is not going to be conducive to a hot date or even a cold one. I've got children to deal with as they come home."

DeeDee nodded. "I figured as much."

"Good, then you'll understand my next move." He took her hand and led her back to his room. "Remember when I said I was a safe date? I meant that, but I want you in my arms and in my bed. Can we try one more time? I can barely keep my eyes open."

She raised her eyebrows. "No sex, just a nap?"

He peeled off his shirt. "The more skin the better it will be. There's a small part of me that might seem willing, but the rest of me is shot."

She laughed and pulled off her sweater revealing a camisole top.

He dropped his slacks as he stared into her eyes. "Don't you think you need to get rid of the pants, too? You certainly don't want them to wrinkle."

"That's all that's coming off."

He pulled open a drawer and handed her a condom. "In case of emergency."

She dropped it back in the drawer. "You've got to be feeling worse than I do."

She removed her pants revealing long, well-portioned muscular legs.

His breath hitched. He pulled down the covers, set his alarm, and climbed into bed. "Promise me, you'll ignore any body part of mine that isn't sleeping?"

***

DeeDee snuggled against Cody, then gazed into his blue eyes. "Ditch the tee shirt. I happen to like skin, too."

He yanked it over his head and then tossed it in the direction of his clothing. "You know you're getting old when this is hot dating."

"Maybe this is better. It's also not hormone driven."

"Better tell that to the area below my waist, because *it* hasn't realized how tired the rest of me is."

"I won't entice it." She giggled.

"Too late. It knows you are here and that's enough."

She tucked her head in that soft spot near his shoulder, and allowed her hand to glide over his chest. A soft silky pelt of dark hair covered most of his chest. Her heart pounded. She was sick of seeing young men who probably hadn't grown three hairs on their chests, and those who could would immediately wax it off.

The memory of being part of the team on a photo shoot for several clothing ads flashed in her mind. There were five young men present for the shoot when the photographer and one of the team members thought it would look better if the guys unbuttoned their shirts and showed off their chests. Except one of the males was actually a tall female with her hair cut short. The other male models knew but never said a word until that incident. They all jumped to the woman's defense.

It was after that day's shoot was over that DeeDee spoke to the female model. DeeDee had thought *he* looked familiar but then discovered they had met in Milan. Most runway models are done by the time they are in their late twenties. This gal was still working well into her late thirties by being a male model. Her strong jaw and features worked in her favor.

The vivid memory faded as DeeDee curled her fingers through the hair on Cody's chest. She couldn't remember ever seeing a man with this much hair. Like a solid male magnet, it drew her hand and held it there.

DeeDee opened her eyes. Slightly disoriented, it took her a moment to realize that Cody was wrapped around her, and that she was in his bedroom. His protective hold on her felt wonderful. Her attempt to move her legs made her aware of his intertwined with hers. At that moment, she realized there was an odd noise growing louder. Cody moaned and rolled away from her.

"Two thirty," his deep sleep-laced voice mumbled as he reached for his alarm. "And I'm getting up because I don't want my children catching me in bed with the most wonderful woman in the whole world." He stood and stretched his arms over his head.

He had just enough body hair to attest to his masculinity. She liked what she saw: a well-defined manly body. She had the worst desire to put him on a remote beach in a gauzy shirt and pants, then roll the pants up to mid-calf, and turn a fan on him. Or leave him shirtless, maybe drop his Stetson on his head and put him in a pair of low riding jeans with a rope casually tossed on his shoulder, while a herd of long horns grazed in the background. He could sell a million bottles of cologne. *Damn!*

She attempted to empty the images from her mind as she scooted into the bathroom. But her entire body shook with need, and the image of him nearly naked was burned forever in her mind.

She freshened her makeup, combed her hair, and pulled on her clothes. She stepped out of the bathroom. Cody was dressed and waiting for her.

"We need to hurry. Melissa will be through the door any second."

"I'm ready." She pulled up the covers on her side of the bed and smoothed them.

He stood on his side of the bed and did the same. In only a few seconds, the bed was made.

She looked at him and grinned. *Your reputation is still safe when it comes to your children, but it's got a few chinks in it where I'm concerned. I*

140

don't believe you'll ever be a safe date - not the way my body feels when you're near it.

Ten

The nap had left DeeDee refreshed and better able to face what was left of the day. When Julia stepped through the salon door, DeeDee inquired about her homework.

"The tech guy at school retrieved my hard disk and put it in a new laptop. Apparently they will bill my dad for the new computer."

"Ouch."

Julia shrugged. "My dad will pay it. Every year at the start of school, we have fees and most of the kids don't pay them. They can't force anyone to pay them. It's a public school. Since we're issued computers instead of textbooks, they can't make anyone pay for them. And we're not allowed to use our own."

"We didn't have laptops when I went to school. There was one room in the library with some computers that we could use."

Julia raised her eyebrows. "That's it?"

DeeDee nodded. "I had to get a computer for college. It was a big deal."

A tractor-trailer arrived. It delivered fifty-five sewing machines, and seventeen sergers. DeeDee had them sent to the second floor. Uncrating them and setting them up was hard physical work, but when she finished, she was thrilled. She looked at her watch and realized time had escaped her.

Gloria had saved her a plate of food and when the last morsel was eaten, she tumbled into her bed.

Tired and achy, sleep failed to come. Instead, her head replayed the images of Cody's half naked body. She wanted him. Thoughts of him withered and were replaced by Richard.

She and Richard had lived together for three years and had plans to marry in the fall. Then she caught him with another woman. The memory of seeing him in a tangled, naked embrace had hit her like punch in the stomach. She never screamed, ranted, or did much of anything. She just began to pick up his things and tossed them out of her little London flat. He laughed and continued humping. Totally disgusted, she swore she'd never bother with another man. Even now, the thought of him sent her stomach churning with acid.

It was easy to understand Cody's feelings of betrayal, for she had experienced it. But she couldn't understand why he seemed willing to try again. Maybe he didn't want a permanent situation. Maybe for him it was all physical pleasure with no strings.

Maybe that wasn't a bad thing. Could it be that's all there ever was? Had she somehow been hoodwinked into believing there was such a thing as a happily ever after?

Her mother's best friend had been married five times and divorced each man after a few years. Had not her two childhood girlfriends been married and divorced twice? She wracked her brain trying to think of one person who was happily married.

She needed to sleep and not ponder such thoughts. Her clock said four minutes until midnight. She got up and paced the room. Her body ached with sexual need. Picking up her phone, she punched in Cody's number.

A sleep-laced voice answered.

"I can't sleep. I'm horny as hell, and I need to talk to you."

"Give me ten minutes and I'll be there."

She greeted him in her flannel sleeveless tee shirt and matching baggy pants. With a finger to her lips, she led him to her room.

***

Cody wasn't certain why he was there, but DeeDee seemed upset, shaken, and not her normal self. He held her in his arms and let her ramble. She too had been burned. Enough to make her never want to be involved with another man.

They were both lonely, yet both had held onto some sort of belief that there was something much more.

Tears flowed down her cheeks as she slipped her hand under his shirt. "Why do I feel this way?"

"I don't know, but I feel it when I'm with you. I noticed it the first time I saw you peering into that dark building and I've fantasized about you ever since." He pulled her to her feet. "We'll never know unless we give into it."

"I can't."

He reached into a pocket, then tossed several condoms on a nightstand. "One step at a time until your body tells you to stop."

He reached under the top she was wearing and caressed her breasts. Her nipples beaded and his breath hitched.

She pulled his shirt over his head.

His lips found that soft spot on her neck and she moaned. In response, he pushed her nightshirt up revealing two luscious natural mounds. He pulled the little flannel shirt off of her and tossed it aside.

She covered herself with crossed arms.

With care, he moved her arms away before hooking his thumbs in the elastic of her flannel pants, pulling them downward past her hips, and pushing them beyond the tops of her legs.

She took a series of short breaths.

Her soft white belly protruded and he splayed his fingers over it. "Pure woman."

She inhaled and chomped on her lower lip, as she stepped out of her pajama bottoms. She turned her back to him. "Why do you want me? I'm not beautiful with a sexy body."

He put his hands on her shoulders. "You are absolutely correct. You are not centerfold material. You're beyond that. You're soft and curvy, and you don't get lost in my arms. There's a lot more to you than just your body. That's what makes you so special."

He could see she was trembling as he slipped his feet out of his boots and removed his jeans. He wished he could control his entire body, but it was impossible. He yanked the bed covers down and pulled her to him.

Her eyes were closed and her body stiff as if waiting for rejection.

He held her tight to him and nibbled on her ear. Inside his chest, his heart pounded, but his head tried to tell him to take it slow and easy. Except it was the fire burning within him that had taken control.

"I see a smart, strong, independent woman, who will do anything to make her dreams come true, and I happen to think that is very sexy." He picked her up and carried her to the bed, then crawled over her before flipping her so she was on top. "Your move. I got you this far."

She buried her face against his neck. "What do you want from me?"

"Whatever you are willing to give me. But what I really want is your love."

***

DeeDee sat up and looked at Cody.

His hands tenderly moved up her sides then cupped her breasts.

She slid to the tops of his legs and looked down at him. The hair on his chest tapered to a stripe that led to his... *Oh my! It's beautiful.* She smiled as she lightly stroked him. Each time, it lifted as if begging to be touched again and again. She ran her finger over the very tip and he moaned.

She'd seen him that one time in the bathroom, but hadn't noticed his length or thickness. It matched his personality. A little voice said to cover it, but she wanted to relish it awhile longer. Her fingers caressed it and each touch caused a response.

"You're torturing me, woman."

She giggled. "You have a beautiful body."

"So do you. I love the way it feels, but it's the woman inside of it that I love more. And if you don't let go of me I'm going to explode."

She gripped him and watched his face.

His eyes closed and his jaw tightened.

She held him against her belly and saw the warning droplet. The thought of watching him sent a hot pulse through her. She held him tight to her and stroked him a few more times.

"Is this what you want?" he asked between clenched teeth.

"Yes."

Watching him release, and knowing what she had done, sent a firestorm through her. Leaning down, her lips found his. Their hips met and she wiggled against the fluid proof of his sexuality.

He held her, tracing her back with his fingertips before putting his hands between them and toying with her nipples.

Her own desire burned brighter. She wanted him inside of her.

She reached for the condoms and grabbed one.

He took it from her, rolled over, and went to her bathroom.

She heard the water run.

When he returned, he had a warm washcloth. "It's one thing to play, but never compromise the situation."

He wiped her hands and then her body with the softest of touch. He covered his penis, and in one long deliberate stroke, he entered her.

Their lips nibbled, parted, and allowed their tongues to dance.

His legs tangoed with hers until hers were tightly together, then he rolled over. Holding her hips, he smiled.

Her own need drove her. She closed her eyes and he met her every stroke. He lifted her upwards until his mouth found a nipple. Almost crying out, she tightened against him and held him tight within her. Fire swept through her. She wanted all of him. His teeth held her nipple while his tongue flicked the very tip. Her hands fisted.

On the verge of losing all control, she begged, "Please."

He mumbled between her breasts as he pushed her towards his hips.

She took all of this length as her body found an ecstasy unlike any other. She collapsed into his arms.

The morning light awakened her. She sat up and looked around the room. Shaking her head, tidbits of images and feelings floated through her, then vanished. It all seemed like a dream. There was no sign of Cody anywhere. Her slippers were where she always left them, her pajamas were folded and lying on a chair, and her washcloth was slightly damp but hanging on the towel bar by the sink where it always hung. She ran her fingers through her hair and jumped into the shower. *I know I didn't dream it.*

***

DeeDee stepped out of the shower and grabbed her towel. A note floated to the ground. She leaned over and picked it up.

You are the most phenomenal woman I've ever known and that was the most intense experience of my life. I want you in my arms every night. If you feel the same way, let me put a ring on your finger. Marry me, Deanne.

She inhaled. *Marry?*

She slipped into her normal office clothes, grabbed an orange from Gloria's kitchen table, and scooted to the small coffee shop.

The bell clanged as she entered and the scent of freshly brewed coffee mixed with cinnamon filled her nose and made her hungry. "Sixteen ounc--"

"You think I don't know what you drink?"

DeeDee smiled at the older woman.

"And where have you been hiding yourself? You can't be brewing anything in your office that is good as I make here."

"You're right. But making my own saves me time."

"Phooey! You don't open for another two hours so sit right over there, and I'll bring you a fresh sticky bun. You need to relax once in a while and smell the coffee not just ingest it."

DeeDee laughed and took a seat. She hadn't had near enough sleep, and for some reason, she wasn't the least bit tired.

Elizabeth brought the breakfast goodie to the table along with a knife and fork. "Thought you might want to keep your fingers out of it, being you're dressed all pretty."

"Thanks. It's not my fingers I worry about. It's what I tend to dribble down the front of me. Do you have a bib?"

Elizabeth laughed as she took the second seat at the tiny table. "The last time you bothered to sit long enough to enjoy your coffee, you looked as though you weren't getting five hours of sleep. Today you are glowing. What's up?"

DeeDee shrugged. "Things are going well. I'm getting ready to hire more people."

"That's old news. Seems you and Cody are getting along. I haven't figured that man out." She looked around the room. "He seems like a terrific catch, but all those children. It's a lot for another woman to tolerate. She's got to really love children."

"He runs a very organized household and the children seem to respect him." She thought back to the night of the food fight. "They aren't perfect angels. But he does well for a single father. I hired Julia and she's been great."

"I know. She comes here once in a while for coffee on her way home."

"Did you know his former wife?"

Elizabeth rolled her eyes. "Never understood how the two of them hooked up in the first place. If she chipped a nail, you'd think the world was going to end. From what I heard, she didn't cook much, and she didn't clean. She was always someplace doing something."

DeeDee nodded. "He doesn't say much about her. The most I've heard is that she liked her garden."

"Oh, yeah. She lived at the garden center on Hilltown Road. And she was on the beautification committee for the downtown district. She's the reason why we have those pretty streetlights and those flower baskets."

"Guess everyone needs to do something if they don't work."

Elizabeth nodded. "It's a shame. Those twins were barely walking when she died. He took it real hard, and just when everyone thought he'd gotten over her death, he seemed to fall into the hole again."

"What do you mean?"

Elizabeth shook her head. "Can't remember which one of his daughters got sick. Never heard very much, but the child was very ill. They were checking for all sorts of horrible diseases. That took Cody out of circulation, real fast."

"You mean he stopped dating?"

"Never really knew him to date anyone. He quit attending the association meetings and in general, he avoided people. He's only stuck his head out of that house in the last year, maybe two. Wouldn't even come in here for coffee."

"Maybe he likes to avoid gossip."

Elizabeth raised her eyebrows. "Looks like I'm getting too busy, I've got to get back to work." She stood and put her hand on DeeDee's shoulder. "Stop in here more often. I need the business."

DeeDee handed Elizabeth her credit card. "Why don't you package two dozen cinnamon buns to go? I'll put them in the break room."

Elizabeth smiled and took the plastic. "Why don't you make that a standing order for every Friday morning, along with at least two of my carry-out boxed coffees? I'll send the bill to Main Street Bridal Salon"

"You drive a hard bargain, but I'll do it."

DeeDee picked up the box that contained two different kinds of breakfast sweets and took them with her as she walked to her office. She had less than an hour to do everything she had intended to accomplish before she opened the doors.

She'd spent most of the morning on the phone contacting those who had applied for dressmaking positions. She had positive confirmations from thirty-eight people who would be starting in the next two weeks.

She had an upcoming fashion show and she wasn't even ready for it. *What have I gotten myself into? And why am I involved with Cody Montgomery?*

***

Cody picked the twins up from Donna's house. She never let them sit around, playing video games. Most days, she sent the boys outside to play in the backyard. Seemed as though half the little boys in the neighborhood played there. Her husband had built a pirate ship out of decking material and it contained swings, a sliding board and a half dozen other things such as a basketball hoop to keep the boys busy. For not having a mother, his twins were well adjusted and happy. He credited much of that to Donna's disposition and loving nature.

That made him think about DeeDee. So far his relationship with her was sans children. He needed to be certain that she blended with them. He didn't want or expect to put his responsibility of the children on her, but he wanted to be certain she would at least care about them. Maybe it was time for a family outing.

But trying to do anything as a family was almost impossible. Sean and Ian were always going in opposite directions, as were Melissa and Chelsea, and with Julia working... By the time he got the twins home, he had an idea.

He checked his calendar. Aside from having DeeDee over for dinner, there wasn't time to do much of anything. Ian had games on Saturdays, and the twins had scouts. With DeeDee's upcoming trip to New York, she wouldn't be free to do anything, but once she returned...

Certainly she'd be swamped with orders. He shook his head. The woman never stopped working. Then he saw it. All the children had a long weekend, as school would be closed on

Thursday and Friday.

He pulled up several nearby resort places he knew and checked. It was off-season and many were closed. He checked another way and spotted what might be the perfect place. A cabin for rent. It would still be cold but not too cold. *Fireplace, outdoor fire pit, gas barbeque, WIFI… this might work!*

He called the number listed and chatted to the owners. "Wednesday night through Sunday morning. Just my family, I have seven children."

"We'll send you the confirmation as soon as we receive the money. We will refund the deposit within two weeks of your departure."

"It's a deal."

After obtaining the address to send the money, he ended the call. Convincing DeeDee might take some time, but his excitement made him want to wiggle his toes. It had been awhile since he'd done something like this with the children. No wild schedule or extra sightseeing, just a relaxed time with the family.

He marked his calendar and then sent messages to his older children. *Family outing next month 6, 7, 8, & 9, we will leave the evening of the fifth. Yes, you must go.*

He picked up his phone, took a deep breath, and put it down. He need to ask her face-to-face. There were eight bedrooms, and he knew the twins would share a room. If DeeDee didn't want to sleep with him, she could have her own room. But then worry crept up his back, as he had the children to consider. He'd always made it a point to be very careful around them. He wanted to set a good example, and openly sleeping with a woman, who was not his wife… *What have I done?*

DeeDee looked up from her computer. "Dinner?"

"Bring your computer and come to my house. You have to eat."

A sigh escaped. "Cody, I'm running out of time."

"You're running out of nutrition, and if you don't eat, you'll be sick."

He handed her the cape she'd worn to work.

Three times she had to excuse herself from the table to take a phone call, twice it was Chrisy and once, it was Karina. But when Chrisy called a third time, she gave up and refused to answer it.

DeeDee swallowed her mouthful of macaroni and cheese. "Are you certain you can hold down the fort while I'm away?"

Julia rolled her eyes. "I took your note into school. They said it was fine and that I had to clear it with each teacher. I'll open the salon on Tuesday and then head for school. I have to be there at nine forty to take a science test. Then I'll do the same thing on Thursday because I can't miss my science lab. My English teacher wants my report this Friday. She said it wouldn't be fair to the others if I had more time to work on it." Julia rolled her eyes. "I told her it wasn't fair that I had less time. As if I'd have more time to spend on it. And my Algebra teacher won't let me miss any classes so I'll be in class every day from twelve twenty to one ten. She says I'm not a strong enough student to miss all my classes."

Cody looked at his daughter with his brow furrowed. "I thought you were doing better in there?"

Julia shrugged. "I'll never ace Algebra. It's okay. Most everyone at the salon is at lunch between twelve and one. I'm going to be zigzagging between school and work. I can do it."

DeeDee smiled. "Julia, you'll be fine. If you need help, call your dad."

Cody put his hand on DeeDee's back. "We've all talked about this. I decided last night I'd use your office while you're gone. I can do most everything from there. I'm a phone call from Carlie, it's not a big deal."

"What if one of the kids gets sick?"

"Do you think it would be the first time I've had one or more ill when I've had a trial to attend?"

"Okay, I get your drift."

"Do we have dessert, Dad?" Sean asked.

"Sorry, no. You may desert the table. Take your plate with you." Cody smiled at his oldest son.

"Me, too?" Ian asked

"Me, too, what? Be excused?" Cody raised his eyebrows.

"Yes, sir. May I be excused, too?"

"Do you have homework?"

"Yes."

Cody stared at his second son.

"Yes, sir."

"Yes, you may be excused. Take your plate. Do your homework. I want to see it when you are done."

Ian pushed his chair back. "Why are you constantly checking behind me?"

Cody rose and picked up his plate, then DeeDee's. "Because

you're not a straight A student. I want to be certain that you do reasonably well on your homework and that it's completed. Who has kitchen duty tonight?"

"Melissa and I do, Dad," Chelsea said, as she put her fork down. "And I have a bunch of homework. This was not the night for me to have kitchen duty."

"Be quick, young lady."

DeeDee knew he'd turn Chelsea loose from the kitchen and take over whatever was not completed. "If I may be excused, *sir*, I have a phone call to return and way too much office work, too."

Cody smirked and nodded.

"Anything I can help you with tonight?" Julia offered as she helped the twins stack their plates.

DeeDee smiled at the teen. "Thanks for offering, but it sounds as though you have an English report to do."

DeeDee went to Cody's home office and sat at his desk. She called Chrisy. "Yes, you needed me?"

"Are you certain everything was shipped?"

"Yes, everything, and Karina shipped cases of shoes."

"And Winnie is coming along with Edith?"

"Yes. Edith is thrilled. She's never been on an airplane. Have you met with all the models?"

"You let me do my job, and you do yours."

"Why can't I say that to you?"

"Baby, for this, I'm the boss. Got that? I'm making you famous."

"You're scaring the you-know-what out of me."

Chrisy laughed. "You've moved to Main Street, and you forgot how to curse."

"Have not!"

Chrisy disconnected the call.

Heat rose up DeeDee's chest to her cheeks as her anger boiled and threatened the contents of her stomach. She opened her laptop and began to double-check every list she had made. Anxiety had taken over her body. *I can't fail.*

Tears began to spill down her cheeks. Panic was taking over. She wanted to be at the salon, running things, but she wanted to know exactly what Chrisy was doing. If only it was all behind her instead of in front of her. Her fingers shook as they ran across the soft pads of her keyboard. She backspaced what she had typed and tried again. "Argh!"

"What's wrong?" Cody came and stood behind her.

DeeDee's phone rang and she picked it up. "Now what?"

"You're flying in a day ahead of schedule. You're flight leaves at five fifteen p.m. and you should be here by ten twenty-seven. I'll pick you up."

"What?"

"Yep. You've got an appointment on Saturday."

"For what?"

"Baby, I'm in charge, just do as I say."

She hung up on Chrisy. Cody was dragging his thumbs over each vertebra in her neck while his fingers massaged her shoulders. She wanted to tell him to leave her alone, but it felt too wonderful. His thumbs worked their way down her back and she leaned forward giving him more access to her spine. "You have no idea how good that feels."

"Oh, I think I do. You are tighter than a drum. You need to relax."

"Relax? Do you have any idea--"

"None. But then you've never handled a high-profile trial with media from around the world shoving microphones and cameras in your face."

"You?"

"Do you remember..."

When he finished, she sat there astounded. "I had no idea that was you."

"I was one of six lawyers who worked to free her."

"I almost don't want to ask, was she guilty?"

"Of being in the wrong place at the wrong time. There was nothing to link her to the murders, absolutely nothing – other than being in the same house and finding the bodies. She was under the influence of drugs at the time of her arrest. She had a two-bit pusher who claimed she confessed in jail. Yet, according to every camera device in that jail, she was never even near the guy - so completely impossible. The cops needed an arrest. People were protesting. No one felt safe."

"Did they ever get the real killer?"

Cody shrugged as he pulled up a chair beside her. "A few years later, a guy confessed. He was in prison for an unrelated crime. He wrote a confession and then committed suicide. Some DNA testing came back inconclusive."

DeeDee searched the web until she found the old photos. "This is you?"

Cody smiled. "Seems like a lifetime ago. Jenna walked out on me three days before that trial started. I was living in Texas back then, and my mom flew down to take care of the children. Chelsea wasn't a year old."

She was barely listening to him. The pictures of the lanky young lawyer were what captured her attention. That same lock of hair fell across his forehead. "It says Charles Montgomery."

"Charles Dakota Montgomery. Cody is a slur of Charles and Dakota. After that trial, I was hunted down by every newspaper and magazine. And every criminal who thought I could get his or her case overturned.

"The fame for the four months of the trial was enough to last a lifetime, but it continued. They wanted me on every talk show. I had three little girls to protect. I went into hiding."

"How did you meet Patty?"

"A cocktail party. She was on the arm of someone else." He shook his head as if to clear the image. "She was educated and pretty, very pretty."

"Was Jenna pretty?"

"And your next question will be to ask if I think you are pretty."

"Maybe, now that you've brought it up."

He chuckled. "If I say yes, you'll contradict me."

"Every woman wants to believe she's pretty."

He took her hands in his. "You are different from Jenna and Patty. Patty was a beauty. That's almost an understatement. Jenna was pretty in her own way. But neither one of them are even close to you."

"Is this where I say thanks?"

"No. Let me explain. You have a natural look about you. And you have something much more important; an inner beauty. I kept looking at the packaging and not at what was under it. It was a tough lesson to learn." He brought her fingers to his lips. "No dragon nails, and it doesn't take you a half hour to apply all your makeup. When I see you, I see a lovely woman with fantastic curves who is soft and wonderful to hold in my arms. I also see a woman who knows what she wants and is making her dreams come true. Your beauty goes beyond your gorgeous eyes and kissable lips."

"If I didn't have you putting up the money for this show, I wouldn't be doing it. But I don't want you to think I'm here because you're some sort of sugar daddy who can make things happen for me."

"And if I thought that was the way you looked at me, you wouldn't be here. There's something very wonderful between us. I turn into a horny teenager when you're near me... I can't help it. You trigger something very primal in me. Which brings me to my next little surprise for you, and I'm not totally certain how to handle it. I suspect I'm going to have to tell my children that you are my lover."

"Now what?"

"When you get back, I have a little vacation planned for all of us. Just a long weekend--"

"I can't--"

"Yes, you can. You'll have Internet and I will respect the fact that you and Julia will need to spend part of everyday at the computer."

"And Julia - that means it's a family thing?"

"Yes. Which is why I'm going to have to tell the children about us. There will be enough bedrooms for you to have your own, but I want you in my arms every night. And I don't want to lie to my children. I've tried hard to set a good example."

He stood and paced the room a few times. "DeeDee, I love you. I want you as my wife. I want to be more than your business partner."

She smiled at him. "I'm not up to making any decisions at the moment. Let me get through this fashion show. Then we can talk about any serious relationship." She watched as he pursed his lips before pressing them tightly together. She wasn't turning down his offer nor was she ignoring it. It wasn't something that she could contemplate with any seriousness under the circumstances. "Taking a few days off sounds wonderful. We'll talk after the show."

***

For all of Chrisy's bluster, DeeDee found herself staring at a very prestigious New York spa. She entered and was immediately whisked away. She was slathered, waxed, heated, massaged, soaked, washed, painted, and bleached. When it was over, she stepped into the cold and was greeted by a limo that contained Chrisy and two other people.

Chrisy didn't have her staying at just any hotel - everything he did was top of the line. She might as well have been one of the première names in design.

It was after ten that evening when she had a chance to look into the mirror and study her hair. The cut had been exaggerated and highlighted with a light ash color next to slightly darker strands, then tipped in a deep brown. It looked… she cocked her head and ran her fingers through her hair one more time… fun and flirty. She smiled at herself.

That was the last time she had five minutes to herself. She dragged out of bed sometimes as early as three o'clock in the morning to do a morning talk show, and fell into bed as late as three o'clock in the morning. Seeing Karina Karr was supposed to have been a fun event, instead they were both so busy, they never had a chance to even share a few quiet moments.

The night before the fashion show, Cody arrived with Julia. They shared DeeDee's suite and she couldn't even be certain if she'd slept with him. She didn't remember when she fell into bed, and she was in such a panic when she awakened, that she didn't remember seeing him.

Two hours before the show, DeeDee sat while someone did her hair, nails, and makeup. Chrisy brought her a cup of coffee and tried to soothe her anxiety that had turned her into a quaking ball of goop.

Chrisy sat on the makeup table and sipped his coffee. "Everyone is here. Everyone is ready. The dresses are perfect. Your teleprompter is set and ready. Just smile and read."

"And hope my tongue doesn't get twisted into a knot?"

"It happens to the best and you know that. You're not new to this."

"I'm not used to being in front of the crowd."

"Calm down. I'm going to tell you, because I don't want you in a total panic when you walk out there, but the place will be packed. You have every bridal magazine and big name fashion magazine out there taking notes and pictures. DeeDee, you're the hottest thing to hit New York in probably forty years or more."

"Omigosh, what have you done?"

"My job. This is why I get the big bucks. You are it! And your dresses are fabulous!"

Tears threatened to spill. *Can't ruin my makeup!*

"Breathe, deep breath in, come on, I'll do it with you. In…" he raised his palms up, "and out." He rolled his hands over and pushed the air under his hands down.

A few minutes later, DeeDee pulled on a watery-blue-green dress that was designed for a bridesmaid. It was the perfect color for her hazel eyes and it showed off her curvy figure. Karina had paired it with electric blue heels and a matching purse that held three-by-five cards that contained everything that should be on the teleprompter. Then she went to chat to the models.

Every show DeeDee worked, she always noticed the designer went to the models for a last minute pep talk. Those models were as nervous and anxious as she.

Chrisy had more models than she'd ever seen for a show. It saved most from the crazy hurried changes and it gave her more body styles. He'd hired several of the well-known runway models along with some new faces, but he had also gone to a performing arts school and hired a variety of young women who probably better represented the average woman. She had chubby women and extra petite ones. She was thrilled.

Cody stood beside her. At one point, he kissed her neck and whispered, "Break a leg."

Four and a half hours later, the final round of brides made their way from the runway to the curtain. Applause had slowed the show on several occasions. The half hour intermission had wound up being closer to forty minutes. Karina had worked the floor visiting with those who had come for the show, while DeeDee remained backstage and prepared for the final round. She even changed into a pearl-beaded, taupe and cream pants suit that shimmered under the lights.

Two hours later, DeeDee smiled at the packed room. "Thank you all for coming and remember every woman wants to feel and look her very best on her wedding day."

Cody stepped on stage and presented Karina and DeeDee with bouquets made of exotic flowers.

Then DeeDee walked the runway with Karina, smiling, waving, and blowing kisses to those who had come to the show. Her feet barely touched the lighted boards. She was wrapped in a magical cloud of success. Several times, she stopped and leaned down to take someone's hand. So many familiar faces and so many big Hollywood stars were standing and clapping. The music that had filled the room no longer could be heard over the thunderous roar from the crowd.

Karina took her hand and they both curtsied before turning and walking back. When they reached the curtains, they turned, took another pause to wave, and vanished behind the curtains as the lights dimmed on the runway.

DeeDee instantly dissolved into tears of joy. Cody wrapped her in his arms while Karina hugged Chrisy who actually wore boots that looked as though they belonged on a man.

Chrisy took DeeDee from Cody. "Baby, I told you. You're hot. Real hot."

"Hot? She's more than hot. She's molten!" Karina purred. "I always knew you were destined for more than a two-bit job working for someone else." She elbowed her best friend. "You're too much like me. Big ideas. Girly, we did it. We rocked this town!"

Chrisy handed over a bottle of water. "No coffee until you're out of that outfit. We'll go celebrate in just a few more minutes. Go thank all these wonderful women!"

No matter how many times DeeDee tried to tell everyone how much she appreciated them, she fell into another round of tears. She found herself in the middle of the biggest group hug with everyone complimenting her on her beautiful gowns and thanking her for allowing them to model them.

***

After a quick stop at the hotel, Chrisy had DeeDee, Julia, Karina, one of Karina's top people, Winnie, Edith, and Cody in a private dining room overlooking the harbor. Cody had been in a lot of places in New York but never here. Glass windows went from floor to ceiling. In the far distance, the Statue of Liberty as she welcomed ships, was lit. Ribbons of light from the buildings reflected across the surface of the harbor. It was picture postcard perfect.

Cody slipped his arm around DeeDee's back and tucked her next to him. "Miz Drayden are you ready to marry me?"

She looked up and grinned. "Give this up to become laundress for seven children? No way!"

A chuckle rose up his throat. "Well, if I can't get you for that job, would you at least consider being my legitimate lover?"

She elbowed him. "Did you sleep with me last night?"

"I wish." He brushed his lips across her ear. You will never believe where I slept."

"Where?"

"The room with the two king-sized beds. Julia had one and I had the other. Talk about awkward."

"Oh dear." The sincerity was apparent in DeeDee's voice.

"She thought it was funny."

"It's not like you were sharing a bed."

"No, but she's not a little girl anymore."

DeeDee smiled. "No, she's not. And I want her full time when she graduates from high school. What did you do, leave the rest of the crew with Melissa?"

"No. Mom flew in to help. I left her with a phone number so she could order pizza tonight. And I threatened the kids if they misbehaved."

"Would you believe I'm almost too exhausted to eat?"

"Yes. But you still haven't answered my question. Are you ready to take me up on my offer?"

Eleven

Cody and Julia boarded the redeye flight to head home. As soon as they had taken off, he pushed his seat back and Julia snuggled to him as if she were still a little girl in need of her daddy.

They had both had almost no sleep, but it had been worth it to be there for DeeDee's show. Julia was sound asleep in a matter of seconds. His sleep refused to come. His mind traveled to Main Street and everything DeeDee had done. *She's accomplished a lot.*

"Sir, you and your wife need to wake up and put your seatbelts on; we'll be landing in just a few minutes."

Cody shook the cobwebs of sleep from his head and righted himself. "Thanks." He smiled at the stewardess standing beside him and then at Julia. "And she's my oldest daughter."

He looked at his watch. He'd had enough sleep for his body to recognize how tired it was and not enough to be rejuvenating. "Julia. Wake up, honey."

Once they landed, and found their suitcases, they each rolled one behind them as they stepped into the cold early morning air. He had a long drive home. The direct flights were not to the airport closest to home.

Julia fell asleep before they had managed to drive a few miles, leaving him to face the rising sun alone with his thoughts. He loved DeeDee, but he had also loved Jenna and Patty when he married them. What made everything different this time? How could he ever trust again? Yet somehow DeeDee seemed completely different. She wasn't chasing him. He chased her, and he still wasn't certain he'd caught her.

He knew better than to trust what was in his pants. He was a sucker for a pretty woman. Responsibilities and general morals had kept him out of trouble. He'd tried to instill those same principles into his children, and he hoped he had succeeded.

Julia had worried him. She had pushed the limits on more than one occasion, but recently she seemed to have matured into a new stage of womanhood that he liked much more. Ever since she went to work for DeeDee, she had changed. Her entire focus had switched. She loved working at the salon and loved being with DeeDee. The woman had taught his daughter all sorts of things - female things, things he wouldn't know about, so there was no question about Julia and DeeDee getting along.

Then his mind drifted back to the flight attendant who had called Julia his wife. Did Julia really look that old or did he look like the kind of man to marry such a young woman? He forced himself to laugh it off, but it bothered him. Julia was still his little girl.

Then the strange mix up at the hotel that had them sharing a room. He let Julia use the bathroom first where she had changed into her pajamas, then he had done the same. Images of camping with the children filtered through his mind. They'd all slept in the big tent together. No matter how he looked at it, all of his little girls were too old to be sharing space with him or their brothers.

Having Julia referred to as his wife hit him hard. He needed to start looking at her as a grown woman.

He had one big hurdle ahead of him. If DeeDee accepted sharing his bedroom, he had to somehow tell his children. There was no way to keep it a secret. Such an action by him flew in the opposite direction of all his preaching about abstinence.

But how did he tell his children that there was a difference between a serious loving relationship and a casual one? Would it be better if he and DeeDee sat with the children and discussed it, or should he do it alone? Should he include the twins? *No. I'll talk to them alone.*

Trying to explain the situation was a thorn that wasn't going to go away. The barb drove deeper into his very fiber. And DeeDee's failure to commit to him only made it worse. A committed relationship was one thing and casual was another. Without DeeDee's commitment, it would be casual and therefore, in his mind, something that he should not expose to the children. But commitment seemed to always be a problem when it came to him and women.

Two marriages…each had tossed their vows aside. *Why? Why me? What did I do wrong?*

***

DeeDee walked the long concourse of the airport, and when she spotted Cody, she ran into his awaiting arms.

"Welcome home!"

"You have no idea how good it feels to put it all behind me." Her body wanted to melt. It was tired and in need of rest. The thought of being cocooned in Cody's love was overwhelming, and if she didn't figure out a way of untangling from his embrace, she really might melt into a puddle on the polished tile floor of the airport. She pushed away from his hold. "I need my suitcase."

Cody lifted the one from her shoulder. "This way."

"Any chance you can stay at my place tonight? I'm totally exhausted, but I'd love to know that you are there with me."

Cody chuckled.

The sound was like liquid gold running over her.

"So this is an invitation to watch you sleep while I die of serious male need?"

She elbowed him. "You're a grown man. Take the five-finger approach."

"Thanks. Just what every man wants to hear." Cody grabbed her bag from the carousel, then escorted her to the parking lot.

She watched as he opened the trunk and placed her bags inside. He had never said anything about working out or visiting a gym, but his physique was excellent. And the thought of seeing his well-defined body made hers twitch. "Maybe we should consider visiting a doctor. We can do it together and receive the results together."

He looked at her slightly shocked. "You're serious?"

She raised her eyebrows. "Why wouldn't I be? I know I'm clean, but it's the only way to prove it."

"I'm clean. I've thanked my lucky stars more than once for that."

"It's not just what you do, but what your partners have done."

"Very true. And part of the reason why I'm extremely thankful, not everyone has been as lucky." He opened the passenger door for her. After taking his seat, he turned to her. "Which doctor and where?"

She lifted her shoulders and let them drop. "I'm due for my once-a-year checkup. Do you know a nice OB-GYN?"

"Yes. Dr. Karen Hoovaar. Do you remember meeting her during the Downtown Business Association's Christmas Dinner?"

The name played in her mind until she put a face to it. "Yes. She sat at our table."

"If that is what it takes, I'm more than willing, but I need to know if this is going to be a serious relationship or just a casual one. If all you want is a little unfettered sex, I want to know that upfront."

She drew her teeth across her lower lip. "I think we've both been hurt. I know my ability to trust has been shaken to the core, yet you've been through worse. Maybe men cope with such things better than women."

"That's an interesting discussion. I'm raising both sexes, and I'd swear up and down that I treat them equally, but the truth is I don't. It's subtle. It's that mysterious estrogen thing. The girls get away with being more emotional. If Sean or Ian tried it, I'd tell them to buck up and be men."

"Oh, so you think estrogen rules our bodies?"

"If I understood women, do you really think I would have had two failed marriages?"

***

Cody stopped at his house long enough to check in with Julia and make certain that all was well. Then he took DeeDee to her place and followed her up the stairs. Gloria was anxious to hear all about the successful show, but DeeDee didn't have the energy to even talk about it. "We'll chat in the morning."

Gloria nodded but never once said anything about Cody's presence.

DeeDee almost stumbled on her way to her shower. She towel dried her hair enough to keep it from dripping, then pulled on a tee shirt and short pajama bottoms. Cody had turned the bed down for her. Mustering her last bit of strength, she curled into bed as Cody tucked her in and sat next to her. He pushed his fingers through her wet hair, pulling it from her face and then stroked her shoulder and arm. Little kisses fluttered over her cheek.

She managed to mumble, "You feel so good."

She opened her eyes to bright sunlight, her gaze flew to her clock, and panic twisted her stomach into an instant knot. *It's got to be a mistake!*

It had been a few minutes shy of eight o'clock when she had tumbled into bed last night, now it was ten thirty. *Fourteen and a half hours of sleep?*

With lightning speed, she dressed and scooted to her salon. Julia was back in school and with no one to open...she didn't want to contemplate the repercussions. Except when she got there everyone was inside working and Cody was sitting at her desk.

He looked up and smiled with a grin that made his eyes crinkle. "How's my sleepyhead?"

"Why didn't you tell me you were going to be here?"

"You were sleeping?" He shut down his portable computer. "I called Gloria and told her to let you sleep and to leave you a note. She said you always grab a piece of fruit so I'll assume she left you a note on the table."

DeeDee put a hand to her forehead. "When I realized the time, I didn't bother to do anything other than come here."

Cody rolled his hands over so they were palms up. "Julia did something from home before she left for school. Then she handed me the keys and gave me her code for security."

"What would I do without her?"

"Want your desk back?"

"No, I want a cup of coffee."

He looked into a disposable cup that was sitting on her desk. "Let's go to Elizabeth's. Her coffee is better than yours."

"I can't just--"

"Yes, you can. Let's go."

"Let me check in with everyone first." She went to the back and then to the second floor. Everyone congratulated her and begged for details. She made a snap decision. "At four, we'll have an informal meeting about the show's success."

The second floor clapped and cheered.

DeeDee smiled at Cody who then walked her to the coffee shop. The familiar clang of the little bell over the door struck something inside of her. This was home, not New York or any of the other famous cities where she had lived. None of them had ever instilled a feeling of belonging the way this place did.

She smiled at the two women sitting at one table with their laptops. She knew they were authors and they were there almost every afternoon working on their newest manuscripts. She raised her hand in a wave as she passed the three young police officers. The town employed a small force, and the county had a slightly larger one. Even a few state troopers would occasionally come in for one of Elizabeth's breakfast treats to go with their coffee. DeeDee suspected they didn't pay for a thing. The place looked profitable and maybe that was because Elizabeth was good to her patrons. She thrived on repeat business.

Cody dropped a ten on the counter.

Elizabeth immediately handed them their coffee. "Morning and congratulations. Julia came in here gushing about how wonderful everything was."

"Thanks. I love New York. I love the energy and the excitement, but I'm so glad I moved here."

Elizabeth laughed. "It's the coffee. I carry the best."

That warm, fuzzy, I-belong-here feeling wrapped DeeDee in its protective coat. She stirred her sugar into her coffee before adding a heavy dose of cream. It was better coffee than she could buy in the grocery store and the rich aroma, coupled with the creamy sweetness was the perfect indulgence.

Cody steered her to a table in front of the big window that looked out on Main Street.

Once seated, she held up one finger to Cody and turned back to Elizabeth. "Any chance you have enough goodies for me to supply my employees during an impromptu meeting this afternoon?"

"What time?"

"Meeting will start at four."

"No, but I'll make two big trays of my famous cream cheese tropical fruit bars for you. Send someone to pick them up about three thirty. I'll be too busy to spare anyone."

"I'll get them." Cody offered.

DeeDee picked up her cup and took a sip. "Are you always this nice?"

"I think the children will tell you I'm not. I'm known for being hardnosed. After all, I am a lawyer."

"I'd like to see you in court. I'd like to see that side of you, because I've never seen it."

"Yes, you did. The night of the big spaghetti fight."

"Your memory is short. I slept through it."

"I think they are all still grounded until they are thirty-five." Cody drank the rest of his coffee. "You'll have to come with me one day and watch me in action. In law school, they called me Ice." He slouched in the pressed-back oak chair. "Law is no place for emotions. Strictly facts. I shed everything except for the job that I must do. It's cold and calculating."

She finished the last drop in her cup. "I'm going to get a refill to-go. What about you?"

He straightened up. "Sounds like a plan. Ready for this weekend?"

"This weekend? No way!"

***

Cody watched DeeDee as she returned to work. Her whole persona changed when she was in the salon. Around him, she was soft and very much a woman, but at the salon she was tough as nails. She was no different from the men he knew with successful businesses. It was considered an asset for a man, but most of the terms used to describe women with the same edge were not flattering. He listened as she ordered fabric and materials.

When she hung up her phone, she turned to him. "Julia has done an excellent job. Any job I left her with is completed. It's almost as though I'd been here the entire time."

Julia had run DeeDee's company with the same skill set as DeeDee. Accounting was up to date, banking done, all orders had been handled and work assigned, everything was as it should be. One high school senior, working far more than part time, had managed to keep things flowing. He knew it was because DeeDee ran a well-organized business, but he couldn't hold back the pride that swelled in his chest for his oldest daughter.

After lunch, he left DeeDee for his own office. Carlie was anxious to get out early and Chelsea would become his afternoon assistant. She, too, had blossomed in the office environment and seemed to really enjoy working there. At first, he wondered if it was because for a few hours, she had her father's sole attention. But then he decided she really did like what she was doing. What had started as a problem, solved by his keeping Chelsea with him, had turned into a good thing.

Melissa stayed busy with school activities, as did Sean and Ian. The children were so different, and he loved each one of them. But watching Chelsea grow into her new job gave the two of them a new bond that was unique.

He didn't want to railroad her into becoming a lawyer, so he kept telling himself that the skills she was learning could be applied to many other jobs. There were days spent explaining things to her, and others re-explaining them. At first, she would send him copious pages that were virtually useless information, but then she learned to actually read what she had looked up. If it were applicable, she'd send it to him. He found himself saving things for her to look up, instead of giving it to Carlie.

His mind wandered to the upcoming trip. He needed to stop by the supermarket and pick up plenty of food for the weekend. He could have easily taken his crew with him in his SUV, but as soon as he added DeeDee he knew that he had to use two vehicles. He'd let Julia drive his car and take Melissa and Chelsea, then he'd drive the SUV with the boys and DeeDee. Taking them into the wilderness for a long weekend was probably going to be a mistake. Could he keep them all occupied and happy? *Please let this weekend go well.*

***

Tuesday evening he sat his oldest five at the dining room table. "We need to talk."

"Now what?" Ian bellyached.

Cody ignored his second oldest son. "We're going off for a weekend, and I'm taking DeeDee with us." He swallowed. "I've told you over and over that I believe that abstinence is the best way to handle things. DeeDee and I are not teenagers, we're gown adults. There's a difference. There are enough bedrooms in the cabin for everyone to have their own if the twins take one room. I'm hoping that DeeDee will chose to sleep in my bedroom."

"Oh!" Julia replied. "That confirms where you've been sneaking off late at night."

He wondered how many of his children had noticed. He looked around and not a single one of the kids seemed the least bit concerned. "I wanted to discuss the situation with you so that you understand, and because I don't want you to think that I'm preaching one thing and doing another."

Sean leaned back in his chair and smirked. "And that is exactly what you are doing. So why are we here?"

Ian laughed. "I think he wants our permission to have sex with his girlfriend."

"Enough!" Cody's hackles rose. "I'm the adult. I'm your parent. I'm trying very hard to raise you to be responsible adults."

Sean leaned forward and knitted his eyebrows. "The gist of this story is that we can't do it, but you can, because you're older."

Cody grinned at his son. "Exactly."

Julia cocked her head. "So when are we adults? When do we get to make our own decisions and not have to worry about your wrath?"

Cody leaned back in his seat. "Good question. You'll always be my kids and I'll always worry about you. I'll do anything I can to prevent you from making the same mistakes that I did."

Julia raised her eyebrows at him.

"I thought when I married Patty, I had changed. I had three little girls and I took on two boys. It wasn't until Patty died that the full impact of my actions hit me."

He looked at Melissa. "When you got sick, my world spun. I

could have washed my hands, hired someone, or stuck you guys in a boarding school, but I didn't. I might have made a ton of mistakes in my life, but I knew I loved all of you. You were my kids, and it's not your fault that none of you are biologically mine."

Julia swiped at tears. "You're my daddy. You'll always be my daddy."

"And my little girls will always be my little girls, and my boys will always be my boys. I had to pick up the pieces of my life and keep going. And those pieces included seven children. I've grabbed for the brass ring several times in my life and it's all turned out to be smoke and mirrors. This time, I believe it's the real thing. I want this chance at happiness. But I also want everyone to feel comfortable with the idea of my marrying DeeDee."

Sean blurted out, "You're going to marry her?"

"And I hope you all will respect my choice and treat her with respect."

"Are we supposed to call her mom?" Sean cocked his head.

Cody grimaced. "I don't think she's ever going to step into that parental role. You're all too old. But I do require that you treat her with a certain amount of reverence when she becomes my wife. She will act in my behalf if I'm not here. Does anyone have a problem with that?"

Julia mumbled, "At least, she's not like Patty."

"Hey, leave our mom out of it!" Ian raised his voice a little too much.

"She was a witch to us!" Melissa retaliated.

"Okay, enough." Cody was determined to put an end to the old contention between his daughters and Patty's oldest boys. "That's all old information. DeeDee is her own person. I want everyone to have a chance to get to know her and for her to get to know you. Other than Julia, the rest of you have had limited contact with her."

He inhaled as he tried to find the right words. "To be honest, I don't expect anything other than tolerance. I think you overwhelm her. She was an only child and she's not been around children very much."

Ian pushed his chair back. "Because of her, we missed going to the ranch at Christmas."

"Yes, we did. And if you had said something, I would have let you go by yourself."

Ian started to stand.

"Wait, have a seat. Communication is important. You failed to communicate that to me. Everyone here knows that I'm not perfect, and I've made some mistakes over the years. I don't want to make another. I want all of you to be comfortable with the idea of DeeDee being part of this family. Will you at least give her a chance?"

***

DeeDee swore she had too much work to take a long weekend, but finally she conceded when she realized she'd have Internet and phone access the entire time. Moving this crew for a long weekend meant suitcases stuffed with clothes, hairdryers, etc. Bags of groceries, which included potato chips and other junk foods that he normally avoided, were packed in the back of the

SUV along with three big coolers filled with everything from bags of salad to pickles and another cooler was filled with meats.

Getting everyone out of the house took some doing, but once on the road, Cody felt confident. His big surprise came when Ian asked DeeDee about her fashion show. Then Cody remembered the conversation DeeDee had had with Ian over athletic shoes. This time the conversation was more focused on marketing.

"Since that was the most difficult thing for me, I brought in Chrisy."

"He's seems weird."

DeeDee laughed. "He calls me 'baby.' But he's the best promoter in the business."

"Why would he call you that?"

"Just his pet name for me. I seriously wanted to choke him a dozen times while in New York, yet I understood what he was doing and why."

"But he wears heels like a cross dresser."

"He does wear heels and very flamboyant clothing, but he's not what I would call a cross dresser."

Cody could see his son's scrunched up face in the rearview mirror.

DeeDee smiled as she answered Ian, "He loves wild colors, but the heels…"

Cody glanced at DeeDee. He couldn't wait to hear what she had to say.

"Look at some of the athletes who wear their hair long or cover their bodies in tattoos. It's the way they express themselves and stand out from the crowd. Chrisy is in the fashion industry, he loves clothing. His choices make him stand out and make him unforgettable."

"And that's what you call branding?"

"Yes."

"But the heels? That's a girl thing."

Cody withheld his desire to laugh.

"I'll let you in on a secret, but don't ever discuss it with anyone." DeeDee's voice grew very solemn.

Cody caught DeeDee turning in her seat to face Ian.

"I don't think he can put one foot flat. I saw him barefoot in the suite we had, and he walks on his toes on that foot. He limps in a regular pair of men's shoes. He wears special inserts in his shoes to try to hide it."

That's interesting.

DeeDee continued, "So being in the fashion industry and tied to Karina, it was easy for him to wear heels. It suits the peacock in him."

"He's not gay?" Ian asked.

"From everything he's ever said…not even a little. He loves women."

"He's still weird."

DeeDee laughed. "He's divorced and he's got grown children… They're adults and he's waiting on one of them to produce a grandchild."

Cody completely understood his son's attitude. He also knew Chrisy was divorced and was looking forward to being a grandparent. Questioning a person's sexuality was never something Cody did. He totally believed in accepting people for who they were. Behind that flamboyant exterior, Chrisy was a mastermind.

DeeDee continued. "He's also extremely intelligent and one of the nicest guys you'll ever meet. Don't ever let the way someone looks influence you. And never be concerned about someone's sexual orientation. The fashion industry is filled with unusual people. In fact, I think anything having to do with an art form tends to attract people who live outside of the box. I'm sure you've been taught never to judge a book by its cover. The same goes with people. Accept people for who they are. Your father doesn't expect you to build robots or to become a lawyer. He expects you to find your own niche and to succeed on your terms."

Cody looked in the rearview mirror and caught Ian's gaze.

"So why are you always on me about grades?"

"Because--"

DeeDee put her hand on Cody's leg. "Because he cares. I was an art major, but I still had to take science and math. I had to show proficiency in all the basic classes in order to go to college. I had to go to college to learn fashion design. I had to learn about some of the strangest things so that I can do my job well."

"Like algebra is ever going to mean anything to me?"

"You're learning more than just how to put numbers together. If you can't make yourself sit for two hours and do your homework, how are you going to do your job? How are you going to have the mental discipline to do something else that is important to you? When you throw a basketball, football, or even a baseball, you are using and applying physics. Geometry will tell you where that ball is going."

Cody continued to listen to DeeDee's lecture. She was good, as she had a knack for making Ian see beyond the sport itself. With a little luck, he hoped this weekend would give her the chance to see past the status quo, and give her an opportunity to realize that their lives could blend into a permanent relationship.

Twelve

Finding the cabin in the semi-darkness was not easy, but the directions had been excellent. Cody pulled in front of a large A-frame with a long wing on one side and admired the clean but rugged lines. He found the key, opened the door, and turned on the lights. *Oh, this is going to be nice!*

Two groggy twins stumbled inside and whined. The girls fought over rooms. Getting everyone fed was first priority. Cody headed outside for the grill and turned it on. Everything was spotless and very inviting, so why was there so much commotion inside? He wasn't surprised to see DeeDee follow him.

"The war has begun. Seems the girls want to watch one thing on the TV and the boys want another." DeeDee sat on the small stone wall that partially surrounded the grill and the patio.

"As long as it doesn't get physical, I try to let them settle their differences. If it gets out of hand, no one will watch anything."

"You amaze me. I don't know too many people who can cope with seven children."

"They haven't scared you away."

She laughed. It was soft and sultry. "They aren't mine. You handle them."

It was not what he wanted to hear. "I'm all they have. I'll be right back. I need tonight's hamburger."

Cody stepped into the house and the noise had quieted. It was almost too quiet. Everyone was in his or her room except for Melissa, who was poking through the coolers looking for her favorite soda. He looked at Melissa. "What happened to the TV argument?"

"They won and no one can make the TV work. Serves them right!"

Cody munched on the insides of his cheeks. He had no idea who *they* were, but he suspected it was the boys. "I'll see what I can do after dinner."

He grabbed the packages of rolls and the box of preformed hamburger patties. He was glad he'd bought them, for it was saving him time. He went back outside. "Sorry to take so long." He put the things down next to the grill and opened the box. *Scissors!* "Darn."

He left DeeDee and went inside. In the kitchen, he rummaged through the drawers until he found a pair of scissors. He looked at them and dropped them back into the drawer. He found a small knife and took that outside.

It didn't take him long to have a dozen hamburgers on the grill. That wonderful aroma filled the entire patio. The sun had set and the cloudless sky had taken on a purple color. A few stars were beginning to twinkle.

It had seemed later and darker when he pulled up to the cabin. He'd forgotten that he'd been driving through the deep shade of the mountain and the tall trees. The thought of his first trip to these mountains filtered through his mind. Having been raised near the Rockies, these mountains were very different. There were no tall peaks and the number of trees almost made him claustrophobic. It took some time to appreciate the beauty of the Appalachians.

He filled in the silence. "Apparently no one can make the TV work."

"Oh, my. It'll be a very long weekend."

He raised the grill lid and flipped the hamburgers. "This looks so good!"

DeeDee smiled at him. "I'm hungry and smelling it is making me twice as hungry."

A few minutes later, he stabbed the hamburger and the juices ran clear. "They are done. Want to hand me the buns one at a time?"

Together they stuffed ten hamburger buns. Then they both turned and looked towards the woods that surrounded the cabin.

DeeDee handed him another bun. "What is making that noise?"

"Maybe a deer." He put another burger onto a bun.

About two seconds later, DeeDee screamed.

Cody turned to see a bear lumbering in their direction. He grabbed the plate of hamburgers and pushed DeeDee inside, then he very carefully went back to the grill, lifted the remaining hamburger off, and placed it on the low stone wall where DeeDee had been sitting. Without turning his back to the bear, he quickly made his way to the cabin. His body shuddered as if to shake the ice off that had flowed through his system. "Dinner is ready. Anyone want to see the bear on the patio?"

Seven kids scampered and pressed their noses to the glass

panes of the big windows that ran in six-foot lengths to the roof of the A-frame section of the house.

Cody went to his suitcases and pulled a gun from the one. He could almost see the color drain from DeeDee's face as she stared at the gun in his hand. "I was raised on a ranch. I know about wild animals. If he wants to come in here, he will. That glass isn't going to keep him out."

The bear rose up on his hind legs and Cody put a twin on Ian's shoulders and another on Sean's. "The bigger we are...the better."

The bear went to the grill but backed off when he realized it was hot. He wandered around the patio, licked at the spot that had once held the buns and the box of burgers, ate the burger that was left on the wall, and wandered off.

Cody let out an audible sigh of relief. "Okay, let's eat. We're going to discuss how we're going to handle this situation. That was a young male. I'm surprised he's not still hibernating, but... Parents will run off young males in the spring. The time has come for him to find a mate."

Sean laughed. "Isn't sending us off to college the same thing?"

Cody chuckled. "Not quite." He grabbed a bag of potato chips and tore it open. "It's taken me almost thirty-nine years to find the right woman." He shook some chips onto his plate and passed the bag to Logan. "And she hasn't said yes."

Chelsea giggled. "She'd have to be crazy to say yes to you."

Cody looked at DeeDee. She raised her eyebrows and took a bite of her hamburger.

"No one wanders outside alone - ever, while we are here. Do not take food outside with you. He's hungry." Cody laid the rules for everyone and they all swore to abide by them.

It took Cody a few minutes to figure out why the TV was not working. Soon the entire family was in the big room watching TV. His great idea for roasting marshmallows in the fire pit just didn't hold the same appeal after becoming acquainted with the bear.

He helped the twins settle in for the night and DeeDee went online to check orders while the older ones watched a crime show on TV. It was eleven o'clock when he got the rest of his crew to head for their rooms. That left him and DeeDee.

"My room?"

DeeDee blushed. "But the kids…"

"I discussed our relationship with them before we came up here. They are aware that we are consenting adults."

"You told them?"

"Not details. I told them that I was hoping that you'd share my bed."

"So you want me to sleep with you here."

"Yes."

She rolled her eyes. "Did you ever turn the gas off on the grill?"

"Yes. I turned it off at the grill before I pulled the hamburgers, just not underneath where the propane is attached."

"Everything locked up?"

He nodded.

"Am I running out of excuses?"

He nodded.

"I'd love to sleep with you."

He inhaled and smiled.

***

DeeDee awakened to an odd sound, then she heard the crash. She elbowed Cody. He slipped out of bed, pulled on a pair of jeans, and put his feet into a pair of boots.

"Stay here and make sure none of the kids follow me." He grabbed his gun and left the bedroom.

Not wanting to miss out, she slipped on a pair of pants and pulled on a tee shirt. After sticking her bare feet into a pair of sneakers, she tied them and followed Cody down the hallway. She froze in place when she saw what was making the noise. One by one, the children opened their bedroom doors to see what was causing all the commotion. The bear had returned and was trying to find food in the kitchen trash.

Chelsea's door was the closest to DeeDee. She glanced at the young girl. "Get your phone and dial 9-1-1."

Chelsea nodded and vanished. When she returned she was whispering to a dispatcher and passed the phone to DeeDee.

Sean had his hands on DeeDee's shoulders and was pressed to her back as she spoke to the dispatcher. "I don't know. We rented a private cabin off of Kiln Road. It's a beauty, all cedar and stone with a big A-frame front. I know the property goes to the water. Can't you GPS this or something?"

"I'm working on that. It's a bear?"

"Yes. He came last night while we were grilling and then left. Guess he's still hungry."

"He'll probably stay in the kitchen area so lock yourselves in the bedroom until we can get someone out there. I have two cars on the way and I've notified the game warden.

"Cody's opened several doors."

"It's not safe to confront a bear unarmed."

"Who says Cody is unarmed."

"Does he have a gun?"

"Yes."

"What kind?"

"I have no clue. I'm a city girl. He was raised on a ranch in the west, but I can tell you that the last thing he would do is shoot a bear. He's not into hurting wildlife; he's not a hunter." She looked at Chelsea. "Is he?"

Chelsea shook her head. "Dad wouldn't kill that bear except to protect us if it tried to attack."

Sean took the phone from DeeDee and told them what his dad was carrying and what ammunition it took. "He knows what he's doing. He's trying to get it to leave. He said earlier that it was a young male."

DeeDee hated not being able to speak to the dispatcher. She felt calmer talking to that man on the phone than she did standing and watching. When she realized there were lights from a car bouncing down the driveway to the front of the house, she turned to Chelsea. "No one takes another step forward, got that?"

Chelsea nodded.

"Cody, I'm going to try to make it to the front door without causing any disturbance."

"Go slow and never turn your back to this bear. He's busy

with the trashcan."

She sidestepped her way until she could open the door and step onto the front landing. Every part of her was shaking with fear as two young men approached with rifles. "Please don't kill it."

"We can't let anyone get hurt."

"Well so far we're all fine."

The two uniformed officers pushed past her and into the house. A second police car approached and a pickup truck followed behind the second cruiser.

The guy with the truck had a tranquilizer gun. DeeDee breathed a sigh of relief. "Please don't kill it. It looks like it has an ear tag on it."

The older man with the tranquilizer gun smiled. "Are you the city girl that dispatch was talking to?"

She nodded.

"You're observant. We know exactly who he is and who his momma is. We've had some teams going through this area tagging our bear population. We're trying to protect them."

He stepped into the house and she followed.

Quickly it became obvious that the men wanted the bear to go outside before he was tranquilized. Instead of leaving the way he came in, the bear knocked through another pane of glass. Two seconds later, a shot rang out, and the men rushed forward.

DeeDee and the kids followed. Several hundred pounds of bear lay on his side and tried to lift his head. Collin and Logan wanted to touch it.

"No!" Cody scolded. "Stay here. And stay away from all this

broken glass."

DeeDee picked the twins up. "You weigh a ton!"

The boys squirmed out of her arms.

"Get your shoes on and a jacket." She watched them scurry back to their bedroom.

The teens had moved forward to the patio to watch.

Julia asked, "What are you going to do with him?"

The ranger turned to her and smiled. "We're going to move him to a less populated area."

"He's out cold, right?"

"Yes, miss. He's not going anywhere on his own any time soon."

She moved forward. "May I pet him?"

The ranger chuckled. "Sure. Why don't you hold this tape measure while I get some more info on him."

Julia knelt down and helped the man. She brushed her hand over the face of the sleeping bear. "I thought he'd be soft but he's not. It's coarse fur."

She helped the man measure the bear's paw, head, and total body length.

"We'll get a weight on him when we lift him."

The ranger retrieved a kit from his pickup that someone had driven around to the back of the house. He took a blood sample and did several other things.

It all seemed to happen rather quickly, but the ranger did allow the twins to touch the bear before he was picked up and loaded into the back of the truck. It took all four police officers, Cody, and the ranger to get the bear moved onto the sling. As the ranger shut the doors that caged the sleeping bear, the ranger's assistant rolled onto the scene.

DeeDee was good at reading people and she could tell that the ranger was not pleased, but the man said nothing in front of the children.

Cody had swept and mopped in an attempt to clean up and clear the broken glass in the kitchen. Julia found the vacuum and began to do the rugs. Sean picked up the larger shards outside and deposited that glass in the trash. Ian took a broom and swept the patio, then Chelsea mopped behind Ian. No one had told the kids to do it. They just did what had to be done. Cody often questioned his parenting skills, but from what DeeDee witnessed, he was raising responsible teens.

DeeDee taped several large plastic trash bags together and covered the broken windows, while Cody made a pot of coffee and the twins ate cereal.

After the pot had finished brewing, Cody poured a cup for him and for DeeDee before asking, "Who wants to go fishing?"

DeeDee had a terrible time telling the twins apart, but she was learning. The boys had snagged her heart a long time ago and this weekend had sealed her love for them. Their excitement over fishing had been contagious. They'd each caught a fish large enough to fix for lunch.

Two hours of fishing had yielded enough fish for the entire family's lunch. Cody scaled and cleaned the fish. Then he pan-fried them. It wasn't the best meal DeeDee'd ever eaten, but it was tasty.

By the time Friday evening arrived, a glass company had replaced one pane of glass, and covered the larger pane with plywood. The children were relaxed and doing well together. Even Ian seemed calmer than normal.

Cody had brought mosaic kits with him and all the kids made tiles on Saturday afternoon. DeeDee was surprised to see Ian patiently helping the twins with theirs. Julia and Sean had laughed as they worked together. When they cleaned up that mess, Cody got them going on edible faces. DeeDee laughed as they cut up salad olives to make eyeballs and Sean made a spider out of celery. Melissa turned kiwis into turtles. DeeDee cut up apples and used raisins to make puppy faces. Then they ate their creations before devouring steaks from the grill.

But what really amazed DeeDee was the TV never went on after that first night. The girls had quit wearing makeup. Ponytails and braids seemed to replace hours of primping. Everyone truly got along. They were not just a pack of kids tossed together. They were a family.

On Saturday night, the twins wore their pajamas under their coats as they roasted marshmallows over the fire pit and made s'mores. DeeDee helped the twins take the sticky, toasted marshmallows off the long sticks and get the hot marshmallows sandwiched between the graham crackers and the piece of chocolate bar. Then she made them blow air on them before eating the sweet, campfire treat.

When Cody decided they'd had enough and suggested it was time to go to bed, both the younger boys begged for DeeDee to tuck them in.

"You stay with the older ones. I'll put Collin and Logan in bed and grab a quick shower before I join you." DeeDee dropped a kiss on Cody's cheek before heading inside with the two little boys.

The twins had clamored for her attention all evening and now they had it. She probably took longer putting them to bed than Cody would have, but it was fun. There were no books to read to them, but they settled in rather quickly after each demanded lots of bedtime kisses.

DeeDee joined the rest of the family on the patio and made a s'more. That's when Cody started telling a ghost story. She knew he was joking, but she hated being scared. Cody was good at storytelling and had the girls glued to him. Even Ian seemed mesmerized by Cody's tale.

Sean sneaked up and poked DeeDee, causing her to scream. That set off the girls. Cody laughed and chased everyone inside before he dropped the big dome lid over the pit suffocating the fire.

"You were horrible for telling the teens such a wild tale. Do you want to give them nightmares?"

Cody laughed. "And they'll be begging to see some horror movie when it comes out. Some of that apocalyptic stuff is ten times worse than any tale I could dream up."

"You scared the daylights out of me."

"Good, now you'll have to snuggle extra tight to me so I can protect you."

DeeDee cut him her meanest face.

He laughed, then his lips covered hers.

The following morning, DeeDee pulled on a jacket, took her cup of coffee to the patio, and Cody followed. He started a fire in the pit, taking the chill from the morning air. She drank her first cup and then returned to the kitchen for a second. That time she picked up her computer and took it with her to the patio.

From the gentle fall of the willow trees by the river, to the curl of the fallen leaves on the ground, DeeDee had found inspiration for dresses. Using her stylus, she drew several bits and pieces that would later become parts of dresses.

Cody looked at what she was doing. "Do you ever stop?"

"Maybe one day. For now I'm enjoying myself."

"You need to design one for yourself."

She looked up at him and grinned. "I already have."

"Do I get to see it?"

"We need to talk."

***

Cody looked at DeeDee as ice water circulated in his system. He could see her tensing as though this was an unwanted conversation. "Yes. We do need to discuss marriage, because I want to marry you."

She dropped her stylus into her jacket pocket. "Why mess up what we have? You have your place and I have mine. I gather from this weekend that our sharing the bed occasionally isn't going to be a problem."

"Did you ever think that your independence is not reliant on you having your own place?"

He watched her heave a sigh. "I've been on my own...completely on my own for almost ten years. I don't want to give up what I have."

"What do you have? You're renting a furnished room from

Gloria Anderson. Does it really make a difference what closet contains your clothing?"

"That's not what I'm talking about. I'm talking about my freedom to do as I please. I don't want to ask permission to take a rep out to dinner, or meet a friend in New York or Louisiana."

"So you think marriage would stop you from doing that?"

"Yes."

"What if I said the only thing I'd like to know is that you intend to go someplace and how long you'd be? Think of it as common courtesy. I have no desire to hold you back from your job. Mine takes me out of town occasionally. I expect that our jobs will separate us periodically, but I'd like to think you'd share my bed the rest of the time."

"And what if you're out of town? What about the children?"

"My mom usually comes or my sister. They enjoy visiting and spoiling the children."

"Do you really think they would come if I'm there?"

He downed the last few drops of his coffee. "Yes." He looked at DeeDee and saw the hard set to her jaw. "I know I have a pack of kids and I'm not asking you to step into some mother role with them, but it seems to me that you do get along with all of them, and they like you."

"So I can keep them if you're gone."

"That's up to you. We both have busy lives. You work as hard as any entrepreneur, and it's one of the things that I admire about you." He stood and grabbed her coffee cup. "I'll refill these."

He returned to the kitchen and poured more coffee. Julia was awake and joined him. He poured the last cup for her. "Will you make more coffee and take care of your siblings? DeeDee and I need some uninterrupted time."

She nodded.

"Thanks."

He returned to the patio and handed DeeDee her cup. "Do you realize that you're the first female that hasn't wanted something from me? We look at each other as equals. I don't see you as some little woman with a cute little job drawing dresses for weddings."

"You'd better not!"

"Don't worry about that because I see a woman who is accomplishing something. I like that about you." He raised his eyebrows. "And I like the fact that under that tough exterior, there's this wonderful woman who is loving and soft with beautiful curves."

"The polite way of saying I'm fat."

"No. You're also not skinny and bony. I like the way you feel in my arms and pressed to my body as we sleep."

She rolled her eyes at him.

"Don't put yourself down. You might work in an industry where women are rail thin, but you figured out a long time ago that you didn't have to be. You're on your feet all day long, you walk when others ride, and you're healthy and very beautiful. Half the women today are afraid to eat a donut for fear of gaining a pound. You enjoy it. What's wrong with that? I think it's great."

She sipped at her coffee. "We've got a good thing going the way it is. I like my life and you're the icing on that donut. End of conversation."

Cody inhaled. "Okay. I'll respect that."

***

After the long weekend, being back in her own room and looking out the window at Main Street, sent a gentle wave of peace through DeeDee. The weekend had been fun. She couldn't believe that she'd learned how to put a cricket on a fishing hook. Visions of the weekend flew through her mind as she watched the vehicles on the street below.

Cody had been a phenomenal lover. Just thinking about his body stirred her. He must have studied the Kama Sutra the way he managed to gently change positions, each time making certain she was comfortable and enjoying every minute of their union. The heat within her burned a little brighter. She chewed at her lower lip and tried to push away the feelings. She convinced herself that taking a shower and doing routine things would make it go away, but it didn't.

Her phone chattered, alerting her of a text message. She grabbed it, seeing it was Cody.

You spoiled me this weekend. How am I ever supposed to sleep without you?

She responded with a smiley face and put the phone on the nightstand before settling into bed. Knowing he was having just as much trouble sleeping gave her some sort of perverted satisfaction.

He was older, but not by much. That bit of gray hair around his temples made him look older. She knew he didn't go to a gym. He laughed about it and said who needed a gym when he had

200

twins to lift and teens to keep him fit.

She had nothing against any of the children. She adored Julia and the twins; Chelsea and Melissa were wonderful young women; Sean was quiet and easy going. Ian was far from quiet, but he had a serious side that she liked. She couldn't imagine any of them ever being a real problem, even though she'd seen the aftermath of probably one of their worst moments. Yet, she'd held the children against Cody and used them as her excuse.

As much as she hated to admit it, she'd fallen madly in love with the quiet, even-tempered man. She thought about his hands. *Piano fingers.* His fingernails were immaculate as were his toenails. *Does he go for pedicures or does he do it himself.* She pondered it for a moment and decided he probably had it done.

Ian had a habit of sticking his fist to his chin and sucking on a knuckle on his little finger. She wondered if he had sucked his thumb or his fingers as a baby.

The image of Patty floated through DeeDee's mind. Cody said Patty's body was the result of a good plastic surgeon. DeeDee believed it. She'd measured too many women. Most women had one breast that was larger than the other, and one hip that was higher. Plus, she knew that most feet were off by a quarter of a size. Patty wasn't but twenty-one in those magazine photos, yet she'd already had implants, a nose job, and several other surgeries.

DeeDee rolled over and faced the wall. *He's been through hell, yet he wants to try one more time? How can he trust me? How can I trust him?*

She wanted to curl against his chest and feel the protective warmth of his arms around her. Her thoughts had come full circle and that fire within was burning brightly. Her phone chattered, she rolled over, and looked at it.

R u still awake? I can't sleep 4 thinking of u.

She smiled and texted him back. *I'll unlock the doors. Lock them behind you.*

She put her robe on and padded down the two sets of stairs and unlocked each door, then scurried back to her bedroom. She ditched the old tee shirt and left the robe wrapped around her knowing it would be much sexier, then wondered if that made her look too anxious. She put the old tee shirt back on and wrapped her robe around again. *What am I doing?*

She sat by the window and watched him stroll down Main Street until he reached Gloria's green door. He was quiet as a mouse as he climbed the stairs to her room. Her body wanted to scream with joy as she watched the doorknob to her room turn.

Wearing a down vest, a gray Henley, an old pair of faded jeans, and an old pair of boots, he was a vision of solid-packed testosterone. She inhaled and waited as he closed her door and turned the knob that locked it. With nothing but a small nightlight glowing in the room, she watched him peel off his clothes and toss them onto a chair. His erection was strong and plastered itself against his abdomen.

She chomped on her lower lip as he walked to where she was sitting in the window. He took her hand and pulled her to her feet, then removed her robe and her tee shirt. Molten lava flowed through her as he pulled her to him. In one swift move, he lifted her off her feet.

"Put me down before you hurt yourself." She whispered as she clung to his neck.

He ignored her, carried her to her bed, and placed her in the center of it as his body covered hers. In a split second, he sheathed himself within her.

She managed to squeak out, "Condoms. They are in the drawer."

"Frankly, my dear, I don't give a damn."

The next twenty minutes of her life were wild, hot, and beyond anything she'd ever imagined. When it ended, perspiration covered her body like dew. His chest heaved, slightly suspended above hers, and his breath flowed over her neck. Her own spasms milked him until they pushed him from within her. She had no voice.

His blue eyes stared into hers. She lifted her chin and his lips covered hers before making their way lower over her body. Then he lifted her hips and entered her one more time. This time it was gentle and unhurried. When it ended, she was lying on his chest listening to the thump of his heart in her ear. His arms cocooned her.

Morning broke and the sun began to stream in the windows. The clock said eight and DeeDee rose from her bed as panic smacked her. She had less than an hour to get the salon doors open, and after being gone for the weekend, she was facing a ton of work.

Cody was gone but the remnants of the passionate night covered her belly and her legs. She jumped into the shower. Lacking some sleep, she didn't mind. The feel of Cody's body lingered on her skin. If she closed her eyes, it was as if he were there holding her.

She stepped out of the shower, dressed quickly, and flew to the salon as though she had wings on her heels. Her office door was open and Cody sat by her desk smiling at her. He had coffee from the coffeehouse down the street and two of Elizabeth's gooey cinnamon sweet buns.

"Did my woman sleep well?"

Your woman? His slightly crooked grin as he spoke warmed her heart. *I should have known you'd be here.* "Overslept. How about you?"

"I don't get the luxury of oversleeping. The older ones can get ready for school, but I have to be there for Logan and Collin."

"You're a good father." She took her seat and pulled up the previous night's orders.

"I try to be." He grinned. "How do you feel about motherhood?"

"What time do I have for it?"

"The same as anyone else who works."

She rolled her eyes at him. "This place is my baby."

"True."

She sipped her coffee and stared at him. "Are you trying to get me pregnant? Or you just like risking your health and mine?"

"I'm clean and I believe you when you say you are. I was joking about the motherhood thing. Besides, aren't you on birth control?"

"No. I have no reason to be on it. I've always been regular and I've not been sexually active except for that one period in London with Richard."

She watched him purse his lips and blow out a deep breath, then gaze at her as though he was beseeching her. "Saying I'm sorry isn't enough."

"No, it's not."

"There's that morning after pill."

"Don't bother. I woke up with my period."

His shoulders slumped.

"You were hoping I'd get pregnant, weren't you?"

He shook his head. "Not without your permission. But I do hate condoms. Once you've lived without them, it's hard to go back." He narrowed his eyes. "I want you in my bed every night. At least, move in with me."

"No. What part of I-have-a-life do you not understand?"

He chuckled.

It was that deep throaty sound of his chuckle that wrapped her in a rich velvet.

He came to where she was sitting and kissed her cheek. "You're as horny as I am. Give into it."

"Damn, Cody. Stop it. Yes, you are wonderful. What's not to like? You're thoughtful and sweet. You treat me like a princess. You've got a gorgeous body and you're handsome to boot!"

"So marry me."

"I told you, no. And I'll say it again. NO!" She narrowed her eyes as she looked at him. "To you, it's a joke. Listen carefully. I have no desire to be emotionally involved with a man. At this point in my life, I don't want to be married or coping with a bunch of children. You had no right to do what you did. So why don't you get the hell out of my life? Get out!"

He shook his head, dropped his empty coffee cup in the trash, gathered up his computer, and left.

Tears filled her eyes. She'd hurt him. Her computer screen became a blurred mess. She shut down her computer, grabbed her purse, and without a word to her employees, she went back to her apartment.

Sitting in her window seat, tears streamed down her face. *What am I doing?* She sobbed. Not since her mom's death had she cried with such abandon. She got up and blew her nose. Tears continued to stream. She removed her fake lashes and tried to wipe away the smudged eyeliner and mascara that ran down her cheeks. But her tears wouldn't stop.

Feeling lower than a cockroach in an abandoned building, she threw herself across her bed until her tears subsided. He might have become her silent partner, along with her best friend… But to commit to marriage? She couldn't think beyond a single day.

She remembered Sean standing behind her while the bear investigated the kitchen. Sean's hands were on her shoulders and he stood several inches taller than her, yet he was still that little boy who was fascinated and scared. Even Ian had captured her heart. Each one of the kids had wormed their way in for different reasons.

I can't be a mother. I don't have time for children.

Then she thought about Cody sitting in her office. He'd obviously taken the twins to Donna's house to catch the bus, and then had opened the salon for the employees. He purposely let her sleep, yet he'd had even less sleep. He was like that, always thinking of her.

Yet she had easily lied to him. She told him she'd gotten her period. She was as guilty as his wives. What if she were pregnant? *No way.* She rolled onto her back and stared at the ceiling. *I'm so sorry, Cody. I should have never lied.*

Like a sad little cloud, remorse filled her. She grabbed her phone and called his number. *I'm so sorry, so very sorry. You deserve better than that.*

Thirteen

Cody heard his phone and opened his eyes long enough to realize it was DeeDee. He put the phone down and drifted back into his fitful slumber. At two thirty, his alarm wakened him. Had he dreamed she had called? No, it was there under missed calls. He had no desire to call her back and listen to her rant, instead he took a quick shower and pulled on a pair of slacks and a white shirt. Maybe he had made a terrible mistake. Maybe this time, DeeDee was the intelligent one who realized he wasn't the kind of guy who should be married. His private life was a total mess. *The children.* That part he'd gotten right, but only after it was forced upon him.

He slipped his belt through his pant loops. *I made another mess of things.*

He was tied to DeeDee because he had become a silent partner in her business, and he stood to make a huge chunk of money, but that's not what he wanted. He wanted her.

He thought about moving home and then dismissed the idea. Julia would graduate in June. Sean and Melissa weren't far from graduating and Ian would graduate behind Sean. By the time Ian finished, Chelsea would be nearing the end of her high school days. At least the kids were happy and they were getting a good education. Private school might give them a slight edge academically, but they were learning more about people in public school. It was better to let the kids stay where they were.

Besides, he was the only lawyer in the in area who devoted his practice to looking for unfairly accused men and women. It would put a huge burden on the agency if he left. He needed to stay put. Why couldn't he just let things ride the way they were? Why couldn't he enjoy a dinner here and there, and maybe some occasional sex with DeeDee? Other men manage to do things like that. No strings. He knew quite a few guys who would kill for such an arrangement. Deep inside it was not what he wanted and he didn't feel like listening to her diatribe over their relationship.

***

DeeDee called a taxi and went to the mall on the outskirts of town. She wandered around looking in all the shops and watching the other shoppers. She stopped at the food court, grabbed a chicken sandwich with waffle fries, then had a slice of lemon meringue pie. Bored, yet anxious, she walked across the parking lot to the big drug store and found the pills. *Plan B, yep, that's me. My entire life is Plan B.* She bought the box, called a taxi, went back to the salon, and checked the doors before walking to Gloria's.

Ideas that had spun through her head over the long weekend seemed to be frozen. She'd drawn a series of curves and as she looked at them, she had no idea why she'd drawn them. It was as though her creative juices had gelled into a useless ball.

She closed her computer and pulled the box from her purse. She read the directions twice. *What if I am pregnant?*

I certainly can't take six weeks off. She'd have to be in the office as quickly as possible. *I'm not doing heavy manual labor. A crib and changing table.*

There was no reason why she couldn't keep her child tucked in the office with her. *Don't babies sleep most of the time?*

The whole idea appealed to her. She'd always wanted a child, but her life seemed to lack a willing sperm donor. She had money, enough to raise a child on her own. And being she was the boss, she didn't have to ask permission to keep her child with her. *I can do this.*

As fast as she had convinced herself she'd be fine, the negatives of the situation began to creep in. All Cody had ever wanted was a child of his own and if she were pregnant…

She pulled the blister packet from the box and held it. *It's a hormone pill, right? It's not murder, is it?* She shoved the packet back into the box and placed it on the counter in the bathroom. *I've got seventy-two hours and I haven't used up the first twenty-four.*

She looked at her cell phone. There had been no response from Cody. *I've really hurt him.*

✳✳✳

Cody caught up on his missing sleep and everything went back to its normal routine. When the children asked about DeeDee, he told them she'd been busy. Julia was the only one who might have suspected otherwise. But she didn't seem to question him, which meant DeeDee wasn't sharing her private life with her teenage employee.

Four days later, his sister sent the blueprints for DeeDee's factory. He had promised DeeDee he'd take care of it. He made several phone calls and waited for the bids, knowing that she didn't care much for glass and steel. Her world was lace and tulle. Steel wasn't part of his realm either, but at least he knew the players.

As the bids rolled in, he went over each one. They were all very close. He watched her bank accounts and the money flow. She was thriving and that didn't happen often with new businesses. Chrisy was part of the reason. The capitol was there. But it was DeeDee's designs and that personal touch that gave her an edge over the competitors.

He was keeping up his end of the bargain, but his heart ached. He made the mistake of overstepping his bounds with her. It was his fault and he kicked himself every day and night for what he'd done. *I don't deserve her.*

***

DeeDee tossed and turned in her bed. No matter what her position, she ached from her knees to her shoulders. It was after midnight when she went into the bathroom. That's when she realized she had blood in the toilet. *My period!* That also meant she was not pregnant. Relief washed over her, cleansing her mind of worry. She had done nothing to stop her possible pregnancy and she was glad. Guilt would have consumed her. Yet she was guilty of lying even though the outcome was the same.

It had been almost three weeks since that fateful night and she missed Cody. He'd been the best thing that had ever happened to her, yet she turned him away. His face, as he tossed his paper coffee cup in the trash, was cold and hard. That was the face she saw when she thought of him.

She took something for her cramps and climbed back into bed. She had resigned herself to being pregnant and now she wasn't. The thought came with the feeling of freedom and yet she wanted to cry. Mixed emotions that had kept her company for the past three weeks seemed to have reversed yet they were just as strong. Tears rolled from her eyes. *I'm sorry, Cody.*

The following day, a smiling Linda Ridgeway came to the salon with a national news team. DeeDee had designed a gown just for her and had pre-made one in cotton for Linda's fitting.

With Winnie Kochang helping, DeeDee made some slight modifications. Linda was almost beside herself as she stared at her image in the mirror. DeeDee's gown showed one bare shoulder and created an illusion for her other with the soft puff of a sleeve that hid what was below.

With DeeDee's help, Linda chose her material. Rhinestones, pearls, and feathers were going to make her the swan princess floating on water with a train creating a watery wake in her path. She dissolved into tears of joy. She had only sought a dress that would actually fit and never dreamed her fantasy of being beautiful would ever come true.

DeeDee had spent the day with Linda. At times it was grueling, and at others it was filled with giggles, but all the salon's employees seemed to be caught up in Linda's dress and what was happening. When DeeDee said goodbye and the cameras were gone, she collapsed into the nearest chair as tears of sorrow and joy trickled down her cheeks. What was intended to be a publicity stunt had turned into the most satisfying experience of her life.

Chrisy appeared and they went to the little Chinese restaurant down the street.

DeeDee's life had become almost hectic. Several small bridal shops wanted to carry her designs but didn't seem to understand that each dress was custom made. Chrisy took over and contacted the shops.

Trying to keep up production was becoming almost impossible. She had four people cutting dresses and she needed more. As soon as Julia came to work, DeeDee'd rush upstairs to help steam whatever was completed. She looked at the rack of finished dresses and knew she needed to hire people to steam and pack.

Her business was growing and she barely knew what she had in her bank account. It was flowing in and out so quickly that she couldn't keep up. Every once in a while she'd see large chunks of money come in or shift out to another account in the corporate name. She knew Cody was behind it and she dreaded to think what she owed him. She figured if it were serious, he'd contact her. And maybe that was why he had scheduled the appointment on Saturday.

***

Cody pulled on his best gray Acquitrino summer suit with a vest and finished it with a black leather bolo tie and silver slide. He wasn't certain why he wanted to be formally dressed for the meeting. It had been almost four weeks since DeeDee had tossed him from her office. He could have met DeeDee in a pair of jeans, but he wanted to keep everything official.

It's a business meeting and nothing more. No matter how many times he tried to tell himself that, his heart refused to believe it. Like iron filings headed for a giant magnet, his heart beat in his chest, pushing him forward. He pushed back the lock of hair that always fell over his forehead. His body pulsed with a desire to pick up a dozen roses and a box of cream mints covered in dark chocolate. *It's not personal. Business. Just business. Get over it.*

He gathered up the folder that contained her tax information along with copies of the blueprints and the bids. They had plenty to discuss. Her building wasn't going to be cheap and it meant he'd be putting up more money. He didn't stop for coffee or pastries. That would have been too familiar.

At exactly ten o'clock, he knocked on DeeDee's office door and there was no answer. He knocked again, then thought she might be on the phone, and unable to answer. He turned the handle and the door opened. She was not in her office. He dropped the folder on the corner of her desk and took a seat. She was probably handling some sewing problem, but he didn't think those women worked on Saturday. There was nothing to do but wait.

Twenty minutes later, he decided that she had stood him up. He wasn't going to wait forever. She was making it clear that she did not want to see him. He heard a slight tap on DeeDee's door and it opened.

Julia smiled. "Hi, Dad. DeeDee wants you to know that she's sorry. She's tied up with a client and she'll be awhile. She said to tell you that if you can't wait, she understands, but you're welcome to wait until she's done. Want some coffee while you're here?"

"How much longer do you think she'll be?"

Julia shrugged. "It's a big wedding party and the woman is insisting that DeeDee handles everything."

"So she could be an hour or more?"

Julia grimaced. "The woman is being a real monster. Totally horrid to DeeDee and everyone else." Julia plopped into DeeDee's chair. "I'd like to tell her to get out and go elsewhere."

By the time Julia was done explaining what all had transpired, Cody wanted to tell the woman were to go. He hated to see someone taking advantage of DeeDee's sweet nature.

"Oh, Dad, it's just appalling. I wish I could do something to put an end to it."

Cody stood and straightened his tie, tugged on his vest, and buttoned his suit jacket. "Let's handle this together."

Drawing himself to his full height, he followed Julia around the corner and waited outside the room where DeeDee was sitting with the woman's mother and friends. He listened to bits of conversation and recognized the voice. He whispered to his daughter, "Is everyone dressed?"

Julia nodded.

Cody stepped around the corner.

The young woman stopped mid-rant and looked at Cody.

***

DeeDee looked at Cody as ice water ran through her veins. Part of her was relieved and part of her was angry about his intrusion.

"I thought I recognized your voice, Candice. Who's the lucky man this time?" Cody grinned at DeeDee's client.

"Why would you care?" the woman snarled.

"Truthfully, I don't." He extended his hand to Candice's mother. "I'll tell mom I ran into you. I'm sure she'll be surprised. What is this? Candice's fifth wedding or is it her sixth?"

The woman wrinkled her nose. "Sixth. And what are you doing here?"

Cody smiled. "DeeDee is my fiancée. We just haven't made any official announcements."

"Oh, scraping low this time?" Candice interjected.

"Not at all." He raised his eyebrows. "I prefer to keep a low profile and when marrying someone as famous as DeeDee Drayden. There are details to work out."

DeeDee watched the interaction between Cody, and the mother and daughter.

"Famous?" the mother asked.

"Living in Salt Lake apparently has removed you from all the action. DeeDee's the top women's designer and internationally acclaimed. She, too, prefers to live a quiet life, but after being pressured into having that fashion show in New York, it seems everyone who thinks they are anyone wants one of her dresses for their wedding."

He smiled at DeeDee. "Why don't you let Julia takeover. You've got that big teleconference in a few minutes." He turned back to Candice. "Who's the lucky man? You've never said."

"I doubt that you'd know him."

Cody cocked his head. "Try me."

DeeDee looked at the screen that contained all the details.

"Walter Mittenhour."

Cody stared at the bride-to-be. "Hmm, I don't. I didn't realize that Walt Mittenhour had any sons, just the two daughters who are my mom's age."

He extended his hand to DeeDee and she took it. Then he looked at Julia, "Darling, I know you don't usually get involved with this trivial stuff, but will you take over for DeeDee. Candice is an old pro at getting married. I'm sure she'll be in and out in nothing flat."

"It was lovely meeting you," DeeDee said, as she left the room. Capable of handling a client without Cody's help, she seethed at his brashness.

The minute she was in her office, she turned to Cody and exploded. "How dare you!"

"Dare I what?" Cody chuckled as he removed his suit jacket. "If she's marrying old Walt Mittenhour, I promise he's got a pre-nup like you wouldn't believe, because he probably won't survive his wedding night. He's got to be well into his nineties."

"You're joking, right?"

Cody shook his head. "I only knew him through my grandfather, who used to drag me to Salt Lake every so often."

"Oh."

"You said that with a twinge in your voice."

"Nothing. Really, nothing."

He grinned. "When a woman says nothing, it means there's something. What do you want to know about Candice?"

"I don't care about her, but what makes you think you can barge in and take over?"

"Julia told me you had the witch from hell. I figured my presence might at least hurry things along, but I wasn't expecting to know your client. Then I couldn't resist toying with her."

"Well, I don't need your help running my salon and now you've thrown your daughter under the bus, so to speak, by putting her that room with my…with that very rude client."

"Oh, Candice will behave herself."

"What makes you so certain?"

"Let's just say I know her."

"You dated her?"

"No way. She was in the same dorms as my sister for about two years. She's all bluster and fluff, and digging for gold. She's also too stupid to realize she'll never get much of anything from old Walt. In fact, I'm certain that he's probably on a limited income because all control was turned over to his daughter probably fifteen years ago. He just wants a pretty face on his arm."

"O-oh. Let me guess. That's where you found Patty?"

He raised his eyebrows and grinned. "I'll never tell." He pushed the folder in front of her chair. "We've got some paperwork to clear up. Personally I think we should have a ground-breaking ceremony."

DeeDee looked at the tax papers first, saw Cody's check attached to it, and gasped. Then she looked at the estimated costs of the building and the various bids. Her heart fell with thud into her guts. "Did you see this?"

"Yes, I've spent the last three days going over the bids very carefully. They are very close. Go with Amory Builders. I know

Gary Amory will do a good job and he's actually come in a few dollars below the others. He's hungry and he's honest. Besides he can start sooner."

"And where am I getting this money?"

"Your corporation is putting up a fair chunk and the rest will come from the bank. Just sign the papers and I'll drop them off this afternoon. You're already approved. Everyone wants this building."

"You like running my company for me?"

"No, but you don't like getting bogged down in the nitty-gritty stuff. You are at your best when you are designing. Chrisy's your handler, and I'm your businessperson. You dream, and we'll make it happen."

"Sometimes, I really hate you."

He laughed. "No, you don't. You love me as much as I love you. You're just stubborn and afraid to give up control for fear of losing something. You think as long as you are in control that nothing will happen." He stood and put both hands on her desk. "And you're right. Nothing will happen because you're afraid to spend money. You are scared of taking risks. You've built a little comfort zone and you intend to stay there. So, you stay in your zone and we'll handle the rest."

She wanted to put her hands around his neck and strangle him, instead they balled in her lap.

He stood there looking down and grinning at her. "Now sign the papers so we can have lunch. The taxes are already electronically filed. This is just a hard copy with our signatures. I'll take you to the hotel and from there to the bank where you are welcome to ask any questions about the loan."

"What if I refuse to sign?"

"I'll still take you to lunch."

"When hell freezes over!"

"Really?"

***

Cody walked around her desk and yanked DeeDee from her seat. He wrapped her in his arms and kissed her. *Damn, you're easy.* She melted into his arms and he probably could have taken her on her desk, except they didn't have the time. But that didn't stop him from running his hand up her naked thigh. "Oh, I love when you wear skirts."

She ground her pelvis to his and his mouth dropped to the low-cut scoop of her neckline. He fingered a beaded nipple through the material that covered it. The way she tilted her head back told him it was going to be a very long afternoon because she wanted it as much as he did.

He broke from their embrace. "We don't have much time. Let's go."

He put his jacket on and buttoned it with the hopes of concealing his erection.

DeeDee reached in a drawer and pulled out a small but wildly printed purse. Her face was tinged with pink and her mouth looked swollen from their kiss. His ability to resist kissing her one more time waned and he grabbed her.

Their lips locked and his hand ran up her leg until he found nirvana.

She leaned into him giving him full access.

His voice was hoarse as he whispered in her ear. "I'm going to ruin my suit."

"My place is closer."

"Why don't I just lock the door here?"

"I won't chance it. My place or nothing."

He plunged a finger into her and she moaned. He nibbled on her ear. "Are you certain you'll make it?"

"No."

"I know I won't." He crossed the room and locked her door. He kicked off his boots and dropped his pants as she shimmied out of her skirt and removed her blouse.

Her hands grabbed his. "Leave the shirt and vest. It's way too sexy."

She grabbed for him and took him in her mouth. He pulled her to her feet and grabbed at one knee. "You got a condom?"

She shook her head.

"Then we're back to square one." He leaned her against the wall and plunged into her. He expected her protest, but none came. It didn't take much for him to find satisfaction and she followed almost instantly. He let her leg return to the floor as he caught his breath.

"Oh, Cody. Why are you doing this to me?"

"Because I love you."

"Damn." She looked into his eyes.

He could see tears welling. "What wrong with my loving you?"

"Everything. The last time we had unprotected sex, I lied."

He reared back. "What do you mean you lied?"

"I told you I got my period the next morning. It was a lie." She pulled her clothes on. "I even went as far as to buy that morning after pill, but I couldn't take it. I know it's just a hormone pill, but I couldn't stand the thought… What if I had conceived?"

"Omigod! You're pregnant?" He handed her the tissue box after he took several for himself.

"No. I just got over my period. But two things happened. One, I realized I'd lied to you and you deserved more from me than a lie. Two, I resigned myself to the idea of being pregnant… You know, coping with a baby by myself. That sort of thing."

"And you never considered marrying me?"

She shook her head. "No. But I wouldn't keep your child from you."

"Why are *you* afraid of marriage?"

"For the same reason you should be."

"I'm not afraid of marriage. I made my mistakes, and I've learned from them." He pulled on his pants and tucked his shirt into them.

"Why do you have to look so damn good to me?"

He chuckled. "Because you're hopelessly in love with me, and you need me."

"I don't need a man."

"Shall we make bets that if I poked around your room, I'd find a battery operated boyfriend?"

She giggled. "You'll lose. What I had died a few years ago and I never replaced it. I figured my sex drive left me before my twenty-seventh birthday."

"I'd say your sex drive is alive and well. You just needed me to awaken it."

"Oh, you awakened it and now I'm back to worrying about being pregnant. You can't keep doing this to me."

"Once you're pregnant, you won't have to worry about it. Marry me and it won't be a problem."

"Why? Why should I marry you?"

"We can discuss it over lunch." He steered her out of the office and to his car.

A few minutes later, they stopped by Cody's house. He ran inside for a moment and returned as if all were normal. Once they were sitting in the hotel's restaurant, Cody passed DeeDee the paperwork. She signed each one where he'd marked with a highlighter. "You completely trust me, because you didn't bother to read a single word."

She blew out a breath through pursed lips. "You're right, I trust you because I have almost no clue as to what I'm doing. I know how to design clothes."

"And I know the nuts and bolts of business. We make a good team. Chrisy is making you famous, and I'm making sure you are prepared. You keep designing."

"You make it sound so simple."

"It is." He picked up the menu, then looked over the top of it. "I should be eating oysters. I'm getting too old for these teenage hormone-driven escapades."

"I feel like eating the taco salad."

"I'll make that two." He closed the menu and put it beside him. "You're going to be writing off some losses for a while. Don't panic."

"But I owe all that money."

"Two different things. Your employee withholdings need to go into a savings account so when you pay them each quarter, it's there."

She put her hand to her forehead. "It's in the account."

"We're going to open some extra accounts and you will put me on them."

"But—"

He held his hand up. "Just say yes."

"To what?"

He reached in his pocket and withdrew a box. "I'm not getting down on one knee. I think that tradition went out before 1900, so here. Now, say you'll marry me."

Fourteen

DeeDee took the box and gasped. She'd seen some big stones over the years but this one was huge. "What is it?"

"A diamond. It matches your hazel eyes."

"I guess it does." She looked at the bluish-green not quite brown stone cut in an oval that had to have been an inch long. Her heart pounded in her chest. "I can't wear something like this with what I do."

He shrugged. "So wear it when you can." He grinned. "It's the Montgomery Diamond and it's cursed."

She dropped the box on the table. "What do you mean it's cursed?"

"You put that on your finger and you'll have to put up with me."

As the waitress came to take their order, DeeDee closed the box. As soon as the woman left, DeeDee opened the box and asked, "You're joking, right? It's not really cursed."

He got that crooked smile that she loved and followed it with his rich warm chuckle. "Oh, it's cursed. I said it comes with me. And this time, it's forever. I'll give you the freedom to rant, and call me every name in the book. I'll let you scream and holler, under one condition. You remember that no matter what happens, that you love me, I love you, and that you will never be unfaithful to me."

Her heart did a flip-flop in her chest. "Why couldn't you have picked out a little one-carat diamond? Do you even realize that you go overboard on everything?" She pointed her finger at him. "No, you can't do simple. You talk about how you're trying to teach your kids that there's more to life than money, and yet you do this?" She shook her head and snapped the box closed. "I don't need some humongous stone on my finger, besides I'll never be able to wear it. And where would I wear it?"

"Will you at least see if it fits?"

She opened the box and slipped the ring from the slot. It was slightly loose. "See. It's too big."

"It won't be when it's tucked into the wedding band. Try this." He fished in his pocket and pulled out what appeared to be a horseshoe. "Give me the ring for a second."

She took it off and handed it to him.

He snapped the horseshoe into the inside of the ring. "Now try it."

This time when she slipped it on, it fit perfectly. "Why, Cody?"

"Just say yes."

Her heart pounded. "And give up everything I've done?"

The waitress brought their taco salads to them and refilled DeeDee iced tea.

Cody shook his head. "You're not giving anything up. I'd never ask you to do that. As I said before, it's definitely cursed. It comes with seven kids and me. Maybe we'll make it eight."

"You are totally impossible!"

He shrugged and picked up his fork.

She picked up hers, but her hand was shaking. She couldn't answer him. Something inside of her kept her from saying yes. She took the ring off, put it in the box and pushed the box back to him.

***

Cody picked up his cell phone and looked at the message from DeeDee. It made him laugh.

Certain he had his mirth under control he called her back. "I'll meet you in twenty minutes for dinner."

It had taken her three hours to get this far and he was certain her answer would be yes. He packed up the things on his desk and went home. Melissa wasn't home yet, neither was Julia. That left Sean. It was time for Sean to step up to the plate and take on some responsibility to the family. "Sean, I need you in the kitchen."

As soon as the young man entered the kitchen, Cody took the computer from his hands.

"NO!" Sean protested and reached for it.

"Yes. The earth is not coming to an end if you're not playing. Something has come up, and I need you to handle dinner."

"That's Julia's job."

"As of tonight, it's yours. Make a salad. Dinner's in the crock-pot. Fix some fruit for dessert. Those bananas are ripe, use them up."

Sean stood there with his mouth agape. Cody didn't dare smile. If Julia could handle it, so could Sean.

Cody opened the refrigerator door. "There's plenty of milk, and there should be some packages of pudding mix in the cabinet. Wash your hands. Don't wait to fix the pudding. Scoop it from the big bowl into these smaller bowls and put them in the refrigerator to set. When it's set, put some banana slices on top of each serving."

"But Collin won't eat pudding."

"Collin may have a dish of banana slices. Save about half of a banana for him."

After looking at his watch, he knew he didn't have time to change. He got back in the car and headed to DeeDee's salon.

He found her in her office, and when she looked up at him, her eyes filled with tears. He wrapped her in his arms and kissed her. As always, she melted. He took his lips from hers and whispered in her ear, "Shall we eat dinner first?"

She nodded.

He took her to a small restaurant south of downtown where they found a quiet booth. The place was locally owned and known for its good food. He ordered the meal for both of them and then took DeeDee's hand in his. His own gut clenched and ice water ran through him as he awaited her response.

Her free hand shrouded her forehead and eyes. "I've tried to think and I keep coming back to the same place."

"That's fine. Spit it out. You obviously want to talk about it."

She nodded. "Marriage is forever, right?"

"I believed that and I still do think it's supposed to be."

"I know you understand my reluctance to say yes."

He nodded.

"I don't know how I can manage to be married and still do all the things that I want to do, but there's this little part of me that says I have to try." She looked up at him. "Why do we think that there's a pot of gold at the end of a rainbow when we know there is no such thing?"

"Because if we didn't, we'd never get out of bed. We have to believe in a certain amount of magic. You came here with a dream and look how far it's gotten you. Did you ever really give up on that dream?"

"No. But I have panicked a few times… Well, more than a few."

"But you've trusted your gut, right?"

She nodded.

The waitress brought their salads.

He looked at the mixed lettuce leaves. Shreds of carrot were sprinkled over the leaves. Around the edges, there were slivers of cucumber, and grape tomatoes had been added and the whole thing had been topped with sprouts. "Life's a little like this salad. Sometimes we have to eat the carrots."

"You don't like carrots?"

"Don't tell the kids, but I despise raw carrots."

She giggled. "I detest the sprouts. Want mine?"

He stuck his fork in the little mound, lifted it off her plate, and dropped them on his. "Maybe marriage is supposed to be sharing the good with the bad. I thought I was done with women, and then you walked into my life. Something in me said I had to try one more time."

"Yeah, I know. I've had that exact same feeling. But I'm scared. What if it doesn't work?"

He poured the dressing from the small container over his salad. "I don't think anyone has an answer to that question. Maybe we have to try to make it work, and keep trying. I only know that I love you." He picked up his icy cold glass of water and drank some. It cooled his hot throat but did nothing to relieve his anxiety that had twisted his innards. "I've looked darn hard at my first two marriages. Maybe I took certain things for granted and made my own mistakes, but I always honored my marriage vows."

"Richard was no prize."

"I give you credit for handling that situation without going into a rampage. It's one thing to bottle emotions for the court and another to do it over private life." He stabbed at his salad and then held his loaded fork over the plate. "I can't imagine what I would have done if I had caught one of my wives cheating on me."

"I think it was shock that kept me from killing him."

He nodded as he took another bite.

"I find it amazing that you've accepted each one of your children."

"You just nailed it. They are *my* children. They belong to me. No one has a choice in his or her DNA. We get what we get. They didn't get mine, but they got me as a father." He finished his salad.

DeeDee finished hers and nibbled on the soft, fresh baked roll that the waitress brought to their table.

"When you first concocted your dream of a bridal design business, did you tell anyone?"

"Just Karina."

"And what did she say?"

"That I was crazy for leaving one of the most famous design houses and the job that ninety percent of the designers would die for." She raised her eyebrows. "I was good and it was recognized. I was designing for the stars on Oscar night. And I stayed glued to the TV that night just to see who showed up in what and what other stars were wearing."

"But you still left and followed your dream. Why?"

"Because I believed it was the right thing for me to do."

The waitress brought their meals and Cody let DeeDee think about what she had said.

DeeDee seemed to have bonded in some way to all of his children. The way she managed to get along with Ian had actually come as a surprise. The teen seemed to connect with her. *Maybe a need for a mother figure?* It was a small, unexpected blessing. He hadn't asked her to mother them, take care of them, or do anything more than respect them as his children. Luckily they all seemed to like her.

DeeDee was in the middle of cutting a bite of her boneless chicken breast when she stopped and put her silverware down. "You're right. I'm just a big coward and there's no reason for me to be wary of marriage. You're the best thing that has ever happened to me."

"Oh, I'd say buying 400 Main Street was the best thing that happened to you."

She waved her hand through the air. "Okay, if I hadn't decided to buy it, I wouldn't have met you. You've made the wheels turn for me."

He nodded and scooped up a forkful of mashed potatoes.

"I know you have money, and so do I. Obviously not what you have, but it's my little nest egg. It's what my mom left me." She picked up her knife and fork and cut the bite of chicken and ate it. "I don't want you to ever think I'm after your money. In fact, if we're going to do this, maybe we should have a pre-nuptial agreement. I know this is going to sound mean, but I want to keep what is mine."

He swallowed hard. The masticated piece of veal medallion seemed to grow into a golf ball-sized lump as it slipped down his throat. He held up his hand until he dared to chuckle. "I don't want your money. How much of mine do you want?"

She furrowed her brow. "How do I say this without sounding like a witch?"

He raised his eyebrows. *Can't wait to hear this.*

"You've put a lot into the corporation. I don't want you or someone else demanding a lump sum in 'X' amount of time. I want that money protected."

He nodded. "I can do that. Anything else?"

"No." She went back to eating.

He watched her swallow and as she reached for her water, he took her hand. "You don't want six hundred million?"

She grimaced. "You're crazy."

"That's not even half of what I'm worth."

"You are full of it!"

"DeeDee, it's the truth. I'll show you when we get back to the house."

She crossed her arms over her chest and leaned back in the wooden booth. "So, why are you living here?"

"You already know the answer to that. And it's nice to know that you aren't marrying me for my money."

She shook her head and resumed eating her meal.

After dinner, he took her back to the house and showed her his holdings and some account figures. "Yes, there's a lot to protect, and I will protect my children."

DeeDee left his desk and sat in one of the comfortable chairs. "So, I've fallen in love with a billionaire?"

"And you still haven't said yes to my marriage proposal."

"What did Jenna get when she walked away?"

"Three million because she didn't take the girls. I was on a short purse back then. I heard she'd spent it all in less than three years. Are you certain you don't want to change your mind about how much you'd get if the marriage fell apart?"

She narrowed her eyes. "No. I have mine and you have yours."

"That's what I like about you." He pulled a file from a drawer. "Come back over here, say yes, and sign this."

She went to where he was sitting, and he stood for her to take his seat.

"I love you, DeeDee. I truly love you. Whatever is between us is very special."

Her lower lip trembled as she looked at him. She whispered, "Kiss me."

He wrapped her in his arms and they stayed in that slow unhurried sway of two lovers who faced a lifetime of togetherness.

She put one hand on his chest and moved away. "Yes. I will marry you."

"Then why don't you try wearing my ring?" He fished in the drawer where he had tossed the box when he returned home. "Here."

She slipped it on her finger. "Now what else must I do before I can sleep with you?"

He opened the folder on his desk. "Sign this."

"What is it?"

"Your pre-nup."

"Don't you have to add the amounts?"

"You didn't ask for anything that isn't already covered, except over here." He flipped a few pages. "You can't take the children I have or any that are the result of this marriage away from me. We can share custody."

"I'd never do that." She initialed the bottom of each page and signed the last page."

"You know we'll have to do this again in front of Carlie so she can notarize it."

"Doesn't matter."

"Don't you even want to know what you signed?"

She shrugged. "I do trust you."

"Good, because you're only three hundred million dollars richer." He chuckled. "Most of it isn't in cash. It's stocks and you'd have to sell it to the children. And they will never know about it until they are nineteen. Maybe you had better read it."

***

Two weeks later, Julia helped DeeDee into a wedding gown. The Renaissance design done in an antique white was perfect on DeeDee. And the tiny inset panels of mossy blue-green brought out the color in DeeDee's eyes. She spun around in front of the mirrors, checking the dress from every angle. She knew it would be beautiful on her, but to stand there with the dress on, gave her the most glorious feeling.

Cody's mom insisted on the wedding being held on the ranch, and Chrisy got involved the minute word filtered from Karina to him. She didn't care. It was insane, and the only thing she had to do was say I do. Then it would be over. Karina would be her maid of honor, and Cody's brother would stand for him. Just simple is what she told Chrisy, and he swore he'd keep it very small. She didn't believe him, not for two seconds.

As quickly as she had slipped into the gown, she slid out of it and went back to work. She had clients who also wanted the perfect gowns for their weddings.

***

A few days before the wedding, DeeDee and Karina turned into the driveway at the Montgomery ranch. DeeDee had worried about Karina driving, but she said she was fine. She swore if she could drive in Italy, she could drive anyplace. DeeDee decided she probably could have driven on the long straight roads that barely contained any traffic.

Karina pulled to a stop. "Are you sure we're in the right place? There's nothing ahead."

DeeDee shrugged. "He said to turn at the arched gates, and he said it's a long driveway."

The car zoomed off again. "You are crazier than crazy. We are in the middle of nowhere."

A few minutes later, they saw something ahead, then they really saw it.

Karina slowed. "Is that a house?"

"It looks like a tent."

It still took them a few more minutes to reach the house and when they did there was a huge set of tents in the front yard obscuring most of the house from view.

DeeDee thought she'd remained very relaxed through this trip and maybe she had, but she wasn't any longer. It was as though her skin crawled with a million bugs and a few hundred bigger ones were marching through her insides. She took a deep breath.

Chrisy emerged from a tent and greeted them. "Ah, my beautiful girls. You're going to love this family."

DeeDee looked Chrisy over. "Your boots!"

"Cody told me where he got his. And look at these heels! Cody's got to get a pair like this."

Karina immediately inspected them. "Oh, I love them! We need to talk to those people."

"I did. They totally ignored me."

"Well, they won't ignore me." Karina ran her fingernail around the metal toe. "How many pairs did you get?"

"Five. Come. You must meet the family."

"But I want to see in the tents. You set them up for my wedding, right?" DeeDee attempted to look past Chrisy.

Chrisy put his arm around her shoulder and steered her to the house. "For starters, tents are for camping. These are marquees."

DeeDee rolled her eyes, and Karina laughed.

Chrisy walked them into the big house. The foyer ran from the front of the house to the back of the house. And trying to take it all in was next to impossible. To say it would have fit in the Hamptons… It was beyond most anything in the Hamptons. But it was exactly the way a wealthy ranch house was expected to look.

When they reached the far end of the foyer, big windows looked across fields to jagged mountains in the far distance. Off to the left, was a cabana house along with several pools.

Chrisy propelled them into a professional kitchen that was manned by a male chef in a tall white hat and a female with a white chef's beret that hid all of her hair. In a far corner near a window, sat a woman sipping coffee while holding an e-reader.

"Mrs. Montgomery, come meet your future daughter-in-law and her friend Karina Karr." Chrisy called as he pushed them forward.

The woman sprung to her feet. "Oh my, which one of you is

DeeDee?"

"I am." She held her hand out to the woman who immediately wrapped her in a warm embrace.

"Welcome home." She turned to Karina. "And you, too, young lady. Anyone who is important to my son or his future wife is important to me. Did Chrisy show you to your rooms?"

"Not yet," DeeDee said. "We just arrived."

"Chrisy, where are your manners? Every woman needs to freshen up after her long trip here. Now go do whatever it is that your doing out there in the marquees, and I'll show them to their rooms."

Chrisy winked at DeeDee, and kissed Mrs. Montgomery's cheek. "Enjoy!"

"Karina, I have plenty of room in the house, but I have a lovely cabana house that I thought you and DeeDee might like to use. It will give you both a little more privacy."

Karina rolled her palms up. "Wherever. I'm very flexible."

DeeDee knew Karina would never complain. She'd been raised in what amounted to a shack with an outhouse and a pot-bellied stove for heat. Now she lived in a modern mansion on several acres overlooking the Gulf of Mexico when she was in the States, and an equally impressive villa in Milan.

"The cabana house sounds lovely," DeeDee answered.

DeeDee and Karina followed Mrs. Montgomery out a door and to the house near the pools. The place was perfect. It had a small kitchen, a living room, and two bedrooms. As soon as they had washed up, their luggage arrived, and they took a few minutes to unpack before joining Mrs. Montgomery in the kitchen.

"Coffee?" Cody's mom asked.

"Yes, please," DeeDee answered.

The woman went to a small nook within the larger kitchen and poured them both a generous cup. "It's decaf. That's what we drink." She waved her hand and furrowed her brow. "There might be the other kind around here. I'm not sure where."

DeeDee smiled. "Any coffee will be fine."

"Wonderful. My staff has been quite busy preparing for the wedding. We have the dinner the night before, the wedding brunch, and then the wedding dinner. My chefs have been making hors d'oeuvres all day. We've had seafood flown in from Brook... Brooker... Brooklyn... no, um, Brooking or someplace like that in Oregon or Washington...oh, or maybe it's some other Puget place."

Karina looked at DeeDee and it was all DeeDee could do to keep from laughing. Cody had said his mom didn't cook and couldn't be trusted to boil water. DeeDee suspected the woman's geography knowledge wasn't much better. She was a pretty blue-eyed blonde and she loved her family.

"Do I smell crawfish?" Karina asked a chef and wandered off to check what was in a pot.

Cody's mom asked if everything in the cabana was to their liking.

"It's lovely. The accommodations are perfect." DeeDee smiled and then carefully broached the subject of Chrisy. "Has Chrisy driven you crazy?"

"Oh, not at all! He's been wonderful. I thought I was going to have to hire someone, but he called and took over. He wants you to have the perfect wedding. The marquee company came in and set everything up, and he's been filling those big tents with all sorts of things. I do wish I'd had him when Cody's sister, Barbara, married. She had such a simple wedding in the Temple and a reception in a nearby hotel.

DeeDee nodded.

"Chrisy wanted everything perfect for you. You'd think you were his daughter." She giggled. "He calls you 'baby'."

DeeDee nodded

"You wouldn't believe what all he's done. He's even talked to the chefs about things like presentation."

Again DeeDee nodded. She realized she began to feel like one of the figurines whose head was attached to a spring. "He's very protective of Karina and me."

"And your gown is upstairs. One of the maids took care of it."

She caught herself nodding again. "I was worried about it."

"Not a wrinkle in it. Elise was shocked when it came. It was in a huge box with air pillows, but she hung it and it was perfect. She thought she'd be ironing it for a day."

I'm not going to nod! "I pack them so they don't wrinkle. Who's Elise?"

"Oh, my maid. She does all the laundry. I don't know what I'd do without her. She's wonderful."

Another nod. DeeDee looked in Karina's direction. The woman was snooping in the kitchen and sampling things. DeeDee was jealous. Her tummy rumbled. She hadn't eaten except for a granola bar at breakfast and now she was starved. Watching Karina eat was only making matters worse. DeeDee looked at her watch. *Four of four? I'll die before I make it to supper.* "How many invitations did you send out?"

"Well, Cody said to keep it small. Including the wedding party, it comes to sixty-three people, not counting the children under ten."

DeeDee nodded. *I only have to say 'I do.'*

"Omigod, DeeDee try this!" Karina called.

DeeDee went to her friend's side and picked up the tiny corn-fried shell and tasted it. "Oh, that is delish!" DeeDee then tried another little rolled up thing. "Oh, this is good, too!"

Karina elbowed her. "Now try this."

DeeDee wanted to eat one of everything and she figured Karina was just as hungry. "We'd better not spoil our appetite for dinner."

"Oh, who cares!" Karina picked up a pastry and devoured it.

DeeDee was actually pleased to see Chrisy enter the kitchen and call them away, or she would have sampled everything in sight.

Chrisy took them to the marquees. The first long tent went between the house and the driveway. Then they walked into a small one where the wedding would take place.

"This is beautiful!" DeeDee walked around the tent.

"The rest of the flowers are coming Friday. I wanted to start simple and then build."

"You've matched my dress."

"Why wouldn't I?" He held his palms up.

"Did you build a waterfall or was it here?"

"Baby, I can practically pick that up in my hands. It's not real stone."

"It's not?" DeeDee poked at the fake stone. "What about the fish?"

"Mrs. Montgomery is having a pond installed in the backyard after the wedding. She's fallen in love with the koi. I ordered everything for her."

DeeDee wandered into the next tented area. It was set up as a place for people to mingle and, with all the tables, she was certain it would contain lots of food. Then she stepped into the dining area. Chandeliers hung from the ceiling. She looked at the boxed items stacked in a corner. "What are these?"

"Table decorations. I can't set anything up until the tablecloths are in place. It's a seated dinner."

"Oh." DeeDee couldn't quite imagine how it was going to look. "And the flowers are coming on Friday?"

"Stop worrying. It will be divine, completely over-the-top and perfect."

"It's that over-the-top I worry about."

Chrisy laughed. "I went to school for marketing and hated it. Tried my hand at interior decorating and found it boring. When I got into personal public relations, I knew I'd found my calling. Now stop worrying. This is a cakewalk and fun for me."

She stepped into the next tent and gasped. Gilded camel seats and pillow-covered seating occupied the space around a generous mossy blue-green dance floor.

"The sultan's den." Chrisy laughed.

DeeDee was calculating the number of yards of fabric Chrisy had used between the four marquees. In less than two months, he had created a wedding oasis that was unlike anything she'd ever seen. Rich cream and white brocades were paired with gold ones and mixed with all of it was the mossy blue-green color that was inset into her gown. Big palm plants sat in planters that contained plenty of room. "Just how many flowers have you ordered? It looks like you've brought in a tractor trailer load of plants."

"Make that two loads of plants, and you don't want to know about the flowers. Your job is to relax. We don't want bags under your eyes for this wedding."

.

Fifteen

Friday the house filled with family and more people kept coming. Dinner that night was served in a large dining room. It was a simple meal of salad, roasted beef, mashed potatoes, peas and asparagus, then followed by a nine-layer chocolate creation that was extraordinary. Cody didn't get there with the children until almost suppertime, which gave DeeDee little chance to talk to him.

He told her he'd intended to spend the night with her but his mom nixed that idea and sent him to his old room upstairs.

DeeDee kept telling herself that she only had to say I do and the rest was just trappings set up by Chrisy. It was all an illusion. After all, it was Cody's third wedding, but she had also learned that his previous weddings had been nothing more than a quick trip to a magistrate, so his mom was quite excited about this one.

Cody's sister, Barbara, looked a lot like her mom, but she shared the strong jaw line of her younger brother. Yet neither Cody nor his sister looked much like their father, other than a general family resemblance. Cody's oldest brother, who ran the ranch, looked more like his dad. But Cody had said he alone was the spitting image of his grandfather. DeeDee hoped to see a picture of that man before she left.

Chrisy had been absent from the house all day and she knew

he was busy in the tents setting everything up. Elise, the maid, had gone out to offer him help, and he must have accepted for she, too, had vanished.

After the meal, the family went to the tents. Chrisy went over every detail of the actual wedding from where everyone was to stand to how to seat the guests as they arrived. Collin and Logan took their jobs as hosts very seriously, and DeeDee had to bite at her cheeks to keep from laughing. Melissa and Chelsea would stay with Julia and DeeDee until the wedding was to start. Then Sean and Ian were to escort their two sisters to the front row before taking their own places. Then Cody's brother would escort Julia to her seat. He'd return for Karina, and the twins would present the bride. All very simple yet it involved all the children. Chrisy had done an excellent job.

The place was overflowing in palm plants and flowers as if it were a tropical paradise. When the wedding ended, Cody and DeeDee would receive guests as they made their way to the next tent. Two big fountains were set up and ready to be filled with juice. But unlike most drink fountains, the fountain sat very high and had nice pour spouts people could use. There would be plenty of hors d'oeuvres and a lot of room to mingle.

The dining room was set up with several round tables. Each throne-like seat had been carefully assigned and clearly marked. The center of each table contained a large Venetian glass vase and in the center of each, a candelabra rose almost four feet above the table. The candles were electronic but looked almost real. Flowers flowed from the vases and trailed onto the table. Matching candelabras hung from the ceiling. Not only did they look pretty with their flickering candles, they also hid additional lights, which provided plenty of light within the tent.

The cake table sat in the left-hand corner of the room. The cake would not be brought out until right before the wedding. It was tiered and way too large for such a small wedding, but DeeDee knew the one chef was so thrilled to show off her skills that she had gone all out to create the perfect cake. It had even been dusted in gold.

As guests left the dining room they were to be encouraged to take a jeweled mask for dancing, thus adding an unexpected touch to the wedding. Chrisy had nicknamed it the sultan's den but lit at night it was beyond beautiful. It all looked like something from a Renaissance castle wedding. Tiny lights flickered overhead like millions of stars. Pierced metal candelabras hung from the ceiling, a few hung low over tables, and others provided additional lighting to seating areas. It was meant to provide an atmosphere of relaxation.

Two musical groups had been hired. One played classical music and the other played a little of everything. DeeDee knew this family considered fancy cowboy boots as being suitable dress wear, so she was certain that a little of everything meant plenty of country-western music.

When they were done, DeeDee, Cody, Chrisy, Karina, and Julia gathered around the pool closest to the cabana house and relaxed. Chrisy was the first to say goodnight, and Julia followed him. Shortly thereafter, Karina vanished to the cabana house leaving DeeDee and Cody alone.

DeeDee watched Cody as he watched Karina leave. She was a beauty with flaming red hair that came from a bottle. Over the years, the woman had left a trail of men swooning in her wake.

Cody turned back to DeeDee. "I can't believe she's not married."

DeeDee giggled. "She is."

"I've never heard you mention a husband, and why isn't he here?"

"She has a wife and her wife prefers to stay in Milan. She's scared to death of getting on an airplane."

"Karina?"

DeeDee nodded.

"But she's your best friend."

"The one has nothing to do with the other. I've always known, and it's never made a difference. And since we're discussing Karina, she's pregnant. She just found out, and she's so excited she can't see straight."

"What?"

"Erika, that's Karina's wife, has a brother who offered his sperm to the cause."

"Oh, that must have been interesting."

"They worked out all the legalities ahead of time."

Cody sat as if trying to wrap his mind around the entire situation. Then smiled and reached for DeeDee's hand. "I'm glad you're mine and not Karina's."

"So am I."

"Are you ready for tomorrow?"

"I only have to say I do."

Cody laughed and kicked off his boots. "Ever feel like doing something totally outrageous while you're still single?"

"Like what?"

Cody pulled off his shirt and undid his pants. "Skinny dipping."

"You're joking."

"There's not a person awake in this house. My parents' idea of bedtime is long past." He pulled DeeDee to her feet and began to remove her dress.

"But--" It was too late. Cody lips crashed over hers and the rest of her clothes fell away.

Cody swept her off her feet and jumped in the pool with her.

She grabbed at his shoulders and almost screamed in fear. "I can't swim!"

Another second later, her feet touched the bottom of the pool.

"Why didn't you say something?"

"I was going to tell you, but you kissed me."

"Then we'll stay at this end where it's not so deep."

His lips took hers and she no longer cared that she couldn't swim.

***

Morning dawned and Karina met DeeDee with a cup of coffee. "I had a heck of a time trying to find real coffee, everything is decaffeinated."

DeeDee rubbed her eyes and took the cup. "Cody's family is Mormon. They don't do caffeine. It's considered a drug or something. Is this real coffee?"

"Is Cody Mormon? And yes, it's real coffee. Ed in the kitchen gave it to me."

"Is there such a thing as non-practicing Mormon?"

"That means it's not a champagne brunch, right?"

"Exactly. It's a female-only thing being held on that big enclosed porch."

Karina tucked her feet under her as she sat on the corner of DeeDee's bed. "Are you ready for this?"

"As ready as I'll get. There's part of me that still can't believe I'm getting married."

"Is it what you want to do?"

"At first, I couldn't see myself married to Cody. I'm not mother material, yet part of me wants that big family and to have that normal life. I was the only child and I didn't want to raise an only child. If I'm lucky, maybe I'll get pregnant. Twice we've failed to use protection and I didn't conceive."

"It's all got to do with timing and body rhythms. We didn't want to be going through this a dozen times with Erika's brother so I've been watching my body rhythm for the last eight months."

"So one shot?"

"No. Three times. It was awkward, but he was so sweet about it. Men are good for some things." Karina laughed.

"Men are wonderful."

"Two different playbooks. I'll stick with Erika."

"And I'm happy with Cody."

"Good." She scooted off the bed. "I've got everything packed up except what I'll be wearing home. I've got a long drive and an early morning flight to New York, then off to Milan."

"Thank you so much for coming. I couldn't ask for a better friend."

"Don't do that to me, you'll have me crying. Go take your

shower."

Two hours later, wearing a plain, creamy-white dress, DeeDee and Karina joined Cody's mom, sister, and sister-in-law, along with a few nieces, and Cody's girls for a brunch on the porch. DeeDee had plain pearl bracelets for everyone including the youngest niece who was just a few days shy of her tenth birthday. The fruity mimosas were sans alcohol, but delicious. There were cream puffs topped with a chocolate and blueberry mixture, and more than a dozen other delightful things. DeeDee swore if she ate another bite she'd never fit in her gown.

Cody's nieces and daughters assembled in the cabana house where they were dressed for the wedding. Then Julia stayed with Karina and helped DeeDee get dressed. The beaded brocade bodice fit like a glove and the long sleeves cascaded in two tiers. Her bodice came to a point in the front and then went up over her hips, accentuating her curves. The bodice was low enough over her chest to show a little cleavage without being revealing. But it was the inset panels that gave the dress its unique look. DeeDee slipped her feet into the heels that Karina had created just for her. And when she thought she was done and her train attached at her shoulders, Karina placed the pearl crown on her head and let the silk veil drape over DeeDee's face and down her back.

Chrisy had hired a photographer to capture all the special moments including brunch and dressing. But no matter how many times DeeDee tried to tell herself she only had to say I do, she knew it was much more. She was committing herself to Cody and that was something that no other woman had ever done to him.

She wore his ring but had removed the little semicircle inside of it so that it would fit into her wedding band. The engagement ring had to be removed before he could place her wedding ring on her finger. It was to be a simple ceremony, nothing more than a formality. She knew he also had a simple gold band for her and would place that one, too. They had bought plain bands together so that they matched. Whatever went with the big stone would be too much to wear on a daily basis. The smooth gold one would be better. Butterflies took flight in her stomach.

She stood silently waiting and opened the little black velvet box that held his ring. *With this ring...*

***

Karina looked stunning in her long jacketed-dress. The mossy green-blue and purple suited her coloring. The style was completely different, but the colors pulled everything together. Once the jacket was removed, Karina had a simple gown under it that she could wear a dozen times.

Tucked in Cody's room was a short dress that DeeDee could put on for dancing the night away, and Cody had made it clear he intended to help her out of her wedding dress. She could feel herself blushing as she made her way through the house to the front door of the large foyer.

Julia groaned. "Be still. I want to fix your train so it ripples perfectly off your shoulders."

Chrisy appeared. "Five minutes. Almost everyone is in place."

"How are the twins doing?" DeeDee asked.

"Adorable!" Mimicking the twins, Chrisy moved his arm in a flourish to his side. "Your seats, please."

DeeDee giggled. "Oh, my."

"No one is complaining. Everything has gone according to plan."

Chrisy turned Cody's girls loose to make the trek to the wedding marquee. "They all look lovely. That was very kind of you to dress the nieces."

"They needed to feel special, too."

"Still it was a thoughtful gesture."

"You look very nice." DeeDee admired the black suit that Chrisy wore with a black leather bolo tie and plain gold slide.

"Thanks. I feel like an undertaker out of some western movie."

Karina dissolved into giggles. "We could have braided your hair like they do to horses' tails."

Chrisy shot her an evil glare. "Don't even consider it. I'm wearing a buckle that won't allow me to bend at the waist without giving myself a Heimlich."

DeeDee frowned. "Cody wears buckles that are bigger than that."

"He's taller than I am."

DeeDee rolled her eyes. "You do look very handsome. The style suits you."

Chrisy frowned. "It's totally lacking color."

"Is the tent filled with people?" DeeDee tried to see beyond the foyer.

"It's not a tent. It's a marquee!" He handed both women their bouquets and opened the door. "Go!"

Karina and DeeDee stepped under the tented walkway and made their way to the wedding marquee.

Karina walked to the front first with Cody's brother, then the twins escorted DeeDee to Cody. Cody and DeeDee took those final steps together.

***

Cody knew DeeDee had a small surprise planned after their rings had been placed but he didn't know what.

DeeDee turned to Cody's children lined up on the front row. "Julia, Sean, Melissa, Ian, Chelsea, Collin and Logan, will you please stand here with me?" She gave them each a moment and turned long enough to have Karina hand her a small box. "Today, I promised your father that I will love and honor him until our deaths. We've given each other rings as an outward sign of our commitment. But I didn't just marry your father - I married a family. I want you all to know that I'm committed to all of you as well." DeeDee pulled a ring from the box and placed it on Julia's pinkie finger. "Julia, will you please accept this ring as my commitment to honor you as I do your father."

"I do." Julia brushed tears from her eyes.

"Sean, will you…"

DeeDee placed a ring on each child's hand and when she got to the twins, they tackled her with hugs before she could place their rings. She looked up at the crowd. "I think that means yes."

There wasn't a dry eye in the crowd and Cody fought to keep tears from forming. DeeDee was special and he knew it. She never asked for the children to call her mom or to even attempt to step into those shoes. She only asked for acceptance as their father's wife.

A moment later, they walked down the aisle, and the children followed. After receiving guests, they stood for formal pictures, then several informal ones. As the children dispersed, Cody caught his wife looking upward and heard her say, "Are you watching, Mom?"

"I hope so." He put his arm around her. "Because you are the most beautiful bride and I've never been happier in my life."

She batted at tears.

"Don't cry. I don't want you to ruin your makeup."

"And Karina put a ton of it on me."

"You look as beautiful as you always do to me. But I love you naked and after last night, I hope you never learn to swim."

"Oh, you like drowning me?"

"No, I love rescuing the damsel in distress." He kissed her gently on the lips.

"Remember, we must remain on our best behavior."

"Oh, I'm always on my best behavior when I'm holding you."

They joined everyone and ate a few hors d'oeuvres as they chatted with family and friends. Then they had dinner and there were toasts to be made. There was plenty of sparkling grape juice but there were also bottles of champagne for those who wanted it. Karina winked and stuck to the juice.

When Karina proposed a toast, Cody hugged her and whispered in her ear, "DeeDee told me. Congratulations to the mother-to-be. We'll come visit you and Erika in Milan."

Karina hugged him back. "I'd love that. Take really good care of my best friend."

"I will. I promise."

DeeDee tossed her bouquet and Julia caught it.

"Oh, no! Not me."

DeeDee laughed. "There's nothing that says when, just that you're next in this crowd."

Cody chuckled. "You're forbidden to marry until you're thirty. That gives you twelve years."

DeeDee giggled and whispered to Julia, "Daddy doesn't want to admit his little girl has a vagina."

Then it was time to remove DeeDee's garter. In a stage whisper, Cody asked as his hand ran up her leg, "Are you wearing underpants?"

Karina leaned over. "Hell, no. Women don't wear underpants when they get married. It's all part of being prepared for later."

DeeDee blushed as his hand drifted higher.

"Oh, I'm all for being prepared." He snagged the garter and pulled it off. Then shot it into the air behind him. A cousin caught it, which sent some cheers through the family.

Then they cut the cake. It was all rather traditional, just done in a very posh setting with fantastic food. Being it was mostly family with only a few close business friends, the attendees were relaxed and having fun.

Everyone put on the fancy masks for the first few dances and DeeDee pretended she didn't know Sean or Ian as they asked her to dance. Ian was more surefooted than his brother and DeeDee seemed to have a grand time.

Cody took a turn with Karina and she laughed as she danced with him. She was an exceptionally good dancer, and he had fun spinning her around the dance floor. After all the prerequisite dances had been completed, Karina whispered in DeeDee's ear. She hugged her friend and Karina disappeared. She had a long night and day ahead of her.

Concerned about her welfare and driving with very little sleep, Cody had one of the ranch hands drive her rental car and another hand followed in a pickup truck. It was the most he could do for her, under the circumstances, and she seemed to appreciate it.

Then he and DeeDee sneaked out of the marquee and into the bedroom of his youth. He intended to change into black pants, boots, and a plain white shirt. But the thought of helping his wife out of her wedding gown heated him.

He loved unlacing DeeDee's dress. The slow revealing of skin set his pulse racing, and knowing there was nothing under it made it even more exciting. Bit by bit the dress loosened and he turned her around before dropping it from her shoulders. It was as if he were seeing her for the very first time. Except this time, she was his wife.

She smiled as the dress fell to her ankles and she stepped out of it. Oh, she was ready for him and he was just as ready for her. What started as slow and sensual, soon built.

He sucked in a breath. "Omigod, I want you."

"Take me."

He did. He rode her hard until she cried out and he joined her. He held his weight on his elbows and knees, as his chest heaved above hers. "Being with you is paradise."

She looked up at him with her beautiful eyes and smiled.

His lips found hers and they stayed that way until he fell from within her. "I hate that feeling."

"I hate to feel you leave."

"They say dogs get tied and don't come apart."

She giggled. "Dogs do. They get a bulbous area that holds them in place. It's a shame men don't have the same problem."

"Oh, I agree. I'd love to stay there forever." His lips traveled down her body. He listened to her squeal in delight. "I'm going to love being married to you."

Only partially satisfied, they cleaned up and dressed for what remained of the evening. Her evening dress was meant to entice and it did. Fire burned within him as he helped her into it. Sheer stretchy fabric covered most of her back and the front was an hourglass of beaded brocade that ended when it joined several layers of sheer white fabric.

She wasn't skinny, nor was she fat. She had curves and he loved every square inch of skin. She was a woman, a healthy, beautiful woman who knew who she was and where she was going. She wasn't afraid to enjoy food. But most of all she was his.

"Ready to join the guests?"

"I don't know. I love to watch a man pulling his pants over his shirttails. It's very sexy."

He zipped his pants, and buckled his belt. He raised his eyebrows. "Any man?"

She grinned. "I don't think so." She crossed the room to where he was standing. "Just one particular man. I want to watch that every day for the rest of my life."

"Then you'd better not sleep in or you'll miss it."

She leaned against him. "I do hope we'll have more pool

lessons tonight. Just because I'm married…" She rubbed her breasts against him. "I hope that won't make a difference."

"Oh, it will make a huge difference, because this time you're mine and I can have my way with you."

"I think I'm going to like that. And what other things will you do to me now that we're married?"

He cupped a breast. "I'm sure we'll have fun discovering all the possibilities."

"I'm so glad I decided to buy 400 Main Street."

"So am I."

***

After spending a week on the ranch, Cody flew DeeDee to Hawaii for two weeks. He had never enjoyed a vacation as much as he had enjoyed this one, and he knew it was DeeDee who had made it different. She brought out the best in him. She loved him. Not his money or what he could do for her… She loved him, the man.

They both worried about being away for so long, but DeeDee kept checking with Julia who assured her that everything as running perfectly. And he knew that Barbara was watching over his brood and spoiling them rotten. Not having children of her own, Barbara loved every minute she spent with his children, plus it gave her a chance to oversee the construction of DeeDee's new building. Phone calls, photos, and Internet kept them in touch, but it was the time alone that he and DeeDee treasured.

Lazy days on the sand or exploring the volcanoes kept them busy. Moonlight dinners and fabulous sensual evenings cocooned them. Money came with privileges, but it also came with responsibilities. His grandfather had taught him well, and he never really knew what it meant to enjoy life until he had DeeDee at his side. She made life worth living.

Book Two

I Thee Wed

One

Julia Montgomery sighed as the buzzer rang for the third time, alerting her of someone at the service door. *Am I the only one around here who can do anything?* She walked to the back of Main Street Bridal Salon, checked the camera, and opened the door to a delivery man and a blast of super hot air. "Sorry to keep you waiting."

"Oh, I don't mind. You're my last delivery for the day. Where do you want it?" The man grinned at her as if she were a hearty meal and he was starving.

"Over there." She pointed to an empty corner in the back room where they received and shipped packages, then took the small computer from him and signed her name on its screen. "It says fourteen boxes and you've brought in six."

"The rest are still on the truck. I promise you have fourteen boxes."

Julia watched as the twenty-something man with bright red hair and a face full of freckles returned to his big burgundy and tan truck and brought in another four boxes, then two more large boxes. Wearing burgundy shorts and a tan, short-sleeved shirt, he revealed a muscular body that had been dusted in more freckles.

"These aren't heavy, just big." Dangling from his waistband was his company ID Badge. But the name Aaron was clearly visible on his shirt.

"That's only twelve."

"There are two more coming."

She waited while he wheeled in the last two large boxes on his hand truck.

"Would you like to recount?"

She held her finger up as she checked each packing slip. Once certain she had everything, she smiled. "All here." She looked at Aaron's freckled face and saw sweat trickling from his forehead, down his neck, soaking his shirt collar and leaving a big sweat-stained vee on the front of the shirt. "Follow me. You look like you really need a drink of water."

"Thanks, I could use it. I started this morning with a six pack of bottled water in my cooler but by two this afternoon, I'd finished my last one."

She led him from the shipping room down the quiet hallway to the employee break room. "It's extremely hot out there."

"We've had record highs this week. I don't mind the heat as much as the humidity, and this humidity is getting to me."

"The thunderstorms every evening are driving me crazy. Seems I lock up and before I get out of here, the rumble starts." Julia walked into the break room and opened the refrigerator.

"No fun driving in it, either. The joy of being the owner's son is subbing for every driver in the area. This is my summer job, also known as a way to lose a few pounds and keep in shape." He ran the back of his hand over his forehead.

"You don't do it year round?" She handed Aaron a bottle of cold water. "This is for the road. Would you like a disposable cup with ice and some water from that?" She pointed to a water cooler.

"Thanks, heaps. I'd love some iced water."

She fixed him a generous cup. "So, what do you do when you aren't driving a delivery truck?"

He chuckled. "Oh, I'm at the university out in Utah, learning animal husbandry. I want to be certain I know how to be a good animal husband when the time comes."

She stared at him. Few people had ever left her speechless, but this crazy redhead was staring at her over his bright blue plastic cup. From the look in his golden-green eyes, she could have sworn he was laughing and not drinking his water.

He lowered his cup. "I was teasing. I'm studying veterinarian science, specializing in large animals."

"Oh." Her heart skipped a beat. He was cute, really cute, with a bright smile.

"When I'm done, I'll have my PhD in veterinary genetics."

"Wow! Never knew anyone really smart like that."

"It's not a matter of being smart; it's doing what you love."

"I love working here. Hated school and couldn't wait until I graduated from high school. My dad wanted me to go to college and I refused. He said I needed to have a real career and to do something with myself."

"He's right."

"Humph! I love what I'm doing. I started part time when DeeDee opened Main Street Bridal Salon. Now, I'm her manager. They don't teach this in school."

"Actually, they do. It's called business administration."

"DeeDee's talked about my taking a few classes at the local college."

"You should do it. Take a few classes that you'd enjoy until you get back into the swing of going to school. It's nothing like high school." He drained his cup. "Mind if I keep my cup of ice?"

"No, not at all. Let me add some fresh ice to it. Would you care for more water?"

"No, thanks. This is great. Between the melting ice and the bottle of water, I'll be fine. I really appreciate the hospitality."

"You're welcome. We're a service oriented business and that extends to delivery drivers on scorching hot days." She smiled at him, then walked him to the back door.

"Thanks, again. Maybe I'll see you tomorrow..." he looked at his computer, "Julia." He returned his gaze to her. "I need to get out of here."

She held her hand up and wiggled her fingers as he jumped in his truck and waved. There was something about him. Those golden-green eyes made her smile. A year ago, she would have had goose bumps over any guy who flirted with her. Now she could appreciate a fine physique without drooling, and he had a very fine one. She put her fingers to her lips. She hadn't felt this way in a long time. He warmed every part of her. *Oh yeah, he's worth drooling over.*

Her pager vibrated and she looked at the flashing lights. She was wanted in the salon. The day she had started working for bridal fashion designer, DeeDee Drayden, was the day she'd given up boys and concentrated on her newfound career.

DeeDee Drayden's sense of style had rubbed off. By copying her boss, who had become her step mom, Julia found a simple wardrobe of dress slacks or pencil skirts in black and a few fancy tops kept her looking her best at all times. She smoothed her skirt and pasted a smile on her face as she entered the salon. But something inside of her still tingled from the sight of Aaron.

"Julia! Oh, you must help me." Meredith crossed her hands over her heart. "I'm getting married September eighteenth and I need something wonderful."

Julia looked at her former classmate with the tiniest bulge to what should have been a very flat tummy. "And who's the lucky guy?"

"Who else but Tommy?"

"Oh, I'm so far out of the loop anymore. You know I just hide away and spend all my hours here. You and Tommy have been together *forever.*"

Julia escorted her old friend to a small Victorian sitting area and offered her a cup of tea. "Let's start by you telling me what kind of a wedding you're planning and from there we'll find the perfect dress."

Trying to keep Meredith on track was as difficult as trying to keep Julia's seven-year-old twin stepbrothers on task. But with patience and months of practice behind her, she managed to get Meredith to admit that she had no real plans. She and Tommy had decided to get married quickly, but she still wanted it to be perfect.

Julia reached over and touched her friends arm. "I understand. But before we choose a dress, if you're pregnant, you'll want to make allowances."

"Oh, no! I'm on a very strict diet. Nothing will change."

"Mer-e-dith, we've been friends for years. I'm not going to tell anyone if you are."

"Oh, no, really, not at all."

Julia knew her former classmate too well and there was no doubt that Meredith was pregnant. "Okay, small, and formal. Let's look at a couple of things that I think will be lovely on you." She steered her friend into a classic Greek style gown. Knowing it would be more forgiving of any waist or bust changes yet still look elegant. "When we're done, I'll show you our fabulous wedding facilities on the third floor."

Julia measured her friend, and when they were finished going through everything, which included the flowers and invitations, she ushered her friend out the door, and began to lock up. It was almost six thirty. *Another late day.*

DeeDee came into the salon from the back. "Julia, what are you doing still working?"

"Had a former classmate stop by. I sold her an entire wedding package."

"Fantastic!"

"The maid of honor and the junior bridesmaid should be stopping tomorrow for their fittings. I've got everything in the computer."

DeeDee walked to a computer. "Is it Meredith Lemanson?"

"Yes. She signed the contract and paid the down payment."

"Sometimes I don't know what I'd do without you."

Julia laughed. "Hire two more people."

"It might take more than two and don't you dare go home tonight and work. Take some time off."

"And do what? Watch TV?"

DeeDee shrugged. "It's a start. If you hole up here and never stick your nose out, you really won't have any idea what people want. You've got to keep it fresh."

Julia sat in a nearby chair and put her elbows on her knees and her chin on her hands. "Two years ago, I couldn't imagine working in a job like this or not having a date every night. What happened to me?"

"You've grown up. You've accepted responsibility and given it your all."

"It's got to be more than that." She frowned as the images of some classmates ran through her mind. "Remember when I took Chelsea shopping last Saturday?"

"That was sweet of you to take your little sister shopping."

Julia shrugged. "Well, I ran into several old friends. I watched what they were doing and the way they acted. Chelsea conducts herself better than they did."

"Are you saying you're feeling older?"

"Yes."

"You've matured. I saw that flicker of maturity when I hired you. I knew you had to start someplace and working for me was as good as any. But I wasn't expecting you to take off like a rocket. You just jumped in and did things. Your computer skills have been a super asset."

"Thanks. You know I love it here."

"I really don't know what I'd do without you."

Lightning lit the interior of the salon and the electrical lights flickered.

"Not again!" Julia groaned.

DeeDee laughed until the electricity went out, plunging them into darkness for a split second until the emergency lighting turned on. "We're out of here."

***

Julia opened the salon, since DeeDee would be spending the morning at the factory in the new industrial park where each dress was made. Julia took care of all the morning chores, and a few minutes before nine o'clock, several employees arrived. DeeDee expected certain things from those who worked for her and no one disappointed, for they all knew what they were to do and how to do it. Julia smiled and said good morning as various people passed her office. People liked working for Main Street Bridal Salon, and Julia did everything she could to help to foster that ambiance.

"Mrs. Prentiss, good morning. Would you like to help me today?" Julia asked one of the saleswomen as she passed Julia's office door. "We got our shipment in last night, and I need to make up the sizing kits for mailing. If we don't get too busy in the salon, I thought I'd start on them around ten o'clock today."

"Certainly." The silver-haired woman had spent most of her life in women's wear. She was also the most adept at handling customers. DeeDee had designated Mrs. Prentiss as the front manager.

"Thanks." Julia went back to working on the online orders and questions that had come in overnight.

She was buried in what she was doing when her buzzer lit, showing she was being called to the salon. Mrs. Prentiss met her holding a pretty bouquet of flowers.

"For you, Julia."

"For me?" *What did I do this time, Dad?* She smiled as she took the arrangement. "Thanks."

Once back in her office, she placed the large bouquet on the corner of her desk and a warm sensation filled her. She pulled the tiny card from the small white envelope that had been attached to the bouquet on a clear forked stake, fully expecting that her dad had sent her flowers. It was so like him - his way of saying thank you for something she had done.

Taken aback, she stared at the card in her hand. *May I take you to dinner this Sunday? Text me. 555-638-2991 Aaron.* She sucked in her lower lip and pressed it between her teeth. She'd never been asked out by anyone who sent flowers as part of the invitation.

It wasn't exactly a small mixed bouquet. Aaron had probably spent a fortune on it, considering the cost of the flowers in it. She sniffed at the beautiful lilies, allowing their sweet scent to fill her.

Aaron wasn't somebody she knew from school. He was older but not old, and obviously very smart. She'd never dated anyone like him. When she thought about it, she'd really never *had* a real date. This was different from one of the guys asking if she wanted to go to the movies or a school function. This was the real thing. She inhaled and knew she had time to respond.

By noon, she and Mrs. Prentiss had put together over five hundred wedding kits. In less than two weeks, as the orders streamed in, they would have to be done again. Julia took off the apron that protected her clothes and pulled on her short jacket. Her stomach rumbled as she thought of the chicken salad sandwich awaiting her.

As she walked past her office, the flowers caught her gaze. A tingle grabbed at the back of her neck. She backed up three steps, entered her office, and pocketed the card with the phone number. Her whole office smelled floral sweet. Then she tried to decide if she wanted to text Aaron now or wait until he was off from work. She wasn't expecting another delivery today, but if he came and she hadn't answered him, she decided it would create an awkward situation. *What do I say?*

Part of her wanted to ask her dad, another part wanted to ask DeeDee, but deep inside something screamed, "Yes!" She went to the break room and found most of the salon employees eating their lunches. She grabbed her sandwich from the refrigerator, fixed a glass of iced water, and sat at one of the tables.

One of the older women turned and asked, "Is it your birthday, Julia?"

She smiled and swallowed her bite of sandwich. "No. Nothing special."

"Well, who sends flowers if it's not your birthday?"

"Just a friend." She took another bite of her food and hoped the flush she felt wasn't going to make its way to her cheeks. She didn't want to discuss Aaron with anyone at the salon.

The talk around her mostly centered on DeeDee's new line of bridal gowns, and the upcoming February bridal show in New York. DeeDee had already told Julia that she'd be going. Pride swelled within her. Her old friends thought she had a sales job, but she knew she was forging a career.

Most of her friends were either leaving for college in a few weeks or they had obtained jobs at the new industrial park. Meredith was considered one of the lucky ones because she had landed a job as an executive secretary in the big corporate headquarters of an insurance company in the new park. Julia wondered how long the great job would last once Meredith had her baby and what would she do with the baby if she continued to work?

Julia was jaded. After watching her dad, the whole idea of a happily-ever-after fairy tale just didn't really exist in her mind, and she never wanted to be like any of the women he'd married. Then she thought about her dad and DeeDee. The whole relationship there was different. DeeDee was different. She was independent and strong. They were lovers, but also best friends. And DeeDee didn't try to mother anyone. She let everyone know that she was there if they needed her, and that she was good at keeping her mouth closed.

Julia slipped her phone from her pocket, stepped out of the break room, and went out the service door to the alleyway between the buildings. In the heat, she breathed in the stale hot air. Water trickled from a pipe and formed a small rivulet that ran down the alley to the street. The dumpster reeked of decomposing flowers, food, and whatever else had been tossed in there. Sweat began to bead on her forehead.

She paced the alleyway for a moment before texting Aaron, thanking him for the flowers. She added yes, but call me tonight after seven.

After deciding that should be sufficient, she scurried back inside where the air conditioner pumped cool, dry air into the building.

She had just turned into her office when she heard a squeal from the salon, and it wasn't a happy sound. Without hesitation, she went to the salon and discovered a young woman in tears. Several other young women milled around her looking totally confused. Mrs. Prentiss was trying to explain that they did not keep hundreds of gowns in stock.

Julia walked up to Mrs. Prentiss. "Please, everyone follow me. Mrs. Prentiss, will you fix a tray of iced tea for everyone."

Julia led them all to a generous private area. "Please have a seat." She handed the one woman a box of tissues. "I'm sorry. Were you expecting a store like those at the mall?"

"Yes! You have nothing!"

Julia touched the woman's arm. "Consider them the fast food joints of weddings. This is five star dining. We don't do cheeseburger wedding dresses. Your gown will be specially selected and sewn for you because we believe every bride is special and deserves to look her very best."

"Everything is custom made?" The woman looked at Julia with tears still running down her cheeks.

"Yes. Everything." Julia smiled at Mrs. Prentiss who entered the room with a large tray.

"Who would like fresh organic mint tea? It's been lightly sweetened." Mrs. Prentiss began handing out tall glasses with iced tea and placed a platter on the coffee table in front of everyone. "Petite chocolate dipped strawberries and petit fours. They are wonderful for any wedding."

Only one gal asked for an unsweetened tea and Mrs. Prentiss served that from another pitcher.

Once the bride-to-be had composed herself, Julia used a remote controller and began to show bridal designs on a large screen as she asked the woman her plans: A Christmas Eve wedding by candlelight, the church decorated with poinsettias. Julia listened and imagined every square inch as the woman talked.

Julia flipped to a special design, a gown with a matching hooded cape. The woman fell in love and when she discovered it could be trimmed in beaded poinsettias, she dissolved into a joyful round of tears. Julia helped the woman choose several shades of green for her bridesmaids and complimentary gowns that they all agreed would be perfect.

DeeDee joined the women and assured them that they would absolutely love their gowns. Soon all the women were being measured. Their names and measurements were added to the computer. All received a tiny gift bag that contained a key chain and some other assorted items to remember the day. Although Julia was certain that none of them would ever forget it.

Julia picked up the last strawberry and popped it in her mouth as she cleaned up the bridal room after the clients had left. It all sounded so perfect. But reality struck, and she couldn't imagine being that excited or that much in love.

She left a little ahead of DeeDee, but instead of heading home, she stopped by the coffee shop on Main Street. The bell over the door clanged as she pulled the door open. Elizabeth, the owner, sat at a table chatting with a blonde woman that Julia recognized. She smiled at both of them and ordered a decaf latte to go. It was just a silly indulgence, a way to unwind from the day before heading back to the family nest.

Cody Montgomery was the man she called Dad. He'd adopted her when he married her mom. He'd been married twice before DeeDee and none of the children in the house actually were of his blood. That left her with two half-sisters and four-stepbrothers.

"Thanks, Luke." She took the cup from the young man behind the counter. There had been a time she drooled over Luke. Blond and blue-eyed, he was two years her senior and going to the local community college. Today, she just smiled. She had changed. She was no longer that boy-crazy teen. She had a career and a purpose. At the sideboard, she stirred a dash of sugar into her coffee before she slipped her phone from her pocket and checked the time. There was plenty of time before Aaron was to call.

She strolled home with new eyes. Houses where she had once Trick-or-Treated now looked different. She waved to Mrs. Caughlin and petted the Calvin's old German Shepherd when he strolled up to her. His face had turned gray and his gait was no longer steady. She stopped for a moment to look at the Jackson house that was recently sold to a young family. She polished off the last of her coffee as she watched two boys doing tricks on skateboards.

When had she changed? She didn't feel any different, not really. She walked up her driveway, tossed her empty to-go cup into the large green trashcan, and went into the house. As she stepped into the kitchen, she wondered what had happened to that wonderful feeling that had followed her home. She sucked in a deep breath, washed her hands, cleaned up the mess her siblings had left, and began to fix salad. She heard her father and the twins, Collin and Logan, come through the front door.

Smacking the stem on a head of lettuce against the counter, she then removed the core and began to tear the leaves into bite-sized pieces. Something in the slow cooker was filling the kitchen with the warm aroma of beef. The refrigerator contained several ingredients she could include in the salad. After adding sliced mushrooms, grape tomatoes, diced zucchini, half a yellow pepper, and a handful of chickpeas, she tossed the salad with a light coating of ranch dressing. A tiny bird at the feeder outside the kitchen window caught her attention. She stood for a moment and watched it. Movement in the kitchen caused her to turn. "Hi, Dad. Guess who has a date for dinner on Sunday?"

Two

Julia had just started to help her youngest sister, Chelsea, clean up the kitchen after the family had eaten when her phone rang.

Chelsea rolled her eyes and Julia scurried to the garage to take the call. With six other siblings and two adults, a private conversation was almost impossible anywhere else in the house. Her heart skipped a few beats as she answered the phone.

"Hi, Julia." Aaron's voice came through loud and clear. "Two things, well three: I need to know if you eat meat, because that would determine where we would be eating, and the address where you live, and if four-thirty would be convenient to pick you up."

She promised him she ate meat, would be ready at four-thirty, then gave him the address. Her insides were turning to jelly as she spoke. It was as though she had reverted back to being fourteen years old and he was the cutest guy on the block. She wanted to dance around the garage while her heart pounded in her chest. Instead, she politely thanked him for his call and told him she looked forward to seeing him on Sunday.

Before he hung up, he said, "Dress pretty."

When Sunday arrived, Julia fixed her hair a half dozen ways before she settled on wearing the sides and crown pulled back and braided while the rest hung free down her back. Then she put on a short green skirt, a bold geometric print shirt, and a pair of green Karina Karr heels.

DeeDee took one look and shook her head. "Too much. Ditch the wild shirt for your strappy black one, and wear that new plum skirt you just bought. Then meet me in my room."

Julia groaned and did as DeeDee suggested. DeeDee was a fashion designer and knew what worked and didn't, so Julia did as she was told. But when she looked at herself in her long mirror, she switched her shoes to heeled sandals that were nothing other than straps that ended slightly above her ankles. It elongated her appearance and it did look more sophisticated.

"Better?" Julia entered her dad's bedroom that DeeDee now shared with him.

"Oh, yes." DeeDee vanished into her closet and brought out a basket filled with scarves. She selected a very elegantly fringed one and tied it around Julia's waist. "There. Now if you get someplace and the air conditioning is too much..." She untied the scarf and draped it around Julia's shoulders. "Just pull it up, and instead of tying it in the front, you can tie it in the back like this."

"I love it!"

"I'm not done with you." DeeDee dropped a set of amethyst stones over Julia's head and handed her some matching earrings. "Now, I'm done."

Julia almost didn't recognize herself in DeeDee's mirror. The amethyst and plum combination made her burnished-brown hair look richer, as it had brought out the deep reddish highlights. So many times she had thought about dying her hair black, thinking it would be more sophisticated, but DeeDee swore the natural color was a hundred times better than anything that came from a bottle. Admiring the amethysts and the way they sparkled and contrasted against the black of her top, she realized that her hair was doing the same thing. She turned her body while still staring in the mirror and looked at how far her hair fell down her back. She grinned.

A knock caused both women to turn towards the door.

"Am I allowed into my own room?" a deep male voice asked.

"Of course." DeeDee smiled brightly as Cody entered.

"Wow! You look very beautiful. Let's see, curfew is at seven. That's long enough to grab a hamburger with some unknown guy."

"*Dad!*"

"I'm teasing." He held out his arms. "I'm not sure what happened to my little girl, but she's turned into a fine-looking woman. I hope I'm still entitled to a hug and kiss."

Julia fell into her dad's protective embrace. "I'm so nervous."

He held her at arms length. "Why? You've been practicing for this moment since you started going to the movies with Billy Kemper when you were eleven."

"Oh, Dad." She groaned at the memories of Saturday dates.

"You have cash on you?"

"Check."

"Debit card and keys?"

"Check."

"Phone?"

"Check."

"You're going to be fine. But I will say, if I wasn't married and your father, I'd be chasing you."

She balled her hand into a fist and punched him in the arm. "Eww! You're my dad. Don't say things like that."

"So, it's wrong for me to recognize a drop-dead gorgeous woman when I see one?"

She looked at DeeDee and then at her father. "No. You're not allowed to see me like that."

"Okay, my darling little troll, from now forward I will only see you as the old hag you have become."

She wrinkled her nose, crossed her eyes, and stuck her tongue out at him.

He laughed and a light flashed. "Gotcha!"

"You didn't! Erase that at once!" She grabbed for his phone but he held it high above his head.

"Nope, that pic is blackmail material. If you're not home by seven, I'll--"

"You wouldn't."

He leaned over and kissed her cheek. "Enjoy your evening. It's just a date and he's just a guy. You're a grown woman, capable of making your own decisions. Remember, I'm always here if you need me. That's why you carry a phone." He flashed her a big smile. "Go wait for your date. I need to talk to DeeDee."

She went into the powder room off the hallway to check her makeup and teeth one more time. Butterflies flitted in her abdomen. *Dad's right. Aaron's just another guy and this is just another date.*

She sat in the living room and stared at the driveway. It wasn't because Aaron sent flowers. His invitation was different. Aaron was special, and she could sense it in his eyes when he looked at her.

"He's here!" She practically leapt for the door.

DeeDee blocked her path. "Chill. Ask him if he'd like to step in while you grab your things." DeeDee took Julia's small purse away from her and set it in the dining room. DeeDee put her finger to her lips. "That's better."

DeeDee stepped out of the line of sight just as the doorbell rang.

Julia's butterflies all took flight as she answered the door. "Hi, I just need to, um..." She looked over her shoulder. "Would you like to come in? I need..." She scrunched her nose. "My purse is in the other room."

She held the door open for Aaron.

"Take your time. I'm probably a few minutes early." He wore a light brown suit, cream-colored shirt, and a multicolored, silk tie. It was all top quality.

She grabbed her purse and winked at DeeDee standing in the kitchen. Then turned and walked towards the door. "I'm ready." That's when she heard giggling coming from the staircase. "Logan, Collin, behave."

She could hear them race up the stairs. She rolled her eyes at Aaron and he chuckled.

"Must be fun to have much younger siblings. I only had an older sister."

"Oh, no. Don't tell me you were that horrid little brother who sat on the steps and giggled when her date picked up her."

He held up both hands. "I never did such a thing. I was older, more mature, and knew better ways to embarrassment my sister."

"Please don't say a word in this house. I don't want anyone to get any ideas. There are four more siblings and they are much older."

He laughed.

The sound of his merriment rolled over her and calmed her nerves. As she pulled the door closed behind them, she called, "Bye, Dad, DeeDee."

Aaron held the car door for her as she slid inside his little foreign sports car. *Nice!* She admired the soft leather seating and the impressive dash. The whole thing screamed money.

They made the usual small talk as they headed north then east.

"I wanted to do something special tonight. I hope you approve." He drove down a lane that ended in front of an old mansion. As he put the car in PARK, two car valets opened their doors. Julia smiled and stepped onto the old granite cobblestones. Aaron joined her and offered her his arm as they climbed several granite steps to the wide porch.

"Where are we?" she whispered.

"The Gray Duck Tavern. I hope you enjoy it." He opened one of two massive doors.

She stepped inside and blinked as her eyes adjusted to the interior lighting. There was a man standing behind a podium dressed in Colonial garb with a white wig.

"Reservations for two. Symons." Aaron spoke with complete authority.

"You are a few minutes early, but your table is waiting. Right this way."

They walked through the elegantly appointed house and Julia noticed the entire staff was dressed in colonial costumes. Julia and Aaron stepped out of the building and onto another porch, down two steps and followed a path to a private garden area that overlooked a wide expanse of the river below.

Aaron held her chair as the man in costume announced that their waiter would be with them shortly. That's when she realized they were sitting under a white semi-translucent canopy.

"This is beautiful. I've never heard of this place." She twisted in her seat to see the flowers that bloomed all around their private outdoor garden room. Surrounding them on three sides was a low wall of stone that appeared to be holding the garden at bay. But flowers tumbled over it and small ones poked from between the crevices of the rocks. It reminded her of an artist's rendering of what a garden should look like, except this was real.

Their waiter appeared, filled their goblets with iced water, and slowly rattled off the evening's menu choices.

"Would you like a glass of wine?" Aaron asked.

She chomped at her lower lip and shook her head. "No thank you."

"May I order for us?" Aaron asked.

Julia nodded. Butterflies flitted through her abdomen and she was certain her hands were shaking. She was so overwhelmed that she was actually glad she didn't have to make any decisions.

The table was covered in a dark gray cloth that fell to the flagstone pavers. Over the dark gray was a pristine white tablecloth, and the pale-gray napkins had been folded into a fancy standing shell.

She heard Aaron say peanut soup before he asked what salad dressing she preferred.

Panic flew through her. "I wasn't paying attention. What are my options?"

The waiter smiled. "What do you normally like on your salads? Then I shall suggest one for you."

"Ranch."

"Why don't you try our buttermilk dill? I'll put it on the side for you."

She nodded as Aaron told the waiter he'd go with the peach chutney vingarette also on the side.

When the waiter left, she looked at Aaron. "I'm not of legal age to drink."

She could see the playfulness in his eyes and the way the edges of his mouth twitched up.

"Please tell me you're not jailbait. Maybe I should have asked the other day."

"I'm almost nineteen. September fifth. More times than I care to remember, I've started back to school on my birthday. It totally ruins the birthday party thing."

He raised his eyebrows and grinned. "I'll be extra good."

"How old are you?"

"Does it matter?"

She scrunched her nose. "It really shouldn't, should it?"

"No." He picked up his water goblet. "I propose a toast to a lovely evening with a very beautiful woman."

"Thank you." Heat crawled up her chest and to her cheeks. "I know you are older. So how old are you?"

He grinned and she loved that twinkle in his eyes. "Twenty-eight. Does that bother you?"

"No." She took another sip and swallowed the cold water, hoping it would cool the heat that spread through her. She wasn't just out on a date with some guy; he really was a man. That sent a trill through her and those butterflies took flight again.

"You're not jailbait, but I don't want your father upset if I'm seeing you."

She took another long swig on her icy water, but it wasn't cooling a darn thing. There was something sexy about him. Dangerously sexy and she liked the way it flowed through her.

"He's my father. He's always been protective of me." She grinned as she gazed into his eyes. "He expects all my dates to be very good."

"I promise. I'm good." He raised his eyebrows. "I'm *very* good."

His insinuation wasn't lost on her. *Oh, yeah, you are definitely dangerous and way too hot.*

Each course was served with a flourish and when the dessert came she was positive that she had no room for even the tiniest bite, but she couldn't pass up the opportunity to sample it.

After dinner, they walked down the path to the edge of the wide river. There were several yachts at the dock that had remained out of view as they ate. It was quiet and peaceful. The only sounds were those of the boats as they sloshed in their moorings. Far on the other side of the water was the outline of trees and farm fields.

She looked up towards the house. It was a beautiful old mansion. She hadn't realized how far down from it they had walked, nor had she noticed the terraced gardens or the two wooden poles, each topped with a big carved wooden pineapple that symbolized hospitality during Colonial times. The entire dinner was beyond anything she had experienced, and her father had often taken the family to fine restaurants. Standing next to Aaron seemed so perfect as if the whole thing were some sort of dream.

Aaron held a shiny copper coin in front of her face. "Penny for your thoughts."

She took the penny and grinned. "I feel as though I'm in a fairytale. And a little brother is going to wake me up and ruin a perfectly wonderful dream."

"No little brothers here. Are you up to walking the gardens in your heels?"

She smiled. "Yes."

One of the terraces contained a reflecting pool and a heron waded at one end. Another terrace contained several fountains and copies of famous statues in marble. Each garden held its own surprises. They talked about the various plants and flowers, and how nature seems to have its own plans no matter how carefully man attempts to control it.

The sun was low and the clouds glowed in pinks and oranges. Aaron escorted her back to their table, which was now lit with several candles. Out of nowhere their waiter appeared, and served them coffee from a pretty silver pot, then disappeared just as quickly.

Aaron picked up a small black book, inserted his credit card, then smiled at her as he took her hand. "I think this evening has been lovely. I know I don't want it to end."

"Neither do I."

"I fly to Utah tomorrow and classes at the university start next week. I won't be back until Thanksgiving, but I'd like to be able to call you."

"I'd like that. Maybe in some way, this evening has been a bit overwhelming. I mean, I thought, you would... That we'd have dinner someplace and maybe see a movie... I had no idea."

He cocked his head and that twinkle showed in his eyes. "I'm asking you now if you'll have Thanksgiving dinner with my parents. Afterwards we'll build a bonfire or maybe have a hayride. I'll ask your dad if he'll allow me to steal you for the few days that I'll be home."

She could see the flush cover his cheeks.

"My mom will put you in the guest room. I promise you'll be very safe from this wolf that she calls her son."

"Hmm." She sat a little straighter. "I don't see you as a wolf. But I'll make bets you've been the class clown."

He laughed. "Ruin my image, go right ahead." When he composed himself, he continued, "I have a question. Never once tonight did you question a piece of silverware, yet you seem to come from a normal household. Where did you learn such things?"

She lifted her shoulders and let them drop. "My dad has always taken us to nice places. Dinner at home is simple, but we travel occasionally. Was this evening some sort of a test?"

"Oh, no. Please don't ruin a perfect night with such thoughts. I brought you here so that we could enjoy a lovely quiet evening together." He blushed again. "I was hoping to steal a few kisses in the moonlight."

She chomped on her bottom lip, then grinned as all the butterflies in her tummy took flight. "Coffee, kisses, and moonlight? I'll think about that while I visit the ladies room."

Her trip to the ladies room meant returning to the mansion and finding the facilities. Candles glowed in wall sconces and reflected in the large mirrors over the sinks in the ladies room. A woman in costume handed her a tiny sliver of soap that had been molded in the shape of a flower. It bubbled and melted almost instantly as she washed her hands. Then she was handed a warm towel and offered a choice of several hand lotions. She chose one and thanked the woman.

She made her way to Aaron who had fresh coffee waiting. But this time instead of seating her, he took her hands and drew her to him.

"Did you come to any conclusions?" His breath fluttered across her face.

"About what?"

"Kisses?"

"Oh." She smiled. "Kisses are always allowed. Anything beyond that would require that two people knew each other very well and had seriously discussed their relationship."

"We need to discuss our relationship." His mouth slanted over hers and she melted into his arms.

Heat flowed through her system and then pooled someplace between her legs. His hand was on the small of her back drawing her tighter to him. Her body begged for release, screaming its need as her pelvis met his.

His lips traveled to her ear. "I know what I want, and I knew it the first day I laid eyes on you."

There was no fumble. She was pressed hard against him. Her body burned. His lips toyed with her earlobe and tugged lightly on the earring that hung from it. Then his lips traveled back to her mouth. Her body smoldered, but his hands stayed splayed on her back.

His lips left hers and as her eyes flickered open, she found golden-green staring at her.

"Oh, yeah, we're going to have to have a very long discussion about this relationship, because I intend to keep you forever."

She backed away from him. Her hands trembled as she took her seat and attempted to fix her coffee.

He sat across from her, but his gaze never left her. "Julia, if that was just kissing, please tell me, because it sure felt like much more."

She blinked, hoping to shut out the intensity of his gaze - a gaze that warmed her blood almost to the point of boiling. Heat still flowed from her chest to her cheeks. "You mean like fireworks and volcanoes erupting?"

"Yeah."

"I know. I don't think I can drink my coffee. I could use a really cold shower."

"I'd better take you home before we're both in over our heads."

***

Aaron took a few deep breaths and then escorted Julia from The Gray Duck Tavern. His car was waiting for him as they walked down the granite steps to the driveway. He tipped the valet and held Julia's door until she was settled, then he climbed behind the steering wheel. "It's been a fantastic evening."

She nodded.

He worried that maybe he had scared her, but she didn't act as though she was. Then he prayed that she wouldn't reach over and touch his leg as they drove down the road. For if she did, he knew they'd find what ever was left of them wrapped around a tree.

He drove most of the way in silence. The electricity crackled and sizzled between them, until he couldn't stand it any longer. He pulled off the road and stopped.

"Julia, I need to be honest with you. I'm too old for games. I'd like whatever it is we're feeling to have a chance. I really thought you were older. I don't have a problem with the difference in our ages. But I also don't want to pressure you. You're only…you know."

She smiled at him. It was that same warm smile she gave him when she invited him to the break room for water. "I was a boy-crazy teen until I started working for DeeDee. I never saw myself having any real future. Once I started working there, I discovered there was this whole world that opened up to me. And being with DeeDee made me see that women could be strong and stand on their own feet." She wrung her hands in her lap. "I've also watched my dad go through two bad marriages. I've done a lot of growing up in the last few months and don't intend to make my father's mistakes."

"I think we'll have a plethora of things to discuss in the coming weeks." He put the car in gear and pulled onto the highway.

When he reached her driveway, he walked her to the front

door, and then pulled her into his arms. "I had the most wonderful evening with you, and I want to have many more."

She pointed upwards. "Smile for the camera. My dad is probably watching."

"No problem. I have nothing to hide." He pulled her back into his arms and held her tight to him.

A small mew escaped her throat as he touched his lips to hers.

The earth quaked. Fire ripped through him as their kiss deepened. Tentatively he touched his tongue to her lips and parted them. She willingly opened to him. With one hand on the small of her back, the other threaded its way through her hair and held her nape. He kissed her until he was certain that he couldn't go on without embarrassing himself in front of the camera. Three months would be a long wait between kisses. But she was worth it.

He'd kissed a lot of women and none had ever rocked him the way Julia did. She oozed the sexuality of a wild cat, yet it was packaged in a refinement that wasn't often seen in young women.

***

Julia found her dad sitting in the kitchen.

He glanced up from his newspaper and grinned. "I wasn't spying on you."

She looked at the remote controller on the table and then over her shoulder at the monitor behind her holding steady on the camera by the front door. "Oh, no, not at all. I can see that."

"That was a serious kiss."

"It was a very serious date." She pulled the chair out across from him. "He leaves tomorrow to go back to school. He's twenty-eight and getting his PhD in veterinary genetics." She dropped the bomb and watched her father's face for any signs of disapproval.

"Yes. I can see why you'd call it a serious date. Where did he take you?"

"The Gray Duck Tavern. Ever hear of it?"

Her father raised his eyebrows. "Not too many young men can afford to toss that sort of money around."

She shrugged. "His father owns a delivery company."

DeeDee walked into the kitchen. "Are you talking about Aaron?"

Julia nodded.

"What's his last name?" Cody asked his daughter.

"Symons. Spelled with a *y* instead of an *i*." DeeDee answered. "He substitutes for the National Delivery drivers."

"Only when he's home from school."

DeeDee poured a cup of coffee and joined them at the table. "Seems as though I walked in on an important discussion. Did your date go well?"

"It was fabulous."

"Good. You're opening for me tomorrow. I'll be at the factory."

Julia stood, then looked at her dad who seemed to be staring at nothing. "I've been invited to stay with Aaron's family over Thanksgiving weekend."

Cody shook his head. "No way. You're spending it with your

grandparents. You know that."

"*Dad!*"

"It's not up for debate. That's the rules. We go home for Thanksgiving."

Julia shoved her chair a little too hard and stormed out of the kitchen and into her room. There were times she hated Cody Montgomery and this was one of them. *You're not stopping me.*

***

Aaron found his parents on the second floor balcony drinking something iced.

"How was your evening?" Ffiona Symons asked her son.

"Good. Very good. I invited her to stay here with us when I return home for Thanksgiving."

"What a lovely idea. Will she be staying in the room with you?"

"No, Mom, I promised her the guest room."

"Very honorable." Barry Symons said. "Who is this young woman you've invited to our home?"

"Julia Montgomery. She works at Main Street Bridal Salon for DeeDee Drayden. She's very much a lady…cultivated."

"Montgomery? Is her father Cody Montgomery?"

Aaron looked at his father and shrugged. "I've never met him."

"Montgomery is a common name." Barry waved his hand through the air as if it were of no consequence. "Choose wisely, my son, or your nights will be cold and lonely."

Aaron watched his father grin at his wife.

"The right woman, when treated with care, will satisfy your

every desire. Just remember what you have belongs to her and no one else."

Aaron chuckled at his father's words and left the two of them. He could hear his mom squeal and then his dad's moan before he got all the way down the hall. *Horny old bastard.*

Aaron chuckled to himself. He'd heard the story of his parents a million times. His father had first met his mother when she was a mere toddler. His father would return to Colwyn Bay in Wales to visit grandparents and Ffiona was the small child who lived with her family on his grandfather's estate. When he returned again after finishing college, he saw Ffiona with new eyes and noticed her budding beauty. Barry Symons returned to celebrate his twenty-eighth birthday with his grandparents and married sixteen-year-old Ffiona while he was there. Petite with flowing golden-blonde hair, she was a beauty and it was easy to see why Barry had fallen madly in love with her. Aaron knew that feeling, for he'd fallen just as hard for Julia.

In the quiet of his own rooms, Aaron stripped off his suit and hung it in the closet. The electricity that had sparked and crackled around him and Julia all evening heated his body and his mind. He wanted to undress her and feel her skin against his. He wanted to ravish her, make her his and never let her go.

He picked up his phone and ran a quick text message. "*Your kisses will keep me warm for as long as I live. Sweet dreams to the most beautiful woman I've ever met.*"

A moment later, his phone buzzed. He looked at the text. "*I took a really long cool shower. Try it.*"

He groaned and headed for the shower. "*I'm taking you with me.*"

"*I'd like that. I'd get to count all your freckles. One by one. Nite.*"

He stepped into his shower and imagined her with him. He leaned back and let the water pour over his body, but in his mind Julia had wrapped her legs around him. Relief coursed through him, but it was only temporary. He wanted her as much as his father had wanted Ffiona.

Still naked from his shower, he stepped onto his balcony and looked around him. At the far end of the pasture, the horses swished their tails. It reminded him of Julia and her long hair. He wanted to lose himself in her hair and feel it cascade over his body. The thought of her kisses, her lips traveling over his body searing him with every touch. Conjuring the image of her naked body made his breath hitch. Desire set him aflame. He could feel her every movement. He relieved himself again of his hot need and headed for bed.

He left the doors to the balcony open, figuring the cool night air would help him sleep. Instead the sheet tented over his body. *Julia. Julia. Julia. Is your body begging for mine, too?*

He got up, grabbed his computer, and checked his tickets online. If he took a later flight… *I need you, Julia.*

Sleep deprived, he stood and stretched when his alarm sounded. He had no time to lose, if he wanted to pull off this wild stunt.

Showered, shaved and out the door before his parents were awake, he intended to see Julia before he left. He drove to Main Street Bridal and rang the doorbell. At eight in the morning, no one came. He went to the back door and rang that bell.

Julia opened the door. "What are you doing here? I thought you had to catch a flight?"

"I do. Tell me you have your own office. I need some time

alone with you before I leave."

She nodded and he followed her past the break room to her office. The room was plain. A desk held three computers and a tablet. There were two extra chairs tucked into a corner. He closed the door behind them, pulled her into his arms, and wrapped her ponytail into his fist. "I need you, Julia."

That electrical current sizzled around him as she ran her nails through his hair. "I know. I couldn't sleep."

He undid the top button on her blouse. "I'll stop whenever you tell me to stop."

Her lips crashed into his. Her tongue invaded his mouth as he slipped the blouse from her shoulders. The wild animal in her had been unleashed. Heat pooled deep in his pelvis.

She wore what he considered to be half a bra. Her areolas peeked over the top of the pretty silky fabric. He dropped the straps and stared at her generous, light pink nipples that beaded and puckered. A groan escaped. "They are even more beautiful than I had imagined."

She arched her back to him, and he took a nipple into his mouth. She mewed and wiggled her pelvis against him until he thought he'd die on the spot. He let go only long enough for her to pull his tee shirt off and then he sampled her other nipple. He found the zipper to her skirt and it fell to the floor.

She reached behind him to her purse that hung from a hook and withdrew a condom. She held up one finger and waved it. "My call, not yours."

She freed his straining shaft, sheathed it, then dropped to her knees. He clenched his jaw and bit back the growl that must have started in his toes. Violent and merciless, his body exploded as fireworks went off in his guts, then his head, leaving him trembling. He whispered, "Stop."

She took his mouth as her hands floated over his body like a gentle breeze. His heart thumped against his chest wall as he tried to steady the rhythm.

His mouth found her ear. "Let me take you."

"No," she whispered into his neck.

"Then let me do this." He slipped his fingers between her legs. The tiny panties she wore were soaked.

***

Julia buttoned her blouse, then picked up her skirt from where it lay on the floor.

"Not yet." Aaron stepped to her and slipped her panties from her hips. "These stay with me."

"You can't take my panties."

"If I can't take you with me, this is the next best thing." He balled them up and stuffed them into his jeans pocket.

"But I'm at work. It's not like I have an extra pair in the drawer."

He laughed. "Go without. No one will know except the two of us."

She loved his laugh, it tickled and tingled something inside of her. "You're terrible."

"No, I'm not. I'm very good, and you, my love, are beyond my wildest dreams." He opened the office door and walked through the salon to the front door. He turned and planted a tiny kiss on her cheek. "I'll text when I can."

She unlocked the door and opened it just as her father was walking past with both of the twins. "Ah, hi. Aaron, this is my dad, Cody Montgomery, and my two little brothers, Collin and Logan."

Aaron stuck his hand out. "Aaron Symons. I'm on my way to catch a flight, otherwise I'd enjoy spending a few moments with you."

"I totally understand. Safe trip."

She watched Aaron drive off and then turned her attention back to her father.

"I'll be at the penitentiary today, in case you forgot."

She noted her father dressed in one of his better business suits. "I can handle the troops."

He raised his eyebrows. "I talked to Sean and Ian at breakfast. I doubt they will be a problem."

"It's okay. Don't worry about us. You do your job." She jerked her thumb over her shoulder. "I have mine."

She ran her nails over the back of Collin's neck, making him squeal and laugh, then she ducked inside the salon. There was plenty for her to do and she had barely started when Aaron had stopped to say goodbye. Now she was behind and didn't want to have to explain why to anyone.

She crossed her arms over her breasts and hoped the tingle he had created would go away.

Three

When Aaron landed, he ran a text message to his father. "*So who is Cody Montgomery?*"

"*Heir to SunWest Oil. The largest oil producers in North America.*"

"*And he's living in an ordinary house, in a middle-class neighborhood?*"

"*That's what I've heard. So does Warren Buffett.*"

"*Cody Montgomery is Julia's dad.*"

"*Best of luck stealing that little girl away from her daddy.*"

Aaron caught his connecting flight and ran a text to Julia before turning off his phone. "*I miss you.*"

It was after eight thirty in Utah when he unlocked the door to his little bungalow on the campus. He flipped on the lights, turned on all the ceiling fans, and opened the windows to let the stale summer air out. He had rented the place during previous summers, but he always came back to such a mess, he promised himself he'd never do it again. He drained off a small amount of water from the bottom of the hot water tank, turned on the gas, and lit the pilot light. Then he checked every spigot before sinking into an easy chair in the living room. He had hoped that Julia would fade into a distant memory once he hit campus, but it was as if she had invaded his very soul. He ached for her.

He took out his phone and ran her a text message. "*I'm home, my home on campus. Long day. Hate flying and all the hassles. Wish you were here. I need to hold you in my arms.*"

***

Julia texted him back, but he didn't respond. She wondered where he lived and what it was like living on a campus. When she went to work for DeeDee, she had jumped in with both feet and found it thrilling even when it wasn't. DeeDee had dropped a huge load of responsibility on her, given her an office, and treated her like an equal. Then DeeDee married Cody. Never once did DeeDee attempt to take on the role of mother. Julia appreciated that. DeeDee was a mentor and friend.

Julia knew Aaron worked as an assistant professor. If she had been a student on campus, she couldn't imagine dating a professor. Wouldn't that be like dating a high school teacher? But she'd heard stories of gals humping a professor to get a better grade. Was Aaron that kind of guy?

***

Aaron awakened when light began to filter into the room and he realized he'd spent the night in his chair. He picked up his phone and looked for a message. Julia had texted him back almost immediately.

He ran a message to her. "*Sorry. Fell asleep. I'll call you tonight.*"

By noon, his little bungalow was spit shined. He stopped by his office and checked in with the department secretary before heading over to the grocery store. By this time, he was starving, and he bought way too much food. As he piled the bags into the trunk of his car, he ripped open the box of granola bars and removed two. He'd eat them on his way home.

Normally, he enjoyed being back on campus and going through the motions for the coming semester, but today there was an empty spot within him; a hole that Julia had created.

His parents had never prepared him for living on his own. He had learned the hard way how to fix his own meals and use the washer and dryer. Failures had taught him what not to do, and YouTube showed him how to do it correctly. Was that why Cody Montgomery was raising his children in a small town?

Aaron fixed a grilled cheese sandwich and made a salad. He ran a quick text to Julia. This was going to be the longest three months of his life.

***

Julia hated that DeeDee has sent her to the factory to learn the sewing end of the industry. And when she cut a skirt and forgot about the weft of the fabric, she ruined over fourteen yards of fabric. Fortunately, DeeDee was more forgiving than Mrs. Hennessey who headed up the department.

Before the week was through, Julia managed to catch her fingertip on the serger and almost removed the padded tip of her finger prompting an emergency room visit.

Sitting in DeeDee's office with tears running down her cheeks, her finger bandaged, and pain medications racing through her system made her feel terribly stupid.

DeeDee sat in the chair beside her. "You're actually quite lucky. It's a hard way to learn a lesson, but you're going to be fine."

She sniffled. "I can't do anything right over there."

DeeDee held up her left index finger and pointed to the tiniest scar. "And I ran the needle and thread through this finger until the needle hit the bone and broke. It only takes a split second."

"Mrs. Hennessey hates me."

"No, she doesn't. She also knows you are my right hand, and she knows I'm teaching you every aspect of this business. You've made some mistakes. Forgive yourself and remember to forgive an employee who makes the same mistake."

"But mistakes are costly."

"Yes. They are. But everyone will make a mistake at some point. We're human, not perfect."

The following morning with one finger wrapped and splinted, Julia was covering buttons with fabric because Mrs. Hennessey didn't trust her to do anything else. Using a die, Julia cut the fabric, loaded the circle into a press along with the blank button, and then pulled a lever to create the perfect covered button. It was boring and she hated doing it. By noon, she'd covered enough buttons for one and a half dresses, for each button took her about eight minutes to complete.

Mrs. Hennessey inspected her work. "You did well. But you need more speed."

Julia looked at the middle-aged woman and forced a smile. "I'm trying, but I don't want to make another mistake."

"Bring your lunch to my office. We need to talk."

Julia's heart fell into the pit of her empty stomach. In a way, she was glad not to have to face the other employees during the lunch hour, but facing Mrs. Hennessey didn't bode well. "Yes, ma'am."

She retrieved her chef's salad she had made that morning and knocked on the woman's office door.

"Come in."

Mrs. Hennessey was in a corner office with two walls of glass that faced over the industrial complex. She knew how to do everything, having anything to do with making dresses, and she was known for being an excellent manager. Her salt and pepper hair had been hot combed and pulled into a twist, but curly tendrils escaped and framed her face and hung over the back of her neck. She had a light, almost almond, complexion and light brown eyes.

Julia sank into a chair and opened the container housing her salad.

"Do you know why you are here?" The older woman lifted her sandwich from a brightly colored, plastic container.

Julia pointed to the floor. "Here in your office? No."

"I mean here in the factory?"

"To learn."

"Are you learning anything?"

Julia emptied the salad dressing from the small container onto her lettuce mixture. "That I stink at this job."

Mrs. Hennessy laughed. "Oh, darling, you've got that much right. But have you learned anything else?"

"That making dresses isn't easy. At it's very best, it's boring."

"No, it's not. We get an order, we pull the pattern, take the fabric from the bolt, and in a matter of a few days, we've created a beautiful gown for someone's wedding - a dress that they will wear once. Probably the most expensive dress that they've ever owned and ever will own. And for a few hours, they will feel like a princess. The salon creates the dream and takes the orders. We make it happen from a few yards of fabric."

Julia nodded. "Like elves in a fairytale."

"Exactly." The woman picked up her sandwich and ate several

bites then washed it down with a few swigs from a can of Coke. "And what else?"

"That everyone out there is skilled in what they are doing."

"True. What else?"

Julia shrugged. "It's not easy."

"What else?"

Julia giggled. "If you aren't there, production slows down and everyone talks."

Mrs. Hennessey laughed. "That's true, too."

Julia ate part of her salad wondering what else she might have learned. Then it dawned on her. "These employees are laborers. Most are minorities and their job means the world to them."

Mrs. Hennessy nodded. "We're all keeping roofs over our heads and putting food on the table. These jobs are important to everyone in here."

That afternoon, Mrs. Hennessey showed Julia how they make allowances in the patterns for the difference in height and bust sizes. Julia understood how certain fabrics had more or less give to them and how that affected the way something would lay and drape. These were things that DeeDee completely understood. This also meant that silk couldn't be substituted for satin or velvet.

Julia knew that sewing was not her thing, but she began to understand production and what it took to do it. DeeDee had an edge because she could sew. But Julia learned to look and see the drape and could see if the fabric had been reversed and instead of flowing down, it was flowing up. It was another set of skills and Julia had to learn them. And after spending weeks in production, Julia did learn. It wasn't her favorite place to work, but she quit hating it. After six weeks there, she wanted to get back to the salon.

***

Aaron counted down the days until he could see Julia again. Seven more weeks seemed like an eternity. The image of her was burned into his mind. As the days and nights cooled, the memories of Julia warmed him and made him hunger for her. Every night, he'd call her and they would talk for about a half hour. It was her voice and that contact, not what they said, that mattered.

His classes kept him busy. Teaching was not difficult, and most of the time, he enjoyed it. But it was the quiet moments that got to him. Those were the times his mind wandered to Julia. There was something about her. She was poised and graceful like a modern day princess. He'd watch the girls on campus and shake his head. They came to class as if they had just tumbled from bed. Tattoos and piercing marred their bodies. He didn't like it. He knew he was being old-fashioned and he didn't care.

Julia wasn't exactly snow white. She carried a condom in her purse, and her actions were skilled. But he had a feeling she was still a virgin and he wasn't certain why he felt that way. But every time he thought about her, his body ignited. Much like a young teen with a new toy, he fantasized and became reacquainted with the daily hand jive.

***

Julia checked the online orders that had come in during the night. She had an odd one and she checked with DeeDee.

"Call Karina," DeeDee said and walked away. Nothing seemed

to faze her anymore. She just went with whatever people wanted. If someone wanted a pink gown with black and white pigs, she'd do it. It was all about fulfilling the bride's dream.

Days ran together for Julia, broken only by the occasional delivery of flowers or some other small gift from Aaron. Each evening he'd call, and when she hung up the phone, her body burned with desire. She remembered their last moments together. It had been all fireworks.

Was she in love or in lust? She had no clue.

"Dad, I don't want to go to the ranch. I want to spend my weekend with Aaron and his family."

"This is not up for discussion. You are going to the ranch."

"Do you want to talk to his parents? I'm staying in the guest room."

"You're going to the ranch and for more than just a long weekend. I've already cleared it with DeeDee. You're leaving here on the tenth."

"What?" Frustration was quickly replaced with anger. "You think you can run my life?"

"For now, yes. And when you are done at the ranch, you can make your own decisions."

"What does a few days have to do with anything?"

"Everything."

Julia stomped to her bedroom and waited for Aaron's call.

"You're never going to believe this. My father will not allow me to go with you."

"Is it because you'll be with me?"

"No. He's determined I must be with the family over Thanksgiving. And he's forcing me to go there early! As if I want to be on the ranch!"

"Ranch? As in west of the Mississippi?"

"Yes. Utah."

"What if I came to you?"

A little pause flowed through her like a puff of air. "Maybe... I'd have to ask my grandparents. I mean... It would be better than not seeing you."

"I want to hold you in my arms and feel your breath on my chest."

She inhaled. "Every night, I think of those last few minutes we had together."

"Oh, Julia. I want to feel your naked body against mine."

"Is this conversation going to deteriorate into phone sex?"

"Do you have a problem with that?"

***

Julia stayed busy. Her knack for dealing with brides, mothers of the bride, and employees increased, and DeeDee rewarded the effort. Julia's confidence grew but so did her workload, and by the time November rolled around, she was ready for a long vacation, even if it was spent on her grandparents ranch. When told to take lots of business clothes with her because she'd be working while she was there, she assumed that was jeans for riding.

DeeDee straightened her out. "No, you need dresses and suits. Prepare to be working in the office with your grandfather, in town."

"Doing what?"

DeeDee never looked up from her computer. "Not sure

exactly. I'll assume you'll be in some meetings. The only thing your dad told me was that it was important that you looked your professional best. I do know that he's bragged to his parents as to how well you're doing here and how proud he is of you."

"Really?" A surge ran through her. *Dad's proud of me? Wow!*

DeeDee nodded. "Do you have this order from Louisiana in the system? The light green bridal dress?"

"Yes. It's under her mother's name. That's who is paying for all of it."

"Okay. Ah, here it is." DeeDee looked up. "You've already sent it to the factory."

"Is something wrong?"

"No. It just surprised me. You're getting very efficient at this."

Julia smiled more to herself than to DeeDee. She'd learned to double check measurements and if all was in normal range, she'd order the material and send the project over to the factory.

The Friday before she was to leave for the ranch, she had the afternoon off. She stopped by the coffee shop on Main Street for a latte, and then walked home in the cool afternoon sunshine. The Calvin's old German Sheppard sat on their porch and wagged his tail. It was too much effort for him to come to her so she went to him.

"Whatcha doing, Prince? Sitting here in the sun warming your old bones?" She sat on the steps and petted him. "Getting too old to greet me?" Memories of a more active Prince flooded her.

"Seems we've both changed over the years." She petted him a little more in all the places he loved. "I've got to go. Goodbye, old friend." She kissed his muzzle, brushed the fur from her fingers, stood, and finished walking home. She had packing to do.

***

"Ready?" Cody called.

"I hope so. Two weeks is a long time." Julia answered as she dragged her second suitcase down the stairs.

Her father took it from her. "Why didn't you tell me you had another. I would have brought it down."

She followed her father to the garage and watched as he loaded the last piece of luggage into the trunk. "Who is going with me?"

"I am. Do you think I'd send my baby girl out for such an important visit all by herself?"

"I'm not a baby."

He chucked her under the chin with his index finger. "I know that. But you're mine, and I've done everything I could to get you to this point in your life."

"What's that supposed to mean?"

"You'll find out soon enough."

***

"Did you tell her?"

"No. I left that honor for you."

"You should have told her something by now."

Julia listened to the muted voices on the other side of her grandfather's door.

"There's never been a need to tell her. She's accepted life. Knows there's money…"

She wanted to press her ear to the solid wooden door.

"We'll leave here at seven fifteen. There's a board meeting at two and I want the paperwork out of the way. Are you coming?"

"Of course."

She heard the sounds of her father and grandfather stirring from their seats. She scooted away from the door. With luck, Aaron would call her, but she wasn't sure when he'd be calling because she had switched time zones.

The next morning, dressed in a suit, she greeted several family members in the breakfast room.

"You look lovely, dear." Grandmother Montgomery passed Julia a plate. "Make yourself at home."

Julia took the plate and added several breakfast foods to it. *Two weeks of eating like this and none of my clothes will fit.*

An hour later, she sat staring at her grandfather as he told her about SunWest Oil. The next two weeks passed in a whirlwind haze as she tried to wrap her mind around the wealth of the family and her part in it. She wasn't exactly angry that her father had never told her, and yet she was. She had always made do on the allowance he had given her, but she had wished it had been more. How many times had she watched friends do things, then she made up excuses because she didn't have the money to do them, too? Now she realized she had almost unfathomable wealth. It tossed a whole different perspective on things.

It was easy to understand why her father spent his time working with inmates who might have been unfairly accused instead of actually practicing law and making money. But it didn't explain why he kept all her siblings after the DNA testing proved that not one of them were his. He could have walked away and no one would have faulted him, instead he did everything to keep them, then he paved the way for all of them to inherit a piece of SunWest just as if they were of his blood.

A fourth of her trust had come into her possession, another fourth would come at age twenty-six, and the final half would come when she turned thirty. Her head spun with all the newfound information. In the course of a few days, her entire life had changed and her with it. She sat in the bedroom, stared out the window over fields, and tried to comprehend what it all meant.

DeeDee was due to arrive later in the evening with the rest of the gang, and Aaron would come on Saturday. Julia wasn't certain she even wanted to see him. Their incredible evening and wild goodbye seemed like years ago. It was as if it had all been a dream or it had happened to someone else. She didn't know what she wanted to do, but she didn't feel like eating dinner. Not tonight. She wanted to climb in bed and pull the covers over her head.

It had taken almost two weeks for her to comprehend who she was. Her world had changed and she wasn't the same Julia Montgomery who had accompanied her father to her grandparents' ranch. But in the process, she hadn't really discovered this new Julia, the one who could financially do anything she wanted. Her head pounded and she was nauseated. How could she possibly explain it to Aaron? And how would he fit into her life now?

Four

Thanksgiving day was much like any other on the ranch. Julia faced it with a smile but deep inside, she felt completely out of place. She looked at her two cousins who had passed their nineteenth birthday. They didn't act any differently, so why did she feel the way she did? Maybe they had known all along?

She walked up to her father and tapped him on the shoulder. "May we talk privately?"

"Of course."

She motioned to the breakfast room and waited until they were both settled at the large table. "Does this mean I can take off for Hawaii, and you can't stop me?"

Her father laughed.

Anger rose from her toes, through her guts, and up the back of her throat. She was certain smoke was probably billowing from both ears. *How dare you laugh at me!* "You drop this little bomb on me and just expect me to deal with it?"

Cody put both his palms on the table and splayed his fingers. "So this is why you've been so withdrawn? Do you want to go to Hawaii or are you testing the water to see how far I can reach?"

"Both."

"It's all quite simple. I raised you to understand that money isn't everything. I taught you the meaning of a dollar. I didn't want you to turn nineteen and figure you could burn it as if there were no tomorrow. I wanted you to appreciate what you have. Yes, you may go to Hawaii or any place you choose. But before you run off, remember your responsibilities and your commitment to DeeDee. You need to request vacation time just like any other employee."

"But you yanked me out of there without that request."

"DeeDee knew well in advance and knew why you were coming."

"So everyone knew except me?"

"Your grandparents and I worked it out, then I talked to DeeDee about it."

"I hate you!"

"No, you don't. If it wasn't for me, you wouldn't be sitting here with a ton of money in your name." He shook his head. "Julia, I've loved you since that first time I held you in my arms and rocked you to sleep."

Her head spun with dizzying images of growing up.

"I'm sure you're wondering why I gave you an older car to drive when you got your license. Did you need a super hot sports car? It wasn't a horrible clunker. It was just a little used car. It was perfect for you and now Sean may drive it."

"And that was supposed to teach me what?"

"To appreciate the next one which will be all shiny and new."

She stared at her father wanting to wipe the smirk from his face. "Do you realize that by omission, you lied to me?"

"Is that what this is about?"

"Yes!"

"Okay. I plead no contest."

"Do you realize that Aaron is coming tomorrow, and I'm not even certain that I'm ready to see him?"

"Why?"

"I've got too much swirling in my head to complicate it with a male relationship."

"Oh dear. I think we need a pot of coffee." He pushed his chair back and went to the kitchen.

She could see him through the doorway. Everything he said to her was true. She was lashing out at the one person she trusted the most. But he was the one who deceived her. It was all too jumbled.

Her father placed a cup of coffee in front of her and then took his seat. "May I make a suggestion?"

"What?"

"Don't make any hasty decisions. Go back with us on Sunday and do your job on Monday. What happened to I-love-working-at-the-salon? Do you still love it?"

She pondered what her father asked as she sipped her coffee. "Yes. I know what I'm doing. I hated school with a passion, but in the salon, I feel totally confident."

"And DeeDee loves what you do for her. You give her the freedom to design. But you are the dream maker. You take those designs and turn them into reality for the brides. You make the dreams happen. That's a gift, just as DeeDee's ability to design wedding dresses is a gift."

"Yeah, but she went to school to learn how to do it."

"Yes, but she knew how to draw before she went to school. She knew as a child she wanted to design dresses. They taught her the fine points of doing it, just as she's taught you about fabrics and taking measurements."

"I'm so confused."

Her father pulled her to her feet and wrapped her in his

embrace. Warm and comforted, she hugged him back. It was always her father who made everything right, from scraped knees to a broken heart. It was her dad who helped her to her feet and got her going again.

"You were not betrayed. I protected you. I kept you out of the press. I hid you away in a small town where no one cared if you were the heiress to an oil fortune. You were just Julia Montgomery who lived in the cul-de-sac. I didn't dress you in designer clothes that cost outrageous amounts. Your clothes came from the same stores as your friends. I also never denied you a fancy pair of athletic shoes. When you wanted those crazy pink ones that flashed light, you got them. When you wanted the purple bike like Markie Anderson's, you got it."

He rubbed her back and planted a kiss on the top of her head. "I'm very proud of you and the way you've turned out."

"Thanks, Dad. But now Aaron's coming tomorrow and I have no idea what to do."

"Okay, I'm the last person who should be giving you advice on your love life. I've certainly screwed that up over the years. Although I will admit that DeeDee is the best thing that ever happened to me when it comes to women. In spite of my mistakes, I have seven wonderful children that I love dearly and wouldn't trade for anything in the world. So, for whatever it's worth, I'm going to suggest that you go into any relationship slowly and with your eyes wide open. I don't want you making a mistake."

She pulled away from her dad's arms and stared into his blue eyes. "I think I understand. You think Aaron has swept me off my feet?"

"I know he has. Put them back on the ground and proceed

with caution."

***

Saturday morning Julia's Aunt Barbara announced that she and her husband would be leaving after breakfast. "I received a text message this morning that they accepted the contract. I don't want to waste a single day."

Julia looked at her eccentric aunt. "They? Do you mean the one in South America that you were telling me about yesterday?"

"Yes. I can't wait to start. They want a year-round ski resort. It's going to be awesome!"

Julia couldn't help being slightly jealous of her quirky aunt who flew all over the globe to design everything from houses for famous people to resorts and lodges for those people to play.

Another thought replaced the green one. That meant the pool house would be free and Aaron wouldn't be stuck in the bunkhouse with her brothers.

"Since you are leaving," Julia turned her attention to her grandmother. "Could Aaron use the pool house?"

"Oh, Julia, darling, the maid won't be here until Monday. Everything would need to be cleaned out there. There would be bedding to wash and a bathroom to clean."

"I can clean it. That's not a problem."

"No, that's too much work for you."

Cody spoke on her behalf. "Mom, she's quite capable. I think you should allow her to do it."

"But, it's so much work. Julia, you should let your young man stay in the bunkhouse. He'll have fun out there with the other boys."

315

Cody looked at his daughter and then at his mother. "Aaron is not a teenager; he's a grown man."

"It's still too much work."

Cody lifted his coffee cup, and the woman who had served the breakfast instantly refilled it. "Julia, if you wish to clean the place, you have my permission. What time is Aaron expected to arrive?"

"He said lunchtime."

As soon as Julia saw her aunt and uncle vacate the house near the pool, she flew out the back door and into the small bungalow that had been built originally for her grandmother's mother. Having once housed an elderly woman and a fulltime nurse, it was filled with lovely amenities that allowed the old woman to live comfortably on her own without being part of the noisy, larger household, but Julia stood with her hands on her hips and looked around. "Pigs! Collin and Logan know better than to leave a room looking like this."

Noise behind her made her turn around. Her father stood in the doorway.

"May I come in?"

She motioned with her hand. "I can't believe this mess."

"Now do you understand why I did not want to raise a bunch of spoiled brats?"

Julia nodded.

Her dad motioned back at the main house. "Mrs. Toberson said she'll help you when she's done in the kitchen."

"I was hoping I wouldn't need help."

"Whining isn't going to get it done. Remember you asked for this."

Julia gathered the towels and stripped both beds. Obviously, her aunt and uncle did not share the same bed. She started the washer and went to work on the bathroom. She only stopped long enough to move things in and out of the washer and dryer. Every cleaning supply she needed was in a large closet off the kitchen. She turned down Mrs. Toberson's offer to help and continued to clean.

When the large California bathroom was spit shined, she made the beds and ran the vacuum over the carpeting in the bedrooms. Then she started on the kitchen. Having no clue where the big trash bins were, she bagged the trash and set it outside of the door. Two people, three days, meals prepared at the main house and yet, they managed to create three large bags of trash.

Julia looked around as she ran the vacuum over the living room carpeting. The dishwasher hummed and the kitchen floor was drying. It had taken her almost three hours to clean the small empty house, but in the end it was worth it. She even filled the candy jar from a bag she found in the pantry. The entire place was decorated in shades of white, then offset in brown, and turquoise. It was sophisticated and tranquil.

"Hello!"

***

Aaron called when his knock had gone unanswered. He assumed someone was inside for he could hear the vacuum cleaner running. He opened the unlocked door and saw Julia with her back to him.

The swish of her long ponytail hanging down her back provided an unexpected sexy visual. And when she turned around, her smile lit up her face like a thousand watt bulb.

"Hi, give me three more seconds. I'm almost done."

He followed her to the kitchen closet. The place smelled of disinfectant, laundry and dishwasher detergents. But when she turned around, he pulled her into his arms. She smelled slightly sweaty and very sexy.

She pushed away from him. "I'm gross. I've got to grab a shower and lunch will be served in…" She looked at her watch. "Yikes! I've got ten minutes. Make yourself at home. Oh, darn, I've got the bathroom towels in the dryer."

"Go, I'll be fine."

He watched her sprint away. Then he looked around. She had originally told him he'd be staying in the bunkhouse with her brothers so something must have changed, and he assumed someone had left the ranch earlier than planned. After brief introductions, her father had sent him to the cabana house by the pool. He looked at both bedrooms and chose the smaller one. He opened a door and discovered part of a bathroom. The second door off the bedroom was a walk-in closet. He went back to the bathroom, washed his hands in a suspended glass sink, and then opened another door. The toilet had its own room with the bidet. A chuckle ripped through him when he realized that the wall contained a table that folded down in front of the toilet. *Morning crossword puzzle or email?*

He left there and found the multi-jet shower and a tub large enough for a party. Soapstone covered the floor, granite covered the walls, and polished granite surrounded the tub and covered other horizontal surfaces. If this was in the bungalow, he could only imagine what the main house had hidden behind closed doors.

"Aaron, hurry up, we're late and my grandmother hates for anyone to be tardy."

"*Tardy?* You're joking, right?"

Julia looked at him wide-eyed. "No."

Lunch looked like any other family's leftovers after Thanksgiving. There was turkey salad or slices of ham for sandwiches. There were deviled eggs, macaroni salad, and potato salad. Everything was scrumptious and he ate more than he should. That's when he discovered there was dessert, a chocolate ganache topped with a raspberry mousse. Decadent and delicious, he ate his entire portion.

As coffee was being served, Julia's uncle, DJ, excused himself and Julia's brothers went with him.

The elder Montgomery male asked, "Your father runs a trucking company?"

"Yes, sir. Express Delivery."

"Ah, the burgundy and tan trucks."

"Yes, sir."

"Julia said she met you this past summer because you were delivering to the bridal place that DeeDee owns."

"I work for my dad whenever I'm home."

"So, he has you learning the company from the ground up."

"Not exactly. I happen to enjoy driving. It's a nice diversion during the summer months. I've been doing it since I was old enough to own a CDL."

"What's that?" the elder Mrs. Montgomery asked.

"Commercial driver's license, ma'am. Have to have it to drive a big truck."

Julia smiled. "He's an associate professor and he's getting his PhD."

Aaron smiled back at her. "Veterinary genetics. It's an important new field and it will help us to understand more about cattle."

"Looking to develop a super breed?" the elder woman asked.

"Nature is a natural selector; I'm trying to understand it. I have no desire to crossbreed a cow with a boar."

Julia cut in on the conversation. "I hate to break up such an exciting debate, but I don't have much time with Aaron. May we please be excused?"

Cody answered, "Yes."

"You do know how to ride, don't you?" Julia asked, as they walked away from the dining room.

"I ride English, but I've tried western on a few occasions."

***

Julia knew she had to tell Aaron something but she didn't know what or even how to begin. To say that she had to slow down the relationship made no sense because when she looked at him, every part of her body burned with desire.

The countryside was all high desert with no secluded place for them to hide. But she wanted to feel his arms around her and his lips on hers. She headed for a grove of scrub that wound next to a dry creek bed. She meandered around, making certain they would be alone with no unwanted critters. The only things she found were a few birds.

She dismounted and found Aaron was at her side. His fingers cupped her waist.

"Um, I-I stopped because I want to talk. I don't... I mean... You know how things happen... I mean..."

His lips crushed to hers and every sane thought left. Her body pressed to his as his arms wrapped her, pulling her tighter to his broad chest. Inside, heat pulsed through her, her heart fluttered, and her body burst into flames. She tried to hold onto some semblance of reality, but it was slipping away.

"I've missed you." His fingers slipped under her coat and then found the waistband of her jeans.

"No. Stop. I can't. We can't. We've got to talk."

His hands left her as his breath left her neck. He stepped away and stretched his arms out to his sides. "What's wrong?"

"Nothing and everything." Tears welled and she tried to wipe them away. "I can't. I don't want to... I'm not going... It's complicated." She took one of his hands and pulled him over to an exposed bit of land near the creek bed. "Please...can we just sit?"

He nodded and sat on the dry sandy land. "What is wrong? You know you can tell me anything."

She gulped some air. "I can't tell you everything, but something happened out here. Something that has changed everything for me." She batted at the tears that formed, and then wiped them away. "This is difficult... How do I explain it?"

His thumb caressed the back of her hand sending a warm pulse through her. The whole time she had cleaned the bungalow she had rehearsed what she was going to say. Now those words were lost to her overwhelming desire to make love to him. "The best way to say this, I guess... I don't know, maybe..."

"Julia, just spit it out."

"I'm not just Julia Montgomery, the adopted daughter of Cody Montgomery, who works at the bridal salon in town. I just found out... There's... I'm... I can't... How do I tell you?"

Aaron laughed. "Let me guess, you're the great-granddaughter of the tsar and you must return to your homeland to rule over your people?"

"No. And it's not funny."

"Okay, let's try this, since you won't tell me, I'm going to take a serious guess. Cody Montgomery is not just a do-good lawyer. This is one hell of a ranch and that house is nothing to sneeze over. From what I know, I believe that Cody Montgomery is heir to SunWest Oil and that puts you as an heiress to that fortune."

His words tumbled into her stomach along with every sane thought and mingled with her brewing anxiety. "Y-y-you knew that?"

***

Aaron watched as the color drained from her face. He'd hit the nail on the head. "You didn't know?"

She shook her head.

"Apparently my dad knows who your father is and knew he was living in the area. My father tried to warn me about dating you. Dad seems to feel as if your father isn't going to approve of me, because I'm not good enough for the heiress to such a fortune."

"How long have you known?"

"After that first date, I had an inkling, but you just confirmed the hunch."

She pulled her knees up and wrapped her arms around them. "Omigod."

"And you didn't know any of that?"

She shook her head.

"You never questioned your father's wealth or even wondered

about the ranch?"

She tucked her head against her knees and mumbled, "I just thought it was the ranch. My dad doesn't want me discussing it in front of my siblings." She looked up with tears in her eyes. "I hate him for keeping it from me, as if my whole life up until now was a huge lie. But when I went to the bungalow to clean it for you, I realized why."

He tilted his head as he tried to connect the pieces together.

"I love my aunt. I always have. When anything ever went wrong, she was the one I'd turn to for advice. And she always stuck up for me when it came to my dad."

"So?"

"Well, when I went into the bungalow, I discovered that she... Oh how do I say this?" She chomped on her lower lip and then lowered her legs and stretched them in front of her. "She lived like a little pig - expecting someone to clean up behind her. As though that was normal. Logan and Collin know not to make those kinds of messes. It was awful."

"So your dad raised you like a normal kid, to make your bed and be responsible?"

"Yeah."

"Guess what? I grew up with maids. If I left my toys, someone picked them up. Then I went to prep school. Talk about a rude awakening." He played with a small white rock next to where he was sitting. "It was the best thing that could have happened to me. I learned to clean up behind myself. My little place on campus is smaller than my bedroom at my parents' house. I like things clean and neat. I like going to the grocery store and figuring out how to cook something. There's a freedom there that isn't easy to explain to someone who's never been coddled."

He picked the small rock up, and rolled it over in his hand. "Not being at the mercy of someone else…" He tossed the small rock into the creek bed. "Your dad did you a favor."

"He said he kept the press away from me."

"Do you question that?"

She nodded.

"I don't know if it is even the same, but look at some of the Hollywood crowd whose parents are mega billionaires. Would you rather be them or yourself?"

"How would I ever know?"

"You won't, but I'm glad you are who you are, or I would have never met you. You wouldn't be doing a job that you love, and we wouldn't be sitting here."

"You make it seem simple."

"It is. You're heir to an oil fortune and I'm heir to the third largest delivery service in the world."

"I never thought of that. I guess you are."

"There's one more thing to consider."

"What's that?"

"I've fallen in love with you and if I don't get to take you in my arms and kiss you the way you deserve, I'm going to explode. And if I do get to kiss you the way I want to kiss you, I'll still explode."

She grinned and leaned towards him. He put his hands on her waist and pulled her over his body as he leaned back against the hard ground.

She buried her face against his neck and then inched lower, unbuttoning his shirt as she went. The cool air nipped at his hot skin.

She gazed at him from someplace near the top of his jeans.

"Got a condom?"

He fumbled with an inside zippered pocket of his coat and produced one. "Before you go further, answer me truthfully. Are you a virgin?"

"Does it matter?"

"Yes and no. If you are, I'd prefer to know because I don't want to hurt you. Other than that, it doesn't matter to me. I'm not going to mind a woman who knows exactly what she's doing."

"Oh, I know what I'm doing and I love doing it."

She freed him from the confines of his pants, covered him, and took him with her mouth.

His hands fisted at his sides as he drew one knee up. Fire burned within him as she ignited firecracker after firecracker deep within him.

Five

Julia had plenty of experience with boys her own age, but Aaron was no boy and this time, she was playing for keeps. She didn't want to go back to the house. She wanted to stay with Aaron except the temperature kept dropping and the sky had gone from blue to pink and orange. She could have galloped back and made it in time to change for dinner, but Aaron wasn't confident in a western saddle. They were going to be late, too late to eat with the family. She pulled her phone from her pocket and called her dad.

"Where are you?"

"West of the house, maybe another twenty minutes. I lost track of time." She giggled to herself. "Aaron rides English and he's not comfortable in a western saddle. Please ask if the family will wait for us. I'm really sorry."

She heard her father expel a breath before saying, "Just hurry up."

"I will." She disconnected the call and then turned to Aaron. "We need to at least trot. We both must be dressed for dinner."

Aaron nodded and nudged his horse. "Are you spending the night in the bungalow with me?"

"If I got caught, I'd be in so much trouble. Keep your butt in the saddle, you don't post when riding western."

"I know."

"But you're doing it."

He grinned. "Habit. So sneak out and join me. You're an adult. What is he going to say? You're a bad girl? If he does, tell him yes and you're very good at it."

"Oh, you are bad."

"And you're very good."

It was almost a quarter after six when Julia joined the family for dinner. Her father had managed to delay everything by suggesting they enjoy some hors d'oeuvres while relaxing with drinks. Julia had warned Aaron that they dressed for dinner, and he looked handsome in his dark brown suit, ivory shirt, and a tie that matched his irresistible golden-green eyes.

She had pulled her slightly damp hair into a bun, then purposely dressed in something with lots of buttons and layers. She wanted to enjoy each article of clothing as it was removed. Her tongue darted between her lips and Aaron caught the movement. A slight smile pulled at her cheeks. *Oh yes. This is going to be fun.*

***

Aaron paced the floor of the bungalow wondering if Julia was coming or not. They had spent the entire evening with her father, DeeDee, and the grandparents. A few times he felt as though her grandfather was skewering and grilling him, but he maintained a relaxed demeanor and coupled it with the business persona that his father had taught him. He was certain he had passed every test they tossed his way.

Images of the evening played through his head, but the thought of holding Julia in his arms clouded his mind as testosterone raced through his system. He felt like a buck during rutting season. He checked the time again. Forty-three minutes since they had parted. Almost ready to give up, he heard the click of her heels on the pavement outside.

His doe had come and he intended to give her a night she'd never forget.

***

Julia never considered herself innocent but up until now, her experience was with one male friend as they figured out where the body parts went. Being with Aaron was completely different. Her clothes were scattered from the living room to the bedroom. She picked up hers and slipped each one on as she found it. She went back, collected Aaron's from where they lay on the floor, then folded them, and put them in a neat pile.

The glow from an electric wall sconce was enough to see his naked body sprawled across the bed. He wasn't quite as tall as her father. As she looked at Aaron, she decided he was the exact opposite of her father in every way. Her father's coloring was icy cold compared to Aaron's buttery warm complexion. She leaned against the bedroom door frame and stared at the sleeping man who had made love to her so many times that she wasn't certain her legs would hold her upright.

Up until meeting Aaron, she would have said that she didn't care for a freckled redhead. They just didn't seem sexy, but Aaron oozed sexy from every part of his body. She couldn't just walk away from him so she tiptoed over and dropped a light kiss on his forehead. His hands found her and pulled her downward.

"Where are you going, my love?"

"Back to my room before I get caught."

"I don't want you to leave. I want you in my bed every night for as long as I live."

"Not going to happen."

His lips crashed over hers, igniting another firestorm within her. She pulled away and gasped for air. "I've got to go, it's almost dawn. You don't want me caught out here with you."

His hand traveled up her leg to her panties. "No, you don't. These are mine."

He rolled her over and slipped them off of her.

"You have some sort of fetish when it comes to women's underwear?"

He grinned down at her. "Only yours."

He played with her until he brought her to another orgasm.

Still trembling, she slipped from the bed and smoothed her skirt over her legs. "I've got to go." Butterflies danced over every muscle in her body as she stepped out of the bedroom. "See you at brunch. Sunday morning is very informal."

She glanced around the small cabana living room and then opened the door that led to the main house. *If I set my alarm for nine-thirty, that's fours of sleep.*

***

Holding her shoes in one hand, Julia sprinted silently across the hardwood floors and started up the stairs to her room. The distinct cocking sound of a shotgun stopped her in her tracks. She waited, listened, and then with caution, took the remaining steps.

At the far end of the hall, rumbled the deep voice of her

grandfather. "Where were you, young lady?"

Her insides clenched into a tight ball and she stopped. There was no point in lying, but maybe she could make it sound more innocent. "With Aaron."

"At this hour?"

"Yes, sir. We don't have much time together and I didn't want to spend it sleeping."

"So you spent the night with him?"

"We fell asleep."

He strode to where she was standing and grabbed her chin.

She stared into his blue eyes. He looked somewhat like an older, slightly heavier version of her father except where her dad was dark her grandfather was gray.

She shuttered her eyes from his intense scrutiny. She could feel every fiber of her body and it wasn't a pleasant feeling. "Please let me go to my room."

"Your room? Do you even know where you're supposed to be sleeping? Did it ever dawn on you that sleeping with a boyfriend is unacceptable behavior?"

"Please, let me go." Her bladder decided to protest the situation and the urgency was getting worse. She squeezed her thighs together.

"What is going on?" Cody's voice boomed as he stepped from his bedroom.

"Daddy, please. I'll explain everything later. I need to use the bathroom." She wiggled away from her grandfather's grip and flew to her room.

"I'll see you in fifteen minutes downstairs." Her father's command sent a shot of panic into her already knotted guts. She knew she hadn't been in this much trouble since she was in sixth grade and was caught cheating on a test.

***

Showered and wearing jeans with a long-sleeved tee shirt, Julia crept down the stairs and found her father, grandfather, and Aaron sitting in the breakfast room. The scent of freshly brewed coffee hung in the air. She listened for a moment.

Aaron was cool, almost cold, as he sat at the table. "She might be your granddaughter but she is of legal age. What we do or don't do when we are together is between us."

Omigod, don't say that to my grandfather. She entered the kitchen and fixed a cup of coffee from the full pot that had finished brewing. She fixed one mug for her father and one for Aaron. "May I fix a cup for you, Granddad?"

"I'll do it myself."

She took her cup and sat beside Aaron. *What's the worst he can do to me? Take my money away?* She waited.

Her grandfather's eyes were narrowed and his lips were drawn in a straight line. Her father's brow was furrowed and he had a slight twitch at the temple. She put her hand on Aaron's leg.

Aaron put one hand on the back of her neck. The gesture was sweet and reassuring.

"Thanks for the coffee." Her father held his mug between the table and his mouth. "But your behavior is inappropriate and I'm disappointed in both of you." He looked directly at Aaron. "You're not a kid. You know better. What you did was disrespectful to Julia and to her entire family."

Aaron rolled his one hand over so it was palm up. "We meant

no harm." He looked at Julia. "We had hoped to have more time together, but she had to come here."

Julia watched her grandfather walk out the back door. Her insides had turned to mush and she knew she only had to get through this interrogation without letting on that they had done anything more than fallen asleep.

Cody nodded. "I realize there's something going on between the two of you that seems serious. I know who your father is and I've met him on several occasions over the years. He has an excellent reputation within the business community. Therefore I believe he's raised you to be a good person and a man of his word."

"Thank you, sir. My father would be pleased with your assessment. He thinks highly of the Montgomery family."

The elder Montgomery came back into the house and dropped Julia's panties in the middle of the kitchen table.

Heat flowed up her neck and over her cheeks.

Aaron reached over, picked them up and pocketed the tiny bright red lace as if it were perfectly natural for him to possess them. "This inquisition is adjourned. We are consenting adults." Aaron stood. "It was a pleasure to meet everyone." He turned to Julia. "Would you prefer to return with your father or do you want to leave with me?"

Cody stood. "I hope that if someday you have a daughter, a man will never ask her to choose between her family and him."

Aaron looked at Julia's father. "I hope that when that day comes, you will never degrade your granddaughter by placing her in such a position because Julia will be my wife."

Aaron put his hands on Julia's shoulders as he stood behind where she was sitting. The gesture sent a comforting warmth down her spine.

"I teach at one of the finest universities in this country and I'm more than aware of the behavior of the students. Julia's mother was no virgin when she married you and I'm certain you spent many a night with her. I am not asking her to choose, I'm giving her an option."

"What is going on in here?" DeeDee asked as she pulled her bulky robe tighter to her body.

Cody looked at his wife. "I've made a grave mistake and treated my oldest daughter as though she was still a child."

Julia saw what appeared to be moisture collecting in her father's eyes. She had only seen him cry twice. Once when his grandfather had died and again when he discovered that none of his children were of his blood.

Cody stood, put his hand out to Aaron, and Aaron took it.

"I'm sorry, Aaron. I should have put a stop to this when it started. I've only tried to protect my daughter from making the mistakes that I have made."

"I accept your apology." Aaron turned to Julia's grandfather. "I'm sorry if I have offended you."

Aaron started to leave. Julia looked at her father, then took off with Aaron.

***

Aaron woke to Julia still curled against his chest. They had both been exhausted as they climbed in bed. He had wanted to make love to her one more time, but their night together had left him incapable of even seriously considering such antics. He had been content to hold her in his arms. He doubted he'd had a total of three hours sleep, but he knew it would be enough. Salt Lake City was not that far away and the ranch was not that far from the interstate. Mentally he made plans to stop for food and coffee about half way. That would allow him to stretch his legs. He made his way to the living room of the bungalow and found several notes that had been taped to the windowpanes in the door.

He peeled one off and read it.

Julia, I hope I will see you later today and that you will return to the salon as my manager. I'm totally appalled at this family's behavior.

The second one was from Julia's father.

I love you and again I apologize to you and to Aaron. Dad

But it was the third one that intrigued him and made him smile.

Julia and Aaron, You are both welcome to have Sunday brunch with the rest of the family. I told that old fart of mine he had no right to stick his nose where it didn't belong. Apparently you set off the alarm when you returned to the house. Don't you worry about a thing. There are too many boys in this family. I'm already putting in my request for great-granddaughters. I want a half dozen of them, little Annies with red curls. Tell Aaron he's welcome here for Christmas and I'll make sure you both get the bungalow. Your aunt and uncle can sleep in her old room. Love, Grandmom

Julia stood in the doorway of the bedroom and stretched as she yawned. When she wasn't wearing those super high heels, she almost looked petite. He handed her the notes. "Your family."

***

After a leisurely but slightly awkward and stilted brunch where the adults all seemed to be extra polite to one another, Aaron said goodbye to Julia's family and prepared to return to his place on campus.

In the privacy of the bungalow, Julia wrapped her arms around him. "I don't want you to go."

"I don't want to leave you. You're spoiling me with your kisses."

"Oh, I think you like more than my kisses."

"I do. It's going to be a very cold winter without you."

Her hands ran over his chest and down the front of his jeans. She smiled at him. "One more time?"

He groaned as she freed him from the confines of his jeans.

***

By that evening, Aaron was back in his small place on campus. He knew Julia was still in-flight. He dropped his duffle bag by the washer and began to sort his dirty clothes. Loneliness settled over him.

This semester was almost over and he had one more to go. With his PhD in hand, he had more than a few choices. He could continue to teach, go into research, or return directly to his father's business. Figuring he'd be dealing with the delivery business soon enough and having come this far, he hoped he'd have a chance to actually do some research beyond the university.

There was a lab in River City and the research looked promising. He wouldn't be far from his father's offices and he wouldn't be that far from where Julia worked. He needed to find that application and apply.

The concept of a house floated through his mind as he closed the door to the washer. If they both worked that meant they'd be sharing the responsibility of the household chores unless they hired someone. There were serious things he needed to discuss with Julia.

Over the next few weeks, they did discuss their future. But Julia was unsure of how she was going to manage her time. She apparently had responsibilities to SunWest, and she was swamped at the salon. And with the upcoming New York fashion show in February, DeeDee stayed so busy that she turned over the day-to-day management of the salon to Julia.

Every night, Julia bubbled with enthusiasm as she spoke about her day. Her people skills were obviously excellent. And the more work DeeDee dumped on Julia, the happier Julia was. He laughed at her passion. Anyone else would have crumbled under the stress but not his Julia. Like a long leaf pine seed after a wild fire, she sprouted, and grew at a tremendous rate.

She had decorated the salon for Christmas and used a red wedding dress embellished with poinsettias made from sequins as center stage. Bursting with pride, Julia had taken several pictures with her phone and sent them to him. He didn't care what women wore for their weddings, but he knew it was a big thing for most women.

When his sister married, he had to wear a tuxedo. There was a cummerbund, and buttons that were like tiny cuff links. He even wore spats on his shoes. It took him forever to get dressed with all those extras and his mom fussed that his shirt wasn't tucked into his pants tight enough. She was tugging and tucking his shirt into his pants as though he was still eight years old. The old memories made him laugh.

A few days later, Aaron discovered he had a Christmas card from Mr. and Mrs. Douglas Montgomery. Doug was Cody's older brother who lived on the ranch, but everyone had called him DJ. This card was from the elder Montgomery family members. Inside the beautiful card, was a note in a hand-written flourish that made it almost difficult to read. Mrs. Montgomery was extending an invitation to spend Christmas with them.

> *Cody and family will arrive on December 26 and will stay through January 2. I will assume you want to spend time with my granddaughter, Julia. As promised, our little bungalow will be available for the two of you. That stogy old man of mine has been very contrite and has apologized again to Julia. I expect he will do the same when he sees you. Please forgive him. Times have changed, but he's failed to realize that. You are welcome at our home anytime. If you'd like to come early (December 24) and spend Christmas with us, we'd love to have you. I'd hate to think our future grandson-in-law would be alone for Christmas.*
> *Lois Montgomery*
> *RSVP*

A chill swept through Aaron as he deciphered the words on

the fancy paper. The idea of spending Christmas there had more appeal than spending it in his tiny place and he had already informed his parents that he would not be home for Christmas. He had expected his mom to dissolve into tears, instead she acted thrilled. She intended to book a cruise to the Mediterranean immediately, saying it was something she had always wanted to do at Christmas. But the thought of being at the Montgomery's house without Julia was a bit awkward, especially after the way the grandfather had acted.

He was living in limbo. He had turned in his thesis. The semester was over, tests graded and final marks were returned. He only had to wait and teach one last semester. But the wait would seem like an eternity and he knew it.

He picked up his phone and pushed a series of numbers. "Hello, I need to speak directly to DeeDee Montgomery, is she available by any chance?" "No this is personal."

His guts knotted as he was put on hold. He didn't want to talk to Julia.

"This is DeeDee speaking, how may I help you?"

He breathed out the tension that had built within him. "This is Aaron, I need to speak privately to you."

"Of course."

"Good, I was worried I was on a speaker phone and Julia was in the room."

"Heavens no, I'm at the factory, she's at the salon. Is something wrong?"

"No. I just need help. I want to buy Julia an engagement ring and I don't know her size. Can you somehow get that for me?"

"That shouldn't be a problem."

Total relief flooded him. "Thanks. Don't let on, I want it to be a surprise."

"I'm very good with secrets. And for the record, if you are looking for a slightly different stone, she loves the color of deep purple amethysts. It really is a beautiful color on her and she wears a size 9 in clothing."

"Thanks, I'll remember that. Do you have one more minute to spare?"

"Certainly. How else may I help you?"

Okay, here goes. "I've been given an invitation to the ranch while you guys are visiting and it includes Christmas Eve and Christmas. What are your thoughts on that situation?"

"You mean spending Christmas there?"

"Yes."

"Cody does Christmas here with his children and then leaves on the twenty-sixth for his parents."

"I gathered that."

"I have to say I'm amazed that they invited you to spend Christmas there considering what happened, but it sounds like something Cody's mom would do. She's a very sweet person."

"Yes. She's the one who invited me."

"Oh, do it. They love company, especially my mother-in-law. The more the merrier." DeeDee giggled. "Go. Don't stay home alone when you can be with another family."

"Okay. Thanks for your time."

"Anytime."

He disconnected the call and made a few more. He needed a ring.

***

The morning of Christmas Eve, Aaron woke to snow falling on top of an old layer of snow. Considering his drive was mostly on the interstate, he figured he wasn't going to have too much trouble. He tossed a few items into his duffle bag, drank the last of the milk in the refrigerator, fixed a sandwich for the road, and took off for the Montgomery ranch. The prediction was for a few inches of snow so he didn't expect any problems, but he was prepared in case the weather worsened. In spite of the flurries, he made good time and arrived at the ranch slightly before noon.

Mrs. Montgomery greeted him with a big smile and a hug. "That's such a beautiful fruit basket you sent. I almost hated to touch it, but we've been nibbling on it since it has arrived."

"I believe it's meant to be eaten."

Mrs. Montgomery laughed. "My husband and I shared a most delicious grapefruit this morning at breakfast. I find it amazing that they manage to have that much perfect fruit."

He nodded. He had more than an inkling of how it was bought and stored. "I'm glad you are enjoying it."

"You know where the bungalow is, so make yourself at home. We'll have lunch as soon as you are ready." She put her hand on his arm. "Oh, and there's a big box that came here addressed to you. I had someone put in the bungalow."

"Thanks. It's filled with Christmas gifts."

It took him a few minutes to empty his duffle, hang his suit, and inspect his shirts for wrinkles. Nothing looked permanently wrinkled and he was certain that hanging for a few hours would be all that was needed. But without Julia, the place was as lonely as his.

He slipped several packages under the Christmas tree that sat in the small living room of the bungalow. He had no intention of giving her those in front of her family. The rest could go into the main house with all the others. Most of the time he gave no thought to money, but this was one time he was glad he had the money to give generous gifts to her family and extended family.

Content with things in the bungalow, he strode to the house. Lunch appeared almost immediately. Mr. Montgomery did apologize for his behavior, but tried to explain that he was genuinely upset with such conduct.

Aaron didn't want a long discussion over any of it. "I'm twenty-eight. I understand your position, so please understand mine. I have no desire to rehash events. I accept your apology and I hope this ends any further contention. Julia will be my wife."

Mrs. Montgomery put down her fork. "Have you asked her?"

"I plan to ask for her father's blessing first and then I will formally ask her."

She put one perfectly manicured hand to her chest. "Oh, that is so sweet. I didn't know if young men still did that. Douglas asked my father for my hand."

"I know my opinion doesn't seem to count." Mr. Montgomery grumbled. "But I doubt Julia will be satisfied being married to a professor."

Aaron swallowed hard to keep from choking on his food. "We've discussed finances on several occasions. I know my father will demand a signed pre-nup in spite of her ability to live comfortably on her own. National Delivery is not a small company. We're not as large as SunWest, but there's plenty at stake, and I do have an older sister who is also part of the company."

Watching the old man's face was worth it. "Your father owns

that company?"

"Yes, sir." He turned to Mrs. Montgomery. "Symons, spelled with a *y* and not an *i*. My father and mother are both from Wales."

***

Christmas morning in the elder Montgomery household was a combination of quiet and then chaos as DJ's children descended on the grandparents. Six boys and two girls ranging from twenty to four were spoiled, noisy, and totally out of control. It was easy to see why Cody Montgomery had chosen to raise his children in a small town and without the trappings of major wealth.

Cody's sister practically snarled at him for staying in the bungalow and he knew why. But when the twenty-year-old grandson picked up an orange from a bowl on the table and viciously threw it at a younger sibling during Christmas brunch, and no one said a thing, Aaron had enough.

He stood and placed a hand on the boy's shoulder. "We're taking a walk and having man-to-man talk. Grab your coat, now!" He gazed at the family. "Excuse us."

He was used to handling insubordinate students, although he never had more than the normal, college-student antics.

Away from the family, Douglas the Third, calmed down. And in less than five minutes, Aaron realized he'd had the young man in one of his classes. "So why do you allow your younger brother to goad you?"

"I don't know. Patterns we fall into when we're together?"

"Okay, it's time to stop it. You're the oldest. You've got to put the brakes on it."

"How?"

"He's your brother. You need to figure it out. But until you do, I'd suggest you stay away from him. You're how old?"

"Twenty."

Aaron shook his head. "No longer are you part of that little boy crowd. I'm not saying you can't enjoy playing video games. I enjoy them, just haven't had time to play in the last few years. But being grown up is more than chronological age. You have to act grown up. There's an old saying that he can't chase you if you don't run."

"You got little brothers?"

"No. I was the little brother. Suddenly the fun was gone because I couldn't tease my sister anymore. That's when I started to grow up and realize I had changed along with her."

"You make it sound simple."

"It's not. Just make certain that you don't stoop to their level."

They walked along the snow-powdered driveway in silence for quite a ways. Aaron knew he needed to say more. "Julia is younger than you. Your paths are different, but I consider Julia a grown woman. I can't imagine her tossing an orange at one of her siblings. She's managing DeeDee's store and the employees in it."

"I heard about that."

"She's stepped away from childhood and embraced adulthood. You need to do the same. You also need to buckle down and work harder. If I remember correctly, you barely passed my class."

"You gave me a 2.1."

"I didn't give you anything. It's what you earned. I only count up the scores."

"I already know I've got you this coming semester."

"Good. And now you know that you can come to me for any help you need. My door is always open to all my students. Just remember at the end of the semester, I only count up the scores. You get the grade that you've earned."

Douglas the Third gazed at Aaron, and he smiled back at the young man. It seemed as though all DJ's children had the blue eyes of their grandparents. Cody's family was the exception. Aaron loved Julia's dark eyes and dark hair. Her hair wasn't as black as her father's. Hers had a warm undertone to it.

In less than twenty-two hours, Aaron would see her and be able to wrap her in his arms.

"Hey, I'm getting cold."

Aaron looked at the young man walking beside him. "Okay, D3, let's head back."

Douglas the Third laughed. "I like D3. Do I get to call you Aaron on campus?"

"Only in private."

The rest of Christmas day progressed with fewer problems. The youngest Douglas had followed Aaron's advice. He stood a little straighter and hung close to his father and grandfather.

***

Julia practically flew into the bungalow and into Aaron's waiting arms. A whole week together was going to be wonderful, but Aaron had one more hurdle before he could relax and enjoy his time with Julia. He shooed Julia to the bathroom to freshen up after her long flight.

She changed into a fuzzy red Christmas sweater paired with

black pants. She looked stunning. It was hard to believe that she was a year younger than D3. Julia was pure woman, and D3 hadn't finished growing up.

Wind whipped between the two houses blowing away the powdery snow that had fallen. In spite of wearing coats as they made the short trek, they were both freezing as they entered the house and hung their outer garments on the hooks by the door.

When Aaron finished hanging up Julia's coat, he smiled. "I need to talk to your dad for just a moment."

Julia raised her eyebrows but didn't question him. The sexual tension between them sparked and sizzled, and no matter how hard he tried to ignore it, it wasn't going away. The heat in his groin grew, but the need to speak to her father kept sending ice water through him.

He greeted DeeDee and the siblings, but when he shook hands with Cody Montgomery, his mouth went dry. "Sir, I'd like to speak with you...alone...for three minutes. If you don't mind."

Cody looked at his watch. "Let's step into my father's den."

Aaron followed the man into a room that was huge. A large ornately carved desk occupied space at one end. Cody turned on several lamps at the far end, illuminating a seating area filled with soft leather chairs and a couch. Two Christmas trees made of welded horseshoes stood like sentries on each side of the large fireplace. In general, the room looked more like a hunting lodge than an office with its large selection of taxidermy animals.

The palms of Aaron's hands were damp and the back of his neck prickled. This was it; no turning back. He'd marry Julia with or without permission, but *with* the man's blessing would be better. Not wanting to sit, he stood behind one of the chairs for a moment and then decided that was the chicken's position. He stepped over to the fireplace, and cleared his throat, but the lump instantly reformed, so he swallowed.

"Sir, I intend to marry Julia. I'd like to know that I have your blessing before I formally ask her."

Cody took a chair and sat. "I gathered that was your intent, and I've heard Julia talking to DeeDee about it. She's still very young. I don't want her making a mistake, but you are older than I was the first time I married. I know she's adamant about marrying you. It's not my job to rule my children's lives or to decide whom they should love. In fact, I've made plenty of mistakes in that department."

Aaron looked at the man sitting there. The tension he'd harbored over this moment dissolved like fireworks fizzling and was replaced by a sense of sadness. Julia had told him about her siblings and her father's failed marriages. They had discussed infidelity and trust. "I'll never run around on her. I was raised to believe that you marry once and work out any problems. I fell in love with Julia the first time I saw her."

The memory of seeing her at a distance floated through his mind. She was talking to someone in another room. It was as though she had a magnetic charge to her. "I tried to ignore the feelings, but they weren't going away. I wasn't sure how I'd manage to approach her, but a few weeks later, I had the chance to grab that route again when the regular driver needed a few days off. She opened the door for that delivery and the rest is history. I'm a science major; cause and effect."

Julia's dad looked up and chuckled. "Treat her right."

"I will. Don't ever worry about that." He reached in his pocket and showed off the ring he'd bought. "I really do love her."

"By the way, I'm not old enough for you to even attempt to

call me Dad so just keep it to Cody and I think DeeDee will feel the same way."

It was all Aaron could do to eat another big meal. Christmas Eve had been turkey, Christmas had been a roast, and tonight it was ham with all the trimmings. He could have quit eating after the salmon and shrimp appetizer, but he didn't. He even managed to eat some plum pudding.

As the plates were cleared and the coffee served, he considered asking Julia then but he wanted it to be a little more special. He waited until everyone had gathered in the living room. He was thankful that DJ's rambunctious family was not present, yet slightly surprised that DJ's oldest son, D3, had joined Cody's family. Maybe it was D3's way of separating himself from his younger brothers.

As the elder Mrs. Montgomery began to pass out the gifts, Aaron stood and called for everyone's attention. "Just a minute of your time." He looked at the twins, Colin and Logan. "This is important, okay?"

Logan nodded.

"Julia, we've talked about marriage, but in general terms. I think it's time we make this official." He dropped to one knee in front of her. "I, Aaron Symons, would like to officially ask the love of my life, Julia Montgomery, to become my wife for as long as we live."

"Oh..." Her eyes began to glisten with tears. "I love you."

"Will you accept this ring?"

She gasped as she took the ring from his fingers. "It's beautiful." She slipped it on her finger and admired it. "It fits perfectly. How?"

"I have my ways."

DeeDee whispered, "Julia, say yes."

"Oh! Yes, yes, yes, yes, until the end of time, yes!"

He wrapped Julia into his arms and the flame within him grew very bright…too bright to let go of her in front of her parents. Like a drop of oil that fell on a puddle and coated the entire surface with rainbows, he suddenly understood his parents. His father was just as madly in love with Ffiona when he'd asked her to be his bride thirty some years ago. Aaron couldn't imagine not feeling this wonderful attraction for Julia.

It was Sean and Ian's teasing that broke Julia from his arms.

"Oh, Julia, I want to see that ring!" DeeDee jumped from her seat. "Aaron, it's beautiful."

"We all want to see it, Julia." Her grandmother beckoned Julia to sit beside her.

Pride filled Aaron's chest like a balloon forcing him to take a deep breath as all the females in the family admired the ring, but when he saw the grandmother's smile, Aaron knew he had done the right thing. He looked over at Cody and the man rolled his hand over enough to give the thumbs up sign. The gesture was small but it meant everything. Aaron smiled back, took his phone from the clip on his side and texted his dad with the news that Julia had accepted the proposal and with Cody Montgomery's blessing.

The twins had waited long enough and began to protest. They wanted to open their presents.

348

Six

Julia watched as her sisters opened their gifts from Aaron and squealed with delight. Cody was never one to spoil them with expensive things and Aaron had bought both of her sisters expensive bracelets from a well-known jeweler. His gifts to her father and DeeDee were more practical, and all four of the boys were delighted with their gift certificates to the local game store back home and several fast-food restaurants.

Cody made the twins hand over their gift certificates so they didn't lose them in spite of the fact that all the boys had received fancy hand-tooled wallets from their grandparents.

The first chance that Julia dared, she bid her family goodnight and went to the bungalow with Aaron. She needed time - time to catch her breath, to admire her ring, and to tumble into Aaron's warm embrace.

But when she entered the bungalow, Aaron had other plans. He made hot chocolate and lowered the lights to just a few wall sconces giving the ambiance of candles. Then he handed her his gifts to her.

She opened the first one to find an amethyst and diamond necklace and earrings. "They are so lovely. You're spoiling me."

He laughed. "Open the other package. I intend to spoil you."

She pealed off the fancy wrapping paper and discovered six pairs of very skimpy, very sexy panties.

"I decided I can't keep taking yours away or you won't have any left. But I'm hoping you'll model each pair for me."

She giggled. "And is there something you'd like me to wear with them?"

"The necklace and earrings would be sufficient for me."

"You are so bad and I love you for it."

He drew her into his arms and kissed her. She had almost a whole week to spend with him, and she intended to savor every minute of their time.

***

Saying goodbye to Aaron was the hardest thing Julia ever had to do. But they both had commitments. Julia just wasn't certain about being committed to her job. There was no reason for her to work, just as her father didn't need to practice law to make a living.

Usually she'd watch a movie or sleep on her flight home from the ranch but this time, she curled up and pretended to sleep. She had to maintain her trust fund secret from her siblings. Not that anything horrible would happen if she let on, it was merely a simple request from her father. He wanted the others to have a normal childhood, even though she didn't consider the teens as children. That fact kept her from discussing the situation with her dad or DeeDee and left her alone for hours with her thoughts.

When she had discovered her wealth, her father had suggested that she take some time before she made any snap decisions and, since DeeDee counted on her, she had promised that she would return to work. It was the smartest thing she could do until she figured out what she really wanted to do with her life.

Spending time with Aaron had taken her mind off the money, even though she had discussed it with him. In many ways, he was in the same position, yet he worked and still went after his doctorate degree. He reasoned he loved what he did and knowing that he didn't have to go to school for his doctorate or teach to make a living, made it even more fun. He did it because he enjoyed doing it.

She thought about Aunt Barbara. Her degree in architecture meant she did what she loved for no other reason than the sheer joy of creating things.

DeeDee didn't have to open her own business or even design clothes. She could have bought a house someplace and lived comfortably for the rest of her life without ever working, yet she worked harder than most.

Julia's dad nudged her and she took the thin blanket he offered and drew it up over she shoulders. Not feeling the least bit cold, maybe the lightweight covering was a shield, something to allow her to hide in plain sight. She smiled at her father and curled on her side, tucking her feet onto the seat with her.

She closed her eyes as bits of her life flashed through her mind. Other kids from school always seemed to have goals. Most talked about college or doing something special. She couldn't imagine ever going to college, even now. Her hatred for school was too strong. There had never been the overwhelming desire to marry and have children. Instead, her teen years had been spent drifting aimlessly.

Then it struck her. From that very first day she went to work at the bridal salon, she had a purpose. It wasn't just a job. Maybe it should have been, but it never felt that way. She loved being there. She loved watching someone's face when they spotted the perfect gown. It was spinning magic and she was the magician. *It's where I belong.*

She sat up and looked at DeeDee. The woman was tucked against Cody while she sketched on a pad with colored pencils. Something inside of Julia wanted to scream for joy. Instead, she asked, "What are you working on?"

"Next Christmas. I have this idea for a white ice and frozen blue, and another for a wine red and sparkling gold."

"The white and blue sounds so beautiful, but what color red were you thinking about? A deep red of a cabernet wine or something lighter like a zinfandel?"

DeeDee smiled without looking up. "Lighter, think frozen. Take the normal wine-red color and drop it in a blender with ice and create a slush. And since when did you know so much about wines?"

She lifted her shoulders and let them drop. "Dad's always got wine around and I've enjoyed reading about them. He's let me cook with them a few times."

Cody looked at Julia and jerked his thumb in DeeDee'a direction as he chuckled. "Did you know that if I get her drunk, her clothes fall off?"

DeeDee playfully smacked him.

Julia giggled at their antics. She was happy to see her father so in love and to see DeeDee appreciate him. Julia knew her mom's name was Jenna, but she didn't remember the woman. And when her dad married Patty, she was furious. Everyone said she was jealous of Patty, but she wasn't. She was only ten at the time, but truly didn't like the woman.

Thinking back, she was too young to really know what was going on, but long after Patty's death and all the DNA testing, she realized that she was witnessing Patty running around on Cody and soaking him for money. When Cody was home, she was nice to all the kids in the house, but as soon as his back was turned, she became a total witch – especially to the girls.

Julia had wanted lime green sneakers with black stripes. Everyone wanted them and they were expensive. She had asked her dad for a pair and he sanctioned their purchase, but when Patty took her shopping the next day, Julia had stopped to look into a store window and admire something. That sent Patty into a rage. Julia had come home minus the new sneakers, with her long hair cut to her ears, and sent to bed without dinner.

Cody brought her a peanut butter and jelly sandwich and asked what had happened, except he didn't believe her. He had sided with Patty. From that moment onward, she refused to have anything to do with the woman, and danced with glee when the women died. As far as young Julia was concerned, the woman deserved to die for being so hateful to her and her sisters.

For weeks, Julia mixed salt into a bucket of water and poured a cupful over every rose bush in the garden along with anything else that the woman had planted. What she hadn't managed to kill became so sickly that her father removed it and had a landscaper redo the gardens. To this day, she couldn't look at a rose or a rose bush without thinking of the thorny woman named Patty.

That thought sent her back to the bouquet that Aaron had sent. There wasn't a single rose in it. Was it coincidence? She must have said something about not liking them, because he often sent her flowers and they never contained roses.

She watched DeeDee sketch for a few more moments. "I enjoyed having some time off, but I'm anxious to get back to work."

DeeDee looked up and smiled. "Does that mean you are extending your commitment to your job?"

Julia could feel the smile that pulled at her cheeks. "Oh, probably for the rest of my life. I knew from that very first day that I loved working there. And since I have your full attention, I was wondering if by chance you might want to consider a partnership arrangement because I'm doing exactly what I want to do."

***

Once back at the salon, Julia faced a mountain of work that had come in during the holidays. She didn't think she'd ever get all of it caught up, but by the end of the week, it was. Chrisy was also at the salon working with DeeDee and preparing for the big fashion show in New York. Most of the time, DeeDee connected with Chrisy by phone, unless there was a show or some other major event.

In a way, Julia liked Chrisy. He was the best promoter in the business. But seeing a man walk around in Karina Karr high heels just struck her as odd. DeeDee called him a peacock. He had a gray ponytail that hung to his waist and he'd wear all sorts of bright clothing. The combinations were almost mind boggling, but under all of it was the nicest man who treated DeeDee as though she was his daughter.

When Julia thought about it, Chrisy was extremely kind and thoughtful towards everyone connected to the salon. Julia knew Chrisy had a daughter who was probably DeeDee's age and a son about Aaron's age. And he wasn't a cross-dresser. He just like heels and outrageous clothing. Julia decided he was one of those people you accepted.

On top of all the normal orders, dresses were being made for the fashion show. The employees at the factory were overwhelmed with work, and Chrisy was always doing something to let them know how much they were appreciated. And if he wasn't at the factory, he was in the salon, which meant he frequently was in the office with Julia.

His ability to woo people was amazing. He admitted his technique was based on solid marketing principles, but he'd done it for so long, it came naturally. He had his own spin on it and his incredible, upbeat personality shined through it. Under his coaching, Julia was adding to her people skills.

As the date approached for the fashion show, DeeDee became a nervous wreck. Her normal calm had vanished, and even Julia's dad could do little to comfort his wife. Chrisy had everything in New York under control. The hotel rooms were booked, the show was booked, all the required fashion magazines and press were given passes. Chrisy even had the models lined up and ready. DeeDee wanted several plus sizes, and she wasn't talking about size twelve. Chrisy went after several budding actresses from some acting school in New York that fit DeeDee's description of curvy figures and booked them. The largest bridal fashion magazine was doing a huge spread on DeeDee. Someone from the magazine came and took photos of the factory and of the salon as well as interviewed DeeDee. The spread had been booked for over a year. It was just a matter of plugging in the images and words.

After working late, Julia would rush home and take a quick shower. There were several times she fell asleep while talking to Aaron. But he always seemed to understand.

February tenth, Julia left for New York. DeeDee had been there with Chrisy for almost a week. On the fifteenth, Aaron flew in and in spite of being thrilled to see him, Julia discovered that being in his arms was calming. For twenty-four hours, his presence was a huge shield from the chaos. But Chrisy swore the perceived madness was normal and that everything was running smoothly.

On the eighteenth, the show began. Julia knew exactly what she had to do and did it. From her spot backstage, she helped to make certain the whole thing went without a hitch. Cody sat in the audience the entire time and beamed with pride. When it was over, DeeDee and Karina joined the models on the runway and waved to the crowd. Julia knew the show had gone beautifully.

Julia looked carefully at the woman who was her boss, mentor, best friend, and stepmother. Standing there in the spotlight gave DeeDee a few additional curves that weren't noticeable in normal lighting. *She's pregnant!* That thought flowed through Julia's mind like a giant roller coaster. *I know you got your wish this time, Dad.*

They had been swamped with invitations prior to the show and after it, there were even more. DeeDee was being asked to do the talk show circuit and Chrisy wasn't going to let her off the hook.

Julia returned to the salon exhausted but happy. With DeeDee gone for several more days, she had even more responsibility heaped on her. She also had her own wedding to plan.

The online orders were pouring in. The magazine ads were creating even more business, and Chrisy was the force behind all of it. He called her more than DeeDee did, and if he couldn't reach her on the salon phone, he was calling her on her personal cell phone.

The dresses from the fashion show arrived and she had several of them altered to fit the mannequins. Then redid the windows. But with more dresses than would fit in the windows, she decided to order more mannequins. There was plenty of space in the salon and she could imagine brides-to-be wandering around looking at all the fabulous designs.

Julia picked up the phone. "DeeDee, you're not going to believe this. I found a company that makes mannequins for all shapes."

"All shapes?"

"Seems that way. And the prices aren't much different from what we've been paying. They are anatomically correct, no sixteen inch waists."

"Do whatever you think is right. See you Saturday night."

She ordered enough to show off almost every dress from the fashion show. A thought formed in Julia's head. She dug through the boxes of dresses that had been returned, and found the super dress. Instead of being embellished with regular embroidery, it had been decorated with spun gold threads. It was a huge hit and featured in several advertisements. It was shown once with white roses, another time with gardenias, and the last time it was modeled, it had been paired with petite sunflowers. The hem of the dress contained special pockets to hold tiny vials where live flowers were inserted. It was to be outrageously expensive and DeeDee wasn't taking orders for it until after May 31.

Julia thought about the work sitting on her desk. *It can wait.*

She locked herself into a dressing room and tried the super dress on. The front of the bodice resembled a trellis with embroidered gold leaves. It covered what had to be covered yet it was sexy and classic at the same time. She couldn't wear it without major alterations. The beautiful Swedish model was probably ten pounds lighter and eight inches taller. She twisted a few times and her nipples showed. *If I move the wrong way…omigod, my father would have my hide!*

She found her pager and called for Winnie to help. The woman barely spoke English but seemed to understand it perfectly. She was the premiere seamstress and did things that no one else could do.

At the tiny knock, Julia opened the dressing room door. "I think it needs a new bodice for me." She wiggled and pointed to her breasts. "Nothing must show. Nothing!"

Winnie said something in French and vanished. She returned with a tape measure and a scrap of paper. She measured this way and that. Once, she poked Julia in the tummy and that caused Julia to suck in and hold her breath. Then Winnie said something about Julia's panties that showed through the lattice that hung very low on her stomach.

"Yes, I know about my panties. I can't wear these."

The woman dropped the bodice to Julia's waist and continued to measure. Jabbering away in French as she did, and stopping only long enough to write a few measurements, she eventually dropped the whole dress and took measurements of Julia's waist and hips.

The older woman mumbled and walked away. Julia wasn't certain, but she had a feeling Winnie Kochang wasn't very happy. There was an inordinate amount of hand-sewn embroidery in that bodice and skirt and obviously the entire dress would be made from scratch for her.

Most 'showcase' super fashions are never meant to be worn, they are one-of-a-kinds that are only intended for wowing a crowd. *I'm going to wear this one.*

Julia slipped back into her clothes and headed for her office. She called Jim Lapinski, the owner and designer at the florist shop down the street. "Mr. Lapinski, what flowers bloom with an amethyst color in June?"

"Considering amethyst covers from the palest of pinks to almost a purple-blue, why don't you send me a color swatch and I'll be able to give you a much better idea."

"I'll do that."

"How many flowers will you need?"

"I'll say two hundred if they are at least two inches in diameter."

"We can do carnations in any color."

"They won't work. Remember those little vials you ordered for us?"

"Oh, that does change things. Send whoever it is down here and I'll show off a few flowers."

"It's for me."

"You? Little Julia Montgomery is getting married?"

"Shh! I haven't announced it yet. Please don't say anything."

"The only thing with ears around here is the cat. Your secret is safe. Who's the lucky guy?"

She grinned. "You'll know soon enough."

Seven

Julia checked the online orders and smiled at the one from Canada. With the wedding planned for July, there was almost three months lead time. *That's rare!* Judging from the styles and colors that had been chosen, she knew this would be a fun wedding and not a stuffy somber one. She dropped all the measurements into the database under the bride's name, Brooke Eldridge, Eastport, Ontario. Then she checked on the amount of pink tulle that would be needed for the bridesmaid's skirts and ordered the extra fabric. There was more than enough ivory-white tulle in stock for the bridal gown. She double checked the beaded bodice fabric, and ordered the pink stiletto heels from Karina before she placed the order in queue. She couldn't explain it, but there was a happy feeling that came with this order.

With a smile still on her face, Julia fixed another cup of coffee, and continued to go through the orders. What is it about today? She looked at one order and reread it. *Shamrocks and lemons? And on the boots?* She picked up the phone and called Karina.

Whoever answered the phone at Karina Karr shoes must have been new, because as soon as Julia said Main Street Bridal, the woman put her on hold. Instead of transferring her to one of Karina's assistants, she got Karina.

After the normal chitchat between them, Julia asked Karina

about the request for the boots. "Yes, that's the request, shamrocks and lemons on western boots. Item #1642"

"Tell DeeDee to email me the design and I'll do it." There wasn't even a hint of surprise in Karina's voice.

Julia probably could have asked for real leprechauns sitting on the toes and Karina wouldn't have flinched. The woman had a can-do attitude that was amazing.

Julia went in search of DeeDee and found her with Winnie. "Excuse me; this is going to need your attention."

DeeDee took the printed order. "Did you call Karina?"

"Yes. She wants you to send her the design and she'll do it."

DeeDee nodded. "I'll create the design and you can send it back to the bride for approval this afternoon. As soon as you have the okay from the bride, send it over to Karina. Just don't process the orders until we have the bride's acceptance."

DeeDee lifted her eyebrows. "Shamrocks and lemons? There must be some reason or significance behind it." Then she smiled. "The color combo will be beautiful. We give the brides whatever they want and if that's what she wants, she will get it."

Some days went smoother than others but no matter what was going on, Julia felt as though she could keep things flowing. She was still learning, but she had a good handle on the day-to-day operations. On most Wednesday and Friday afternoons, she'd sit with DeeDee and they'd discuss whatever was happening. They were still a small business and DeeDee preferred to keep them somewhat exclusive, even though most of her dresses were very affordable.

"I don't want to ask you to do it. You've taken on way too much as it is. But what I need would only be extremely part-time work if I hired someone." DeeDee sat back in her chair as she tapped her pen on the edge of her desk.

"I'll do it. I don't mind. Really I don't."

DeeDee shook her head. "I'm thinking I should hire someone who can handle all our Internet needs. We need to expand our presence. I was hoping you would know someone."

Julia touched the tip of her fingernail against a front tooth for a second before holding up her finger in front of her. "Actually, I do know someone, and he has a part-time job working for Elizabeth at the coffee shop."

DeeDee knitted her eyebrows. "Who?"

"Luke. He's been going to the community college for computers. He's a lot like Sean, but Sean is a gamer. Luke is...well, Luke. I can't explain him. He's just darn good with computer stuff. And if he doesn't want to do it, I'm sure he knows someone if he's getting his degree in computers."

"Maybe you need to visit the coffee shop. You could ask him."

"I have a better idea. I'll ask if he knows anyone who would be interested in the job. He might want it or he might know who to pass the opportunity to. Really, it is a girl job."

"You know I don't make gender distinctions, even though this is primarily a female business."

The phone rang and DeeDee answered it. "Amy Nguyen? Yes, I remember you. You came to the salon with your friend when she needed a bridesmaid dress." "Madeline Quinn?" "Let me check."

From where Julia was sitting she could see DeeDee searching a database.

"Yes. I have her. It was a bridesmaid dress." "Oh, not really. Um, sometimes. Give me a second. Let me put you on hold." "Julia, do we have anything that would only require some slight alterations to fit…" She scribbled a few measurements onto a pad of paper.

Julia looked at the measurements and grabbed the other computer in DeeDee's room. "Got it. Ivory, embroidered silk, strapless, full skirt, Item #458."

DeeDee pulled up the number. "Amy, do you have a computer handy? It's in my wear-again collection." "Tell me where you want it sent, your place or to your hotel room in Las Vegas?"

DeeDee typed the information into the database. "No problem. This laces, which is very forgiving and it looks like the only thing we need to do is hem it. If you had called me last week, we could have done anything you wanted from scratch."

DeeDee sent the order to the printer, cupped her hand over the phone, and said, "Handle that for me before you head down to Elizabeth's for a cup of coffee."

***

A few days later, Julia was ordering fabric when the salon beeped her. Mrs. Prentiss had a bride and the bride's mother, and things weren't going well. Julia was good at smoothing feathers and this bride's mother had her feathers ruffled. That's when Julia decided that often their biggest problems didn't come from the brides, but rather their mothers who were determined to do things against the daughters' wishes.

By the time Julia got back to her office, she was way behind on her own work. She closed her door with the hopes it would allow her to concentrate. It didn't work. She looked up and answered the knock.

Mrs. Prentiss came in with a box. "Hate to tell you this, but this just came with a *rush* note attached to it."

"Another dress?"

Mrs. Prentiss nodded. "I don't understand."

"I think there was so much pressure on everyone over the show - mistakes were made."

"I looked up the original order and attached it to the top of the box. Do you want me to send it to the factory?"

"Thanks for printing the order." Julia stood and went to check the paperwork. When she saw the name Main Street Bridal in Kentucky, her stomach clenched. "Oh, no! There's not much time. I'm sure the bride is panicking. We don't have time to let this process normally. I'll take it to the back, right now. There's not enough time to send it to the factory. It will have to be handled here."

DeeDee and Chrisy had worked hard to get dresses into quite a few privately owned bridal and dress shops in the United States and even a few in Canada. DeeDee had even made sample dresses that she could send to these salons. The last thing they needed was a problem. Julia grabbed a note pad and wrote the name and phone number down. She would call to profusely apologize and assure them that Claire Ramsay would have a new dress in just a few days.

Chrisy always said that the vast majority of problems could be handled smoothly. This was a fixable problem, but to the bride, it probably seemed impossible. Julia's job was to bridge that gap.

"Thanks, Mrs. Prentiss, for bringing this directly to me. I'm going to give it to Miz Edith and when I return to my desk I'll call the shop."

"Do you have enough time to fix it?"

Julia smiled at the older woman. "Yes. Claire Ramsay will have her dress in time."

Most of the seamstresses worked at the factory, but DeeDee kept about forty people at the shop. They had specific jobs, but often handled overflow from the factory. Even if all other work had to be suspended, this dress would be done in time.

It was two in the afternoon when Julia stopped working long enough to eat her salad. She calculated the time difference and checked her phone for Aaron's schedule. He wasn't in class. She dialed his number.

"Is everything okay?"

Julia giggled. "Can't you say hello like a normal person?"

"You never call during the day."

She stabbed at her salad. "If you don't mind my rabbit crunching, I thought I'd talk to you while I ate my lunch."

"Really, are you okay?"

"Yes, I'm fine. It's been hectic today and I just wanted to hear your voice. Sometimes it feels as though you are so far away."

"It won't be much longer." He chuckled. "Want some good news?"

"Oh, wesp." Carrots crunched in her mouth.

"I assume your mouth was full and that was a yes, so…Stockton Bridge Pharmaceuticals has offered me the job in their research division."

She swallowed. "Omigosh! That's wonderful. That's right here, right? They're putting up a building behind the dress factory. A month ago, it was an empty lot with a sign, now it's a steel frame."

"I know. Taking a subscription to your town's newspaper was a brilliant idea. As soon as I heard they were building a new lab there, I applied. They won't open their doors until October. The only thing left for me to do is convince my dad to let me have a few weeks off from being a delivery driver this summer. I do want to give you a proper honeymoon."

"Oh, I don't want anything fancy. I just want to stay in bed and kiss freckles. There's that one favorite--"

"I have a student who just walked into my office. I'll get back to you concerning that this evening."

She made a kiss sound and said goodbye. Talking to him had lifted her spirits and knowing he had a job that would allow them to stay here made her want to dance for joy.

Apparently Luke had turned down the part-time job, but he'd sent a classmate to the salon. Julia handled the preliminary interview. Megan Johnson was extremely interested in the position.

Julia smiled as she spoke to the woman who was a few years older. "For the time being, we're looking to have someone take care of our website. DeeDee is constantly adding to it with colors, embroidery, and even new dress designs. We've always handled it, but...we thought that it would be best to hire someone who could do it and handle some of our other media. DeeDee's looking to expand her online presence."

Megan nodded. "I still have a year of school left and with two children, this would be perfect."

"If you go to our website, under careers, there's a job application. We'll need you to fill that out." Julia understood divorced with children. She had a feeling that DeeDee would hire Megan. The woman seemed qualified and very anxious to have the added income.

She bid Megan goodbye and she spotted Cassie coming

through the door. She smiled at the young woman who was several years her senior. "Are you getting married?"

Cassie put her palm to her chest. "Not me. Always the bridesmaid, never the bride! It's not in me. At the rate I'm going, I'll never marry. Is DeeDee here? We chatted the other night."

"I'll call her for you." She picked up the phone that connected everyone. "How's the photography business going?"

"Great. I just need more work."

"Tell DeeDee." Julia grinned at the woman who had been a neighbor for years. "We're always looking for local people to handle things."

"I will. Thanks, Julia."

Julia held up her hand when her boss answered. "Hi, DeeDee. Cassie is here for some melon-colored bridesmaid dresses." Julia looked at Cassie. "She wants to know which color melon. Watermelon, cantaloupe, honeydew--"

Cassie's eyes grew wide and her hands came up as if to say stop.

"She's not certain. The bride had said melon." Julia listened and then smiled. "She's going to bring you several colors."

DeeDee always tried to at least stop long enough to visit with every client. But occasionally she'd handle everything. People liked that personal touch. It made them feel very special.

Julia returned to her office, but Cassie played in her mind. She was adorably cute, smart, funny, and she deserved to find someone wonderful. *Why hasn't she? Why does it have to be so difficult for some people to find the right person?*

As Julia sat at her computer, her dad drifted through her mind. She knew her dad was good looking and would always be considered a good catch but until DeeDee, his luck with women had been in the toilet. *Why?*

Someone by the name of Julie Beckman in Hamlin, New Hampshire, had ordered that beautiful wrapped fish gown. Four times she typed *Julia Beckman* into the database and each time had to correct it to Julie, but it kept coming out Julia. *Some sort of subconscious slip? I love that gown, but I've got way too much figure for it.* This gal had the perfect figure for that phenomenal dress.

DeeDee never used super-thin models. She wanted real people with real figures. She didn't want to see shoulder bones protruding; she wanted people who looked as though they actually ate meals. The memory of the model for this gown floated through her mind. She was Asian, and she and another gal modeled all the gowns meant for the extra petite woman. But as Kim Sue Lang walked the runway in this dress, Julia had drooled. There had been the sounds of inhaling throughout the crowd. It was so beautiful. It showed every tiny curve and flowed into a soft wake. It definitely took someone special to wear it.

Lubbock, Texas. The name struck her and she wasn't certain why. She even had a sense of where it was. If she'd had a map she could have poked her finger almost onto the spot in the north-western part of that big state.

Mandy Wagner. She entered the bride's information and double-checked everyone's measurements before entering them into the computer. The woman had chosen a classic gown that had a split in the front and laced up the back. She was pairing it with white dress boots that had been stitched in gold. The six bridesmaids were wearing teal with teal boots. And there was even a flower girl to match.

Julia's imagination ran away with her as she pictured the dresses. She wondered if Mandy's groom was a cowboy, all handsome and hunky. And with that split in the skirt, would the bride and groom ride off into the sunset on horseback?

None of the gowns were very expensive, but they were formal and would create a fairytale wedding. This was not going to be a small wedding, not with six bridesmaids. Teal was one of those colors that looked great on everyone, from the palest blonde to the darkest of dark.

Julia put a halt to her daydreaming of cowboys in Stetsons and finished the order. She didn't have time to waste on fairytales, sunsets, and romance. *Besides, I've got Aaron.*

She flipped to another screen and filled out the order for all the cowgirl boots to Karina.

***

The first week of May, Aaron had begun to pack up the place he called home when he was at the university. He couldn't believe all the personal things he had collected, along with the books and papers related to his chosen field. He wasn't keeping much. His intention was to sell the little house furnished. He looked at the oil painting he had bought during a charity auction. A very talented student at the university had done the oil of cattle in a field with the mountains in the background. *I can't take everything, but this is coming with me.* He slipped it from the wall and stacked it behind some boxes of books that he was shipping home.

His phone rang and he smiled when he answered. "You're calling early."

Julia purred, "I want your arms around me."

"I'm counting down the days." He glanced at his calendar on

the wall. "Maybe absence does make the heart grow fonder."

"Oh, just hearing your voice… You have no idea what you do to me."

"Don't say that. You know what you do to me and I don't even have to hear your voice to make it happen."

"And I love knowing that I have that affect on you."

***

Julia barely had time to consider her own wedding. Aaron would be here in a few days and as much as she wanted to spend every spare moment with him, she knew she couldn't. DeeDee swore she'd be fine and she could handle things. Julia doubted it. She had started coming in sometimes as early as seven a.m. to start on the orders. What had once taken an hour took the entire morning, if she wasn't interrupted.

She processed all the incoming orders and then checked her email. She read the note twice. Corrine Woods and Claire Woods…*Wait a minute!* She went back and pulled the order she had processed for Mimi's Bridal Shop in Lake Willowbee. *Claire is the bride and Corrine is the bridesmaid?* The easiest way to handle the order was to re-enter it but ship to Corrine Woods. Julia's palm went to her forehead. *Seriously? How do you surprise a bride? I'd love to be a fly on the wall for that one.*

She checked everything one more time. That bronze silk was beautiful and she thought about having the pants suit made for her to wear while she was working. DeeDee's wear-again collection contained some lovely outfits and that halter-top with beaded chrysanthemums was classy.

Another email struck her as slightly odd. This one requested a color swatch of Mandy Wagner's teal bridesmaids' dresses. Whoever it was wanted to make a hatband.

Julia called the factory and talked to Mrs. Hennessey. "Do we have any teal left over from Mandy Wagner's bridesmaid dresses?"

"Yes. We do. Is there a problem?"

"I hope not. Someone wants a swatch. She wants to make a hatband to match."

"That has to be cut on the bias."

"Will you cut enough for that?"

"No problem. Give me the address and I'll ship it out of here this afternoon."

"Thanks." *I'll make bets Mandy Wagner is wearing a white cowboy hat to match.*

***

Managing the salon for DeeDee was more than just processing paperwork, although there was a ton of that. She kept a close eye on the front and it seemed there were always one or two brides at any given time. She handled any additional perspective brides, took phone calls, collected the mail, then sorted and processed as much as she could. She ran upstairs and checked on the women working on the second floor.

One thing for certain - Julia was not a seamstress. But she did know how to prepare and package a dress for shipping. On occasion the two women who did that would get backed up in work going out. When that happened, Julia would step in and help. Lately, they needed help almost daily.

Julia knew DeeDee needed to hire another person and probably two people. It was considered unskilled manual labor. Truthfully, it took skill and common sense. She made a mental note to talk to DeeDee about it.

Julia grabbed the steamer and dropped a dress over the form. There was no fast way to steam a dress. To call it boring probably would have been an understatement. They weren't her designs, she didn't sew them, and they weren't her dresses, but the pride she felt inside as each was completed bubbled within her. She managed to do three before being paged to the salon.

Julia fixed a cup of coffee before returning to her desk. She figured she'd check the online orders one more time before she left for the evening. A groan escaped from her throat. Between the fashion show and the full-page ads in several magazines, the orders were barreling in faster than ever. She shook her head and started processing. *What is DeeDee going to do if I'm off on a honeymoon?*

She laughed to herself. She could picture her dad sitting at her desk, attempting to process all the paperwork. *At least Mrs. Prentiss knows how to do it.*

With that, Mrs. Prentiss tapped on Julia's door. "We have a problem on line three. Tina Normand from Boggy Bayou, Louisiana, wants to cancel her order. Do you want to take the call or should I send it to DeeDee?"

"Let me look it up first." Julia searched the name and found it. "Oh, no can do! This dress has already been shipped." She pulled the tracking number and checked. "According to National Delivery it will be delivered no later than noon tomorrow. Line three?"

Mrs. Prentiss nodded and walked away.

Julia took a breath and picked up the phone. "Good afternoon. I'm Julia and you wanted us to stop your dress order?" Julia winced. "I can't do that. It's already been shipped." "Yes. It should arrive no later than noon tomorrow." "I'm sorry, Miss Normand. But we can't do that. This dress was custom made for you."

Julia lifted the phone from her ear and could still hear the woman ranting. "Oh, I do understand." "I realize you are upset. I would be, too." "Yes, we do. We guarantee the *fit* of the dress. We don't refund your money. You have four days from the day you order it, to cancel. After that, you own the dress."

Julia cringed as the woman's tirade was filled with curse words. *Lucky man, you got out before you married her.*

"Please, Miss Normand, look at the bright side of this. You have a lovely figure and you are all prepared with your dream dress when your prince charming does come along." "No, really. I'm sure Boggy Bayou is filled with frogs. Just keep kissing them until one of them turns into a handsome prince." "Oh, yes. Lots of kisses. Consider it practice, because you want to be ready for him." "Oh, yes! I promise, I've kissed a lot of frogs. It wasn't until I tried kissing a redhead with freckles that I found my prince."

Julia chewed on the insides of her cheeks to keep from laughing. *Swim, little froggies from that soggy boggy bayou before you discover she's dining on your legs.*

She hung up the phone and went to processing orders. Most orders went smoothly, but it seemed as if she'd had a ton of problems these last few weeks.

I'll ask DeeDee. Maybe Cassie could take some photos of the interior of the salon and the factory. We could put it on the website. Maybe it would help people to understand that everything is custom made for them.

She pulled up the next order. Dani Brand from Lubbock, Texas. The name struck her. She went back through some older orders for dresses. There it was, Mandy Wagner. *What now?* Last week, they had to completely remake one bridesmaid dress for Jean Jackson. That time extra darts were added in case it needed to be let out again. She had checked with Miz Edith and she agreed that this was possibly an unconfirmed pregnancy.

Earlier today, Julia had overheard Mrs. Prentiss suggesting several styles to someone on the phone who apparently was pregnant but not far enough along to want a maternity gown. According to the order, this wedding was two weeks away. She wanted something off the rack.

Anything white and pretty but I really like Item #412. I'm pregnant. Julia giggled. *Since when do we do anything that isn't pretty? And when will they learn that there are no rack items!*

Quickly she scanned several items in the catalog. She chose a simple gown very close to what Dani had suggested, except this one was more forgiving of any changes. The pretty crisscross design of the bodice would allow for any expansion in the breasts and the way the skirt attached to the bodice, it would allow for probably two inches difference in the waist. She made the notation to add flounce for additional increase in the waist. Pregnant women were known to suddenly change size.

She thought about DeeDee and giggled. So far there had been very few changes but DeeDee wasn't skinny. She was hiding it well.

Six months ago, she wouldn't have considered it a rush job, but with the incoming orders streaming at an unbelievable pace, Julia began to wonder if any of the jobs this week would be completed in time. Julia inhaled as she looked at the order on her computer screen. She'd keep this job at the salon instead of sending it to the factory. Just as she was about to push the send button, she stopped and looked at Mandy Wagner's order. *It's a double wedding! No bride wants to pale next to another, and Mandy's gown is much nicer.*

She ran to the back and checked in several drawers where beading was kept. There it was. DeeDee had dropped it from her line because the manufacturer had quit carrying it. White on white, it would be perfect and so easy to attach to the skirt. It was nothing more than a floral flourish. But it would add to the plain gown and make it special. She pulled it, placed it in a large packet envelope, and wrote Dani Brand on the outside.

DeeDee never questioned certain decisions and often said to give the bride a little extra. Julia added no charge to the beading, discounted the price of the gown and added a garter to the shipment. Dani deserved to look as pretty as Mandy.

She continued to process as many orders as she could. *A beach wedding, if we only had a beach.* The polished cotton dress contained appliquéd seashells with pearl beading along the hemline. She typed in Sandcastle Dreams Item #389. In a sandy white color with muted seashell colors to match, it was also an elegant resort cover-up. She sent the request to Karina for the cork-lined sandals that left JUST MARRIED imprints in the sand.

Thoughts of her chosen dress filtered though her mind. She tried to imagine walking down the aisle with her dad and then tried to envision actually being married. It seemed too far away.

She looked up when DeeDee came into the small office and collapsed into a chair.

"I'm beat. Totally beat. I'm so tired. I'm not even certain I have what it takes to go home."

Julia grinned at her boss. "When are you going to admit you're pregnant?"

"What gave you that idea?"

"Oh, I don't know. The fact that you've given up coffee, you wouldn't touch a glass of wine in New York, you're so tired you can't see straight, you've quit wearing pencil skirts and have taken to tunics with pants, or that you tossed up your dinner the other night? Hmm, which one could it be?"

"Oh-h-h…"

"Have you told Dad?"

She shook her head. "I don't want to get his hopes up and have something go wrong. He knows I've gained a few pounds. I have my first ultrasound tomorrow. I thought I'd tell him after that appointment."

"Dad's going to be over the moon. He loves you so much."

"I'm crossing my fingers that this baby spreads his legs and smiles for that ultrasound. I know how much he'd love to have a son of his own."

Eight

Saturday morning in late June before the sun had arisen, Julia slipped out of bed and into the kitchen. Too excited to sleep, she was pleased to have this time alone. This was home and it contained countless memories of good times and bad. She pushed away the memories of her father's second wife.

Julia's tummy was filling with butterflies as she sipped another cup of coffee. After organizing so many weddings, she had been certain her own would go smoothly. But instead of being confident, every possible problem that might occur was flitting through her mind.

When Melissa and Chelsea found her, they chased her into the bathroom for a quick bath. She poured the lilac bath oil into the tub and gently washed her body. When she was done, she buffed her skin dry with a fluffy towel. Her every move sent the butterflies into motion. She slipped on a white robe and went back to her bedroom. Her sisters had coffee and a light breakfast waiting for her.

In a way, it was strange. Her wedding had brought the three of them closer than they had been in years. Now they chatted and giggled like sisters were supposed to do.

Chelsea, the youngest, maintained a checklist of everything that was to be done. As Julia had taken the last bite of her breakfast, the gal came to do her hair and nails. Julia showed her the diamond and amethyst earrings and necklace that she would be wearing.

The woman matched the nail polish perfectly to the jewels. Julia sat quietly through the whole nail thing. While her toes were being done she was able to finish drinking her coffee, but when the woman started on the fingernails, she was no longer allowed to touch anything.

A knock on the door startled everyone.

"May I come in?" Cody asked.

"Yes," Chelsea replied before anyone else.

"I just wanted to see the bride." He grinned but there was a touch of sadness in his eyes.

Julia smiled at her dad. "I'm fine. A little nervous…maybe…if the butterflies would settle down… I'll be fine. How's DeeDee?"

"She went to the church first and then she's headed to the hotel for your brunch with the ladies."

"Yes, she has a champagne brunch planned for all the female family members." Julia held her left hand out in front of her and admired the fantastic manicure.

Cody raised his eyebrows. "Well, she's called me about ten times so far this morning."

Chelsea giggled. "She's only called me six times."

The butterflies took flight again as a thought surfaced. "Please tell me you didn't get Aaron drunk last night."

Cody chuckled. "No, he wasn't really drunk – over the limit to drive." Another chuckle erupted. "We made sure he was going to sleep through the night."

"No one brought in a stripper, right?"

"No one did anything that crass. It was a mild party - lots of toasts and telling of tales. His father is quite a guy. Funny, funny man. Excellent sense of humor."

"I'm glad to hear it."

Cody leaned over and kissed his daughter on the cheek. Then quickly left the room.

I'll always be your daughter.

As soon as the woman finished Julia's nails, she did Chelsea's and Melissa's. Then she did their hair before coming back to Julia.

Julia's hair was done in cascading buns with braids wrapping them. The woman tucked several bits of baby's breath under the braids. The look was stunning. The whole thing was sprayed to make certain no hair drifted from its place. The last thing was to have her makeup done.

Melissa's curls were pulled up and contained in a large clip. Bits of lilac and baby's breath were tucked into her hair. Chelsea's dark hair was allowed to hang down, but it was flat-ironed and sprayed so it stayed perfect. She had a crown from lilacs and baby's breath.

When the doorbell rang, Melissa sprang from her seat. She returned a minute later with two little girls in tow. "Look who I found!"

Lily and Rose were the twin daughters of a worker from the salon and their grandmother worked in the factory. They were dressed and ready. Even their corn rowed hair had been finished on the ends with ribbons that matched their dresses.

"Oh, you both look so beautiful." Julia grinned at the tiny things.

Not quite in unison, the girls said thank you.

Without their mother around, no one could tell them apart. The one child rushed to Julia's side. "Grammy bought us new earrings to wear. See?"

"They are perfect!" Julia admired their purple cubic zirconium gems. "Are you ready to be my flower girls?"

They both nodded.

Chelsea inspected their nails and then turned to the stylist. "Do you mind doing their nails? They look clean, but I have a feeling they'd love to have a fancy manicure."

Julia suggested that the girls go to the kitchen for their manicures while she got dressed, and everyone agreed.

After Julia slid on her plain white chemise-like dress, her dad took her, her sisters, and the two little girls to the hotel to join the champagne breakfast. Aaron's mother and sister were there along with several other women from his family, including his grandparents who had flown in from Wales. Julia's Aunt Barbara and Uncle DJ's wife were with Cody's mom. What Julia thought was going to be small, had turned into huge. Between Aaron's family and hers, almost every room at the hotel had been reserved.

The breakfast went well, but Julia was pleased she had eaten at home for she really never had much of a chance to eat anything from the beautiful buffet. A few family members she had met at the dinner the night before, but many had arrived later. Ffiona Symons, Aaron's mother, looked more like she was Aaron's sister than his mother. Tiny and petite, she was a natural pale, golden blonde with a very light dusting of pale freckles; a real beauty.

After the breakfast, Julia and her sisters went to the room that had been reserved for them. Melissa helped Julia into her wedding dress. The slightly wider lattice contained wire to hold everything in place and the lattice had been embellished with white leaves containing gold embroidery. Winnie had done a beautiful job and now nothing would show that shouldn't. Winnie Kochang even added little knit panties into the dress. Julia wiggled her way into it and Melissa zipped it into place.

"Please do not tell me you're going to have to go pee between now and the wedding," Melissa pleaded as she placed the gold trimmed veil on her sister's head.

"I hope not, but may I have another cup of coffee. I promise I won't spill it."

"You're out of your mind. That will be your third cup! You're going to have to pee a million times if you don't stop drinking stuff."

"Please!" *It's not my third; it's my fifth.* "I know what I've drank; I'm dying of thirst and nervous as hell!"

"Don't curse."

"DeeDee does."

Melissa laughed. "Dad will let her get away with anything. Don't forget to count the orange juice concoction that you drank during the breakfast."

"Or the champagne that you weren't supposed to be drinking." Chelsea fussed with the flowers on the dress. "Think we'll always be little girls to Dad?"

"Probably," Julia answered. "And that champagne punch didn't have a bit of alcohol in it. I think it was sparkling white grape juice. DeeDee isn't drinking, Dad's family doesn't usually drink. Do you really think there was any champagne in it?"

Chelsea rolled her eyes. "Then why didn't DeeDee tell me that I could drink it?"

Julia shrugged.

"Don't go anyplace and don't sit! The limo will be here soon to take you to the church. I want to check on Collin and Logan,"

Melissa ordered.

Julia looked at one sister and then the other. "They're here?"

"Yeah. Dad brought them here before the breakfast," Chelsea answered.

"What about Sean and Ian?"

"I saw them earlier with Uncle DJ. They looked very handsome in their tuxes, and they're on their best behavior. I have no idea what Dad has threatened them with, but they are being extremely good," Chelsea said. "Dad had something going with the men in the family for breakfast."

"I want coffee!" Julia called as Melissa closed the door behind her.

Julia wanted to sit, but with a bunch of water vials on her dress, she didn't dare. The butterflies weren't just in her stomach; they were crawling all over her skin and biting her fingers and toes.

Chelsea appeared with a spill-proof cup and a big towel. She draped the front of Julia's wedding dress before handing her older sister a travel mug. "Here. Press to drink from it."

"I know how to use it."

The warm brew slid down Julia's parched throat. She knew she shouldn't drink another cup of coffee. But maybe she could drown the butterflies with this one.

Chelsea slipped the blue garter on Julia's leg. "There's your blue. And here's the old. She taped an old penny to the bottom arch of the Karina Karr shoes just before the heel began.

Karina had made the shoes especially for Julia. They were sandal-like with lots of straps and made to match the lattice and leaves on her bodice. They were also the same color as her amethysts. So much for the plain white shoes she had ordered.

Karina was here for the wedding and had handed them to Julia last night.

Chelsea gazed at her older sister and smiled. "Guess your shoes are the new. I thought you were going to cry when Karina handed you these."

"I almost did."

"She was nothing like I expected after hearing DeeDee talk about her."

"That makes two of us." Melissa replied as she walked into the room.

"Karina is a wonderful friend to DeeDee. She's just one of those people who live outside of the box." Julia grinned at the thought of the woman whom she had met on several occasions.

"Like Chrisy?" Chelsea rolled her eyes.

"Here's your borrowed. DeeDee was going to give you something but according to DeeDee, Aaron's grandmother insisted that you wear this." Melissa pulled a diamond wristlet from a box, then slipped the bracelet on Julia's left arm.

Huge diamonds circled her wrist. "When did you get this?"

"Dad passed it to me early this morning."

"It's beautiful." Julia fingered the bracelet. "Has anyone seen Aaron?"

***

Julia stood in the small room next to the church's vestibule and looked around. Several coat racks had been pushed against one wall and the opposite wall contained three long, skinny windows made of some sort of yellow, wavy glass. She watched people entering the church. As the crowd thinned, Julia's anxiety climbed. She gazed at her sisters and realized she had a serious problem. "I've got to pee!"

Chelsea broke into hard laughter and Melissa frowned. "Come on. I just knew this would happen. You're going to be doing this all afternoon."

"No, I'm not."

"I know you. Three cups of coffee?"

Julia grinned at her sister. *I'm not telling how many cups.*

In the tiny bathroom at the back of the church, it took almost ten minutes for Julia to wiggle out of the dress and then back into it again. Melissa fussed the entire time.

"The last time I looked, it was twenty minutes before two. The wedding is to start at two. Besides, I can't help it."

"We all told you not to drink another cup of coffee."

"I was thirsty."

Melissa zipped the dress one more time. "Remind me to wear something very simple when I get married, like a tee shirt and jeans."

"Oh, you'll do exactly what I've done and pick out the most splendid thing there is."

"Maybe I'll never get married."

Julia giggled. "You sound just like me until I met Aaron."

"Wait a minute; you've got a flower out of place." Melissa fixed the sprig of lilac blossoms.

"Who put all my flowers on the dress this morning?"

"DeeDee started it, and Chelsea and I finished while you took your bath. You look absolutely beautiful."

"Thanks." Julia leaned over and air kissed her sister's cheek. "I really do love both of you."

"You're just saying that because you're going to need our help every time you'll need to use the bathroom."

***

From where Julia stood, she watched her sisters being escorted down the aisle by their stepbrothers and then she watched the little flower girls enter the sanctuary. Carrying nosegays, they were so cute in their lilac-colored taffeta dresses that had been trimmed with lots of white lace. The same lace was on their white socks and they wore ballet-like slippers that had been dyed to match their dresses. They were so thrilled to be in the wedding.

Her father stood opposite her on the other side of the doorway in the large church vestibule. He looked extra handsome in his tuxedo. *He's giving away one daughter but in another four months, he's gaining a baby daughter.* Suddenly she had the urge to cry.

Her father shook his head, then wagged a finger at her and whispered. "Don't you dare. You'll mess up your pretty face. Look up."

She did and batted at the tears until they went away.

The music changed and she stepped forward. Her father took her arm and they slowly walked the long aisle. Time stood still. She noticed everything - the flowers that were arranged by every pew, the ones in front of the church and on every windowsill. She spotted the man video taping the wedding; the minister draped in a black robe; Collin's partially tied shoelace, and Logan's cowlick that was threatening to flick a lock of hair straight up. Her hands were sweating as they held the bouquet of white and purple lilacs mixed with small white carnations and baby's breath. DeeDee stood next to Cody's dad and smiled, while Cody's mother wiped tears away.

The room was filled with haves and have-nots, as most of the people from the salon and the factory came, along with many of the merchants from town who knew DeeDee and Cody. Julia spotted several close high school friends and smiled at them. The other side of the room was filled with friends of Aaron's family. She continued to smile as she approached the front of the church. Her father patted her arm and she stopped walking.

Her dad kissed her cheek, and she knew if she looked at him, she'd burst into tears. Instead, she riveted her gaze on Aaron's golden-green eyes. The minister said something and her father answered. Ice water ran through her veins, yet she felt hot. Aaron stepped forward and took her arm. They walked up the steps to the altar and waited.

The minister had her and Aaron face each other then bound their left hands together with a satin cloth as he spoke about marriage. Julia gazed into Aaron's eyes and saw his love. *Windows to the soul.*

She remembered those eyes staring at her over a bright blue plastic cup. His shirt had been soaked in sweat. Sparks flew between them and continued to flash and sizzle whenever they were together, but today, it wrapped them in an electrical blanket and kept them riveted together.

"I, Aaron Trevor Symons…"

She listened to what he was saying and watched the way his mouth moved with each word. Her handsome Welshman was dusted in freckles from his toes to the top of his head. They dusted his broad shoulders and muscular chest, arms, and legs. In a few hours, they would be alone and she couldn't wait to kiss every freckle.

She held her fingers out as he slipped the wedding band on her finger.

Now it was her turn. "I, Julia Lynn Montgomery…"

She repeated each line as the minister gave it to her. Melissa handed Julia the gold band for Aaron and she placed it on his finger. "I thee wed."

Aaron grinned at her and his eyes sparkled.

She loved that mischievous-looking grin of his.

Another prayer was offered. Their hands still bound together, Aaron had captured her fingers in his and gently squeezed them.

She knew what he meant. That silent communication passed between them. Never had she dreamed she'd fall this much in love or find someone as wonderful as Aaron.

"I now pronounce you husband and wife. You may kiss the bride."

Aaron's lips fell upon hers. Sweet but with an urgency, the kiss, the first marital kiss, a love like none other, sent a wave of heat through her.

The minister unbound their hands. "You came as two, now go as one before God and the world."

She smiled as the music started. Aaron filled her with complete joy. Together, they walked down the aisle. There were toasts to be made, food to eat, a cake to cut, a bouquet to toss, dances to dance, and friends and family to wish them well. She was having the perfect wedding. Everything was going according to plan.

At the end of the day, they would hide away before heading off on a cruise to the Symons' estate in Wales. She had three glorious weeks to count freckles and make a baby, for they both wanted a large family and were anxious to get started.

But before any of that could happen, Julia became very aware of the fact that she had a problem, a serious problem. *I should have never drank all that coffee.* She leaned over and whispered in Aaron's ear, "I've got to pee!"

Book Three

To Have

&

To Hold

One

Drexel Cunningham looked over the rental applications for the small gatekeeper's house on the back end of his property. Not much bigger than a doghouse, it needed a single, quiet renter, not a party animal. One application intrigued him and might be worth pursuing if he had a cup of coffee while he did the background checks. He stood, stretched, and fixed a fresh pot of coffee. As it brewed, he looked across the estate's lawn to the garden that he had tilled and then covered in dark plastic to sterilize the soil and kill any weed seed the tilling stirred up. He had eight cubic yards of compost to add to it. Visions of fresh tomatoes made his stomach rumble. The clock said three twenty-eight. *Too soon for dinner. I'll be fine with coffee.*

Pouring a cup of the fresh brew, he returned to his computer. In that short length of time, he had received another application. This one was from Melissa Montgomery. As he looked the application over, he raised his eyebrows. *Actuary with SunWest Oil?* He continued to read. *Need a quiet place to stay when I'm home and telecommuting. The rest of the time, I'm traveling.*

Taking a sip of his coffee, he thought about the application. He wasn't anxious to rent to a female. For years, it had been rented to an older man who kept the place immaculate. Then in three years, it had been rented four times. The last two were females. Both had left without notice and left the place in bad shape. *I have a right to rent to whomever I please and I don't feel like getting burned again.*

The background check showed very little other than she owned a new Lexus and had apparently paid cash for it, for there was no loan. She had attended Brigham Young University, and had grown up in an older but nice local neighborhood. There was one credit card in her name with an excellent rating. A few more keystrokes and he confirmed she worked for SunWest Oil. *Why is her name familiar? Actuary?* He called her.

***

Melissa called home. No one answered. Next she called her dad's office, only to get a recording, and then she tried his cell phone. Frustration was taking the edge off her news. She tried the one phone number that she knew someone would answer, Main Street Bridal Salon.

"This is Melissa Montgomery; Julia please." She waited a moment as the phone call was transferred several times.

"Julia speaking, may I help you?"

Melissa let out a breath that she realized sounded more like a huff. "Oh, thank goodness. Where is everyone?"

Julia giggled. "Dad's in Texas, DeeDee is probably en route from the factory to the salon. Collin, Logan, and Charley should be at Donna's house. And I'm here. What's up?"

"I got my own place."

"Super. Where?"

"The Claxton Estate."

"Are you crazy?"

"Not the mansion. Do you remember the gatekeeper's house by the bridle path? It's way in the back of the property."

"Sort of…maybe."

"We used to go ice skating on the pond sometimes."

"Little place. I remember that."

"It's only one bedroom. All newly renovated. I've only seen the photos online, but it looks adorable. I'm coming home this weekend to sign the papers and move some stuff in. Want to help?"

"Not really. Aaron and I have made plans for the weekend."

"Darn. When is Dad due home?"

"Thursday. What are you taking?"

"You mean to the house?"

"Yes."

"I have no clue. I figured I'd do some shopping after I see the place."

"Shopping sounds like fun. Were you hoping to take DeeDee with you?"

"Not really. I figured I could do it myself. Remember when we used to redo the house on Dad?"

"Oh, those were the days." Julia giggled.

The warmth of that special bond between sisters came through the phone. "I've got to run. Tell Dad to call me when he gets in."

"I will."

Saturday morning, Melissa sat at the family table and sipped on her coffee as her dad fixed breakfast. His premature gray was no longer confined to his temples. Silver strands were turning his hair to salt and pepper, but he was just as handsome. He slipped their bacon and eggs onto plates and joined her at the table. She heartily gobbled up the hot meal.

"You are very quiet this morning," her father said, when he finished his glass of juice.

"Thinking."

He raised his eyebrows. "Second guessing your decision to have your own place instead of living here?"

"Not really. I love my little apartment in Utah. And I promise to come home for dinner occasionally." She crunched on a piece of bacon. "Did you want to come see the place?"

"You don't need my approval. Maybe you'll invite me to lunch after you've moved in. And since I fixed breakfast, you get to clean up."

"But I didn't ask for you to fix it."

"I know. Wasn't that nice of me? Now you can return the favor." He kissed her cheek and walked away.

She laughed to herself as she stacked the dishes in the dishwasher and cleaned up the pan he had used for the eggs.

The unseasonably warm weather was often referred to as a Dogwood Winter. After Utah's cold, this was a welcome reprieve. She drove to the Claxton estate with her driver's side window down and let the fresh air fill her car.

The Claxtons had been family friends. As a child, she could remember being invited to their house to see their Christmas displays, for Fourth of July picnics, and fall hayrides. The elderly couple would lavish attention on the Montgomery girls as if they were grandchildren. But it all stopped when Mrs. Claxton became ill and then died.

Then Dad married Patty Shillings. The thought of her father's second marriage soured in her stomach and tossed a foul mood over the glorious day. She flipped on the car's radio and tried to clear her mind. *Who owns the house now? Do they live in it or are they breaking it into apartments?* She pondered that and then found herself singing to the song on the radio.

The big wrought iron gates were open as she pulled into the driveway. Everything looked the same, except she didn't see any horses in the surrounding fields. The house loomed into view. Made from rough-hewn granite blocks, it sat like a majestic lady on top of a slight rise. Three stories with a mansard roof - the home was a beauty.

She slowed, fully expecting Mrs. Claxton to open the door and wave. The memory of the woman's gray curls framing her face, "sensible" heels, and a dress always adorned with a jeweled brooch flooded her mind. As a child, Melissa had been fascinated by the elderly woman.

Drexel Cunningham said to come to the guesthouse behind the main house. As she drove past the mansion, she realized the curtains were all closed. A sadness descended over her. It was as though the house reached out to her and begged to be loved and filled with laughter and children. *Such a shame.*

Staring at the house, she could have sworn she saw curtain movement at an upper window. There were two nondescript cars behind the house, and the guesthouse sat off to the left with an old pickup truck in front of it. She was a half hour early, and she didn't care.

After parking the car next to the pickup, she strode to the door. As she raised her hand to knock, she realized she had more anxiety about coming than she wanted to admit. She squared her shoulders and drew in a deep breath.

The door opened to a man in his early thirties. He looked awake but not exactly ready to face the day. Wearing cut-off jeans and an old tee shirt, he appeared as though he'd just tumbled from bed, except sexier.

"Hi. I'm Melissa Montgomery. Sorry. I'm early. I do hope it's not too inconvenient for you."

His hand flew to his jaw and he rubbed the stubble that covered it. "You are early, and I wasn't exactly ready, but you might as well come in. I'll give you the paperwork in case you have any questions."

A feeling of lust flowed through her, but she had no interest in getting involved with any guy. But she couldn't help noticing his broad, well-muscled chest, slim waist, strong legs and bare feet. *Oh those feet! Ick!*

"Make yourself at home." He pointed to a seating area and vanished.

The image of his feet was stuck in her mind. His second toe was long and each toe sprouted long dark hair. The same dark hair that covered his legs continued to the top of his instep. *Gross!* She shuddered. So much for sexy, it departed when she noticed his feet.

He handed her a manila envelope and disappeared again. She could hear water running as she read the lease. It was standard. He had sent it in an email, and she had passed that to her father who was a lawyer by trade. The only thing strange about the lease was the hefty cash deposit, but she knew that ahead of time and had the cash.

She put the paperwork down and looked around the room. The place was beautifully furnished and didn't look like it belonged to a single guy, except for the large screen TV. Where were the beer cans and pizza boxes? Where were the dirty clothes?

Plants sat in pretty containers and floor plants were tucked in corners. Each looked healthy and happy. An array of African violets bloomed near a window. *What guy keeps African violets? Maybe he's got a wife?*

***

Melissa Montgomery? She even looks familiar. The inability to place her shook Drexel. She was impeccably dressed and hadn't balked at the deposit. He wasn't certain what actuaries made, but he was confident it wasn't peanuts. Soft dark curls spilled down her back from where they had been contained in some sort of clip. Her dark eyes were framed in long dark eyelashes and were perfectly arched by dark eyebrows. The image of a little, dark-haired girl flashed in his mind.

Showered, shaved, and dressed, he went back to his living room. "Ready?"

She looked up at him and smiled. "Very."

"Okay, follow me down the drive. I'll show you where it is."

She laughed. "I know where it is, unless you've moved it."

Her comment punched at his gut. She had to be at least ten years younger than him. *How would she know?* He'd only been here for a few years, and prior to that, the house had remained vacant since his grandfather had passed. He had flown home for the funeral. *Seven years?*

He jumped into the pickup and prayed it would start. Tapping his foot on the accelerator pedal three times to put some gas into the carburetor, he turned the key in the ignition. The truck sputtered and caught. He tossed it in first gear and started down the road.

Two Tennessee Walking horses wandered through the meadow. The mare was heavy, and he smiled. He'd carefully chosen both horses with the idea of breeding them and he intended to find another pair. Those tall elegant horses appealed to him unlike any others.

Through the woods and beyond, sat the small house in the middle of a clearing. Unless someone was used to being on the bridle paths, the bungalow was virtually nonexistent. The original building was stone and had been added onto. He had no idea how old it was until he gutted the place and renovated it. Hand hewn beams had fascinated him, but some of what he found scared him. Open wires ran through the attic and batts of grass had been used for insulation. He was surprised that it had never burned to the ground. Now it was properly insulated, with new wiring, plumbing, and energy efficient windows. He had knocked himself out fixing the old place and turning it into a mini showpiece. The last thing he wanted was for a renter to ruin his hard work.

He pulled to a stop and she parked next to him.

"It's different. It doesn't look the same," she said as she exited her vehicle.

Her quizzical look gave him pause. "I said in the ad that it's newly renovated."

"There was a porch over there."

"It wasn't worth saving. I turned the footprint into a laundry room."

"Footprint? What's that?"

"The existing…um, foundation… The area that housed the porch."

She turned away from the house and looked towards the creek that flowed into a pond. "Wasn't there a bridge over the creek?"

"Who are you?" He didn't mean to say it aloud.

"I used to come here as a little girl to see the Claxtons. Mr. Claxton would let me ride his pony and sometimes my dad would bring me to ice skate on the pond."

"How old were you?"

She shrugged. "Maybe nine or ten the last time I came. My dad remarried and life changed."

The image of the dark-haired little girl flit through his mind, but it had been so many years ago and the image wasn't very clear.

She smiled brightly. "Mostly I ride Western. But Mr. Claxton taught me English."

"Do you still ride?"

"Of course. I just haven't ridden English in years."

He opened the front door. "Ta-da."

He watched her face as she stepped inside.

"It's adorable." She wandered around, opening every door and cabinet. "It's perfect. It's all old and new. Someone did a great job on this. Even the colors are perfect - earthy and wood toned."

He couldn't keep the swell of pride contained. "Thanks. I did every bit of it."

She turned back to him with a look of horror on her face. "You did it? I do hope you hired out the electrical and plumbing."

"No. I did it."

"But there are codes… It's not safe--"

"Yes, I know. I had to pass every inspection along the way. Every code has been exceeded. Do you want to see the building permits?"

"Yes!"

He swallowed. "They're at my place."

***

A few minutes later, Melissa sat at Drexel's kitchen table while he hunted for the permits. He handed her an accordion file filled with receipts and permits. The city's building inspector had signed each one. Satisfied, she picked up the lease. "It says you are to have access to the building at all times for inspection. I do hope that will be during normal business hours."

He nodded. "You already said you aren't home much. If a pipe were to break…"

"Fine. I get you." She reached in her purse. "I want a receipt."

"Naturally." He took the money, counted it, and gave her a receipt.

She signed the lease and prayed her elation was not showing. The place was beyond perfect. She never realized how much she enjoyed quiet until she had her own apartment in Utah. Having grown up with a pack of siblings, total quiet was a real luxury.

With a copy of the lease in hand, she bid Mr. Hairy Feet goodbye and returned to the cottage long enough to collect some measurements. Then she set out to do some shopping. Her first intended stop was Byrum's Furniture in town.

She didn't have a lot of space in any of the rooms. She chose several Shaker-styled items and some fancy curtain rods. But choosing upholstered furniture made her rethink her plans when she fell madly in love with predominately white floral print. It would change everything. *Why did I think this was going to be easy?* She chided herself.

She left for a late lunch at a small downtown café. That gave her time to mull over her furniture choices and look at several brochures the store had handed her.

"Hi, Melissa. I almost didn't recognize you." The mother of a childhood friend smiled, as she stood ready to take Melissa's lunch order.

Melissa looked up and grinned. "Hi. I haven't seen you in ages. How's everyone?"

"We're doing great. You do know Kathy got married two years ago?"

"Yes. Julia told me." Melissa chatted amicably for a few moments.

"I shouldn't keep you. I'm sure you are hungry."

"It's been fun talking to you." She pointed to the menu. "I'll have the tuna salad plate."

The woman motioned towards the brochures. "Picking out

new furniture for your dad?"

She didn't want to get into a discussion about renting the house at Claxton's. "Just daydreaming. Do you have any herbal teas?"

"Oh sure." The woman left and returned with a box of teabags, none of which were herbal, and a small pot of hot water.

Melissa picked out a white tea mixed with peach and dropped the bag into the pot. Then went back to reviewing the brochures. She was stuck on the Shaker idea. Those clean lines appealed but so did the English cabbage rose print on the super stuffed upholstered pieces. Did she dare mix the two styles? Would the one soften the other?

Her lunch was served and she ate it as she debated with herself. *The big white blooms...* She envisioned pillows in various colors to spell the seasons. All feminine and pretty, it appealed to her soft side and was completely different from the Danish modern look of her apartment. By the time she'd taken her last bite, she knew what she wanted. Drexel's face loomed before her mental eye. Tall, dark, and handsome, he appealed to her, and she had no clue why.

She returned to the furniture store, confirmed her order, and chose a few more things as decorations along with several pillows. Everything would be delivered on Monday. She headed for the mall. But the image of Drexel wasn't leaving her mind. She had no intention of getting involved with a man who was some sort of groundskeeper or maintenance man for the Claxton estate. But the image of him in that tee shirt and cut offs with muscles bulging... *Remember his feet.*

Sunday afternoon was spent filling her kitchen cabinets and

stacking new, laundered towels and sheets into the small linen closet. The place was coming together and elation built inside her. She liked doing her own decorating and couldn't wait for her furnishings from Byrum's. She sat on the floor facing the back windows and crossed her legs. The view of the pond was delightful. On the water's edge closest to the cottage, someone had created a small Japanese garden, as she recognized the weeping cherry and the little pagoda. An edge on the far side of the pond appeared to be under construction, and she wondered if the pond would be filled with flowers when spring came.

Her original plan to put her little table and chairs by that one large window had changed, and now she intended to put her computer desk there. The view was too good to ignore and would be a welcome relief from the computer screen. She looked to her right at the pocket doors that were open, exposing her empty bedroom. By the time she put her bed in there, there was no room for furniture, but the generous closet would hold whatever clothing she'd keep here. She pictured the pencil bed with its tall skinny posts and the tiny tables that would sit on each side of the bed. The tables were nothing more than plant stands with granite tops, but they matched the house.

Her reverie broke when she heard a knock on the door. She scurried to her feet and answered it. It took her a moment to recognize Drexel in a suit. "Hi."

"I saw your car earlier and I wanted to make certain everything is okay. No questions or anything?"

She looked at the suit and knew it was not a cheap one. *How can you afford something like that?* "Not really. My furniture comes tomorrow morning. I'll meet the Byrum's delivery truck at the main gate at nine."

He nodded. "My phone number is in the laundry room. Don't hesitate to call twenty-fours a day."

"Thanks. I saw your number and I've added it into my phone. Plus I have your email address."

"If you need help tomorrow, call me. I'm very good at hanging things on walls. I prefer one solid nail to a mess in the sheetrock."

She grinned. "I won't mess up your walls. But thanks for the offer."

He bid her a good day. She stood and watched him drive away in the old beat-up pickup truck. Nothing about him made any sense, nor did the feeling he had on her body.

***

Drexel went into the mansion and up to the second floor. He knocked on the door and was greeted by Nanny Peaches. The name fit her golden red hair that was streaked strands of white. The woman had once been his mother's nanny and then his.

"How's my girl, today?"

"Margo is fine. She's dressed and ready for her tea party."

"Ah, it's a tea party today? Does she have plans?"

Nanny Peaches laughed. "When does she not have plans?"

"Byron! There you are. Are you ready for our tea party?"

Drexel rolled his eyes at his nanny and kissed Margo on the cheek. "I hear we're having a tea party this afternoon."

"Oh, yes. Come." Margo dragged him across the room and made him sit at the table and chairs. A moment later, she put a string of beads on him and plopped a big floppy-brimmed, floral hat on his head.

In a way, it unnerved him to see her like this, but she seemed totally happy. There were worse things in life. He played along and Nanny Peaches brought them dinner and warm sweet milk. Little chicken bites were not his idea of food, but considering how often Margo fought during mealtimes, it was good to see her eat everything on her plate. Then after dinner she insisted they play a board game, except she couldn't actually play it. Eventually she wound up sitting on the floor and sucking her thumb. Nanny Peaches came and coaxed her into her bedroom.

Drexel pulled the hat from his head and left it on the chair. He fought tears as he left the room. She was still alive and had done well. Unfortunately her mind was that of a child's, and she played as if she were still three years old. She no longer knew him by his name and called him Byron. *Byron. She probably doesn't even remember Byron's last name or that he was her husband.*

Drexel stepped out the back door and crossed the lawn to his house. He raised his hand in a wave as Melissa's car lights panned the yard as she came around the curve. *Wonder what she was doing?*

He opened the door to his place and stepped inside. He poured himself a glass of apple juice and pondered his dinner date. Every Sunday, he dressed and joined her. The last two years had seen many changes. *At least she isn't in pain.*

He stood by his kitchen window thinking about his evening and spotted headlights. The car pulled in front of his place and came to a halt. It wasn't until Melissa walked in front of her headlamps that he realized who it was. He opened the door before she could knock. "Hi. Is something wrong?"

***

Melissa opened her mouth but nothing came out. Mr. Hairy Feet stood there with a string of pearls draped over his tie. She tamped down her initial surprise and tried not to smile. *Whatever rocks your world. That explains the African violets.* "I'm sorry, I didn't mean to interrupt your evening. I only stopped to ask about the gate. When does it close and when does it open?"

"You weren't interrupting a thing. Would you like to come in?"

"No thanks."

He raised his eyebrows. "As for the gate, I never bother to close it. There's an electronic beam that transmits to the security company and alerts me of any late traffic. That's part of the reason why I wanted to know what you drove."

Anger crept up her back. "So if I have a hot date…"

"If a strange car leaves or comes late at night, I will know about it."

"So am I supposed to keep you informed of my--"

"No. That shouldn't be necessary, unless you want to inform me of a frequent late night visitor. But the system picks up on a frequent vehicle. It's a good thing and yet there's a flaw in the logic. So if you know you will have late night or very early morning traffic, you might want to consider giving me the vehicle information, because I do like my sleep."

"Whatever. I'm sorry to have bothered you." It was no one's business who came or went to her little place, and she wasn't into hot dates. Yet she could visualize her sisters, Chelsea or Julia, coming and pouring their hearts out at some unreasonable hour.

The discomfort over what felt like an invasion of her privacy made her want to lash out. She knew it was wrong, but after years of practice on siblings, she couldn't stop herself. "By the way, the pearls add a nice touch. Not many men have the guts to pull off the look."

She turned on her heel to return to her car, but not before catching the look on his face, which was priceless and well worth the jab. *Still in the closet?*

The drive to the gates gave her time to ponder the situation. She was wrong and she knew it. Slowing as she approached the gate, she looked for whatever it was that would identify her car and saw nothing. *This is no different from living in a gated community or having the added security of a doorman. Damn. I should be thankful.*

A gust of wind caught her car, brown leaves blew across the road, and by the time she reached her father's house, the temperature had dropped. *Goodbye, dogwood winter.*

At eight thirty in the morning, Melissa sat in front of the mansion's gate and checked her email on her phone while she waited for the delivery truck. Icy cold rain pelted her windshield and her wipers slapped at the offending water that blurred her vision of the world beyond. By nine fifteen, she was getting antsy. Ten minutes later, she called the furniture store and was assured that the truck was indeed on its way.

Her mind wandered to Drexel standing there in pearls. It bothered her, and she wasn't sure why she even cared. The more she thought about it the more she decided he needed help - serious help. *What kind of a guy is going to want you if you look like that? Those hairy feet…* She shuddered.

She spotted the delivery truck and all extraneous thoughts vanished from her mind. *Why did it have to rain?*

The men put special mats just inside her front door and they wrapped the furniture in plastic sheeting to protect it from the rain. It didn't take them very long to bring everything inside, assemble her bed, collect the mats, and leave.

She loved where the desk was, but that had changed the placement of her table and chairs. It took her a minute to figure out how to drop the sides of her small harvest table. Once she did, she moved it against the one wall. Totally unsatisfied, she pushed it around a few times and still wasn't contented. Byrum's had promised her that if she was unhappy with anything… But she had loved the table.

On the verge of tears, she heard a knock. Pulling herself together, she answered the door.

Drexel stood there smiling at her. In a pair of jeans and a tee shirt under an open leather jacket, he was, as her sister Julia would say, positively *lickable*.

"Just being nosey and offering my help."

"Come on in. I don't need help; I need to return the table and chairs that I bought."

"Why? What's wrong?"

She explained how she had made a last minute decision to move her computer desk to the window.

"So for the most part, it's just you and no one else for meals, right? And you want to keep the view of the backyard?"

"Right."

"Here's your mistake." He moved her desk so it wasn't directly in front of the window, then moved the table at a right angle to the desk. "There, that's much better. Except you'll need a floor lamp if you intend to be at your computer in the late afternoon or evening."

She crooked her finger for him to follow. "Like that one?"

"It's perfect. Besides you really don't need a light in that bedroom when you have the ones in the ceiling and on the fan."

He brought the lamp in and set it beside the desk. "Now all you need are some plants to continue the view into the interior."

"No plants for me. I have an ugly brown thumb."

He grabbed her hand. "No, you don't. It's a lovely thumb."

A jolt of electricity flew through her and instantly warmed her.

"You just haven't been trained to care for plants. I'll teach you."

She stared into his blue orbs and hoped that he'd never let go of her hand. She didn't care what he was. He was incredibly handsome and very sexy. Her entire body seemed electrified and the sensation was pooling deep within her.

***

Drexel realized how warm her hand felt in his. Her eyes seemed to widen and sparkle. Dark curls tumbled and escaped from the big claw clip that was supposed to have contained them. Her pretty pink lips were slightly parted as if begging for a kiss, and he wanted to kiss them. He moved closer to her and she didn't flinch. Her tongue slipped between her lips and he decided he might die on the spot. *Just one little taste*. He inched closer and her eyes closed as her chin lifted. *Oh yeah, baby. You want it, too.*

He hovered by her lips as his mind raced. Getting involved with a renter was totally wrong, but she was too luscious to ignore. His lips touched hers. Fire ripped through him as she leaned into him and he felt her pelvis against his leg. There was no question that he was falling into hell, but it certainly felt like heaven.

Two

Tuesday morning, Melissa left for Utah. From her office in SunWest, she could see the mountains. But between her and the mountains there were lots of buildings and then a flat open area. It was so different from what she saw out that back window of her little cottage. As much as she tried to forget Drexel and their awkward kiss, she couldn't. It niggled at her. She wanted to talk to someone, and she didn't know who, certainly not her father. She also realized she wasn't paying enough attention to the stats on her computer screen. The feelings Drexel had stirred in her had clouded her ability to think.

She turned off her computer, went to the break room, and fixed a cup of decaf coffee. The rich earthy taste filled her mouth but didn't help her thoughts. Various co-workers wandered in and said hello. It was one thing to take a few minutes away from her desk and another to lounge over a cup of coffee, yet she couldn't clear her mind. Then it struck her.

She scurried back to her office and dug through her list of contacts. Jack Corosa. *My neighbor.* She called the number she had for him and waited. She wound up in his voice mail. "Hi, Jack, this is Melissa Montgomery. I was hoping you'd be able to join me tonight for dinner. I'd like to talk to you about something.

Your partner is welcome to come, too. I promise, no scams, I'm not selling anything, I'm just looking for some answers, and you're the only person I can think of who might be able to shed some light. It'll make sense when I see you. Text me, and we can decide where to eat."

Feeling as though a huge boulder had been lifted from her, she threw herself into what she was doing for the remainder of the day. At four, her phone pinged with an incoming message. So engrossed, she forgot she was expecting a text message. A half hour later, it dawned on her, and she grabbed for her phone. They decided on the little restaurant not far from where they lived.

Melissa made reservations and was waiting in a corner booth for the two men. Jack was probably in his mid-thirties with dark hair and even darker eyes. His partner, John, was a blue-eyed blond who was slowly turning white. Suddenly all her questions fled, and she swallowed. She was crazy for even thinking she could ask them something so personal.

They did the normal, polite small talk and then Jack asked, "What was so important that you wanted to talk to us over dinner?"

She ran her fingers over her forehead and grinned. "It's stupid and I should have never even thought of asking you guys. Just forget about it and let's enjoy a pleasant meal. How often does a woman get to ask two handsome men out to dinner and not worry about being kissed goodnight?"

John guffawed. "Who says we don't like goodnight kisses from a beautiful young woman?"

"Oh geez. What have I done?"

"What do you mean?" Jack asked as he cocked his head and his dark eyebrows knitted.

Melissa smiled at the waitress as the woman placed the bowls of onion soup in front of them.

Melissa looked at Jack. "Okay, maybe John just answered my question."

"Does this have something to do with us being gay?"

Melissa nodded at Jack. "Only because you two are the only gays I actually know who are. I think I need to know more." She pushed her spoon into the bowl of soup breaking the cheese seal over the top of it. Steam rose. "There's this guy and I thought he was gay, except he kissed me."

The conversation about sexual orientation continued through the course of the entire meal. She knew she'd been sheltered, but she had no idea to what extent. Suddenly a whole lot of things fell into place. But the guys could not give her anything definitive on Drexel. She'd have to noodle that situation out by herself. And the most likely explanation was that he might be bisexual or enjoy dressing in women's clothing.

She thought about Chrisy who worked for DeeDee at the bridal salon. He was DeeDee's handler and had propelled her into the limelight. Apparently he was straight, but loved bright clothing and wore women's heels because they were more comfortable. Melissa decided she was more confused than ever.

After dinner, they walked to their apartments. John had taken her hand and talked most of the way, and then invited her to their apartment for an after dinner drink.

"I'm not much of a drinker. Probably the worst I did when I was home was drink coffee, the real stuff - filled with caffeine."

Jack laughed. "Melissa, we need to teach you a few things. There's nothing really wrong with drinking alcohol, but getting drunk is not good. The problem is most people can't be responsible, so it's easier to say don't do it."

She knew her father and DeeDee did drink on occasion. "Something very light?"

"No problem. I have a very nice sweet wine that I think you might like. Just drink it slowly and savor the taste."

Once ensconced in their apartment, she watched as John removed a cork and poured wine for all of them. Cool, tangy, and tasty, it was delicious. She just wasn't prepared for the next two hours to pass as quickly as they did.

"Time to send you home." John pulled her to her feet and wrapped his arms around her. "This is where I'm taking that goodnight kiss."

His mouth slanted over hers. She held onto his arms to steady herself. The kiss was heady, and she felt the warmth of that tender kiss clear to her toes. "Oh. I think I understand."

"You don't have clue, but you're a damn good kisser." John laughed, glanced at Jack, and grinned.

"Come on. I'll walk you to your apartment," Jack offered.

She followed him and as they rode the elevator up another level, she couldn't stop smiling at Jack. "Is John bisexual?"

"Not even a little."

"Oh. You?"

"Not even a little."

"Okay."

As she slid her key into her door, Jack grabbed her and spun her around. She closed her eyes and waited for his kiss.

He brushed one on her cheek.

"That's it?"

He raised his eyebrows and nodded. "I have about as much interest in kissing a woman as I would kissing a baboon."

"But John kissed me."

"To each their own. John enjoyed playing with you, and I suspect teasing me."

"Oh. Should I apologize for this evening?"

"No. You'll probably have more questions as you review the things we talked about tonight. Don't be afraid to ask, I'm just not sure we'll have answers for you. And maybe the person you really need to be talking to is your friend Drexel."

He gave her a hug and started to walk away. He turned back to her and said, "One more thing. You're a big girl. Use condoms. They can save your life."

She nodded. "I'm not stupid."

"Didn't think you were, but people do stupid things in the heat of the moment."

She grinned. "Enjoy what is left of your evening."

He laughed. "I will. I know what's in store for me."

She watched him push the call button and the elevator doors opened as though they were waiting for him. *If only I had someone wonderful waiting for me.* The image of Drexel sprang before her and with it, the heat of his kiss that triggered a pulsation that wasn't going away. She mentally kicked herself. She had learned a lot while talking to John and Jack, but that information failed to answer her questions about Drexel.

***

Drexel walked out of the board meeting and into the exhaust stench of city air. A limo awaited him. Four days of sitting in an office and wearing a tie had set his nerves on edge. Then he thought of the money. Sixteen to twenty days a year was all it took. The company didn't need him. His job was to review, oversee the course, and make the stockholders happy by appearing. The real work went on behind the scenes and the company honchos knew what they were doing. Drexel only had to wine and dine them while in the city. Then he'd go home for three months.

He stepped into the limo and pressed the button that called to the driver. "Do you have my bags?"

"Yes, sir."

"Fine. To the airport."

He loosened his tie, partially reclined his seat, and closed his eyes. The gentle hum of the vehicle was relaxing, and his mind drifted to the cottage and Melissa. Having promised her some plants, he needed to stop and select some on his way home. Various varieties of plants filtered through his mind and he could picture them nestled by that large back window.

Melissa had seems disappointed that the porch was gone. But if he added a deck off the back door and covered it... Images flipped at high speed through his head. He liked Melissa and wanted to please her. He wasn't certain how old she was, but she had to be quite a bit younger than he was.

She was a beauty, but she was also feisty, and obviously smart. A woman with brains, he liked that. He also liked the way she treated him. Certain that she thought he was hired help, she was still courteous and respectful.

That one night, she looked at him flabbergasted and then recovered quickly. He hadn't figured out what had unnerved her until she made the comment. That's when he realized he still had Margo's pearls draped around his neck.

He went back to thinking about creating a deck. He liked working with his hands, liked making things, liked keeping busy. The buzzer interrupted his thoughts. "Yes?"

"We're arriving at the airport."

"Thank you."

The flight home gave him plenty of time to mentally design a deck and the garden area around it. It would be almost as large as the house. That thought made him chuckle to himself.

It was after four p.m. when he landed and that didn't give him much time. He headed to the greenhouses on the far side of town and pulled into the parking lot a few minutes before closing. He sprinted towards the greenhouse filled with tropicals, grabbed a dolly, and began to fill it with plants. He looked at yucca and grabbed the Ponytail Palm, a coffee tree, an Aralia, a Staghorn fern, a split-leaf philodendron, several varieties of Crotons, a few more ferns, a fig, another palm, a tri-colored Hoya, a Hawaiian Ti, a few Dracaenas and several small flowering plants. He looked at the orchids for a moment and skipped them. He went to the Hilltown Garden Center's showroom floor and grabbed several pots, including several stands and loaded them onto another dolly.

He motioned for the young teen and tossed him the car keys. "I'm parked by the greenhouse. Load the plants carefully into the car and keep a running tally of what you load. Then bring my car around here."

The young boy nodded and took off.

Mike appeared. "Hey, Drexel, what are you doing here? Buying the place out?"

Drexel chuckled as he picked up a bottle of fertilizer. "I need a mat. What do you have that's ten by four?"

"Are you crazy?"

He nodded. "What do we have?"

"Go look in the back room. Are we writing all of this off?"

Drexel ignored his friend, headed to the storeroom, and spotted several mats still wrapped in plastic. The largest he could find was eight feet and said Hilltown Garden Center in bright green. *Covered with plants, it won't show.*

"I found one. I'll call and order one directly, but until it comes, I'm using this."

The one young man returned with a list of plants.

"Thanks." Drexel took the list. "Now go load the rest of this stuff starting with this rug into the trunk."

"Ah, sir, that rug isn't going to fit. There's too much here."

"Fine, grab the company van and load the stuff in there. You can follow me home."

"Drexel! You're going to put him into overtime."

"Fine." He called back to the boy. "Clock out. I'm paying you. You'll drive my car and I'll take the van."

The boy's face fell and recovered with a smile. "I really get to drive your car?"

"No." Mike said. "That will leave me with a van stuck out

there at your place. I'll drive the van. Jason, clock out. You're done for the day." Mike turned back to Drexel. "Where have you been, dressed in that suit? Practicing for your funeral?"

"I just got back from corporate."

"Ah, poor baby. Had to actually work for a living?" Mike fished under the register for a cashier's gun.

"Hey, don't knock it. That job is what allowed us to bankroll this place."

"You scan and I'll load it."

Drexel did as he was told, and Mike very quickly loaded everything into the van.

"Just write it off inventory. We need an excuse to update the security cameras and our computer system."

An hour later, Drexel pulled up in front of Melissa's cottage. Relief flooded him when he realized her car was not there, but he knocked on the door anyway, and then let himself in. Mike offered to help, but Drexel turned the proposal down. This was going to be a labor of love, and he didn't want to share it. They unloaded everything, and Drexel thanked his friend.

He washed his hands and headed over to the main house. Mrs. Pollard, the woman who did the cooking, was just cleaning up as he walked through the door. "Hi. Any chance of some leftover food?"

The woman made him a plate of boneless stuffed pork chops, creamed corn, and asparagus straws. He inhaled every bite. "Delicious. You're the best."

"Tell that to Margo who won't eat it."

He shook his head. "I'm sorry. The most we can do is console ourselves knowing that we're giving her the very best there is."

"There's no hope that it can be reversed?"

"None. But they really don't understand the human mind." He picked up his empty plate and poured a cup of coffee. "This is decaf, right?"

"Yes, it's decaf. That's all that's in the house."

"What's really scary is that could be me in a few more years."

"Don't say that. Your grandparents were fine until your grandmother had that stroke. Once she died, your grandfather didn't care about living. He never lost his marbles nor did your grandmother. Was there ever a problem on your father's side?"

He shook his head as he took a sip of the hot brew. "Nothing. Just Margo."

"She always was rather delicate. Lived her life afraid of everything."

"I know she was never afraid of the horses until she was thrown and had that concussion."

Then she wouldn't sleep without a light on in her room and often wouldn't leave the house."

"Yeah, I knew about that. Such a shame, she was so beautiful."

Mrs. Pollard shook her head. "It's not Alzheimer's. They can label it anything they want today. I think she just fell apart when your father was killed. Who would have thought a car bomb would go off while he was having lunch in a café in London?"

"I know." He didn't want to think about having lost his father. Everything in his life slid downhill after that. Somehow he finished his degree, but Margo spiraled out of control until he was forced to hospitalize her when she tried to commit suicide. The thought of placing her in a nursing home was too much. He brought her back to her childhood home where he provided the finest care. Six days a week, she had specialists who worked with her. Money was never an issue.

But the circumstances with Margo had cost him his relationship with Adele, and after that failed relationship, he had no desire to even consider being involved with another woman… *Until Melissa.*

"Thanks for the meal. I really appreciate it."

He walked out the back door and went to his place. He needed to change, and then take care of Melissa's plants. His mood instantly lifted.

The first thing he did when he returned to the small cottage was to lay the mat in front of the window, and then using his ladder, he began to insert several hooks into the ceiling to hold hanging plants. Sitting on Melissa's kitchen floor, he placed the plants, one by one, into the pots he had chosen for them, gave them a drink of bottled water, and then covered the soil with dried moss. When he was done with all the large plants, he arranged them on the mat. Satisfied, he took plant stands and nestled them between the large planters before transferring the smaller plants into pots and arranging them. When all the plants were where he wanted them, he looked at the small box of air plants and the tiny terrariums he had for them. Planting them was fun and finding the perfect places to tuck the tiny plants that grew on bark in their natural habitat was like sprinkling stardust.

He stood back and admired his work. Then scanned the mess he had on the kitchen floor. *Oh well.* He found a broom, swept up the floor, and grabbed some paper towels so he could wipe the floor until it was spotless. He put her desk and chair back into place. *Beautiful.* Certain she'd be thrilled, he closed the door and left. He had a deck to plan.

***

Melissa drove through the gates of the Claxton mansion and wondered if Drexel would notice her entry to the property. Then wondered why she would even think about him. Did she care?

She drove past the house and slowed as her gaze scanned the second story windows. *Nothing. Maybe it was my imagination.* She drove past the guesthouse and there wasn't a vehicle in sight.

She pulled in front of her little cottage, jumped out, grabbed her small bag, and went inside. She stopped dead in her tracks and stared at all the plants. Colorful leaves, long skinny ones, and fat plump ones sat side-by-side looking perfectly happy. *Omigosh!*

There on her desk was note. She picked it up and read it. *Oh, that was sweet of him.*

Then she noticed the deck. She stepped out the kitchen door and realized the deck wasn't completed. Overhead was the beginnings of a roof. There was a table saw and slightly beyond was a large stack of lumber. She sat on the edge of the deck and her feet dangled a few inches from the ground. She looked across to the pond and enjoyed the serene view. This was heaven on earth.

After a few minutes, she went back inside. Her kitchen sink contained a large covered cup and her refrigerator contained a pitcher of water and jug of juice. *Drexel.* In a way, it was unnerving to think he used her place when she wasn't there, yet if he had asked to place those items in her refrigerator, she would have given him permission. She walked through the cottage. There was a roll of paper towels in the bathroom and the wastebasket contained several used ones. That was too much. Anger welled within her like a small volcano. Using her bathroom was an invasion of her private space and he had no right to just use her place even if he did bring her all those plants and was building a deck. He could have at least said something. *You do have my email address!*

She returned to her car and drove to his guesthouse. She beat on his door and waited for him to answer. Nothing. She tried the handle and it was locked. She looked around. The sun was setting and the place looked deserted. When she thought about it, there were always cars around, and now there were none, other than that old truck of his. It was eerie, as though something was terribly wrong. She returned to her cottage. She'd chew him out tomorrow.

For four days, she returned to the guesthouse. He was gone. If she could accuse him of not trying to contact her by email, then wasn't she doing the same to him? She wrote an email to him and kept her note very short. *I want to talk to you.* She pushed send.

An hour later, she had an answer.

I'll be home on Saturday. But you don't have to thank me in person.

"Grr!"

Saturday afternoon cars appeared at the house. Melissa knocked on the guesthouse door but didn't get an answer. She tried again in the evening and still no answer.

Sunday morning she got up early and left to spend the day with her family. It was at dinner that she brought up the fact that her car was acting strangely.

"What do you mean?" Cody Montgomery asked his daughter.

"The steering wheel feels like it's jiggling. When I flew in this past week, I picked up my Lexus from the long term parking garage at the airport, and the car was fine, at first, but I hit a pothole on the way home from the airport and ever since then, it's jiggled."

"Leave me your keys and I'll take you home tonight. You may have damaged something in the front end. I'll have the dealership pick it up first thing in the morning. It probably shouldn't be driven. You'll ruin your tires."

"Well, I've been driving on it for a week."

Cody shook his head. "I thought I taught you about cars."

"You taught me to change a tire and pump my gas."

A little while later, her father drove her home. She kissed him goodbye and went into her cottage. Showered and dressed in a peachy-pink summer-weight nightgown, she felt pretty. It was her favorite gown. The lacy bodice showed off her curves and the almost sheer skirt fell to mid-thigh. She loved looking sexy without really being extreme about it.

Julia had given Melissa several pairs of very sexy underpants when she graduated from BYU. After years of being very devout, it didn't take much to convinced her to always wear sexy underclothes. To Melissa, it all became a game. Under her dark suits, she hid a sexy vamp. Except she didn't have an Aaron in her life who loved sexy underwear. In fact, she'd never had a serious relationship. But the fun of owning sexy underwear had spilled into buying very feminine nightclothes.

She wandered out to her kitchen and fixed a glass of juice. She loved the freedom of her own place, and the cottage was secluded, giving her a greater feeling of tranquility. She sat at her computer and checked her email.

I have no life. It's nothing but work and family. Her mind drifted to when she had been a teen. She looked at her hand, flexed her fingers. For six painful months her hand had cramped and her fingers curled. When the pain ended, the hand and the arm were almost useless. She'd had therapy and still to this day when she got tired, her right hand became very weak. The doctors had tested her for everything and had even done DNA testing, but they never found a cause. But the experience had left her leery of having any serious relationships and twice as leery of having children. That was a deal breaker for most men, especially when her religious beliefs encouraged women to have children. *Not mine. I'll adopt.*

She looked at both of her hands. They looked the same. When they did the DNA testing, it had opened a can of worms. Her father had married her mom when he thought he'd gotten her pregnant. Jenna already had Julia when Cody met her. Jenna and Cody had been an item for several months and Cody wasn't surprised at the pregnancy. Five months after they were married, Melissa was born. Everyone commented about how much she had looked like her father with her dark brown hair. Then they had Chelsea. A few months later, Jenna walked away. All she and her sisters had was Cody. Then he married Patty Shillings. She already had Sean and Ian from a previous marriage. Patty almost ignored Chelsea but was horribly wicked to Julia and her. She'd lie in bed and listen to Cody and Patty argue, praying they'd get divorced. Instead, the woman got pregnant with twins. Then two

E. Ayers

years later, Patty died.

Cody was left with seven children. Four were his and three came with marriages. But after the DNA testing, he realized that none of the children were his and none other than the twins shared the same fathers. Melissa had watched her father unglue with the news. His life had fallen apart. The betrayal had been more than he wanted to accept. Yet, he didn't take it out on them. Instead, he collected them together and held them tight. He was their father, if only in name, and he wasn't going to allow anything or anyone to usurp that position.

She wiped tears from her cheeks. Her dad loved her as much as if she had been from his seed.

She scanned her emails and opened the one. Her college friend, Anita, was getting married in June and wanted Melissa to be her maid of honor. Thrilled for her friend, she accepted the position. *Oh, to find someone wonderful.* She thought about her sister, Julia, who already had three children and was working on her fourth child. Julia and Aaron were so happy together.

Melissa wanted that sort of bliss, but she was nothing like her sister. Melissa was the one who always had her nose in her studies - the serious one. And it didn't take her long to figure out that guys didn't ask girls out who were... *Nerds.*

As an adult in Utah, she'd meet a guy and it didn't take him long to figure out that if her last name was Montgomery and she worked for SunWest, she was one of *those* Montgomerys. It either scared them off or they wanted the money. To make matters worse, she was an actuary - a math wiz. How boring was that? No one ever wanted her for the person she was.

DeeDee Drayden was now married to Cody Montgomery, and

DeeDee often said that finding the right guy was a matter of luck, but had warned Melissa not to settle for anyone other than Mr. Perfect. *Yeah, there's a Mr. Perfect on every corner waiting for his chance with me. I don't think so.*

She wandered onto the deck and gazed across the yard at the lake. It was a cool night, but the air was still. Above her, stars twinkled and a sliver of moon was about to slip away in the western sky. A dozen or so Canada geese honked and settled onto the still water, creating ripples that reflected in the moonlight.

The only men who had ever shown genuine interest in her were ones who were more interested in her money. It never took long for her to figure out what they really wanted. The chill in the air caused her to rub her arms, but she didn't want to go back inside.

The image of Drexel appeared and wasn't going away. He didn't seem to know who she was. No one in this little town ever knew who the Montgomerys were, including her, until the Thanksgiving after her eighteenth birthday when the little bomb was dropped upon her. That's when she learned she had a trust fund from SunWest Oil and enough money to last multiple lifetimes. She didn't need a man to support her or even add to her wealth.

Julia and Aaron had married, and Aaron was wealthy. Except the only thing that mattered to Julia was their love. She wouldn't have cared if Aaron were nothing more than a driver for Express Delivery. *Why should it matter what Drexel does for a living?* She shook her head as if to clear the images of the dark-haired caretaker, but they wouldn't shake loose.

The hope that the cold air would cool her body and her mind

didn't materialize into reality. Heat pooled deep in her belly and part of her twitched at the thought of the handsome man. When she decided she was freezing, she wandered back inside and went to bed. But Drexel wasn't leaving her mind, and her thoughts of him were anything but pure.

She opened her eyes to the screech of a power saw. She didn't know what time she actually fell asleep for she had tossed and turned for what seemed like hours. Now her peaceful slumber had been disturbed. Fury raged within her. She stomped out of her bedroom and realized her back door was open, chilling the house with morning air. The volcano inside her erupted as she stormed out of the kitchen door and found herself staring at Drexel's muscled back as he cut a piece of wood.

"How dare you!" she screamed over the noise of the saw, but he never flinched. When he stopped sawing, she repeated herself.

He turned and then smiled.

She realized he was wearing some sort of earphones. She stomped her foot and again said, "How dare you!"

"Sorry, I can't hear a thing with these." He went to his toolbox and handed her another pair. "Here. Mine play music, but these will protect your ears if you want to watch."

He adjusted the headset on her and went back to sawing. She tried yelling again, but couldn't even hear herself. She watched what he was doing and then saw the cord for the saw and followed it to the outlet on the side of her cottage. She unplugged the saw, whipped off her headset, and screamed, "I'm trying to talk to you."

He didn't respond so she balled her right hand and punched his arm.

428

It was like hitting a brick wall. Pain radiated clear to her shoulder.

He whipped off his headset. "What *is* your problem?"

"I'm trying to sleep! You've got my kitchen door wide open. You've used my bathroom. I had no clue you were just going to make yourself at home in my rental."

He stepped close to her and smiled. "You're beautiful in that nightgown. An absolute angel with a perfect figure." He cocked his head. "Do you traipse around in such things all the time?"

"Have you listened to anything I've said?"

"Of course, but I'd rather look at you than discuss my building your deck." He blew air between pursed lips. "You've got the body to give a man a hard-on that would last for weeks."

"You have no right to use my house and you have no right to look at me that way."

He raised his eyebrows. "Then wear a robe. If you're going to flaunt it, I'm going to look. And I like what I'm seeing."

She knew he'd won that battle, but it did nothing for the anger boiling inside her. If anything, she was twice as furious. She raised her hand to take a swing, but he caught it and drew her close to him.

His lips crashed over hers, as he enveloped her in his arms. Exasperated, she tried to hold her ground, but her rage was waning and heat was pooling deep in her lower abdomen. His hand gripped a butt cheek and drifted lower to the bare skin of her leg before sliding back up again.

He groaned.

The feel of his hand on her bare skin should have set off every alarm within her, but it didn't. She wanted to be touched. It was exhilarating. She couldn't remember feeling more alive or sexy. Her whole body had betrayed her. Her arms were wrapped over his shoulders and her fingers threaded his hair. She didn't want it to end.

His hands gripped her shoulders and his lips left hers. He moved her away and held her at arm's length. Unsure her legs would support her, she gripped his wrists as she stared into his blue eyes. Her chest heaved with each breath as though she were attempting to find oxygen where there was none.

Three

Drexel stared at the vision before him. He wanted to sweep Melissa off her feet and make love to her. He could hardly remember the last time he'd been with Adele, but she had packed her bags faster than lightning when he took over the responsibility for Margo. Now he was staring at a dark-haired angel who was built better than anything he'd ever seen. He swallowed.

"You wanted to talk to me?"

"Grr! Yes." She stomped her foot.

She was comical when she was angry, and he couldn't hold back the chuckle that burst from within.

"You think it's funny? I rent a place and then you use it. That's unethical."

He raised his eyebrows. "It's wrong for me to buy you plants when I told you I'd get some for you? It's wrong for me to add a deck when you said you missed the little porch and I thought you'd enjoy sitting outside in the evenings? You weren't here. So I used the refrigerator. You aren't paying utilities for this place. I am."

"And my bathroom!"

"Oh, that's insane. Would you prefer I use the bush? Or write my name in the dirt?"

Her mouth opened and then closed.

"I put the paper towels in there so that I didn't have to touch your towels. Unless you'd prefer that I didn't wash my hands after using--"

"Never mind."

The magnetic draw to her was too great. He stepped up to her and kissed her again. Burning heat seared his body and the bulge in his pants begged for release from its tight prison. She tentatively touched the tip of her tongue to his. Certain she wasn't resisting in any way, his lips left hers and traveled down her neck.

She mewed and wiggled in his arms.

He eased the straps of her gown from her shoulders and exposed the most beautiful breasts he'd ever seen. He held them in his hands as his lips explored her dark pink tips. Running one hand over her hip until he found bare flesh, he made his way around her leg to paradise. He thought he'd die, or maybe he was dead. Either way he'd found nirvana.

Her hips responded to his touch, and her mews fed the beast that was brewing in his pants. The need to take her, to release the pent up desire that was becoming painful and glowed like an industrial furnace. He collected her nipple between his teeth as his tongue teased it.

He let go long enough to ask, "Condom?"

"None."

His mouth covered hers again and her pelvis tipped to him. With one hand, he lowered the zipper that painfully confined him as he plunged a finger from his other hand inside of her. He stopped dead and slowly backed away as his mind and body fought.

Finding his voice, he asked, "How old are you?"

"Twenty-four." The numbers came out in a breathy whisper.

"You're a virgin."

She nodded and pressed her chest to his. "You feel delicious. Don't stop."

"Oh we're stopping, and we're going to talk."

"Is it because you're gay?"

"Gay?" The word didn't even feel right in his mouth. "I'm trying to do what is best for you."

"I understand. You think that because you're gay, you'll confuse me and send me the wrong signals?"

"You think that because we stopped, I'm gay?" He looked into her dark eyes that were washed in tears. "Whatever gave you the idea that I'm gay?"

"The pearls."

"Pearl-- Oh, them." He lightly chuckled. "They were... It's a long story. I didn't want to lose them or damage them by shoving them into a pocket." He hoped his explanation seemed plausible. "I wasn't expecting anyone to see me. I'm not gay, nor am I a cross-dresser. I was trying to do a dozen things that night, which included putting the pearls away someplace safe. I just hadn't gotten that far."

An hour later and after several rounds of tears, it was apparent that Melissa Montgomery was probably the most inexperienced twenty-four-year-old woman imaginable. She sat beside him and told him probably more than she should.

He held her hand in his and realized how soft it was. Every nail was neatly trimmed and unadorned. She didn't wear any flashy jewelry, just a tiny gold band on a pinkie finger, a simple gold chain on her left wrist, and small gold loops in her ears. She had no tattoos marring her silky skin. But the thing that struck him was that they both shared the same religious background, yet both loosely practiced what they had been taught.

"You're very handsome, and very sexy."

"Thanks." He gave her his best grin.

She frowned. "Don't interrupt me." She blinked as if trying to regain her train of thought. "And it really shouldn't matter what anyone does for a living, right?"

"It shouldn't, but it does. We all have responsibilities and often the difference in classes can clash, because what is important to one is not to another."

"So you're saying it would matter that I made more money than you?"

He raised his eyebrows and looked at her. He wanted to laugh at her. What she made in a year is what he probably spent in one month on Margo's care.

"I don't care if you're the groundskeeper of this estate or that your hands are calloused from manual labor."

He leaned back on the deck and shielded his face from the sun as he laughed. *Groundskeeper?* He loved it and the more he thought about it the funnier it became, until he laughed aloud. "I'm a little more than a groundskeeper. I'm a landscape architectural engineer. I'm trained to build mountains and put a house on the top of it."

"Really?"

"Yeah." The sun warmed him, but not like her presence.

"So why are you here?"

"Beats working in a boring office." He reached over and pulled her down on him. "If I was in an office, I wouldn't be able to do this." He kissed her again.

Exhilaration whipped through him, but with it came another feeling - one he'd never experienced. She was a virgin and that scared him. It was a responsibility that he wasn't expecting. *Now what?*

***

Daily, the deck changed from just a deck to a sheltered area with a wide-open expanse on two levels. Tucked in one corner, there was a barbeque and even an area with built-in benches. Sitting at her computer, she could watch the whole thing taking shape, but when she awakened to the weeping cheery covered in pinkish buds by the pond, her heart leapt for joy. Spring was truly springing and the feeling made her ecstatic.

But watching Drexel was fun, especially when he pulled off his shirt. He didn't have a body like the guys on the covers of those muscle magazines; he had the natural muscles of a man who used them. She attempted to stay out of his way and to avoid another session like they'd had. She knew she was on thin ice as her body betrayed her feelings towards him. But she loved when he came in and planted a kiss on her cheek or neck. He'd kiss that spot just under her ear and she'd almost wet her pants when he did it.

She'd make pitchers of cold drinks for him. Sometimes it was orange juice and other times she'd make a pitcher of white tea mixed with fruit juice. He'd wander in and out of her kitchen, and occasionally used her bathroom. Now it didn't bother her. She just made certain her bathroom was always neat and clean.

She watched him mix up batches of fertilizer and then water her plants. And she hated the days she awakened to drizzle or hard rain, because she knew she wouldn't see him. But it was just such a day when her phone rang.

"Hi." Drexel's voice was crystal clear. "Any chance I can interest you in dinner tonight? There's this little place called the Gray Duck Tavern that I thought you might like."

Melissa remembered that Aaron had taken Julia there on their first date and she never stopped talking about it. "Oh, I've never been there, but I know about it. Sounds like fun."

"Great. I'll pick you up about four thirty."

"Um, we can use my car, that way you don't have to drive your pickup."

"I wasn't planning on using the pickup. I do have a car."

"Oh. Okay." She looked at the time and knew she had hours before she'd even need to get ready.

After a few polite exchanges, Drexel said goodbye and she echoed him. At least she'd see him. She went back to work on her computer, but her mind kept drifting to Drexel. She worked on the latest problem until three o'clock and then quit for the day.

After a quick shower, she fixed her hair into a fancy figure-eight bun and put on some makeup. A little mascara always made her eyelashes look twice as long, as though she wore fake ones. She wasn't into color on her face so she had only used a wee bit of neutral shadow and highlighter over her eyes. And since she couldn't draw a straight line, she totally skipped any attempt to use eyeliner. But using a lip pencil, she colored her lips a deep red before glossing them.

From what Julia had said, the Gray Duck Tavern was swanky. She looked at several dresses that hung in her closet and settled on one, a simple black sheath with spaghetti straps. With an over dress of a sheer fabric that shimmered and was adorned in a geometric print done with gold thread, the ensemble looked elegant. If it hadn't been raining, she would have worn her gold heels that were trimmed with rhinestones, but since there was no sign of the rain abating, she wore a pair of patent leather Karina Karr pumps that wrapped to her ankles. She grabbed a small, matching purse and decided on some jewelry.

She knew DeeDee would have suggested wearing something bold and contrasting, but she wasn't a bold person and preferred something understated. Settling on a set of onyx and gold beads with a matching bracelet and earrings, she looked in the full-length mirror and admired her choices. The whole outfit suited her. She turned and looked over her shoulder. This was a sophisticated look she could rock.

With fifteen minutes to kill, she took a selfie and texted Julia with the news that she was going to the Gray Duck Tavern.

A moment later Julia replied. *OMG U look fantastic!!!! Who is the lucky guy?*

Don't LOL. He's the groundskeeper here. Says he has a degree in landscape architecture.

Groundskeeper? R U nuts?

Yes. He's very handsome & a good kisser. Hoping I get kissed again

2nite.

LOL Kissed or laid?

Melissa couldn't hold back her laughter as she typed: *Both*

Enjoy!

Melissa sank into a chair and contemplated the situation. She remembered when Julia lost her virginity. Julia had always been boy crazy and had never lacked a date. She had planned to lose her virginity and had chosen her long-time buddy to be the one to take it. Being the younger sister made it all sound exciting, but when Julia had returned home that night, she admitted it wasn't exactly a wonderful, earth-shattering thing. Shortly after that Julia went to work for DeeDee and quit dating until Aaron came along. Julia and Aaron were like an explosion in a sawdust factory.

Chelsea was the quiet sister. She had hooked up with a guy shortly after she started college and everyone in the family expected them to announce their engagement anytime. Melissa had met him and wasn't impressed. *To each their own!*

Melissa pulled on her black, trench-style raincoat when her doorbell rang.

Drexel greeted her with an oversized umbrella. "Hi, you look ready."

"I am." She looked at the Ferrari he was driving and just about died. "Where did you get the car?"

He laughed. "I get to use anything in the garage. It's a perk to my job."

"Nice perk." She settled into the soft seat and prayed he wasn't going to drive it as though they were in a Grand Prix race.

An hour later, they pulled to a stop in front of the posh, Colonial-style restaurant. A canopy protected them from the rain as they made their way inside.

Drexel helped her remove her coat. "You look stunning."

"Thank you."

They were seated at a table by a window. A long, dark gray tablecloth went to the floor and was topped with a lighter, almost silver gray cloth. A candle in a glass globe glowed on the table and more candles were in sconces on the wall and in the chandeliers. The staff wore Colonial period costumes. The crystal and silver were real.

The waiter came and rattled off the evening's meals. Each one sounded delicious, making it difficult to choose. After a quick mental debate, she picked the lamb.

They chatted about growing up. He was an only child and she was from a large family.

"I can't imagine being an only child," she admitted.

"And I can't imagine what it must have been like to have that many kids in the house."

She lifted her shoulders and let them drop. "Maybe there are good points and bad to both. I know how much I enjoy my peace and quiet. But even now, I'm still close to my sisters. I can't imagine life without them."

"You're lucky." He grinned at her and she could see the sparkle in his eyes.

"Sometimes I think about having children, but I wonder if I'd have the patience to raise them." She fingered the edge of the cloth napkin on her lap.

"I'd love to fill the house with a dozen kids, but it's not going to happen."

"Why not?"

He chuckled. "That little bit about being married first."

"Well yeah, but if you found the right woman, you could fill a house with children."

He picked up his water glass and took a sip. "I found the woman I want. She just doesn't seem anxious to fill a house with children."

She cocked her head and looked at him. "If you're in love, why are you having dinner with me?"

"She doesn't know I'm in love with her. I think if I told her, she'd run in the opposite direction. I figure it's going to take time for her to realize it. And maybe I need to know more about her. Besides, my life at the moment is complicated, and I can't just say hey, I love you and I want to marry you."

"But if you know her, you can."

"Maybe I don't know her well enough. How do you tell another person that you're interested in them?"

She pondered what he said. It hurt to think that he had someone else. "Maybe frequently asking her out might help to get the message across."

"I was thinking that, too."

"Have you ever sent her flowers?"

"No. Not flowers. I've given her some plants, but not flowers."

"Try flowers. Women love to get flowers." Inside her heart was breaking, but she kept her emotions under control. She had no reason to fall in love with him. None. Just because he was sexy and turned her body into a molten mess, didn't mean she loved him. *I barely know him.*

"Really?" He raised his eyebrows for a moment. "How would I know what she likes? I don't know anyone to ask."

"That's tough. My sister abhors roses, and I wouldn't say I dislike them, but we had a rotten stepmother who loved them so there's this tie to roses and her."

"Oh, dear. Guess that means you wouldn't like the rose garden next to the main house that I worked on last summer."

"They don't bother me the way they bother my sister. They just aren't my favorite flowers."

"What are your favorite ones?"

"I don't think I have any favorites, but I do like pansies with their little faces, and irises with those fuzzy caterpillar things on them. And my dad has a vine with red flowers and the hummingbirds love it. They would dive bomb me trying to get to the flowers."

"Interesting."

"And we have these bushes that get tons of white flowers on them and they smell delicious."

"Philadelphus?"

She rolled her palms up.

"Well, I'm glad you told me about the roses, or I would have planted some around your deck. Your sofa is covered with roses."

"I thought cabbage roses were peonies."

"And you like peonies?"

She nodded.

The waiter brought them decaf coffee, and they talked some more as they waited for their dinner to be served. But Melissa couldn't shake her disappointment. She didn't want to think of Drexel with another woman.

Throughout the entire candle-lit meal, rain had pounded the window next to their table. Raindrops had collected and rolled down it, creating wiggly patterns on the already wavy glass. Now those drops matched her mood and their constant downward journey reiterated the feeling of sadness spiraling like a whirlpool deep inside her.

She didn't care that he was the groundskeeper. Her father had raised her to accept all people no matter what they did for a living. Drexel dressed well and had impeccable manners. The only thing negative was his job choice. And what was wrong with doing what made him happy?

When dinner was over, they rode home. As they pulled to a stop in front of her little cottage, Drexel reached over and took her hand. "I won't be around tomorrow. I have some things I need to handle away from the estate. I'm not certain how long I'll be. Otherwise I'd ask you to dinner."

It was all she could do to nod her response. She started to open her door and Drexel jumped from his seat to hold hers and hold the umbrella over her as they walked to her front door.

Standing under the roof of the tiny front porch that barely held two people, she fought with tears. She wanted Drexel to be interested in her as more than a fill-in when he wasn't around the one he loved.

"I had a wonderful evening with the most beautiful women I've ever met."

A tear slipped down her cheek and she brushed it away. She hated being slung a line of malarkey, especially when she cared, and he didn't.

"You're crying. What's wrong?"

"I must have an eyelash or something in my eye."

He took a key from his pocket and opened her door. "Let's look where there's more light."

"No. I'll be fine. Maybe it's already washed out. It feels better."

"Are you sure?"

"Yes."

"If it doesn't or if you think there's something still in there, I'll drive you to the hospital and let them look at it. You need to protect your eyes."

Stop being so nice to me. I can't handle it. She forced a smile. "I'm fine now, really I am."

He leaned over and kissed her cheek.

"Thanks for the dinner, but I need to do some things this evening." She scurried inside as the dam broke along with her heart and tears flowed down both cheeks. *Why? Why did I have to fall in love with him?*

***

Drexel stared at the closed door and waited for a moment before returning to his car. He didn't understand her. In fact, the more he thought about it, the less he understood her. She was dressed to kill in understated elegance. Instead of the evening progressing as he thought it would, she withdrew. Now he was confused. Had he not dropped enough hints?

He sat at his computer and pulled up the website for Lapinski's Florist on Main Street. He asked for iris and peonies, if possible, but no roses. But he wanted lots of sweet-scented flowers delivered to the cottage. No card.

He paced the room and wondered what it was going to take to win her heart.

***

Dawn arrived bright and clear. Melissa tumbled from her bed and looked out that big back window. The world sparkled as the sun kissed every raindrop that clung to new grass, baby leaves, and the beads of water that lay on the deck. She stepped outside and breathed in cool moist air. Then she poured a glass of orange juice and booted up her computer to check in at work. It was too early for them. She constantly forgot about the difference in time zones. Maybe it was just as well. A lazy morning would be a good thing. She pulled up her favorite sudoku game website and played until someone knocked on her door.

Fully expecting it to be Drexel, she opened her door wide only to discover it was the florist. Surprised, she sputtered hello to the younger brother of a classmate.

"Hi, Melissa. I guess these are yours. It says to deliver to the cottage and there's no card." He passed her a huge bouquet.

The sweet scent of flowers filled her nostrils and she inhaled deeply. "These are beautiful."

"Glad you like them. I'll tell Mr. Lapinski." He turned and started to walk away.

"Kevin, wait." She put the flowers down, fished in her purse for her wallet, and passed the young man a generous tip. Then went back to the flowers. *No card? Who sends flowers without a card?*

She called the florist and asked for Mr. Lapinski. "Hi, Melissa Montgomery. Someone sent me flowers, and they are beautiful, but there's no card."

"Well, young lady, I do believe you have a secret admirer. He asked for no card."

"Who did?"

She listened to the man's soft laugh.

"Let's just say it's not your father."

"Someone paid for them and I want to know who."

"I'm not at liberty to divulge that information."

"Oh, don't give me that. I want to know who sent me flowers."

"Melissa, I didn't even know they were going to you. The order was to deliver to the gatekeeper's cottage behind the Claxton mansion. Aside from that, I was instructed which flowers to use and not to use."

"What were you told?"

"Let's see."

She heard him at his computer.

"No roses, prefer peonies and iris, if available, mixed with sweet scented flowers."

"Okay. If you want to play games, will you confirm his initials?"

"Sorry, honey. I need to get back to work. Call your dad, because it's going to take a court order for me to tell you who sent them."

"Beaver house!"

"What?"

"Never mind. Thanks for the info; I think I know." She disconnected the call and sniffed at the flowers. *I need to go to the grocery store and pick up a few things.*

It took her longer to buy a week's worth of groceries than she expected, but she was thrilled to see some of the fresh vegetables in stock. She knew she needed to watch what she was eating or her clothes wouldn't fit, but she wasn't into dieting.

In Utah, she walked more than she did here. Even when she was a teen, she'd walked all over the place. Now she was in a remote area and everything was too far away. *Maybe I need to get into the habit of at least walking the length of the driveway to the gates and back.* Satisfied, she returned home and unloaded her groceries.

After lunch, she dressed in comfortable clothes and slipped her feet into rubber-soled flats. *Perfect! My new fitness regime.* Uncertain how long the driveway was, she contented herself with the idea that it was long enough to burn off some extra calories. She sniffed the flowers one more time and left on her weight-control fitness trek.

New leaves appeared on most of the trees. Several had flowers. She admired the beauty that surrounded her as she walked the drive towards the house. As usual, two cars sat near the back door to the house, but the truck was gone and the Ferrari was nowhere in sight. As she walked past the house, she looked up at the second story windows but saw nothing. *Maybe it's haunted.*

She stopped once and admired the horses in the field. They were exceptionally tall and regal looking. One of the horses spotted her and walked to the fence.

"I'm sorry. I have no treats today. I'll bring you a carrot

tomorrow." She petted the long nose and decided the horse looked pregnant. Soon the other horse joined the mare and wanted attention, too. Memories of riding at her grandparent's ranch last summer filtered through her mind. She loved riding and would have loved to have the time to do it every day. Suddenly she realized she was almost jealous of her brother Ian, for he had bought a ranch and settled down with his girlfriend. They were raising fancy sheep for wool.

Why am I thinking this way? I don't hate my job. She pet the horses some more and realized that she might not have hated her job, but she wasn't feeling fulfilled. *Julia loves her job at Main Street Bridal. What's wrong with me?*

She moved away from the fence and the horses to resume her hike to the gates. She didn't have to work, but to do nothing would have been boring. "Even Dad works," she mumbled. "What's wrong with me?"

She walked to the gate and turned around. As she passed the house, she swore she saw a white haired woman at the window holding a baby. From everything Drexel had said, the house was empty. Except it wasn't, and she knew it wasn't. *I'm not crazy and that was not a ghost. There's someone there.*

She walked to the back of the house and tried the door. It opened easily. Trying not to make a sound, she stepped inside and closed the door. Her heart pounded in her chest. Melissa could hear her father saying that curiosity killed the cat, but she was determined to discover why the empty house seemed to have people in it. She heard a muffled buzz and followed the sound to the kitchen. Then to a laundry area where the washing machine hummed as something spun inside the commercial-sized machine. Slightly beyond, she spotted a woman in a gray and white uniform with a white-bibbed apron reading what appeared to be a cookbook. Melissa retraced her steps. The woman accounted for one car, but there were two vehicles out there.

Melissa passed the library. Drop cloths covered the furniture. She remembered playing under the big table in that library with Julia who was always her coconspirator on such adventures. A little further, she passed a room that she almost didn't recognize until she saw the fireplace. Mrs. Claxton always called it her room, which Melissa thought was funny because it wasn't a bedroom. It was more like a living room. The fireplace stood out with its carved cherubs in the white marble. Memories of sipping lemonade and listening to Mrs. Claxton read books seemed like yesterday.

Across the hall was the dining room. The long table was hiding under cloth, and the tall candelabras Melissa remembered were missing. A little further was the ballroom. The door creaked as she opened it. The last time she was in that room, it was Christmastime. Melissa closed her eyes and could hear Christmas music playing in the mental image. A big tree stood at one end and was surrounded with little presents for everyone.

Whenever she thought about Prince Charming, she imagined him dancing with her in this very room just like in the storybooks. She would be wearing a blue ball gown with lots of white ruffles and he would be dressed in a white suit with a blue sash that was covered in jewels.

She silently giggled at her childish imagination, stepped out of the room, closed the door, and walked to the very front room. *The living room.* More memories flooded her mind. Children's parties, people, late nights, and sunshiny days.

Peanut! The name of the pony came to her mind. He was a creamy peanut shade and he had a white tail and mane, a true Palomino color. Mr. Claxton would sneak Melissa a lump of sugar to give Peanut. There were several children that often rode with Mr. Claxton and usually her dad would ride, too. But she remembered wanting to ride on the bridle path while the others walked around in the big pasture. It must have been summer because she remembered hot sunlight beating down on her and she wanted to be in the cool shade of what she considered deep forest where she could explore. She recalled an older boy taking her to the path and letting her go first. He was Mr. Claxton's grandson, but she couldn't remember his real name or if she ever knew it. Mr. Claxton always called him Sonny.

She turned from the living room, intending to leave, when she saw the big staircase. She stood at the bottom and looked up. The handrail's sweeping curve begged to be ridden, and she and Julia got into trouble for sliding down the large railing. But she never forgot how much fun it was.

She heard voices and listened. Not well enough to make out what was being said, as only a few words drifted down the stairs and a bit of laughter. If no one lived here, then who else was in the house and why?

Suddenly she was flooded with other memories of spending a few nights here and sleeping in what Mrs. Claxton called the nursery. Julia always claimed the lavender bedroom, leaving Melissa to take the plainer blue one. There was a miniature china tea set that she loved and eventually her father bought her one so that she and Julia could have tea parties at home, too. She loved the bear from Germany and the cradle that contained the beautiful life-sized doll, with a stuffed body and porcelain head, hands, and feet.

This house was filled with wonderful recollections. Silently, she walked up the steps, hoping to at least catch a glimpse of the nursery. *Does it still exist?* She heard a door and then footsteps that faded away. Her heart pounded in her chest. She was trespassing, sneaking around, doing things that she shouldn't, but some part of her kept egging her on and making her want to see more. She had loved this house and loved this family. The feeling of home wrapped her in a protective blanket. She wasn't doing anything bad. Just exploring.

She walked down the long, wide hallway and past Mrs. Claxton's sitting room. Melissa paused for a moment and held her breath as if she expected to see Mrs. Claxton knitting little baby sweaters. But that room was draped in heavy white cloth like the rest of the house.

At the end of the hallway was a set of double doors, and on the other side was the nursery. Her heart raced and the back of her neck tingled with the excitement of seeing it all once again. Was that beautiful doll still there? Would someone have covered the cradle...doll and all? She pushed down on the latch and opened the doors. The room wasn't covered. She stepped into the room. The tiny table and chairs were missing and in their place were a real table and four chairs. The cradle was there, but it was empty.

"Hello. Did you come to play with me?"

Four

Melissa's heart hit the back of her throat as she spun around and faced a woman of undetermined age. Pure white hair had been plaited in two long braids and tied with blue ribbons. In her arms was a baby.

Melissa put her finger to her lips. "Shh! Who are you?"

The woman put her thumb in her mouth and sucked for a moment before removing it to answer. "Margo. What's your name?"

"Missy." The childhood nickname Mrs. Claxton used spilled out, surprising Melissa.

"Do you want to hold the baby? My arms are tired. I'm always holding her."

Melissa looked at the woman and accepted the baby, except it was the doll. Not the doll that she had remembered. This one was vinyl, but very realistic. "She's a beautiful baby. Is she yours?"

Margo nodded. "Mommy got her for me. And I had a little boy, but I lost him."

"Do you want me to help look for him?"

Margo pouted. "Everyone has looked for him, but he's gone. They say he grew up, but I know that's not true. Will you have tea with me? I love having tea parties." The woman turned towards another door and began to call, "*Nanny Peaches! Nanny Peaches! I want a tea party! Missy is going to have tea with me!*"

Melissa tried to shush Margo, but the woman ignored the plea. A door opened and a woman entered, looking about as shocked as Melissa was feeling.

"Who are you?" the elderly woman demanded.

Melissa swallowed. "Melissa Montgomery, I… I rented the cottage, but I used to visit this house as a child. I'm sorry. I didn't know anyone was here. I just wanted… I haven't done anything other than look into the rooms and I haven't touched anything other than a few door handles." She looked at the doll in her arms. "That is until Margo handed me her… her baby. Really."

"You're little Missy Montgomery?"

She nodded.

"Oh my, have you changed. The last time I saw you…"

Margo stomped her foot. "She's my friend and I want a tea party with cream cheese sandwiches and cake!"

"I'll ask Cook if she can make you a tea party."

"With birthday candles. It's Missy's birthday and we're having a party."

Melissa looked at the woman Margo called Nanny Peaches a little wide-eyed and shrugged.

"Are you up to a party with Margo?"

"I guess. Is it all right…I mean is it safe?"

Nanny Peaches nodded. "Mentally she's three. She just likes to play."

"Alzheimer's?"

"No one is certain. They call it brain damage. She fell apart when her parents died, but when her husband died... She couldn't take it and attempted suicide. Now she's like this, but constantly slipping backwards in time."

Melissa nodded and smiled at Margo. "A tea party sounds like great fun."

Years of Melissa's father making her work in the soup kitchen had taught her plenty, and she'd met lots of mental patients who survived on their own, but this was different. This woman was well-tended and obviously happy.

"I think the baby is asleep." Melissa laid the doll in the cradle, and Margo rushed to pick the doll up.

"She never wants to sleep in her cradle. She cries when we lay her down. She always wants to be held." Margo went to the big rocking chair and began to rock with such force that Melissa feared the chair might tip.

A few moments later, Margo put the baby on the floor. She grabbed some big hats from pegs on the wall and placed one on Melissa's head. "It's perfect on you." Then she draped Melissa in a white shawl and added some pearls around her neck along with a fleur-de-lis broach that appeared to be encrusted in diamonds.

"There. We always must wear pearls when having tea parties. It's the thing to do. Here." She passed Melissa a tutu and a pair of heels. "You must be properly attired for a tea party."

Melissa slipped the pink tulle over her hips but the shoes were two sizes too small. "The shoes don't fit. Do you have something else I could try?" She peered over Margo's shoulder and into a chest of dress-up clothes. "May I try these?"

The open toed, open-back shoes were still too small, but she'd survive. This was not the way she had intended to spend her afternoon, but in a way it was almost fun to be a little girl again and play pretend. And Margo was filled with such joy as she pulled on what looked like a prom dress over her clothes. *She must get terribly lonely.*

A moment later, the woman who had worn the gray uniform appeared with a tray of tea, and plates of sandwiches. "Now you must eat all of your sandwiches before you're allowed to have cake."

Margo whined, but Melissa's stomach gurgled at the sight of the tray. "Oh, how beautiful. I've not seen such lovely finger sandwiches since I was little."

"Good luck getting her to eat them. She only plays in her food."

Melissa looked at the child-like woman and smiled. "Isn't this exciting, Margo? Doesn't everything look yummy?"

The tea was barely warm and very weak. Margo served the tea in fancy demitasse cups and put two lumps of sugar in each china cup and then added milk. Margo placed a lump of sugar in her mouth, looked at Melissa, and slipped it out.

Worried that the lump was headed for the bowl that contained more cubes of sugar, Melissa instantly grabbed the bowl. "It's okay to eat a lump of sugar. May I have one?"

With a little prodding and lots of giggles, Margo managed to eat all of her petite sandwiches. She then called for Cook to bring cake. Margo devoured the cake and insisted on singing several children's songs and dancing around in a circle while they held hands. She was more than a little spoiled, but then how did they manage with an over-sized child living in a fantasy world?

Melissa watched Margo pick up her doll and start sucking her thumb. The woman probably hadn't played so hard in ages. Melissa slipped out of the heels and found a book. "Which room is yours?"

Margo pointed to the blue one.

"Oh, that's my favorite room, too!" She led Margo to the bed and began to read.

Nanny Peaches tiptoed in and whispered, "There's someone who wants to know who had tea party with Margo today."

Handing over the storybook for Nanny Peaches to finish, Melissa left the blue bedroom. Fully expecting another servant, Melissa found herself staring at the one person she didn't want to see.

***

"I can explain." Melissa stammered.

Drexel wasn't certain if he wanted to be angry or if he found the whole situation funny. His vision of loveliness stood before him wearing a tutu over her jeans, wrapped in the white shawl while wearing the pearls and broach he often wore. His dirty little secret was out. The secret that had cost him one relationship, and he hadn't intended it to cost him this one, too. But now it was too late.

As silly as she looked, he knew he looked ten times worse when having Sunday tea parties.

"Ditch the dress-up stuff. We need to talk," he hissed at her.

She pulled off the hat and hung it on a peg. The shawl and tutu she put back in the big chest, and the pearls and broach she put in the jewelry box. She slipped her feet into her flats and walked out of the nursery. "I didn't do anything. You said the place was uninhabited, but there were cars here all the time. I was curious. Besides, it's not like I didn't know my way around. I'd certainly spent enough time at the Claxtons.'"

"Just how much time did you spend here as a child?" He steered her down the stairs and to his place.

"I don't know; I was little. But I loved coming. The house is filled with all sorts of wonderful memories. I wasn't touching anything or stealing anything."

Anger boiled within him as he opened the door to his guesthouse. "What were you doing upstairs?"

She rolled her palms up. "I wanted to see if the nursery was still there - the china doll and the bear from Germany. My sister would sleep in the lavender room and I'd sleep in the blue one. But those rooms don't look the same."

"No, they don't." That blue room was his when he spent the night at his grandparent's house and the thought that she, too, had used it stabbed at something inside of him.

"The little table and chairs are gone, along with the tiny rocking chair, replaced with adult-sized ones to hold Margo? And what happened to the china tea set?" Tears slipped down her cheek as her lower lip rolled out. "I guess you really can't go back. No Smokey to sit on my feet, no Peanut to ride, no Mrs. Claxton to knit baby things for some charity. It's just a house."

Smokey was his dog. The one his mom didn't want in the house because he grew too big. Melissa knew too much. It was strange. Something inside of him shredded.

"Do you remember Margo?"

She shook her head. "No, just the Claxtons and…"

"And what?"

She sat on his leather sofa, kicked off her shoes, and curled her feet under her. "There was a boy, Sonny, who used to take me riding on the bridle paths."

He coughed. "Sonny? What do you remember about Sonny?"

She shrugged. "He was nice to me. He'd let me ride first on the path, but he wouldn't let me try any of the jumps. He said Peanut didn't know how to jump."

"Peanut didn't. You would have both been hurt."

"You remember Peanut?"

"Oh, yeah." How could he ever forget that tiny pony?

"What was he, this high?" Melissa giggled. She held her hand about four feet from the floor.

The image of a dark-haired girl riding Peanut became clear. She'd grown too tall for that pony. "He was taller than that. Those last few times you should have been on Jingles. She was much taller."

"My sister always rode Jingles."

"When did you sleep at the house?"

"A few times. The last time it seemed as though we had stayed forever. My father had to do something and Aunt Barbara couldn't come. He didn't want to take us out of school to go to our grandparents, so we stayed with the Claxtons, and Mr. Claxton took us to school everyday."

Memories of little girls staying at the house with his grandparents ran through his mind. But he was a teen and they were much younger, yet he still couldn't place Melissa.

"So explain what you were doing with Margo."

"Doing?" She giggled. "We had a tea party. Totally crazy, but she was so sweet. I didn't want to upset her."

"So now that you've spent time with her, what do you think?" He wasn't certain he wanted to hear the answer.

"I don't know. I'm not sure I understand what is wrong with her. Obviously there's something very wrong. But it's not her fault, right? So what is the harm of giving her two hours of pleasure? She had fun."

"Did you?"

"In an odd way, it was fun. But she's not my responsibility. I mean…she's not my sister or family member. It must be a very sad situation for someone. She said she had a little boy and he grew up and… went away. Omigosh, were you that little boy?"

He pressed his lips into a fine line. "I'm responsible for her."

"But are you the little boy who grew up?"

"No." He didn't like lying, but he didn't want to lose Melissa. Then he remembered his manners. "Would you like something to drink?"

She shook her head. "I really need to get back to my computer. I've been gone for hours and the office might be trying to reach me."

"May I give you a lift?"

"I need the exercise. I'll walk."

"I'll walk with you." He offered her his hand and she took it as she rose from the sofa.

"There was no card, but I do believe you sent me flowers. They are lovely. Thank you."

"Since there was no card, what makes you think I sent them?"

***

Melissa walked with Drexel and she enjoyed the quiet peace between them. He wasn't the kind of guy who had to fill every moment with words. There was an understated confidence about him that she liked. Her dad had that same sort of sereneness about him.

She squeezed his hand and asked, "Do you watch sports? I never hear you say anything about any team."

He grinned. "I'm a Green Bay Packer's fan, always have been. I love NASCAR racing, I root for the Red Sox, and I follow North Carolina college hoops. Does that answer your question?"

"Which North Carolina team?"

He raised his eyebrows. "UNC. Is there any other?"

"They're the ones in the pretty blue uniforms?"

He chuckled. "Melissa, am I going to have to educate you in the fine art of sports?"

"Probably. But please don't. I had enough with a brother who did nothing but eat, sleep, and drink sports."

"I didn't know you had brothers."

"Stepbrothers. My dad remarried, and they came with the marriage."

"How did that go?"

She couldn't hold back her laughter. "Ninety percent of the time it was fine, but that other ten percent was wicked. It's only been in the last few years that Ian and I have gotten along. Now I like him. He's grown up and turned into a decent guy."

"You're lucky to have come from a large family."

"I'd love to have my own big family. Don't laugh when I say this, but I'd rather adopt."

"Why?"

"As a young teen, my right hand and arm cramped. It was unbelievably painful and as they tried to figure out why, they did some DNA testing. My gene pool could use some chlorine. Seems I'm a carrier for a few things. I decided I didn't want to pass that along to anyone. There are so many children that need to be adopted. Why not give them a chance at a good life?"

"I've never had any DNA testing, but about two years ago, I decided I didn't want to be fathering children. I didn't want to pass along... I got snipped."

"Isn't that against everything the church teaches?"

He laughed. "Be fruitful and multiply? The fruit is rotten."

"Are you opposed to adoption?"

"Not at all."

As they neared her little rental cottage, Drexel stopped her and pointed to a bird in a bush. "A rufous-sided towhee," he whispered. "They are quite shy."

"So you know about birds, too?" She watched the small colorful bird that reminded her of a robin going from branch to branch.

"Not really. Just enough to recognize most of the common ones and enough to know what plants encourage them to visit."

"Don't get upset with me for saying this, but you are a very strange man in a good way."

He laughed and that sent the towhee flying. "I'm strange because I'd rather be in the fresh air than behind a desk? Is there something wrong with me…being happier when surrounded by plants and all the beautiful colors of the seasons? I'm an artist that prefers working with living things. I get my kicks from making things happen."

"Maybe that's my problem. I can't make anything happen. I just give the odds to the what-ifs. I'm bored. I love playing in numbers, but not when important stuff hinges on what I do. I'm one of many and when my numbers don't agree with everyone else, then my bosses think I'm wrong, yet I know that the math is right."

Drexel shook his head. "I'd be climbing the walls if I had to sit at a desk all day."

"Sometimes I do. There's a frustration level to what I do. I can be deep into a problem researching and working it, and then someone will toss in a curve ball. It throws everything off and I'm told to ignore things that shouldn't be. It makes me want to stomp my feet and throw a temper tantrum."

"Have you ever thought about doing something else?" he asked, as they stepped up to her front door.

She shrugged and pushed her door open. "Want to come in?"

He followed her inside and she turned on her computer.

"This will only take me a few seconds." She hit several keys and checked for messages. "I really thought being here would increase my productivity. I thought I wouldn't have any distractions. I was wrong. I'm constantly distracted by the view or by my thoughts." She paused and touched a few keys on the computer's keyboard. "I have this amazing landlord who is building a deck outside my window and I love watching him." She turned and grinned. "I love looking at him and what it does to me."

He came up to her and wrapped his arms around her. "I hate to tell you this and break some magical spell, but a man is more than muscles and a penis."

She looped her arms over his shoulders. "There's nothing wrong with enjoying the view."

"I could say that about you." His hand slipped lower and he cupped a cheek.

"And what if everything you know about that person makes you want more?"

"Like now?" His lips touched hers and he drew her tight to his hard body.

She wanted him to strip her naked and take her. She wanted his lips on every inch of her skin. She didn't want the moment to end. But it did.

He pulled back from her and undid the clip that contained her hair. He gathered two handfuls of her locks and pulled them forward to drape her breasts "A few more inches and you could play the part of Lady Godiva."

"With you around, I doubt they would ever cover enough to remain modest."

"You're right; they wouldn't. Besides, I doubt you've ever ridden sidesaddle."

"No, but I've ridden bareback many times. Furthermore, sidesaddle really didn't exist back then. I think she was a few hundred years too soon. She had to have ridden astride." She pushed a lock of hair from his forehead and giggled as another thought flew through her mind. "My little sister can stand bareback and ride."

"O-oh. That's dangerous."

"She doesn't think so."

"And I don't want to talk about your little sister. I want to talk about you." His breath fluttered warm across her face.

"What do you want to know?" She stared into his blue eyes and felt her whole body turning to mush.

"What will make you happy?"

"Your lips on mine."

"That's not easy to do because I want to do so much more."

"I want you to do more - much, much more." She closed her eyes and waited.

***

Drexel stared at Melissa and fought with the demon urging him to give in to his own desire. She was young, nine years younger, and a virgin. She was a good girl and his father had taught him not to mess with good girls. They were the ones you married, not the ones you played with, but he wasn't playing this time.

He gripped her shoulders. "Open your eyes. I'm not going to touch you." He blew out a long and hard breath. "You're a virgin. You've saved yourself for someone very special, for the man you will marry. I'm not crossing that barrier or taking that from you."

"But I want you--"

He placed his fingers on her lips. "No." He removed his

fingers and replaced them with his lips to give her a sweet kiss. The demon stabbed him in his groin. "I'm not going to do more and don't ask for more, because one day I might not be strong enough to turn you down."

He turned on his heel and left. His heart pounded in his chest, but it didn't match the pulsing in his groin that wanted her as much as she wanted him. *Damn!*

The cool air did little to eliminate the sexual heat that burned within him. *Why? Why am I being punished? I've done nothing wrong. Is it my fault my mom is…*

The next morning, dawn emerged clear and bright. But Drexel struggled to drag himself from his bed. His desire for Melissa had kept him awake. He poured a glass of juice, and as he pondered the situation, his phone rang. "Yes."

"It's Margo."

He listened and instructed the obviously distraught woman, who had served as a nanny for two generations, to call the ambulance. He jumped into the shower and then dressed quickly. By the time he arrived at the hospital, the neurosurgeon had already performed another brain scan. Margo Cunningham was hooked to several pieces of equipment including an IV that was pumping antibiotics into her system. He sat in the small curtained room and waited for all the results.

A young Pakistani doctor stepped into the cubicle and introduced himself.

Drexel rose from where he was sitting and took the man's hand. "I remember you from the last time. You're Dr. Richards' resident."

"Dr. Richards and I went over this scan." He showed Drexel

the results of the latest tests. "Do you see this area right here?"

Drexel nodded and listened intensely to what the young doctor said.

"We're doing everything we can. She doesn't appear to be in pain."

"May I take her home?"

"Not yet. I'm sorry, Mr. Cunningham. Each fever seems to do more damage. We just can't reverse it."

"I understand." Another slide down the slippery slope and where it would end this time no one knew.

"We want to keep her until tomorrow. Then we'll do some more testing. We'll take it one day at a time. We've given her something for her fever and to make certain she's comfortable. She'll probably sleep most of today. Tomorrow she'll appreciate having you here."

"So you are telling me to go home?"

Two hours later, Drexel left the hospital and went home. Margo had no one other than him, and now he'd become the parent. Sitting there holding her hand when she was sleeping that soundly, made no sense and he knew it.

He went directly into the library of the mansion and pulled out the photo album. Years of good memories were stored in the photos: Christmases of him by the Christmas tree playing with his new toys, toothless grins of the summer before he turned six, and more pictures of him playing with his light sword, skateboard, etc. His mom dressed for the fox hunts. As he turned the pages of the old album, there were family vacations in famous locations both here and abroad, and more riding pictures.

His mom had always been so happy and composed. Her beautiful blonde hair either spilled over her shoulders or was neatly confined in a bun. In one photo, she looked pregnant, and he remembered her disappointment when the baby didn't survive. He later discovered she had tried several times to have another child.

Everyone said he was his father's clone, but he never saw it until now. The difference was his father had slightly longer hair. The entire album was Drexel growing up, his high school graduation and his college graduation. She must have taken a dozen photos of him in his cap and gown. His mom had been so proud of him, always doting on him and telling her friends about him. All the wonderful memories of a happy family were tucked in that album.

He picked up another album that had belonged to his grandparents. Pictures of his mom when she was a little girl filled the pages. If she wasn't on a horse, she was in the pool, or holding a doll. Her high school graduation photos and then the photos of her years at Bryn Mawr College filled several pages in the old album. Pictures of his mom's wedding. The pictures of her were fewer, but she was there in the pictures of family events. He stopped dead and stared. *Missy.*

The name came to him when he looked at the photos. *Missy and Julia.* Missy on Peanut, her long dark curls pulled into pigtails. *So cute.* Memories surfaced of the vivacious little thing who loved to ride. She had won the hearts of everyone. There was even a picture of her with a dark-haired man, and then another picture to which his grandmother had added the names of all those present. Above the dark-haired man...it took a moment to decipher his grandmother's handwriting. *Cody Mont…gom… Cody Montgomery. Omigod. Missy Montgomery…Melissa. They are one in the same.*

Going back to the picture of Missy on the pony, he removed the photo from the four black, archival mounting corners that held it in place, and pocketed the picture. He'd make a copy of it and return the original photo to the album. He put the albums away and went to the kitchen.

"How's your mother? Will she be home for dinner?"

He kissed Mrs. Pollard on her cheek. "Not tonight, maybe tomorrow. They are keeping her sedated and comfortable while they treat the infection, but she's spinning downhill again."

Mrs. Pollard made a tsking sound. "It's so sad. I hate to see her like this. She was always so lovely."

"I know." He fixed a cup of coffee and took a seat at the old butcher-block table. "Any chance that you'd take pity on me and make me a sandwich?"

She opened the refrigerator door. "Sonny, I'll fix you anything you want. What would you like?"

***

Melissa first talked to her father and then called her grandfather. "As your granddaughter and not an employee, may I discuss my position with SunWest?"

"Go ahead. Let's hear it."

She swallowed. "I've been thinking about my job. I think I made a mistake. Not in anything that I've done, but in my career choice."

She tried her best to explain that she wasn't happy. Her grandfather wasn't an unreasonable man, but he expected the best from her. She fought tears as she talked to him and prayed that he couldn't hear it in her voice. "Just because I can do something doesn't mean it's what I should be doing. Right?"

"I understand. But I want you to be certain that you're not making a mistake."

"How will I ever know if I'm making a mistake?"

"Maybe you need to come out and spend some time tucked at my side."

"Okay. I can do that. What do you want me to tell my boss?"

"I'll handle that. How soon can you be here?"

She looked around her tiny place. "Give me a few days. Will Monday work?"

"Yes."

She hung up the phone and cried. She knew what he intended and she wasn't certain that's what she wanted. It was a huge responsibility.

She looked out her window and saw Drexel planting something next to the lake. The way he used the shovel was like watching a man working at full throttle. She wanted to join him. No, that wasn't right. She wanted to wield a sledgehammer and tear something apart. She wished she wasn't the levelheaded one. She didn't want to be the bright math student. Why did her last name have to be Montgomery? She called her father.

A few hours later, Melissa sat in a booth at a small local restaurant with her dad.

"Did you really expect your grandfather to brush the matter

away as though it was nothing and just let you quit? You're not simply another employee; you're a Montgomery. And if you sneeze, he knows about it. He knows you disagreed over that last well. Do you realize he stopped it, pulled the plug, and said no?"

She looked at her dad. "Because I disagreed?"

He nodded. "He called me. Asked if I knew anything about it. I told him I didn't. He told me that your numbers dumped it, yet everyone else in that department only saw glowing sales figures. He didn't ask you any questions?"

She slowly shook her head. "Nothing."

"What did you see?"

"Some instability in the ground when combined with the angle, three houses, a road, a cattle lane and an aquifer. It was a bad combo."

"What do you mean, a cattle lane?"

"Without a map in front of me… Here's a pasture and here's one with this strip in here. The only way between the two spots is here." She ran her fingers over the tablecloth as though she was drawing with a pen. She moved her water glass. "If this is pierced…" She passed her hand near the glass. "And the layer becomes unstable, then water seeks or maybe I should say seeps… Are you following me?"

"Yes."

She continued.

"So why did you see this and the rest of the department didn't?"

"They did. But the value of this surface land as compared to--"

"I agree with you and obviously so did your grandfather. Don't ever forget we're a ranching family, and we know the value of land and clean water. As you just said about yourself, just because we can do something doesn't mean we should do it."

A little smug righteousness flowed through her. "But how did Granddad know?"

"He did. And that's between you, me, and this table."

"Between or among?"

He chuckled. "Hey, you're the math major, what do you know about grammar?"

"I did have to take English classes."

"Eat your dinner."

She forked her vegetables. "Is Chelsea following in your footsteps?"

"Looks that way. She's very taken with Project Release - sees the merit in what I'm doing. Wants to be part of it." He ate a piece of his fish. "Sometimes I wonder how I raised you girls and you've all come out so differently."

"You never forced us to do anything but our best. And you've always supported us each step of the way." She ate some more and then looked at her father. "What do you know about the Claxtons?"

"Super nice people. They had a daughter, maybe about ten years older than I am. She married and they had a boy who is maybe ten years older than you. The Claxtons were wealthy, but the daughter married a man who dwarfed the Claxtons when it came to wealth. He was quite a bit older than she was. Not sure exactly what company he owned - maybe insurance or something. He was tied to Silicon Valley somehow. He died in a foreign country a few years ago. Don't know what happened to her. Never heard another word about her. I never see her."

"Who is Margo?"

Five

Cody looked at Melissa. "The Claxtons' daughter. Why?"

She shrugged. "I guess living at the cottage has renewed some memories. Who is Sonny?"

She watched her father furrow his brow. "Geez, I'm not sure. He might be the Claxtons' grandson - Margo's son. Seems the boy was named for his dad but he was called Sonny. If I could remember the name of the man Margo married…"

"Drexel?"

Her father shook his head. "Everyone called him Ron. But that wasn't his name."

"Was the last name Cunningham?"

"Maybe. It's been too many years." Her father chuckled. "Ask Elizabeth the next time you go for a cup of coffee. She knows everyone." He took a sip of his water. "Care to share a molten chocolate fudge cake with a scoop of ice cream, and do you want me with you when you talk to your grandfather?"

***

Thursday morning Drexel took Nanny Peaches to the hospital

to help Margo, who was lucid, but it was obvious that she had slipped further down. "The ambulance will be here in about a half hour. I'm going home to make certain everything is ready for her."

"I want my mommy. Where's Mommy?"

"Nanny will be staying with you." He leaned over and kissed Margo's forehead. "You get to ride in an ambulance."

"We-e-e-e!" she grinned.

He blew out a breath. *It could be worse.* "That's right."

He slipped from the room and went home. As he opened the back door, he called, "Mrs. Pollard!"

"How is she?" The woman scurried towards him.

"A simple urinary track infection. She's coming home. Mrs. Peachtree is with her." He looked at his watch. "They should be here in about twenty minutes."

"Oh, that's wonderful."

"She's slid further down."

"Oh, no. How far?"

The emotional pain of watching the downward spiral that he couldn't stop grabbed at his gut. "She wanted her mommy."

"Don't you worry about a thing, Sonny. Nanny Peaches and I will take good care of her. Let me make her a snack, so it's ready for her when she arrives."

"This afternoon a nurse will be here, and tomorrow she's getting a new therapist."

"Now, I already told you. Don't you worry about a thing. We'll take care of her."

***

Melissa left a note on her kitchen table, grabbed her small carry-on and left the cottage. In a few hours, she'd be back in Utah. Her heart was heavy in her chest as she walked out the door.

She had no intention of staying in Utah. She'd break up her apartment and return home. Still uncertain about her future, she knew only one thing. She hated the corporate world. The desire to leave grew with every passing day. Trying to explain that to her grandfather was near impossible.

Maybe watching Drexel and seeing how happy he was made her re-evaluate her own life. She didn't have to work. She didn't have to do anything. But the thought of doing nothing had more appeal than it should.

I know what I want. A houseful of children. She thought about all the beautiful houses and where they were located. She didn't want modern and sterile. She wanted old and warm, someplace that had been filled with love and laughter. *And where am I supposed to get a pack of kids?*

The movie *Annie* went through her mind and then the child's book <u>Madeline</u>. She knew all the stories about orphans. As a child, she was abandoned by her mother, but Melissa had her father, except he wasn't really her father. But he was the man who raised her and loved her, and that's what made him a father.

As all of her siblings crossed into adulthood, they had forged new bonds with the man who had raised them. Seeing the situation from an adult perspective made them realize what he had done and how much he cared. He could have stepped away, but he didn't.

She could adopt. She certainly could prove ability to support.

I've lost my mind. I didn't have a mother so I want to be a mother? I hated not having a mother. So why should I consider adopting when there is no father? I'd be doing a disservice to a child by denying that child a second parent. Why must everything be so complicated?

She pulled into the airport and parked her car. With a little luck, this might just be her last flight to Utah for the corporate world. She flew so much she had the whole procedure down pat. She cleared security and walked the long hall to the gate. Flying first class gave her a slight advantage. She was more comfortable, but no matter how she looked at it, it was still riddled with problems. There was no direct flight, which meant transferring. She sat and waited for the gate to open.

By the time she reached her destination, she was frazzled. To make matters worse, she couldn't remember where in the long-term parking lot she had left her leased car. By the time she pulled her vehicle into a guest parking space at corporate, the anxiety of facing her grandfather had soured her stomach. She pulled open the door to SunWest's headquarters and her heels clicked on the stone floor as she walked to the bank of elevators. One set of polished metal doors opened and she stepped inside the posh elevator. She pushed the button for the top floor and caught the stares from several people.

"Excuse me." She made her way to the back corner of the elevator and watched as people came and went at each stop. She was alone as she stepped out. She started to walk past the reception desk when someone called her name.

She stopped and turned. "Yes."

The woman handed her an envelope.

Popping it open, she discovered her grandfather had written

her a short note. *Meet me at the house.*

She wanted to scream. It had taken everything for her to make it this far and he wanted to meet her at the house? *Grr!*

An hour later, she sat in her grandmother's kitchen and sipped on a cup of decaf coffee while nibbling on some cheese and crackers. Finally, her grandfather joined her.

"So, what do you want?"

"Out. I want to quit. I hate my job. What do you want me to say?" She didn't want to look at him. She knew he could be hardnosed. Her grandmother wasn't, but her grandfather was.

"I want the truth. Has something gone wrong?"

She looked up at him and saw the concern in his face. "No. They know I'm your granddaughter. They treat me with white gloves and half the time act as though I'm going to run to you and tattle on them if they grab a cup of coffee when it's not break time."

"I don't want any employee goofing off, but I've never faulted anyone from stepping away from their desk for a minute or two."

"Granddad, I'm not happy. There's no passion to what I'm doing. I'm just crunching numbers." She touched her fingers to her eyes with the hopes of staving off tears. "In the beginning, it was fun. It was oh, wow, this is for real. Then it just became a drag. I'm incredibly bored. I hate getting up every morning and coming into work. And I hate being confined to a tiny room. I know I'm going to sound like a spoiled child, but I want to get up in the morning and enjoy watching the sun as it comes up. And I want to hear the birds chirp. Maybe go riding or stay in my fuzzy slippers past lunchtime."

"This doesn't even sound like you. What has changed your

mind?"

She rolled her hands over so her palms were up. "I moved out and got a little cottage back home. There's a guy--"

"Ah, a guy. So you're in love."

"No, hear me out. My feelings towards him are a whole different thing. He's the groundskeeper where I'm living. He'd got an engineering degree, a…um, he's a landscape architect or something like that."

Her grandfather laughed. "That's dumping an education that probably cost a fortune. He's what your aunt is but with an added degree."

"He said he could build a mountain and place a house on it."

"Or put a bridge between mountains or drill a tunnel through that mountain, or build a city deep in the ocean."

"Yeah, something like that. But he's happy, really happy. He says just because you can do it doesn't mean you must."

"True. That applies to many things."

"I feel as though I've never had a chance to…" She looked out the window, across the fields, and to the mountains beyond.

"To what?"

"I don't know. I only know I'm not happy." She watched her grandfather stand and pour a cup of coffee. Not knowing what he was thinking was killing her.

He took a sip and returned to his seat. "Now what about your feelings for this young man?"

"He's not young. I'd say he's in his early thirties."

Her grandfather guffawed. "That's not old."

"Okay, it's relative. He's a whole lot older than I am and not as old as Dad." She swirled what was left in her cup and watched the dark liquid rotate around the sides. "He's handsome. We've kissed. But… He's made it clear that he's not rushing into anything. And I know who I am, I've got my job, and I know that no one wants me mixed up with some guy who likes to play in the dirt and plant flowers for a living."

"Good girl."

"That's the other problem. I am a good girl." She looked at her grandfather. "I'm a virgin, and he knows it." *Did I really just say that to my grandfather?*

"Good. That's the way it should be. And I'm glad to hear that he respects you for it."

"You don't understand. No one is a virgin anymore. I'm a dinosaur. It's not like it used to be. Guys expect to have sex. It's all about recognizing and enjoying one's sexuality."

"Maybe you should talk to your grandmother about this."

"No. You asked and I'm telling you. I scare the hell out of guys. I'm smart. I'm a Montgomery. And I'm a virgin, too?" She blew out a breath. "No way. A guy isn't coming near me. And if one does, he either wants some notch on his conquest gun belt or he's after the money. This guy doesn't know who I am. He's just nice to me."

"And you're in love with him?"

"Whatever my feelings are… I'm not about to be swept off my feet by a good looking guy."

"I like your level-headed attitude." He swigged at his coffee and then drained his cup. "Will you give me this week before you turn in your resignation?"

She nodded.

"Fine. Report to me tomorrow morning at seven thirty, right here at the house. You can ride into the office with me. I want you to shadow me all this week. We'll talk again Friday evening, and you can tell me what you think."

She nodded and stood. "Thanks, Granddad. I don't know what I want. I just know what I don't want."

"We'll talk Friday."

She returned to her apartment and began to make plans. She wasn't certain what her grandfather had in mind, she only knew she wanted out of the corporate world.

She wanted to go home - back to her cottage by the pond, and she wanted to get as far away from Utah as possible.

***

Drexel stopped at the cottage and when he didn't see Melissa's car he wondered. He had stone being delivered and he didn't want to panic her. He had tried her phone, but she didn't answer or return his call. Maybe she had run errands and left the cottage without her phone. He let himself into her cottage and called her name.

Her computer is missing.

He glanced around and the place looked as though she'd gone off again. He wandered into her kitchen and found her note. He blew out a breath. *Damn.*

After watering her plants, he returned to his place. He had plenty to do and the sky was clouding. With today's gray skies and rain forecast for the next few days, his mood mirrored the weather.

He checked the schedule at the house. Between visiting nurses twice a day, two new therapists, and Margo's normal caretakers, the schedule was packed. He just hoped it wasn't too much on his mom. He looked at the extra copy of the old photo he had made. *Missy Montgomery.*

He poured a glass of juice and went to his computer. *Cody Montgomery.* He typed the name into the search engine and waited. The only thing that showed in the results was the law office of Cody Montgomery. There was virtually nothing on him other than a few ties to Project Release, a nonprofit group that helped innocent felons.

He played in the search engine again. *No one is this hidden.* He tried a few more things and came up empty. "Okay, Mr. Montgomery. I'm going to find you. You are someone important. My grandparents didn't have friends who weren't."

C. Montgomery, Esq. It returned dozens of hits. Someplace near the bottom was a newspaper article, along with several other news feeds on a Charles Dakota Montgomery and a huge court case. There was no mistaking the man in the photos. This man and the man in the photos that his grandmother had in her album were one in the same.

He now had a full name and he continued to dig. *SunWest Oil. She's working for her family's company.*

One of the wealthiest families in the USA, yet she had grown up in town and now rented the little cottage. A twinge of anger rippled through him. It was as though she had lied to him. *Well, at least she's not after my money.*

He found himself laughing. She was steering clear of him because he was the groundskeeper and way below her status. Yet she never looked down on him. She treated him as an equal. He was the one who had led her to believe he was nothing more than the groundskeeper.

Rain pummeled his windows and the truck carrying stone rolled down the driveway. It was going to be a very long day.

Several hours later, he was cold and completely drenched. He returned to his place and took a hot shower, but it didn't seem to help the chill that went to his bones. His throat was scratchy, and then his nose began to run. *Ah! I don't need this.* He couldn't even remember the last time he was sick. He found some Tylenol and went to bed. *It's just a cold. I'm not going to die.*

It was Friday according to his computer when he dragged himself from bed. In the vague recesses of his mind, he remembered telling Mrs. Pollard to go away because he didn't want her to carry whatever he had back to his mom. A fresh bottle of Tylenol sat on his kitchen counter, his refrigerator contained homemade chicken noodle soup and an array of juices. He looked at his phone. Melissa had called him three times. His email was overflowing. He was too tired to deal with any of it.

He stretched out on the sofa and flipped through several TV channels before settling on an old movie. He got up once and climbed back into bed. He needed to do so much, but he didn't have the energy to do a thing.

***

Melissa flew home on a Saturday. One week had turned into

two. On her way through her hometown, she stopped at the coffee shop. The place was busier than usual and every table was occupied. One blonde-haired woman had her nose to her laptop. The woman was an author and came to Elizabeth's to write for as long as Melissa could remember. "Miz Carol, may I join you while I drink my coffee?"

"Of course, honey. I haven't seen you in ages. How are you?"

"I think I'm fine. I just quit my job." Saying it made the whole situation so much more final and it pricked at her.

"Oh, dear. Do you want to talk about it?"

Melissa shook her head and then looked at the long-time resident who was Elizabeth's close friend. "I haven't told my dad. He's going to be upset with me."

"Why would he be upset? Certainly you didn't quit one job without having another."

"That's just it. I don't have another job lined up. I don't know what I want to do with my life, but what I was doing... It was wrong. I want to see sunshine and smell the flowers. I don't ever want to go back to an office environment."

"Oh, my. You do have quite a dilemma."

"I know." She took a sip of the sweet, whipped cream laden drink as Elizabeth joined them.

"What are you doing in town, Melissa?"

She shrugged. "It's a long story, but I think I'm home for good."

Miz Carol patted her arm. "Seems she doesn't like sitting at a desk. She wants sunshine and flowers."

"Well, there is Hilltown Garden Center. But I would think that you'd want something that was more than minimum wage. But I have an opening if you're interested. You'd be good because you know most of the customers here."

"I'll think about it. Um, since you seem to know everyone, maybe you can fill in my foggy memory. What do you remember about the Claxtons?"

Elizabeth raised her eyebrows. "Not much to know. They weren't part of the downtown. They had their own friends. They were horse people…fox hunts and that sort of thing."

Melissa knew this info fishing expedition wasn't going to be easy. "Did they have children?"

Elizabeth nodded. "I'll be right back."

Melissa knew she couldn't tie Elizabeth to a table when her little coffee shop was busy. But she wanted answers. "Did you know them, Miz Carol?"

"Too wealthy for my blood, but my son took riding lessons out there one summer. Margo Claxton used to teach when she was home from college. That must have been thirty-three years ago. Kenny was only ten at the time."

Melissa had to close her mouth. "You have a son who is forty-three?"

Miz Carol smiled brightly. "He's grown into such a handsome man. I couldn't be any prouder of him."

"Forgive me, but I thought you were only about fifty years old."

Miz Carol laughed. "Oh honey, you just made my day." She patted her blonde bob as if to smooth it. "Yes, I was a young mother. But seven would be a little too young. I was barely eighteen when I had him. I fell in love with his father when I was in high school. We got married and I've never regretted it. But it wasn't easy with my husband in college and me with a baby. If we hadn't been madly in love, I don't think we would have survived those years."

"I wish I could fall madly in love."

"You have to let it happen. Your heart will tell you when the right man comes along."

"But what if your heart says one thing and your head says another?"

"Then you're going to have to listen to your head but trust your heart."

"Whatcha want to know?" Elizabeth joined them again.

Torn between the two subjects, Melissa turned her attention to Elizabeth. "Miz Carol said something about a Margo Claxton."

Elizabeth rolled her eyes. "Margo was their daughter. Ran off to some fancy women's college someplace up north. Then she comes back and has this big society wedding out there at the mansion."

"Who did she marry?"

"Byron Cunningham. He was a good bit older than her. An Englishman from Hong Kong, but was tied to something out in California. The family was involved in shipping to and from China. They were extremely wealthy. He actually took her to Hong Kong to live, but when she got pregnant, she came back to the States. She wanted her nanny to raise her son." Elizabeth shook her head. "Rumor had it that she didn't trust the Asians. If you ask me, ever since she was thrown from a horse during a fox hunt...she's been daft."

"That's not at all like you to say something unkind about a person."

Elizabeth frowned. "I know what I know. She must have suffered more than a mild concussion. Do you remember Paul Pollard?"

Melissa looked at Miz Carol who shook her head.

"Paul worked for the Claxtons and his wife was their cook. Margo was constantly accusing them of all sorts of horrible things. One minute she was fine and the next..." Elizabeth looked around and in a low voice continued, "When Mrs. Claxton had a stroke, Margo said that Mrs. Pollard had poisoned her. Called the police and everything. Then shortly after Margo's husband died, the son had to rush his mother to a hospital. Rumor had it that she tried to kill herself."

"What was the son's name? Do you remember?"

Elizabeth pressed her lips together. "Everyone called him Sonny. He had his dad's name, but he wasn't a junior. He was something like the fourth or the fifth. It was a long name. You know those English like to give their sons lots of names. Handsome guy. Seems he went to college with the guy who owns Hilltown Garden Center. Heard Sonny's tied into it. They bought it about six or eight years ago. Built all those greenhouses and expanded the whole company. They're breeding and selling exotic and tropical plants - quite an operation. But I don't know of anyone who has actually seen Sonny in years."

Melissa's heart fell into stomach. "So he's not in town?"

"Not that I know of. His mom lived about two counties over. Heard they had a big horse farm out there - raised and trained horses for steeplechase. Why all the interest?"

"I've been renting that cottage out there on the Claxton estate. Lots of memories of things from my childhood, but everything is isolated and disjointed."

"You must have been little. Right around the time your father married Patty Shillings, would have been when Mrs. Claxton had her stroke. That put an end to all the fun events she used to have out there." Elizabeth took Melissa's empty cup. "Decaf, right?"

Melissa nodded.

She returned with another cup of the delicious orange and almond-laced chocolate and coffee mixture coated in whipped cream, along with a regular cup of coffee for Miz Carol. "Do you remember the Easter Egg Hunts?"

Melissa shook her head.

"Mrs. Claxton would invite the whole town. Hundreds of dyed eggs and some were specially marked. The children could trade in those marked eggs for special prizes. My son won a bike one year." Elizabeth smiled. "He was so proud of that thing."

Miz Carol stopped typing on the keyboard of her old laptop long enough join the conversation. "One of Penny's little girls won something out there one year. The child didn't want to give up her hardboiled egg."

"Oh, I remember that." Elizabeth laughed. "She cried."

Melissa searched her brain for any memories of an egg hunt and couldn't think of a single one. "I remember the hayrides, the Fourth of July events, and Christmas parties."

Elizabeth raised her eyebrows. "If you went to a Christmas party there, that must have been private. The only things I know that they did for the community were the egg hunts and that fundraiser for the volunteer fire department in the summer."

Melissa drank the rest of her coffee, thanked Elizabeth, and left. She had a little more information, but not enough. She made a quick stop at the supermarket and then went to her cottage. A huge pile of stone blocked the spot where she normally parked. *Now what?*

Inside everything looked the same, except an envelope from Drexel lay on her desk. She opened it. Inside was a picture of her on Peanut. No explanation, just the picture. *Wonder where he came up with that?*

Those beautiful plants by the window seemed to thrive. She knew if she touched them, the leaves would probably instantly turn brown and fall to the floor. Two of them had sent up shoots with white flowers and another was covered with tiny star-shaped flowers. *Amazing.*

She went to her bedroom, found her old jeans, and took a shower. She was putting Utah behind her. *Fresh start! If I only knew what I was doing, I'd feel more enthusiastic.*

She puttered around until darkness fell and then convinced herself that tomorrow would be much better. But no matter how hard she tried she couldn't turn off her mind as she lay in bed staring at her bedroom ceiling. Thoughts spun through her brain so quickly that she barely would think of one thing when another would overlap it. Every thought became a jumbled mess. *My whole life is a jumbled mess.* She really wasn't certain how much sleep she'd had when she realized the sun was shining.

She dragged herself from the bed and brushed her teeth. Looking into the mirror sent another wave of thoughts through her mind. She wanted to be a success, to prove that she could do anything. Instead, she'd thrown it all away. She had failed simply by giving up. *You're a total idiot.*

After berating herself, she went to the kitchen, poured a glass of apple juice, gazed across the room to her desk, and finally had a good cry. It was as though she'd lost something, as though some part of her had died, and now there was a big gaping hole.

Feeling as though she were weighed down by hundreds of pounds, she forced herself to get dressed and make her bed. With all her little chores out of the way, she decided that a walk in the warm afternoon air would do her some good.

Drexel's truck was gone and there were two cars by the back door of the mansion. She thought about the woman inside and how lonely she must be. *Oh why not?*

She opened the back door, went to the large staircase, and then to the nursery. She knocked and opened the door. Margo sat in the rocking chair sucking her thumb.

"Hi, Margo. I came to play with you."

The woman just rocked.

"Don't you want to play today?"

The woman continued to rock.

"You need to tell one of us if you come up here." The woman Margo called Nanny Peaches said, as she came into the room. "You're not going to get her to play. She's been like this for a week."

"Oh. I didn't know." She looked at the older woman. "May I ask you something?"

"Can't say I can answer it."

"Have you worked for the Claxtons for a long time?"

"On and off for most of my adult life. Why?"

"What's Sonny's real name?"

The woman laughed. "Byron Cunningham, the sixth. That's a few hundred years of those boys. Heard that family went all the way back to the Roman Empire. Margo was tracing the family roots. She was into stuff like that. Byron wasn't even an American. He was English...born and raised in Hong Kong. He talked with a real funny accent, but Margo loved him. And he'd do anything for her. Took real good care of her. It would have broken his heart to see her like this."

A woman entered and the nanny told Melissa that it was time for Margo's therapy. "Come back another day. Maybe she'll be doing better."

Melissa looked at the woman with her hair neatly combed and pulled into two soft braids. She was well tended, but there was a sadness about seeing her. Melissa forced a bright smile and waved. "Bye-bye."

As Melissa walked out the back door, she came face to face with Drexel. "Hi."

He frowned. "Were you visiting Margo? She's been ill. We don't want germs being brought to her."

She didn't like his accusation. "I'm not bringing her germs. I'm perfectly healthy and clean."

She pushed past him, but he grabbed for her arm.

"How dare you! Let go of me."

"No. We need to talk. My place in an hour." He let go of her and went into the house.

Anger boiled as she strode home. She had a whole love-hate thing going on with Drexel, and it was all very confusing. He was horrendously sexy and whenever he was near her, she could feel the electricity between them, but her head kept her at a distance. There were too many things she didn't know about him, and she didn't want to be involved with someone that she really didn't know or with man who thought he could order her around. Just the fact that he grabbed at her sent red flags through her system. *No man has a right to grab me...ever!*

She stepped across the threshold of her little cottage and there was a large vase of flowers on her desk. No card, just an abundance of pink, white, and rose colored peonies. She put her nose to them and inhaled their sweet scent. Part of her wanted to dump them in the trash and part of her wanted to throw them in his face. And someplace deep inside there was a little tiny piece of her that melted at his kindness.

Why do you do this to me, Drexel? I know you are behind the flowers.

Pacing around her tiny cottage wasn't doing her any good. And it didn't take much for her to decide that she wasn't about to be at his beck and call. Being a sitting duck for his nonsense stuck her as wrong. *No man will control me.*

Her low-cut fuchsia dress was the perfect thing to wear when she had no place to go. She laughed as she slipped it over her head and hooked the cloth loops over the tiny covered buttons. She slipped her feet into matching Karina Karr shoes and grabbed the purse that matched the shoes. She dug her case filled with makeup from the bathroom cabinet drawer and made certain that she looked her very best. With her hair turned loose, she only needed to use a tiny barrette to keep it from falling in her face. Then she added a diamond bracelet and her earrings that were each a string of dangling diamonds. *Nice touch.*

She looked at herself one last time in the mirror as she pulled her black silk scarf over her shoulders and tied the two points behind her back, so that it wrapped her shoulders and stayed put. *Eat your heart out, Drexel!*

She put the flowers on the seat of her car and drove to Drexel's guesthouse. She took her time getting out of the car, walking to the passenger side, and retrieving the vase of peonies. *He has to know I'm outside.* A moment later, she rang his doorbell. When he opened the door, she smiled sweetly. "These obviously weren't intended for me." She pressed the vase to his chest. "Sorry I can't hang around and chat. I've got a date."

Watching his face was worth it. She turned and made certain that her hips wiggled as she returned to her car. *A super high pair of heels always enhance the sway of the hips. Like what you see?* She wiggled her fingers at him as she got into the car and then drove off. She wanted to cry, but she wasn't going to ruin her makeup.

She pressed a button on her car. "Call. Dad. Home."

Her phone dialed and she waited for him to pick up. "Please put on your best suit and meet me at the hotel for dinner in a half hour."

Six

Drexel stood there watching Melissa drive off, and then his brain kicked into gear. She was dressed for a hot date and he intended to find out whom she was seeing. He grabbed his keys and took off in the old truck. He couldn't have been more than a minute or two behind her. There was nothing for miles to right of the gates, which meant she'd probably turned left. In all likelihood, she was headed for town, and dressed like that he didn't think she was meeting someone for pizza. That meant she was headed for the hotel.

At one point, he caught a glimpse of her distinctive blue car and he hung back. As he draw near the town, he circled around so that he wasn't behind her. He approached the hotel from the far side and waited. He didn't see her car.

The concept of being in town bothered him. Aside from a few doctors' office visits and an occasional hospital run, he avoided those who might know him. He didn't want to answer questions about his mother. The less people who knew the better.

Where did you go, Melissa? There is no other place in town, not dressed like that. He stewed. *Maybe I've made a mistake.* Then he saw her car and another car followed her into the parking lot. The hair on his body rose. He wasn't a man to fight, but he wasn't about to lose her to someone else. A delivery truck pulled to a stop for a red light, blocking his view of the parking lot. When it moved, she was gone.

He jumped out of the truck and crossed the street. Outside the hotel's door, he stopped. *And what am I going to do when I see her? Pick her up and drag her away? That crap happens in movies. She was mad that I touched her. I didn't hurt her. I only wanted her attention. What the heck am I doing?*

He wasn't wearing a suit jacket. He wouldn't be allowed in the big dining room. *I'm insane!* He looked in the small café figuring she wasn't there, but it was worth a try. He went to the main dining room and tried to see her from the door.

"May I help you?"

"No." He held his hand up. "Yes, I'm looking for a young woman in a pinkish-purple dress."

"A women went into the bar a few minutes ago."

He turned, peered into the bar, and saw her sitting by herself at a high-top table. She was reading the menu. "Thanks." He strode to where she was sitting, grateful she was alone. "Can we talk now? I'll buy the dinner."

She looked up at him and he saw a combination of anger and sadness in her eyes. "I already have a date."

"Really? Where is he?"

"Right here," a male voice answered.

Drexel spun and came face to face with Cody Montgomery. Whatever anger he had harbored slipped as he stammered, "S-sir."

Cody put a glass down and held out his hand. "Sonny, good to see you! It's been quite a few years... Your dad's memorial service?"

Drexel took the man's hand and swallowed. It was one thing to fight for his woman when it came to another guy, but there was nothing he could do when she was with her father. He glanced at Melissa, and she looked away. "I didn't mean to interrupt a father-daughter date."

"Oh, I wouldn't say you are interrupting this date. I get the distinct feeling you are the reason for it. Have a seat. Let's clear the air."

"Never mind, I'll be on my way." He looked at Melissa. "Maybe you'll consider stopping by my house if it's not too late."

Cody's hand was on Drexel's back. "Nonsense. Have a seat."

Cody grabbed another chair and pulled it to the small table. He smiled at his daughter. "Are all your pieces falling into place now?"

Melissa looked at her father and then at Drexel. "You have the manners of a swine."

"No name calling," Cody interjected.

"Dad, he grabbed me!"

"I didn't grab you."

"Yes, you did."

Cody looked at Drexel. "Did you grab her?"

Drexel swallowed. "You're making it sound as though I did something horrible. I touched her arm."

"You grabbed me."

Cody put his hand up. "Did he hurt you or fail to release you?"

"No."

The waitress came to the table and asked if they'd like to order anything. Melissa shook her head.

Cody smiled. "We'll have the nachos. I don't think anyone is very hungry."

The waitress turned to Drexel. "Would you like something to drink?"

"Carbonated water on tap will be fine."

The gal looked at him as if he'd lost his mind. Maybe he had. Why was he sitting here? He looked at Melissa. *Oh what you do to me.* "I didn't hurt you. I'd never hurt you."

Melissa pouted, but her eyes flashed with anger.

"I only wanted to talk to you." He glanced at Cody and then returned his attention to Melissa. "Margo has been ill. She just came home from the hospital. Her immune system is very weak and she's not doing well."

Cody jumped into the conversation. "I'm sorry to hear that. If you don't mind my asking, what's wrong with your mom?"

"She's spiraled downhill from a combination of things."

Cody knitted his brow. "She's not much older than I am. Rumor had it that she'd fallen apart after Ron died."

Drexel nodded. "Losing my grandparents took its toll, but when dad died... She's rather fragile."

"That's tough. I watched my maternal grandmother slide downhill with Alzheimer's. At least my paternal grandfather's death was quick."

"It's not Alzheimer's."

Melissa looked up. "It's not?"

"It's complicated." He didn't want to get into all the medical details. "I prefer not to discuss it."

Cody nodded. "I understand. She's lucky she has you."

The waitress put a large bowl of nachos on the table along with several dips. "If you need more nachos or dips, let me know."

"Thank you." Cody grabbed a chip and stuck it in the salsa.

Melissa mumbled, "Margo is your mother?"

Cody nodded. "Beautiful woman. Always was. And you've turned out to be a clone of your father."

"So I've heard."

Cody turned to his daughter. "I'm certainly not the person to ask about falling in love, but I can vouch for his family and for the young man that he once was. But I think the two of you need to have a few serious conversations and see what you can work out."

***

Drexel walked Melissa to her car. She knew she had jumped the gun with him. Maybe what he did really wasn't as terrible as she thought it was. He did apologize.

He followed her home and to the cottage. Her father had convinced them to spend some time talking and not keeping secrets from each other. She knew her dad was right.

As the pieces came together, she realized that Drexel was Sonny and more than just a groundskeeper. They had plenty to discuss. She still hadn't made up her mind what she wanted in life and to make matters worse, she'd added Drexel to that mix.

Drexel opened her door and waited for a moment. "Are you

sure you want me?"

"Yes. Make yourself at home. I'll fix some lemonade for us. The nachos have made me thirsty."

He followed her into the kitchen. "Didn't know it in the beginning, but I figured out exactly who you were. I did have the feeling that I knew you. There was something familiar about you."

"I remembered Sonny, but I didn't equate him with you. In fact, I asked you once if you were Sonny and you told me no."

He shook his head. "I didn't say no. I just dodged the question."

She turned around. "I asked you point blank, and you said no, you were only responsible for Margo."

"I'm sorry. I didn't mean to lie to you. I just didn't..."

She handed him a drink.

"Thanks." He took the glass. "About being honest... I... Oh, how do I say this without sounding... My mother cost me one relationship. I didn't want to ruin any chance that we might have had, and I figured if you could love me as the groundskeeper, then I could be assured that you weren't after me for my money."

"Well, I don't need your money." She motioned for him to follow her into the living room area.

"I know that now." He chuckled and took a seat at one end of the sofa. "And for the record, I'm half owner and silent partner in Hilltown Nursery and Garden Center."

"Well, rumor has it that Sonny was tied to it somehow."

"Damn. I wonder how that got out?"

"It's a small town. But back up to something you just said.

Why would your mom cost you a relationship?"

He pressed his lips together, and glanced at her once before lowering his gaze to stare at nothing. "It was shortly after my father died. I had to step in, take over the company, take care of my mother - I... It was a rough time on me. I moved out here and chose not to move into the main house. My mother flipped between crying all the time to thinking I was her husband."

He looked up and Melissa could see the added moisture in his eyes.

"I was grieving the loss of my mom. She's still here in body, but *my mother* is gone." He shook his head. "I couldn't walk away from her. That doesn't make me some sort of momma's boy. And if someone can't figure out that I'm responsible, then we have a big problem."

"And your girlfriend didn't want to accept it?"

He heaved a breath. "Worse. She acted as though it was a contagious disease and I was next. She was vicious about it." He drank the rest of his lemonade. "In a matter of a few months, I lost my dad, finished my education and graduated, lost my mom as I knew her, wound up responsible for a mentally and physically ill woman, took over as head of a company that I knew almost nothing about, had to give up a job that held a great deal of promise, moved home and then moved here, Adele broke up with me and socked me for what ended up as being a million dollars in palimony as if I were the one who walked out on her, and the whole time I fought my own demons of anxiety and loss over the death of my father."

"But you seem so happy and content."

A slow smile spread across his face. "After a few months of

being here, I realized that I could wallow in my fate or grab the reins and do something with my life. I started to ask myself what I wanted to do. What would make me happy?"

"Considering I just quit my job at SunWest, and all I've done is ask myself what will make me happy - I can't wait to hear how you found happiness."

"Don't expect the sky to glow in neon letters with an answer, because it won't."

"I know that."

"I started working outside in the yard. It was something to fill in the hours. Then I realized how much I loved it. I went to a landscape and nursery conference, partially to keep up my accreditation, and because I was looking for some odd plants for the yard. I ran into someone I knew from my early years at college. One thing led to another and we bought Hilltown Garden Center."

"And this place?"

"Necessity. My last tenants trashed it, and then a pipe broke while it sat idle. I was going to tear it down. I started to tear it apart and was fascinated by much of what I was seeing. The place is quite old, so I made the decision to restore it."

"My aunt is an architect and I doubt she could install a faucet."

"I watched a lot of YouTube. Who's your aunt?"

"She's married, but she uses her maiden name, because that's what's on her diplomas. Barbara Montgomery Designs, Inc."

"I should have known. Her name is always cropping up in trade magazines."

"She's doing some library building on some campus in South

America right now. Seems she's always doing some major project. She's super passionate about her job. Kinda like my sister and DeeDee are about Main Street Bridal Salon."

"What are you looking for?"

"I don't know and that's the problem. Maybe watching you has made me realize how miserable I've been. I've been the good girl, the straight-A student, top of the class, the smart one who could do it all, except I forgot how to have fun along the way."

"So, how did I make you change your mind?"

"You were doing things that you enjoyed. I could tell that you liked building the deck."

"It *is* fun."

"You are having fun and I'm crunching numbers that no longer mean anything to me. It was just a job - a thankless, horrible job. A job that was weighing on my shoulders and dragging me down further and further."

She got up and refilled their glasses. "Remember when I saw you wearing the pearls?"

He put his hand over his eyes and rubbed his forehead. "Yeah."

"Well, I understand now, or at least, I think I do. It's easy to see how it happened if you had a tea party with your mom. But I didn't know about her then."

"And you thought I was gay."

"Or something. So I asked my neighbors, Jack and John, in Utah. They're really nice guys. Anyway, by the time they talked to me, I was probably even more confused. But there's this woman I know and she said to listen to my heart... It's all rather convoluted."

"I'm not gay or a transvestite or even remotely interested in--"

"I know that. But I had to figure out the answers even though my heart was telling me--"

He held up his hand and put his phone to his ear. "I'll be right there." He stood. "It's Margo."

Almost dumbfounded, Melissa watched him leave. She wasn't certain what had happened, but standing in her little living room wasn't going to help him.

She changed into a pair of slacks and took off in her car for the mansion. She arrived as the ambulance was pulling in. Unsure what to do, she motioned for the emergency people to follow her. She flew to the nursery and could hear someone screaming as she approached.

She opened the door and gasped. Margo was on the floor, her nightgown was torn, and she was covered in blood. Drexel was also bloody, as was a woman that Melissa had never met. Two windows were broken. Glass and blood were everywhere. The entire room looked like something from the set of a horror movie.

Melissa backed against a wall and watched as the emergency people began to access the situation and work on Margo.

"Go downstairs. They are calling for backup. Show them where we are," Drexel ordered.

Melissa stepped out of the room and caught her breath. Her hands shook, her heart pounded, and her knees felt weak. The nachos had mixed with the lemonade and weren't going to stay put. She flew to the nearest bathroom and emptied the contents of her stomach. *What happened?*

***

Drexel watched as they wheeled his mom away. He was under investigation. Everything he'd done for his mother would be questioned. The agency that sent the evening nurses to stay with his mom would be questioned, and Jackie Santos would be questioned. For three years, she had been his mother's night sitter four nights a week. She was as diligent as they came, and what had happened was a nightmare.

"Ouch!" Drexel flinched as the emergency medical technician swabbed his arm with something. "What are you doing?"

"We're trying to clean this wound." The EMT continued to wipe the cut on his arm.

He looked at Jackie who had been injured while trying to stop Margo. Jackie's eye was already swollen shut. Blood still ran from her nose and she was spitting blood into a tissue. Two police officers were waiting to talk to him and from what they were saying another team was coming. *Crime lab. End of my low profile.*

"No! No bandage. Not on my arm." He looked at the tape in the one gal's hand and imagined it wrapping the hair on his arm.

The EMT giggled. "I'll circle your entire arm in gauze and then tape it. You really do need this wound covered."

He nodded at the young woman in uniform.

"You've got a glass shard in your back. It'll be easier if we cut your shirt off."

"Cut it. The shirt is ruined." He heard the first snip on the material and his shirt seemed to fall from his body in a matter of seconds. Then he felt gloved fingers on his back.

A voice behind Drexel said, "We'll let the hospital remove the shard."

He looked at Melissa and realized she was a pale shade of grayish green. "Go to the kitchen and call Mrs. Peachtree. That's Nanny Peaches. Tell her I'm asking her to come now."

"Mr. Cunningham, you have three places that probably need stitches, including the one with the embedded glass shard. We need to transport you," an older female said as she began to pack up their gear.

"But the police want to talk to me."

She smiled broadly. "They can talk to you when the doctor clears you to talk to them."

He nodded. "Melissa just left. I need her to get some clean clothes for me."

A few minutes later, he was sitting in an ambulance with Jackie and they were on their way to the hospital. Melissa promised to stay at the house until Nanny Peaches arrived and then she'd bring him some clothes and meet him at the hospital. He had told the police what he knew.

"I'm sorry, Jackie. I never dreamed this would happen."

"Mr. Cunningham, I never imagined such a thing could happen. Margo is always so sweet. Normally if she wakes up, she cries. I just go to her. Sometimes she wants to go to the bathroom or she wants a drink. Usually I just tuck her back in bed and she goes off to sleep. I never heard her until it was too late."

"I don't fault you." He glanced at the police officer who climbed into the ambulance with them. "I know they want to ask questions, but it's probably best if we consult with an attorney."

Jackie looked at the policeman. "Are we under arrest or something?"

"No, ma'am. We're just investigating."

Drexel put his hand up at Jackie as if to tell her to stop. "I know you are thinking we've done something wrong. We haven't. This totally took us by surprise."

The officer leaned back in his seat. "Just doing my job, sir."

"I understand." He glanced at Jackie. "Maybe we shouldn't talk."

Jackie nodded.

The next few hours only added to the nightmare as anxiety built within him. He still hadn't found his mother, but he did find Melissa.

"Where's Margo?"

***

Melissa sat in the hospital's emergency department waiting room. *How do I tell him?* She wrung her hands in her lap as she debated the situation. *No point in sugar coating it. He probably suspects.*

The sound of the heavy doors opening between the waiting room and the actual emergency area caused her to look up. Drexel looked better, wearing clean clothes. He walked directly to her but his eyes franticly searched the large room.

"Where's Margo? Do you know?"

She nodded. "I'm so sorry. She didn't make it. They took her to the hospital's morgue. I lied and said I was family."

He nodded and slumped into the seat beside her. "What happened at home?" Melissa looked at Drexel and wanted to cry.

The horror she had witnessed was almost minor to what followed. Two people dressed in surgical gear combed the place. From listening to them she had pieced several things together. Margo must have awakened when she wet the bed. But Melissa couldn't fathom someone purposely inflicting pain upon themselves or even breaking windows with their bare hands for no reason. But Margo had done it.

Drexel had wrapped his mom is a warm protective environment, yet she had managed to create havoc. Melissa could feel her heart breaking for Drexel. She knew he had done everything imaginable for his mom and she was certain that the staff that cared for the woman on a daily basis were just as kind.

Two police officers greeted Drexel. An hour later, he was free to go home, but it all came with stern warnings.

Melissa drove home with Drexel. "Why don't you stay at my place? They have my phone number. You're beyond exhausted and you need someone to look after you."

"You have one bedroom and one bed."

"I think you're probably the safest bed partner I could have."

He chuckled. "Don't count on it."

In spite of his protests, she took him to her place. He washed up at the sink and went to bed. She checked on him once and he was sound asleep. After taking her shower and slipping into the bed beside him, she lay there and wondered why she had made such a suggestion. What if he had not gone straight to sleep? If it had been her parent? She would have tossed and turned her way through whatever was left of the night. What if it had been her dad? She couldn't fathom something like that happening.

At some point, she must have drifted off to sleep because she awakened to the scent of bacon.

"Hi, did you get some sleep?" Drexel stood at her stove.

"Not much. I couldn't stop thinking." She made coffee while he finished fixing breakfast.

Her phone rang and she scurried to retrieve it, but the caller had disconnected before she got her phone. *Twenty-three calls?* "Who do I return first - the police?"

He nodded. "I'm the bad son. I failed to protect Margo."

"No, you're not."

"But they don't know that." He ran his piece of toast around his plate and sopped up the yellow yolk from his fried egg.

"I'm calling my dad. I think you need a lawyer."

"Probably."

"We'll use my car. You don't need to be driving."

Cody Montgomery met them at the police station and Jackie Santos was also there with her husband.

"Let's talk to Jackie first. She's obviously in pain and needs to return home." Cody suggested to the investigating officer.

Melissa watched her father and Jackie disappear with the officer and in less than a half hour, the three people returned.

Drexel was next. The waiting area was stark. There wasn't even a magazine, just a few flyers on crime prevention and some brochures on being a witness or a victim. People around her came and went as she played a few sudoku puzzles on her phone. She checked the time once, and after another long stretch, she checked it again. Drexel had been gone for almost an hour and a half. Boredom and fear wormed its way through her body until she couldn't stand it any longer.

She walked to the reception desk. "I'll be outside."

The warm air felt good, but it wasn't relieving the strain of the situation. She walked across the street and bought some gum and a pack of cigarettes. She never really smoked. It was a stupid teen thing she had tried on a few occasions. Something to say, "I'm bad," and a way to fit into the high school crowd. It was part of the "look" of being cool. But everyone said it helped in a crisis. *This is a crisis, right?*

She lit a cigarette and thought her lungs had instantly collapsed. Then she coughed until she wasn't certain if her breakfast would remain inside her body. *Let's try this again.* She felt like a fourteen year old, except this time it wasn't illegal.

She wandered back towards the precinct and stood near the smokers' butt collection stand. Several men stood there smoking, and she thought maybe she'd die between the smell of their cigarettes and what she was holding. She moved upwind and kept waiting for some sort of relief - some settling feeling, except there was none. Her concern for Drexel increased and with it came a headache.

She saw the familiar black boots with silver toe tips and looked up. Dumping the cigarette into the little slot in the smokers' stand, she tried to smile at her father. "Want a piece of gum?"

"No thanks. When did you take up smoking?"

"Five minutes ago. Isn't it the thing to do when you're upset?"

"Has it helped?"

She shook her head.

Her father put a protective arm around her shoulders. "Let's go back inside. It's your turn. And go to the ladies room and wash your hands. I really don't want to smell cigarettes on you."

"Where's Drexel?"

"Inside."

"Is everything okay?"

"They want to talk to you and then to the doctors."

She nodded and walked with her father into the police station.

***

Drexel was certain he was in the clear. But elder abuse wasn't uncommon and the scene probably looked more like murder to the ambulance crew. At least he had his phone back. One of the officers asked for it while the medic was attending him, and he had turned it over without thinking. He checked for incoming messages, but all had been silent.

Cody had suggested that Drexel just stay with the facts and give the timeline of events and what transpired. Several times he looked at Melissa's father, who nodded and indicated to keep going. But Drexel did notice that Cody made notes as they talked and often referred back to other notes. Drexel was certain that a lunar moth was lodged in his stomach, and the thing was constantly flapping its wings during the entire interview. He didn't like someone questioning him or second-guessing the care that his mother had received. But he had never seen his mother do anything like this before - except when she had attempted suicide, but even that was nothing like this. She had simply overdosed on something the doctor had given her for depression. He didn't understand her behavior, but he hadn't understood it for a long time.

With nothing to do but simmer with his thoughts while he waited for Melissa and Cody, he tried to piece together a mental timeline of the last few years. Was she trying to jump from the window? Had she hallucinated?

Melissa appeared without her dad. She jerked her thumb over her shoulder. "He said for us to go home. He'd call me later. I know my dad and I'm certain that all is well."

They walked out of the building.

Melissa opened her purse and fished for her keys.

"You said you didn't smoke. I don't want smoke in the cottage nor do I want a fire outdoors."

"I feel like a kid who's been caught smoking on school grounds. I bought the pack because I couldn't stand sitting in that waiting room for another second. I've heard people say it calms the nerves. My dad caught me."

"Smoking is very bad for your health." He reached over and removed the pack. "Where's the lighter?"

"I got a pack of matches."

He held out his hand, and then promptly lit a cigarette. "I quit when I moved here. Damn, this tastes good."

He leaned against her car and finished the cigarette. It didn't do anything but set his anxiety a little higher. He stomped it out and then looked for a trashcan to deposit the butt. When he returned, he smiled. "Okay, we're even."

"No, we're not. I think I turned twenty shades of green and purple."

"Let's go to the funeral home."

***

At Drexel's insistence, Melissa dropped him off at his guesthouse and she went to her cottage. The leftover aroma of bacon still filled the air. Drexel wasn't off the hook, not yet. There would be a full investigation, and an autopsy. But it wasn't her mother. No matter how Melissa looked at it, she saw it as one less burden on Drexel. She also realized it freed him.

There were no signs of him grieving. She wondered what, if anything, he was feeling. As darkness approached, she tumbled into bed. Exhaustion should have put her to sleep, but her mind spun with events and her tea party with Margo. She tossed and turned, until she finally got up. She went to her deck and stared into the night. The fire pit called to her.

Grabbing a flashlight, she went to the pile of trash and found several small pieces of wood along with a few twigs. Uncertainty overtook her as she struck a match to some paper and watched the wood scraps catch fire. *Isn't outdoor lumber treated with something?* She moved so she wouldn't breathe in the smoke.

She stared into the flames, watching them leap and dance in shades of yellow, red, orange, white, and blue. *A painter's palette or DeeDee's dresses, chrysanthemums in the fall.*

"Melissa!"

She jumped as her heart thumped to a stop. "You scared me."

Drexel stepped onto the deck. "You scared me. I could smell the smoke and panicked there was a fire. I tried your phone and couldn't get you."

"Who calls at this hour?"

"Who starts bonfires at this hour?"

She patted the deck beside her.

He sat on the deck next to her, stretched his legs out, and smiled. "I'm glad you're awake. I couldn't sleep."

"I'm really sorry about your mom."

He shook his head. "My mom has been gone for a long time. I shed those tears years ago. But I was still responsible for what was left of her." He crisscrossed his legs. "In a way, it's a shame she didn't succeed with her first attempt. I'll content myself with the fact that she spent her last few years in a childhood paradise. Even her therapists played with her as part of her therapy. Most Sundays were tea party days. Occasionally we'd do something else like picnics on the front lawn. Then twice a year, she'd go to a spa-like place for a week of special treatment and evaluation. I tried hard and it wasn't easy." His voice broke. "I did it for my father, because he wasn't here."

Melissa reached over and rubbed his back. She poked at his rolled sleeve on his tee shirt. "What's this?"

"Cigarettes." He slipped them from his sleeve, lit one, lit a second one off the first, and passed her the first one. "Feel like being really bad?"

"Yeah. And there's no one to catch us."

"Just remind me not to buy any more when these are gone. It was hard enough to quit the first time."

She took a drag and coughed. "What are you going to do now that you are free?"

"Not really free until the investigation is over."

"Dad said it was all crossing *t*'s and dotting *i*'s. He called me tonight. She has a mental history and she was being well tended. The medical records are there." She tossed her cigarette into the fire pit and looked down at his feet, which were now tucked under his knees. "What are you going to do when you are free?"

He chuckled. It was low and throaty. "Nothing. Maybe I'll spend more time at the garden center. I've already spoken to Mike about expanding our Christmas offerings, and I'd like to start an online catalog for Gesneriads and orchids."

"Oh, I know lots about online catalog stuff because of DeeDee."

"You do?"

"Yeah." She looked at his feet and winced. "Since we've decided to be really honest with each other… Um. Have you paid any attention to your feet?"

"What's wrong with my feet?"

"Let's start with those really hairy toes."

"I can't help that."

"Yes, you can. Laser treatments. Takes off any body hair you don't want."

He laughed. "And you want it off my toes?"

"Oh, please, yes!"

"And my chest and my arms and everyplace else?"

She touched his arms and ran her fingers through it. "No, this is fine. But when you're done with the laser treatment, you can get a pedicure."

"If that's all it takes to make you happy, I'll do it."

"And you can finish my deck."

He raised his eyebrows. "Anything else?"

"Yeah. That pile of stone. What's that for?"

"I'm going to build planters on each side of the deck."

She scrunched up her nose. "Can you skip the plants and make a Koi pond?"

"I can, but it will change my plans. I'll need more rocks. Any other requests?"

She giggled. "Do it with your shirt off. Especially since I'm no longer distracted by a job and a computer screen, I can concentrate on watching you build it."

"Maybe I should finish it in my birthday suit."

Her body instantly warmed at that thought. "O-o-o that might be more distraction than I can handle."

"Are you in for the long haul?"

She nodded. "I've been waiting a very long time for the right man to come into my life."

"And you think I'm that man?"

She nodded. "I know you are."

His lips touched hers and fire consumed her as his hands explored her body. Her nightgown vanished over her head as his lips left trails of fire on her skin. She heard herself mew as he took a nipple into his mouth and then dipped lower.

Undoing his zipper on his cutoffs, she freed him. He groaned as she wrapped her fingers around him. This was it and she knew it. Never had she been more ready.

His lips returned to her mouth. "Are you certain?"

"Yes."

"I'll be gentle."

He kissed her some more and their tongues danced to the

ancient music of lovers. Her hips rose against the caress of his erection. He reached between them guiding the head to her opening.

She grabbed at his muscular butt and pulled him to her. Her body pulsed with need as his kiss deepened. He pushed against her. A gentle thrust and he was there. Her body screamed for him.

His lips were on her ear. Hot and breathy, she heard his words. "I don't want to hurt you."

Seven

Drexel had never touched a virgin. His father had only warned him to stay away from them. Not knowing what was true and what were boyish tales, he worried that he would seriously injure her, but he wanted her. His body burned for entrance and that burning desire had overtaken him.

The thrill of a virgin enthralled him. *To be her first. To be her only. This is what I want.*

Slowly he pushed some more and felt the head slipping further inside.

Melissa mewed.

She was tight and it felt wonderful. He pushed some more and suddenly slid deeper than he expected, but with it came the sound of her inhaling.

He whispered in her ear. "Are you all right?"

"Oh, yes. You feel glorious."

"No pain?"

"Not pain, I can't explain it."

He thrust again and she gasped. He gave her a moment to recover as his lips found hers. His heart pounded in his chest. *You are mine forever.*

She pulled him to her, rocked her hips to his, and opened her eyes. "You feel amazing."

He grinned back. "No, my darling, you have no idea what you do to me and how fantastic you feel."

He moved slightly, and she gasped. Yet her walls pulsed and tantalized him. "For tonight we will do no more. I don't want to hurt you."

"Then promise to hold me until you must leave."

Her walls continued to squeeze him and he kissed her until her mews grew into something more. His own fluid spilled and she gripped him tightly to her. His hands floated over her soft curves until he slowly fell from within her.

The fire had faded to a handful of glowing coals. He stood in the darkness, helped her to her feet and wrapped his arms around her. "I don't want to spend another night without you for as long as I live."

She pulled away from him and scurried inside. He placed the lid on the fire pit, gathered their clothes, and followed her. He found her in the bathroom in tears holding a tissue between her legs.

"Did I hurt you that much?"

"No. I really don't hurt at all."

He withdrew her hand and looked at the fluid that had spilled. He looked at himself in the light and smiled. "Your menses? Breaking the hymen should have only been a bloody tinge or a few drops. That looks like much more."

"I don't know…maybe. It would make me a day or two early."

"Let's take a shower and we'll figure it out."

"You're not upset?"

"A little. I would have preferred to awaken to another chance to make love to you. Shall I give you a moment to take care of things?"

"Please."

He kissed her cheek. "I'll make some tea."

He found her tin of herbal tea and boiled some water. He set the tea to brew and went back to the bathroom. She was already in the shower when he stepped in with her.

He ran the back of his finger over one breast. "You are the most beautiful woman I've ever known and you are mine. I'm keeping you until the end of time."

***

Drexel took her to Hong Kong. In a small shop, she found the ring that she wanted. It was perfect. The diamonds were not too big or too small and the whole thing fit her finger perfectly. She met several of his family members and was welcomed into this distant family. But when she returned home, she ran to DeeDee's bridal salon and dragged Drexel with her.

DeeDee might have become her legal stepmother, but she was more of a friend.

Julia gushed over the ring and offered to help Melissa pick out a dress.

"You really don't need me for this," Drexel protested.

"You're right, I don't need you, but I'd like for you to help me pick it out."

Drexel rolled his eyes. But when Julia showed off one particular dress, Drexel almost salivated. "That would be beautiful on you."

Julia smiled. "That's what I thought."

Super-white satin with touches of lace made it a fairytale dress. It was then that it hit Melissa. "I want to be married at the main house. And to have the reception in the ballroom."

"Whatever you want." Drexel smiled.

Julia took Melissa's measurements and DeeDee hovered nearby making sketches of Melissa in a bridal gown.

DeeDee looked at Drexel. "It's that off the shoulders thing that you like?'

"I guess. It just looks like it belongs on her. It's all feminine, but not frilly. It looks like a bridal dress."

Melissa grinned. "You like the cleavage."

"What man wouldn't?"

"On Melissa, you'll get lots of cleavage." DeeDee tipped her sketchbook and showed them. "I want you to have something special - a real one of a kind."

"Oh, it's beautiful."

DeeDee went to a computer and pulled up a page. "This. Like this."

Melissa instantly agreed.

"Shall I call Chrisy?" DeeDee returned to her sketching.

"Yes!" Julia's face lit up.

"Who is Chrisy?" Drexel asked.

DeeDee answered. "He's my promoter." She giggled. "He's a very unusual man, and he's very good at what he does." She turned to Melissa. "You'll break his heart if you don't let him in on this wedding."

"Chrisy is a guy?" Drexel looked at them with disbelief on his face.

Julia laughed. "And he's straight, too. He just doesn't look it."

"He likes bright colored clothing," DeeDee said, with a smile.

Julia rolled her eyes. "And he wears heels."

"He's more comfortable in them," DeeDee said, and then looked directly at Drexel. "Talk to Cody. He's gotten to know Chrisy, and the guys get along great."

Melissa thought for a moment. To Chrisy, weddings, especially involving a Montgomery, were worthy of a Hollywood setting.

"Oh, come on, Melissa," Julia pleaded. "You only get married once."

Melissa looked at her family and then at Drexel. "Okay. But tell him I want small and quiet."

DeeDee laughed as she picked up her phone. "Explain that to him."

***

Drexel open the doors to the ballroom. It was the perfect day for a wedding. The sun shone and warmed the air, yet there was a gentle breeze. Mrs. Pollard was in the kitchen fretting over every morsel, and Chrisy was checking every flower arrangement.

The Montgomery women were right. Chrisy was a very unusual man. He wore a peacock blue suit with matching boots that were heeled and his long, gray ponytail hung down his back. But under that colorful exterior, Chrisy had a heart of gold and wanted Melissa to be totally happy.

Chrisy had opened windows letting fresh air blow through the house. Rooms had been repainted and everything scrubbed clean. Drexel's grandmother's antique furniture shone with a satiny finish.

But Drexel watched Melissa's excitement as she had walked through the house the other day was worth every penny spent on renovations. Her smile was so bright, and she was so thrilled. That enthusiasm spilled over on him.

Everyone had panicked when Melissa flew off to be a bridesmaid for her friend's wedding, but Drexel knew Melissa would be fine and be back in time for her own wedding. She was good at keeping promises, and she wasn't about to disappoint her best friend or miss that wedding.

Last night, they'd had the rehearsal and the dinner to go with it. Then they partied until the wee hours. Somewhere between last night and this morning, the ballroom had changed. *Chrisy must have stayed up the entire night to do it.*

Drexel worried a little about his ability to dance. At sixteen, his mother had sent him to take ballroom dancing. He had turned his nose up at the lessons, barely paid attention, and begged to quit. He knew a few basic steps and Cody had tried to show him enough to survive this event.

He took the stairs two at a time, and knocked on one door. He called the woman Aunt Patrice, but she was really a distant cousin who had come from Hong Kong to attend the wedding. Altogether there were twenty-three family members who were from Hong Kong.

Aunt Patrice's husband opened the door.

Drexel smiled. "I do hope everything is to your liking."

"Oh, my dear boy," Aunt Patrice said, from where she was seated by a window. "This is wonderful. The view is spectacular. But I've been totally fascinated watching that baby horse trying to find some legs."

Drexel flew to the window. "I had no idea." He stood there next to Aunt Patrice and watched the tiny foal. "Looks like they did fine without me. And what a perfect day for birthing."

The older woman patted his arm. "I'm sure you'll be making lots of little Cunninghams to keep the line going. You know you are the last. You need to produce some heirs."

He leaned over and kissed her cheek. "Melissa and I have talked about filling this house with children. Now, if you will forgive me, I have plenty to do today."

He passed Nanny Peaches in the hallway, and greeted her with a kiss. She was helping in the kitchen and doing a fine job of taking care of the family guests who were staying in the house.

He knocked on another door and his mother's cousin opened it.

"Just checking that you have everything you need," Drexel said with a smile.

"Lovely. Simply lovely. You couldn't ask for a nicer day. Audrey and I were just talking about that." He waved his hand. "Things are so different here in the States. Much nicer than England, don't you think?"

Again, Drexel chatted for a few minutes before excusing himself and returned to the downstairs. He grabbed up a few cubes of sugar from a sugar bowl that had come down on a tray from someone's breakfast. Chrisy wandered past and appeared to be talking to himself, but Drexel knew the man had an earpiece for his phone. Pushing the back door open, Drexel stepped outside. He went to the meadow and his mare instantly came to him. Her mousy gray foal was all legs and still wobbly.

"You had that little filly without me, didn't you?" He stuck his hand into his pocket and then fed the mare the lump of sugar. "I thought you were going to need help."

He stood petting the horse's muzzle and contemplated his life. It wasn't that long ago that he looked across this land and thought that his life had crashed. Now he saw it as the beginning of a better one. He understood what it was to have a multibillion-dollar business under him and how to handle it. He had the garden center, and his dream of an equine center was taking shape with his Tennessee Walking horse foal. But what made him the happiest was having Melissa.

"When did she have her?"

Drexel turned and saw Chelsea and Melissa standing beside him. "Aren't you supposed to be hiding from me and getting ready?"

Melissa shrugged. "Old wives tale. I needed some exercise and doing nothing is killing me. When did she have her baby?"

"Maybe in the last hour or so. Isn't she a beauty?"

"She's a pretty color."

"She won't stay that way. She'll be solid black once she sheds her foaling coat."

"Shed like snake skin?"

"No. In a couple of weeks, you'll notice the change in her coat."

"Oh." Melissa stared at the animals for a moment and then turned her attention to him. "Are you nervous?"

He shook his head. "How about you?"

"A little. Chrisy makes everything a big production." She looked up at him with her sweet smile. "But I'm not the least bit nervous about being married to you." She turned and spotted a car. "That's Julia. Got to run." She scampered away with Chelsea in tow.

He rubbed his mare's muzzle and walked to the rose garden. There in the center under the sundial, he had buried his mother's ashes. *You would have loved to be here for this. At least you got to meet Melissa.* He wiped away the tears that rolled down his cheeks.

In a way, he wished the wedding had been scheduled for earlier in the day. Killing time was killing him.

***

Julia ordered Melissa into the shower. "I can't believe you are this nonchalant about this whole thing. This is your big day."

"No, it's not. It's just a big production produced by Chrisy. I'm only getting married, making it all official."

"Are your suitcases packed?"

"Yes!" She wiggled her fingers in a wave and headed into her shower. Drexel had spent the last few nights at his guesthouse because of all the family buzzing around. They had to keep up appearances according to him. She just wished he were with her. They hadn't been able to do more than steal a few minutes alone in almost a week.

She dried off and pulled on her white terry robe that Julia insisted she needed. As she stepped out of the bathroom, she announced, "I don't want a bunch of nail polish on my nails. All I'll do is chip it off."

"Too bad. You're getting a French manicure. If it chips tomorrow, you can take it off. Let me see your nails. You didn't cut them, did you?"

"No! And they are driving me nuts. I hate them this long."

Chelsea giggled. "You two are darn funny."

Melissa snarled, "You're next. Wait until she starts ordering you around as though you're still eight years old."

Chelsea laughed. "It probably won't work. Maybe I'll elope and skip all this."

"Don't even think about it! Grandmom will have your hide," Melissa shot back.

"Let's not talk about our grandparents." Julia whined.

"Why?" Melissa asked.

"They are driving Dad nuts, and all Dad is doing is cleaning up behind Aunt Barbara." Chelsea laughed. "You have no idea what it's like at the house. I almost called the other night to see if I could stay with you." Chelsea left and answered the knock on the door. "It's time to get beautiful!"

Julie peeked around the corner. "Yep, hair and nails."

Melissa sat through the manicure and pedicure totally afraid to even breathe for fear of messing something up, but she, also, didn't like the odor of nail polish. "Please open my back door before I die from the fumes."

"It's not that bad," Chelsea said.

"Yes it is." Melissa didn't want to let on that her anxiety over the wedding was building within her.

At noon, her hair was done and she was wearing her white day dress. Julia drove Chelsea and Melissa to the mansion for a garden lunch. Apparently the men had a buffet inside, but the bride's event was outside.

Melissa caught Julia frowning at the rose garden and smiled at her sister. "They aren't Patty's roses, they were Drexel's grandmother's roses."

"I know. It's been a long time, but Patty Shillings was the most hateful woman I've ever known."

"She was jealous of us. I can see it now, but I didn't back then. She wanted to protect her boys, and we, by virtue of our existence, stood in the way."

Julia grimaced. "I still hate her."

"Let it go."

"I'm sorry. It's your wedding day and I'm talking about the witch."

Melissa laughed and greeted her grandmother. On the far side of the garden, she could see Drexel. Standing there dressed in his light gray suit, he almost looked out of place in the yard dressed like that as he inspected a shrub. He had fussed over the outside more than Chrisy had fussed over the interior.

It had taken months to restore the interior of the house. Furniture came and furniture went, and what was kept was cleaned, polished and buffed. And through it all, Chrisy oversaw every drop of soap, paint, oil, shampoo, and polishing compound as this house was combined with antiques from Drexel's parents' home.

She and Drexel had traveled back and forth between the two houses, making decisions on all sorts of things. The blending of the two houses meant they were keeping the very best of everything. The Claxton Mansion was incredibly beautiful - better than it ever was - but with the same warm charms that Melissa had loved since childhood.

She had openly fought with Chrisy over his outrageous wedding plans and several times thought Drexel was on Chrisy's side and not hers. But Drexel wanted her to have the perfect day, too. In just a few more hours, it would be over. They only had to survive the hoopla and make the families happy. She smiled and Drexel smiled back before vanishing around the front of the house.

***

Chrisy stuck his nose in the kitchen and Mrs. Pollard threatened him with her wooden spoon. "You are not going to come in here and tell me what to do. I've been cooking for this family since before you were born."

"Okay. I understand."

"You had better."

"But--"

"Don't give me any but!"

"I only wanted a cup of coffee."

The woman frowned. "Well, be quick about it."

He grabbed his coffee and retreated to the front of the house. Normally after two cups of coffee, Chrisy felt wide awake and energized. This cup made his fourth one and he still felt as though he needed a nap. *What's wrong with me?*

The men were having lunch in the main dining room, and from the library window, he could watch the women with their garden lunch party. He watched the three sisters and DeeDee. It seemed like yesterday when the girls were teens and they had grown into confident women. He loved them as he did his own children. Pride filled him as though he had made them what they were.

He moved from the window to check the ballroom one more time. The crystal chandeliers twinkled from the sunlight causing them to toss rainbows over the floor and walls.

Drexel had given Chrisy free run of the greenhouses and he promised not to empty them. But before Chrisy had a chance to do any of it, Drexel had done it. Rubber trees, ferns, and several ponytail plants softened the corners. Chrisy was impressed with Drexel's ability to select and arrange the plants. *He's got a good eye.*

Julia had worked out the seating plan for the sixty-eight attendees. Place cards sat on the tables. On the back of every chair was a white satin pocket filled with little wedding favors. With an attendee's name embroidered in blue, the pocket was attached to the chair with blue ribbons. Snowy white tablecloths draped over floor length blue ones and each table displayed a tall, antique silver candelabra decorated in white and blue flowers.

One table held the cake. He couldn't believe that Mrs. Pollard had made it. Three large tiers, a set of columns and two more tiers sat on top. At the very top was a china bride and groom figurine that had once belonged to Drexel's great grandparents on his mother's side. The sides of the lower tiers had clusters of sugared blue violets and between those were Chinese dragons made of icing for luck. The top layers had sunbursts between the violets. *I wonder if anyone will even notice the intricate design.*

Chrisy stepped out of the room and locked the big doors. The kitchen still had access, but the room was closed for all visitors. As soon as the men dispersed from their noon meal, Chrisy would set the smaller dining room up for the hors d'oeuvres to be served after the wedding. He slipped his father's antique, gold engineer's watch out of his pocket and looked at the time.

Lapinski's florist shop still hadn't delivered the bridal bouquets or the final arrangements of flowers for the wedding. Chrisy's stomach churned with bile and wasn't going to settle down until he saw that van and those flowers. There was plenty of time, but he'd breathe easier knowing they were here.

Julia had hired two local bands to play music and a string ensemble for the actual wedding and dinner. He knew that something was up between Cody and Melissa when it came to dancing, because DeeDee had sent Chrisy a warning not to interfere. All he knew was it would start with a drum roll on a beatbox, and it worried him. He trusted Cody more than he did Melissa, but figured if Cody was content, it couldn't be too bad.

The wedding would take place in the waning afternoon sunlight. Chrisy leaned against the doorframe. The ballroom was understated elegance. It matched Melissa's quiet but often playful demeanor.

He hadn't slept in over thirty-six hours. Adrenalin, pumping through his system, had kept him awake and functioning. It was almost time for the main event, and he lived for these moments. He slipped his phone from his pocket and checked his list one more time. Everything was on schedule - everything was running smoothly.

One last peek at the front yard assured him that this wedding would go without a hitch. Drexel had built the arbor and intended to use it in a garden afterwards. He had also insisted on choosing the flowers to decorate it. He didn't want tropical plants being burned in the bright sunlight.

Slipcovered chairs were in a perfect semicircle facing the arbor, and each chair was tied with a blue bow. The arbor looked perfect, and the florist had sent lovely bouquets that complimented the flowers on the arbor. A pale blue carpet runner went from the steps of the house to just slightly beyond the arbor. The runner covered a hard surface underneath that would allow Melissa to walk in heels over the grassy area. Brass posts with blue velvet cords kept people from stepping on the carpet and roped off the entire area.

Chrisy remembered Melissa hounding him over this wedding. She didn't want anything over the top, just a simple wedding. The photographer's video person was setting up several tripods to capture the actual wedding. The photographer was local, someone the girls knew. Chrisy had looked at samples of the photographer's work and loved it. Satisfied, he stepped back inside to pace until the flowers arrived.

I swear I'm not getting any kick from this coffee!

***

Melissa stood in front of a full-length mirror while Julia fastened the tiny covered buttons down the back of her wedding gown. Its off-the-shoulder design was perfect on her. DeeDee had recently designed the gown as part of her new wedding collection and then changed it slightly to show off Melissa's figure.

Julia had called it Melissa's princess dress as it was befitting royalty. Melissa smiled at that thought, because she felt like the princess in a fairytale who was about to marry her Prince Charming.

"Who the heck is knocking at the door? Don't they know we're trying to get Melissa dressed?" Chelsea huffed.

"Probably Chrisy with some last minute thing. Just answer the door," Julia commanded.

A minute later, Chelsea returned and handed Melissa a box. "That was Drexel. He said this is for you. For the wedding."

Melissa took the box and removed the blue bow and the white wrapping paper. Underneath the paper was a box with the logo from the jewelry store in Hong Kong. As she lifted the lid, she gasped. Beautiful blue sapphires, diamonds, and pearls sat in a filigree of dragons and sunbursts in white and yellow gold. So beautifully crafted and intricately designed, the two company logos were virtually lost unless someone looked for them. Melissa smiled as her sisters ogled the gift. "Well, which one of you is going to put it on me?"

Chelsea took it and draped it around Melissa's neck.

Melissa slipped the diamonds from her ears and went with the ones matching her necklace. "How do they look?"

"Like a million bucks!" Chelsea stood with her hands on her hips. "You are so lucky."

Melissa handed her younger sister the diamond and pearl set she was going to wear.

"But DeeDee bought these for you."

Melissa laughed. "I think Drexel trumps DeeDee. Besides, I did wear them to the luncheon. And when do you two plan to get dressed?"

"Now." Julia giggled.

Pregnant again, Julia didn't want to be part of the wedding party. She slipped into her blue street-length dress and changed her shoes. Then she helped Chelsea into her into her dress. Chelsea's blue dress was similar in style to the bridal dress, but not as full or embellished in embroidery. Chelsea didn't have her sister's figure, but DeeDee had made Chelsea's dress so that it appeared that she had more cleavage.

The gal doing their makeup draped all three of them in special capes and touched up their faces. When they were done, Chelsea announced that she had to sneeze. Julia handed her a box of tissues and threatened her not to mess up her makeup.

Six times, Chelsea sneezed. Each more forceful than the last and when she was done, Julia dusted a little more powder on her nose.

"Did you take your allergy medicine this morning?" Julia asked.

Chelsea nodded and grabbed another tissue.

Melissa laughed. "I will kill you if you sneeze during the wedding."

"Maybe it's the powder." She sneezed again.

"Okay, no more powder." Melissa giggled.

Charley burst through the door with her normal six-year-old enthusiasm. "Hi, Mommy and Karina are coming.

DeeDee called to the girls as she walked into the tiny cottage with her best friend, Karina. "Look who finally made it!"

They each hugged Karina and thanked her for their fabulous shoes. Karina Karr shoes were the most sought after shoes in the world and having her design something special just for them really was an honor.

DeeDee looked at Melissa's necklace and earrings. "They're beautiful. Drexel?"

Melissa nodded. "I hope you aren't disappointed. I'm letting Chelsea wear what you gave me."

"Drexel wanted a sketch of your bodice. I just didn't know why. And yes, letting Chelsea wear the set is perfect. I don't mind at all."

Karina looked at Melissa. "I hear you need something old and something you can borrow." She reached into her purse and withdrew two items wrapped in tissue paper. "The hankie is very old. I found it in a tiny shop in Madrid. And since you don't have a pocket, just stuff it between the girls."

"It's beautiful. Thank you." Melissa giggled as she stood in front of the mirror and poked it out of sight between her breasts. "I could hide a ton of stuff down there."

Chelsea grabbed another tissue and sneezed. "I think it's the--" She sneezed again. "Powder."

Karina raised her eyebrows. "Well, aren't you going to open your borrowed item?"

Melissa opened the elongated package and found a metal stick with a pearl on the end. "What is it?"

"A hatpin. But here, turn around." Karina slipped it into the fancy bun that held Melissa's dark curls. "I can't imagine it falling out. Just remember it's borrowed. It's also old. It was my great-grandmother's hatpin. Probably not worth a thing, except for the natural pearl, but it looks lovely in your hair."

"Oh, Karina, thanks. You are so gracious and wonderful."

"Oh, don't let that out to the public. You'll ruin my image of a bitch who makes the best shoes on the planet."

They all laughed.

"Let me see!" Charley complained. "And Mommy says you're not allowed to curse."

"I'm sorry, sugarchild. You're right. I shouldn't curse," Karina purred in her old Southern accent that she normally tried to hide as lifted the child up.

DeeDee laughed. "Cody is on me all the time for my word choices. He's managed to raise all his other children without using foul language, and then we have Charley and I undo everything."

DeeDee placed the veil on Melissa's head and secured it, as Julia made certain the sheer lace lay perfectly.

Cody opened the door a few inches. "Is my little girl ready?"

"Don't do that to me, Dad. You'll make me cry."

Charley stomped her foot. "I'm your little girl."

Cody laughed and picked Charley up with one arm and deposited her on his hip. "Yes, you are my youngest little girl, but all my girls are my little girls. I love each one of you." He turned to DeeDee. "Take these bouquet boxes. Chrisy was having fits."

Melissa looked at her dad standing there in black tails with a silver and black tie over a gray shirt. His black boots with silver toe tips gave the tux a slightly different look. "I think I really love you dressed like that. You should sport that look every night."

"Great. You want me in a tux at night, and DeeDee prefers me naked. Would you like to weigh in on this, too, Karina?" Cody kissed Karina's cheek.

She laughed. "Well, if I ever wanted a man, you would probably... Yeah, maybe. So for now, I'll just take you in jeans and a tee shirt. I can appreciate a nice body. But I'll stick with Erika. You can keep your clothes on, and yes, you do look very handsome."

"Oh, Karina, you are quite safe around me." He turned to Charley. "Are you ready to marry off your big sister?"

They all followed Cody out of the cottage and drove to the house.

Melissa's stomach tied itself into an unexpected knot. *I'm only going to have fun. Fun. This is fun.*

DeeDee, Karina, and Julia walked down the long hallway and onto the porch to be escorted to their seats. Chelsea, Charley, Cody, and Melissa stayed in the hallway of the main house.

Chrisy stood near the front door. "Ready, ladies?" He looked in Cody's direction and grinned. "And gentleman."

Melissa nodded and inhaled a deep breath.

Mike, from Hilltown Garden Center, was Drexel's best man, and he walked with Chelsea to the arbor as the music played.

Charley walked the carpeted path by herself, sprinkling aromatic blue blossoms of lavender along the way.

Chrisy fixed Melissa's train and shooed Cody through the door to await Melissa. Then he whispered, "You look breathtakingly beautiful. Knock'em dead!"

Chrisy's hand on her back propelled her forward, but she stopped, smiled, and planted a kiss on his cheek. "Thanks, Chrisy. And thanks for this lovely wedding."

He grabbed her arm. "Where's your honeymoon?"

She held a single finger to her lips. "Cruise, down to the Caribbean, through the canal, over to Hawaii for a week at a resort on one of the little islands, another cruise to several Pacific Rim countries, up to Hong Kong, onto the Chukchi Peninsula, over to Alaska, and then we'll fly home. Seven weeks."

He grinned. "Ambitious. This is your day, have fun."

Melissa took her father's arm, and together they descended the steps from the house. It wasn't that far to the arbor, but the walk seemed to take forever. Chelsea stood to one side looking lovely, and Charley stood patiently waiting to hold the bridal bouquet, and on the other side, Mike stood next to Drexel.

Drexel, also wearing long tails, looked as though he was trying to hide his smile. As much as she wanted to smile at her family and friends, she couldn't take her eyes off of Drexel. His broad shoulders and narrow waist were accented by the cut of the tuxedo. The boutonnière made of a semi-opened peony and blue hydrangea flowers matched her white and blue bouquet. But it wasn't until he stepped forward to claim her that she saw pearls mixed into the boutonnière. She wanted to burst into laughter, and it took everything she had to control the desire.

Fortunately, the ceremony was quick and simple. Mike handed Drexel Melissa's wedding band and Drexel slipped it onto her finger. When the time came, Chelsea passed Melissa the larger gold band to place on Drexel's finger.

Melissa took a deep breath and repeated the vows as she

placed the band. She hadn't noticed until that moment that his nails had been manicured. She looked up and saw the twinkle in his eyes.

When he took her into his arms to kiss her, she only expected a simple kiss. Instead, he leaned her over until she was balanced on one foot and held her there. Returned to an upright position, she began to giggle.

"What?" he whispered.

"You are the only man I know who can wear pearls."

"I almost died when I saw them in my flowers," he whispered back, as his grin widened.

When they took that first step, as husband and wife, paper confetti rained on them. They practically ran to the porch where they waited to greet each guest. Then the photographer took all the traditional wedding party photos.

"What happened?" Cody asked. "I noticed you looked as though you were about to burst into laughter."

Melissa waved her father off. "Let me leave it as an inside joke between Drexel and me. Was it that apparent?"

"I'm your father. I know you."

With cocktails, hors d'oeuvres, toasts, dinner, and then the cake cutting ceremony, the next few hours were busy and passed quickly. Then the dancing started. Drexel moved her to the dance floor and whispered, "Wish me luck."

The music began to play a waltz. Drexel wasn't exactly a great dancer. His timing was good, but his feet didn't seem to move as they should. She could hear him counting to three under his breath. It wasn't exactly the fairytale moment of her childhood, but Drexel had done his best.

She danced with her brothers and with several of the men in Drexel's family before the crowd seemed to notice that she hadn't danced with her father. She smiled as her father came to claim her. As a little girl, she used to stand on his toes to dance with him; now she could really dance. And dancing with Cody Montgomery was very easy - until the band set up and the drummer started playing on the beatbox. Cody stopped mid-step, looked at his daughter, and fell into the band's music. Everyone started clapping. After a minute or so, the chamber musicians turned up their speakers and drowned out the band. The violinist began to play a lively country two-step, and Melissa and Cody danced to it. But when Cody picked his daughter up and tossed her into the air, the crowd gasped. The fancy lift ended between his feet and she returned to hers as though it was all quite normal. She laughed, as he had been doing that lift with her since she was probably no more than eight years old. They finished their dance as her family members joined them.

When that was over, Melissa and Drexel scooted out the door and upstairs to a small, unused bedroom. Melissa slipped out of her wedding gown and into her white dancing dress. The short gored skirt with frilly blue and white bloomers were adorable on her, and Drexel agreed as he changed into a pair of slacks and a more comfortable pair of shoes.

He winced and rubbed his feet.

"What's wrong with your feet?" Melissa asked.

He pulled off his socks. "What do you think?"

She looked at his now bare feet and giggled. "Waxed?"

He shook his head. "Permanent hair removal by the doctor

and a pedicure to boot. I did it the other morning while you were busy with your sisters and DeeDee."

"They look so much better!"

"Are they sexy?" He pulled a small tube of gel from a pocket and applied some to his feet.

She reached over and touched his long second toe. "You will never have truly sexy feet, but the rest of you is just fine."

He put his socks and shoes on. "Are you ready to dance the night away?"

"Yes. And I've been thinking. Let's wait a little while before we start adopting. I'm enjoying my freedom."

"Sounds fine to me. I think we'll both know when we're ready to become parents." He planted a kiss on her lips that said there was more to come. "There's enough love between us to fill the entire house with children. But just because we can do it doesn't mean we should." He grinned and took her hand. "Let's go have fun."

Did you enjoy reading *A Rancher's Woman*
by E. Ayers?

Please let your local bookstore know and be sure to tell a friend! Independent authors count on your reviews and word-of-mouth to help them succeed. You can write to the author directly at the following website: **http://www.ayersbooks.com**

About the Author

Born and raised with wealth, E. Ayers turned away from all of it and married a few days after turning eighteen, to the shock and dismay of family and friends.

A firm believer in love conquering everything, there was never cause to look back. The newlyweds' life-long love became the springboard for many future novels.

Fascinated with the way people deal with everyday problems, E. Ayers has always been an observer and a listener. A simple problem for one person is a mountain for another. Utilizing those common predicaments, the subsequent novels have touched many lives.

Today finds E. Ayers writing while living in a pre-Civil War home with a dog and a cat. Rattling around in an old money pit provides one's muse with plenty of freedom. A perfect day is spent at the keyboard, coffee in hand, and everything in the house actually working as it should.

As the official matchmaker for all the characters who wander through a mind full of imagination and the need to share, E. Ayers enjoys finding just the right ones to create a story.

More Great Books From E. Ayers!

A Rancher's Woman (A Creed's Crossing Historical)

A Rancher's Dream (A Creed's Crossing Historical)

Wanting (A River City Novel)

A New Beginning (A River City Novel)

A Challenge (A River City Novel)

Forever (A River City Novel)

A Son (A River City Novel)

A Child's Heart (A River City Novel)

Coming Out of Hiding (a novel)

A Fine Line (a novella) *

Mariners Cove (a novella)

Ask Me Again (a novella)

A Skeleton at Her Door (a novella)

A Snowy Christmas in Wyoming (a novella) *

A Cowboy's Kiss in Wyoming (a novella) *

A Love Song in Wyoming (a novella) *

A Calling in Wyoming (a novella) *

Sweetwater Springs Christmas (anthology) *

*Sweet Reads

www.ingramcontent.com/pod-product-compliance
Lightning Source LLC
Chambersburg PA
CBHW050059120726
47904CB00004B/1152